STORMI

By Dale Brown

FLIGHT OF THE OLD DOG
SILVER TOWER
DAY OF THE CHEETAH
HAMMERHEADS
SKY MASTERS
NIGHT OF THE HAWK
CHAINS OF COMMAND
STORMING HEAVEN

DALE BROWN

STORMING HEAVEN

HarperCollins*Publishers*

HarperCollins*Publishers*
77-85 Fulham Palace Road,
Hammersmith, London W6 8JB

Published by HarperCollins*Publishers* 1994
3 5 7 9 8 6 4 2

First published in the USA by
G. P. Putnam's Sons 1994

A catalogue record for this book
is available from the British Library

ISBN 0 00 224137 4
ISBN 0 00 225230 9 (SPECIAL TRADE PAPERBACK)

Set in Baskerville

Printed in Great Britain by
Redwood Books, Trowbridge, Wiltshire

Acknowledgments

As a full-time Guard unit, and with one of the largest flying squadrons in the U.S. military, the men and women of the 114th Fighter Squadron (Oregon Air National Guard), Kingsley Field, Klamath Falls, Oregon, are in a class by themselves, and I relied on them for much of the information on air defense fighter procedures and for a vital orientation in the F-16A Fighting Falcon ADF (Air Defense Fighter), which was a real thrill for this ex- bomber crew dog. Thanks to Colonel Donald "Scott" Powell, commander; Captain Sandra Kaufman, Chief of Public Affairs; Captain Ken Muller; and to all the other instructors and pilots I met with, for your generous support and assistance.

Interestingly, my old friends of the 119th Fighter Group, 178th Fighter Squadron "Happy Hooligans," North Dakota Air National Guard (whom I wrote about in many other stories as the fighter unit that gets jumped by one of my high-tech bomber "battleships"), pull alert at Kingsley Field, and I had many opportunities to speak with them and learn firsthand about fighter intercept procedures. Thanks to Lieutenant Colonel Tom Tolman, commander of Det One, and his pilots and crews for a tour of their facility and their help in understanding the air interceptor game.

Thanks to the pilots of the 194th Fighter Squadron, California Air National Guard, at March AFB, Riverside, California, for their help in learning firsthand about life as an air defense pilot. Also at March Air Force Base is the Southwest Air Defense Sector Operations Command Center (SOCC), commanded by Colonel Russ Everts and Colonel Pat Madden, SOCC Director, and I thank them and their staff for the time they invested in me to tell me about air defense sector operations.

For information on ground-based air defense operations, I relied on the U.S. Army Air Defense Artillery School, Fort Bliss, Texas, commanded by Brigadier General J. M. Garner. Thanks to First Lieutenant David Reardon and Sergeant First Class Rich Glynn, of base Public Affairs, for putting together a terrific research itinerary for my visit. Thanks also to the men and women of the 6th Air Defense Artillery Brigades, especially LTC Larry Johnson, commander of 3-6th ADA (Patriot), U.S. Marine Corps Captain Brian Yeager, Hawk systems instructor; Mr. James Pool, Patriot systems instructor; First Sergeant Lanham and Sergeant Hayes, Stinger and Avenger instructors, and Sergeant First Class Kilgore and Sergeant Brown, Stinger simulator instructors. Thanks also to 11th ADA Brigade at Fort Bliss, especially LTC Ben Hobson, commander of 3-43rd ADA (Patriot), and Captain Valerie J. Meadows, commander, 2LT Staggs, Sergeant Ken Macchus, Sergeant Ray Gorman, Sergeant Talbot, and Sergeant Rory Reed of F Battery, 3-43rd ADA.

For information on airborne surveillance operations in the E-3 Sentry AWACS (Airborne Warning and Control System) radar plane, thanks to the men and women of the 552nd Air Control Wing, Tinker Air Force Base, Oklahoma City, OK, especially the commander, Brigadier General David J. Oakes; Captain Mike Halbig, First Lieutenant Tim White, and Staff Sergeant Chris Haug, Public Affairs; Captain Jerry Krueger, 964th AWACS; and Major Steve Lisi, First Lieutenant Mike Ruszkowski, and Staff Sergeant Mike Savage, 963rd AWACS, who showed me a bit of what integrated air defense is like during Tinker's CORONET SENTRY 94-1 air supremacy exercise.

For information on the Federal Aviation Administration and air traffic control center procedures, thanks to Tony Longo, Assistant Manager for Training, Federal Aviation Administration, and Glenn W. Coon, Jr., Training Instructor, for a great tour of Oakland Air Route Traffic Control Center and for explaining the intricacies of domestic air traffic control, emergency procedures, and terrorism issues. Thanks also to Barry Maxwell, Debbie Yarborough, and David Jolly for a great tour of the air traffic control tower and FAA facilities at Memphis International Airport.

Thanks to Lieutenant Diane Ramsey, Sacramento Police Department, and Dr. Jim Poland, Ph.D, criminal justice professor and terrorism expert, California State University–Sacramento, for their help in understanding the organization of the U.S. government's antiterrorist forces.

Special thanks to flight instructor, aircraft broker, and good friend Bob Watts, Jr., president of Capitol Sky Park, Sacramento, California, for helpful information on civil aircraft purchasing, licensing, and transport operations, and for all his long hours accompanying me to all the military bases we visited as he checked me out in the Piper Aerostar 602P. It was a first-class way to travel thanks to this first-class gentleman. Thanks also to Chip Manor, Media Relations Director, Martin Marietta Corporation; and my good friend and fellow AirLifeLine pilot Jim Rahe, and his wife Lin, Houston, Texas, for their suggestions and assistance with this story.

Finally, very special thanks to my hardworking and very patient executive assistant, researcher, and friend Dennis T. Hall, for helping me develop this story, for ideas and research on stock-option investment strategies used in this story, and for all-around maintaining a pretty good sense of humor while dealing with all my typical harried author's nonsense. Few authors work in a vacuum, and I'm lucky to have Dennis's help and advice.

This book is dedicated to the hundreds of volunteers who coordinate missions and fly every day for AirLifeLine, a national charity medical air transportation service based in Sacramento, California. They fly needy medical patients free of charge to receive treatment, and I dedicate this especially to its founder and president, my friend Tom Goodwin. Thanks to this great organization, I've been able to give back so much to the people of this great country who have given so much to me.

Author's Note

This story is a work of fiction. The persons and events used herein are a product of my imagination. To understand the difficult and dangerous world of air defense, I enlisted a lot of assistance from the real-world persons and organizations I describe. I thank all those who took the time to help me, and I hope I've done you proud. But the final result, however true-to-life and technically accurate, is fantasy.

I hope it all *remains* a fantasy.

Folsom, CA
April 1994

Real-World News Excerpts

SUMMARY REPORT, Executive Committee on Terrorism, National Security Council (June 1979): . . . The resolution of a serious domestic incident might conceivably be beyond the capabilities of available civil police forces. The use of specially trained and equipped military forces might be necessary in order to restore order and preserve human life.

. . . The FBI and other civil authorities have a substantial capacity to deal with terrorism situations, and the use of military forces would be necessary only in extreme cases of highly sophisticated, paramilitary terrorism operations in the United States.

U.S. DEPARTMENT OF TRANSPORTATION, Federal Aviation Administration Order 7210.3K, 16 September 1993, para. 6-1b(4) and para. 6-5a — The air traffic manager shall take whatever steps are necessary to ensure that the Presidential flight, airplanes, helicopters, and entourage are given priority. . . . Honor any request of the pilot concerning movement of the Presidential aircraft if it can be fulfilled in accordance with existing control procedures . . .

WALL STREET JOURNAL, 2 December 1993: . . . In a bizarre case of mayhem and apparent market manipulation, Mr. Ramiro Helmeyer [of Caracas, Venezuela] is charged with heading a group that carried out a flurry of terrorist bombings in order to profit from the resulting decline in the price of Venezuelan stocks and publicly traded government debt . . .

. . . Some speculate that Mr. Helmeyer and his alleged confederates might have been political terrorists, who engaged in market speculation in order to finance their activities . . .

WASHINGTON TELECOM NEWS via Phillips Publishing, December 3, 1993: Acquisition officials from the Department of Justice's Immigration and Naturalization Service (INS) and NASA are briefing potential private-sector telecommunications and information services partners in separate meetings . . . The partners are being asked to provide ultrasophisticated telecommunications and information services networks for politically sensitive missions mandated by the Clinton administration.

INS was told by the White House that it would support a "sweeping" antiterrorist strategy throughout the federal government . . . that could help identify "potentially dangerous" foreign immigrants . . .

CBS NEWS' "60 MINUTES," 26 December 1993 (reprinted with permission from Burrelle's Information Services)— . . . It's called GPS—global positioning system: 24 orbiting satellites launched by the Pentagon that transmit mapping and targeting information with an accuracy never before known. It's free for anyone to use, and the scariest use would be in what the military calls the "poor man's cruise missile," which could enable any Third World nation, any madman, any terrorist, to send a missile right down the smokestack of the Pentagon . . .

Nothing is too high for the daring of mortals:
we storm heaven itself in our folly.
—*Horace*

Prologue

"What you're about to see," the talk-show host began, "is a videotape of what is a historic but tragic occurrence—the last time since World War Two that territory of the United States of America has been attacked by a foreign power. Our guest today says this can and will happen again, and he should know. You will see a videotape log of the control room of an American drug-interdiction station, located just off the east coast of Florida. Roll the tape."

The studio audience was deathly silent as the monitors came to life.

"Attention, all platform personnel, this is the command center. We have received notification that the aerostat radar unit on Grand Bahama Island has just come under attack and has been destroyed by hostile aircraft. I am placing this platform on yellow alert. Clear the flight deck and prepare for aircraft launch and recovery. Off-duty crew report to emergency stations."

There were about ten people in a large room of computer consoles and radar screens, a room resembling a smaller version of Mission Control at the Johnson Space Center in Houston. Men and women were on their feet, expressions of confusion and fear visible on their faces. "Take your seats and watch your sectors," an officer was shouting, his voice visibly shaking. He was obviously the senior officer, returning to a console slightly raised above the others. "Get your life jackets on but continue monitoring your sectors. Do it!"

Technicians quickly moved back to their consoles, working with quiet efficiency, but the tension in the command center was obvious.

"Sundstrand-351, acknowledge," came the voice of one of the female controllers. "You are exiting the entry corridor and approaching restricted airspace. Turn left to heading three-five-zero immediately."

"Twenty-one, your target is at eleven o'clock, nine miles. You are cleared to engage. Suggest left turns to evade. Seagull One is at your four o'clock, five miles, on auto intercept."

"Mike, Homestead is launching alert fighters in support. We've got one F-16 designation Trap-01, thirty miles out and closing at Mach one-point-two."

"Damn it," the senior officer could be heard saying, "keep making warning calls. Tell him he's about to be blown out of the sky."

"Michael . . . ?" The senior officer's head jerked toward the speaker.

"Tell twenty-one to intercept and identify that bastard," the officer named Michael responded quickly, as if startled into answering. "Tell the F-16 to break off the attack and stand by." A few seconds later, they heard a loud, sharp boom. *Heads visibly rippled across the command center at the sound. "I want a standard intercept, light signals, and warning flares. Get on his ass, get a light in his cockpit, but don't attack until he sees your* FOLLOW ME *lights. Is that clear? Get beside him, twenty-one. Close to gun range. Try a warning shot . . ."*

"Warning shots are for losers," the guest interjected.

"I don't understand that, Admiral," the host said. "You've got to be absolutely, positively sure. Can you do that from a radarscope?"

"If you break the law, if you violate restricted airspace, you should suffer the consequences," the guest responded.

"Shoot first, ask questions later, eh, Admiral?" the host asked.

"It would have saved lives in this case."

"In another, it may have wasted innocent lives."

"I don't buy the argument that we should be prepared to let a hundred guilty persons go so that we make sure one innocent life is saved," the guest said. "The fact is, the innocent rarely are involved—we just end up letting the guilty go. It's time we stop this insanity." No one replied, but heads in the audience were nodding in agreement.

The host saw himself losing control of his audience to his guest's arguments—this audience wasn't quite as liberal as he wanted. He made a mental note to speak with the producer about this. "Let's continue with the scene, shall we?'' he said quickly, and the attention turned back to the replay.

"He's heading right for the platform—he's too close . . . I've got a missile lock," another excited voice being transmitted over a radio shouted. "Am I clear to engage?"

"Hold your fire. Get beside him. Make him turn away."

"He's going to hit. Am I clear to engage? Am I clear to fire?"

Suddenly, a different voice boomed over the radio, a frantic, completely terror-filled voice: "Don't shoot, don't shoot, can you hear me, don't kill me!''

"Get him turned away from the platform, Angel," the senior officer shouted.

"Target turning right, heading zero-four-zero, climbing . . . well clear of the platform." The audience could see shoulders slumping in relief all across the control center—in fact, the audience's shoulders relaxed as well. But just a few moments later, they heard the same female radar controller call out, "I've got two targets bearing zero-seven-zero, ten miles, altitude five hundred feet, speed four hundred knots, closing on us fast. One more up high, near the F-16."

Then, a high-pitched male voice: "Mayday, mayday, mayday, Trap-01, five miles southwest of the Hammerhead One platform, I am under attack. I am hit. I am hit."

"Three planes . . . no, I count four, four planes just appeared out of nowhere . . . coming at us at high speed . . . no ID . . . attack profile."

The videotape stopped abruptly.

The audience was stunned into silence.

''Of course, we all remember what happened then,'' retired U.S. Coast Guard Rear Admiral Ian Hardcastle said to the studio audience as Phil Donahue stepped to his mark to make his guest introduction. ''The U.S. Border Security Force air operations staging platform called Hammerhead One was hit by two cluster bombs and two Argentinean-made antiship cruise missiles. Forty-one men and women lost their lives.''

''The videotape you just saw was taken inside the command center of a U.S. Border Security Force platform in the ocean between the Bahamas and Florida, when it was attacked and destroyed by exiled Cuban military commander-turned-drug-smuggler Agusto Salazar a few years ago,'' Phil Donahue said to the camera by way of introduction. ''My guest is no stranger to danger, or to controversy. Ladies and gentlemen, meet Admiral Ian Hardcastle, former Coast Guard admiral, former commander of the Seventh Coast Guard District in Miami, and former commander of the U.S. Border Security Force.'' The audience applauded politely, perhaps cautiously. Ian Hardcastle's reputation had definitely preceded him, and few persons could really say they had a firm fix on his views or motivations.

''He's retired from twenty-seven years of government service, but now he's waging a one-man crusade to, as he said in the Op-Ed page of the *Times,* 'stop the hemorrhaging of America's self-defense capability,' '' Donahue continued. ''You've seen him on the cover of everything from *Newsweek* to *People,* shouting it from the rooftops: America is in danger because we've led ourselves to believe we're safe. The enemy is the shadowy, faceless world of terrorists, something of which America has not had any real experience. Are we really in danger or is this the sour-grapes tirade of a frustrated drug-interdiction guru who found his frontier-justice programs slip out of control? Your calls and comments for our special guest, the champion of America's pro-military hawks, Ian Hardcastle. Stay with us—we'll be right back.''

The audience followed the prompts from the stage director and the overhead lights and dutifully applauded.

Donahue raced away to get his makeup touched up, and Hardcastle was left alone on stage, so he stood up to stretch.

Hardcastle was tall and lean, with gray hair, a bit longer than he wore it in his Coast Guard days, swept gracefully back from his forehead. ''Character lines'' were deeply etched around his narrow blue eyes, giving him a hawklike visage to match his politics. He wore lightly tinted glasses now, a concession to the hard years of a former Marine Corps and Coast Guard officer finally catching up with him. He wore a dark suit that looked a size or two large for his thin, wiry frame, which only served to accentuate his rather fanatical Captain Ahab–like presence. He looked fearsome, but was a riveting personality.

Hardcastle, age sixty, was a retired Coast Guard rear admiral. He was a Marine Corps officer during Vietnam in a bomb-disposal unit, and ultimately the stresses of the job and war turned him to drug dependency. Upon finishing detox, his commission was transferred to the Coast Guard, where he began a long and distinguished career, rising to become district commander of the busiest Coast Guard district in the U.S.

In 1990, because of his efforts, Hardcastle was placed in operational co-command of a joint Coast Guard–Customs Service border security/drug-interdiction unit called the U.S. Border Security Force, colloquially known as the Hammerheads (after a 1920s-era Coast Guard alcohol-smuggling interdiction unit). The then–Vice President of the United States, Kevin Martindale, was one of its biggest supporters. Although it was responsible for many successful operations, the unit was under constant criticism for not adequately doing anything to stop the flow or the market for illegal drugs, and for its military-style weapons, aircraft, and tactics used against civilians. The Hammerheads were under intense pressure during the Presidential campaign to curtail their offense-oriented tactics, and were disbanded in 1993 under the new administration.

Hardcastle retired in 1993, but became very active on the lecture and political-pundit circuit as a conservative political activist. He associated himself with a large conservative political action committee called the Project 2000 Task Force, which sought control of both the White House and Congress by the year 2000. Although his expertise was widely sought by many in Washington and nationwide, and although he was considered an effective, believable, and popular get-tough speaker, Hardcastle's views were often considered too reactionary and extreme for political office or for a major government appointment.

His personal life was also considered too politically distasteful. He successfully overcame a severe period of post-traumatic shock and depression from his tours in Vietnam, but that episode in his life, although far in the past, was always dredged up by critics, especially when Hardcastle was on one of his broadcast tirades about an issue that he felt strongly about. Others worried about his on-again off-again affair with alcohol. He was divorced and had repeatedly lost regular visitation rights to his minor children. More interestingly, he had a few rather liberal ideas, including legalization of some drugs and stricter gun control, that made him unpopular with far-right conservatives.

A few moments later, Donahue came trotting out, gave Hardcastle a thumbs-up, took his microphone, and stepped briskly into the audience, which had just been commanded to start applauding as they rolled the intro. "We're back with Admiral Ian Hardcastle, former commander of the drug-interdiction unit called the Hammerheads,'' Donahue said when he got his cue.

Some videotape started rolling on the monitors as Donahue did a voice-over—it showed a large orange tilt-rotor aircraft with the words U.S. BORDER SECURITY FORCE and FOLLOW ME in large letters on the side, firing missiles from fuselage pods and dropping off heavily armed assault officers onto a beach.

''You all remember the Hammerheads, with their high-tech aircraft and robot helicopters fluttering over the beaches chasing smugglers—and I'm sure you remember the 1992 incident that sparked the controversy over the need for a unit like the Hammerheads.'' Donahue all but smiled.

Videotape was rolling on the monitors.

A shot from a low-flying helicopter circling overhead, showing a woman lying on the beach, surrounded by two small children and by armed men in orange flight suits. One of the large V-22 tilt-rotor aircraft was landed nearby, stirring up great clouds of sand as the huge double rotors on the plane's wingtips turned at idle speed.

''This pregnant Mexican woman was killed during her arrest, in full view of horrified spectators and TV viewers. In their short history, the Hammerheads are gone, disbanded, certainly discredited. Admiral Hardcastle says the danger is still with us—but not just from smugglers, but from terrorists. What do you think?''

Donahue's staff had already picked out a prescreened audience member who was liberal, highly opinionated, well-spoken, not afraid to speak her mind, rather pretty—she would be perfect to use coming out of commercial. ''You'll stand, please,'' he said as he plucked her out of her seat and handed over the microphone to her.

''Mr. Hardcastle, it looked to me like you were out there fighting a war,'' the woman from the audience said. ''You got fighters all over the sky, guys with radar and guns and all—''

''What's your question, ma'am?'' Donahue briskly interrupted.

''My question is, I don't see much security here—just a lot of killin', like a bunch of neo-Nazis in ugly orange suits ready to bomb innocent people if they don't play by your rules.''

''Ma'am, the Cuban drug smugglers under Colonel Agusto Salazar used civilian planes faking distress to distract us, then *bombed* us with Cuban military aircraft,'' Hardcastle responded. ''We didn't start this fight—*they* did.''

''But you were supposed to be on guard for this type of attack, weren't you, Admiral?" Donahue needled. "With all due respect to your troops, it seems like the attackers got you pretty easily."

"We're sworn to play by the rules, Phil." Hardcastle shrugged. "Our rules of engagement at the time said we could fire only if fired upon. We knew there was a threat of attack—retaliation for being so effective—but Congress and the courts left us virtually defenseless.

"But let me point out something here," Hardcastle said. "At the height of the Hammerheads' manning deployment levels, we were able to conduct radar surveillance of the entire southeast United States and seal off all of Florida with rapid-response aircraft. Drug use dropped significantly because availability of drugs like cocaine and marijuana plummeted—"

"But gang violence and violent crime increased because the pushers and users were fighting for whatever product was on the street," Donahue added.

"Phil, my mission was to get drugs off the street by cutting off the supply lines into America," Hardcastle insisted. "We *did* that. We were successful. No one can doubt that."

"I think we're here because we *all* doubt, Admiral," Donahue said, rolling his eyes.

"What we have now are borders that are wide open to invasion of all kinds," Hardcastle warned. "No Border Security Force. A downsized Border Patrol, Custom Service, and Coast Guard. Back then, I could call on four Air National Guard fighter units for help—now there is just *one.* A hurricane took care of one unit—Congress killed the other two. Ladies and gentlemen, we have only twenty air defense units in all of North America—yes, *twenty.* That's about forty planes ready right now to stop an intruder."

"What intruders are you talking about, Admiral?" Donahue asked. "The Russians? The Chinese? The North Koreans? Who wants to take on the United States these days? Aren't you being just a bit . . . paranoid?"

"Phil, we proved in Operation Desert Storm and the fall of the Soviet Union that no nation can beat the United States in a conventional military conflict," Hardcastle said. "But we have no defense whatsoever against *un*conventional conflicts. Terrorists are better armed, more mobile, and more sophisticated than ever. How do we respond to the threat? We cut funding for defense, security, and counterterrorist programs."

"Admiral, I've got some *real* threats to America's security to tell you about,'' Donahue blasted back. ''We've got forty million Americans with *no* health insurance and over a million homeless Americans—men, women, and children. We've got an average of three hundred Americans gunning each other down per *day,* and we've got fifty thousand Americans rotting in overcrowded prisons, getting no help for their drug addictions and violent, dysfunctional upbringing. In an era when we can't take care of the people living on the street outside this building, here you are, collecting a generous pension from the Coast Guard as well as a very generous stipend from the conservative Project 2000 Task Force, asking for funding for programs to stop these shadowy bogeymen that no one has heard of and that don't directly affect anyone's lives.''

''Tell that to the fifteen thousand people working in the World Trade Center back in 1993, or to the one hundred thousand people affected by the 1994 terrorist mortar attacks on Heathrow Airport,'' Hardcastle snapped. ''Ladies and gentlemen, America is becoming a target for terrorism because we're allowing ourselves to become a target. And I'm no longer just referring to a hijacker or kidnapper or letter-bomber or gang warfare—I'm talking about a *campaign* of terror against America, on the scale that nations in Europe and the Middle East have experienced for decades. We need a military—and more importantly, an administration in the White House—ready to deal with the dangers before they impact the lives of millions of Americans.''

''You're talking about isolated incidents of fanatics, or of terrorist attacks overseas between factions that have been fighting for years,'' Donahue said dismissively. ''I don't see the connection.''

''Ladies and gentlemen, what if I told you that there are over three thousand *known* terrorist groups operating in the United States right now?'' Hardcastle interjected. ''What if I told you that over three hundred pounds of enriched plutonium, enough for thirty nuclear weapons, is reported as missing *every* year? The United States had three long-range radar systems patrolling the skies four years ago. Now we have one, and that one operates only forty hours a week. We sent a hundred Patriot air defense units to Saudi Arabia last year—any guesses as to how many Patriots we have operating in the United States? That's right, *zero.* The sky is filled with unidentified aircraft.''

''Your point is . . . ?''

''What I'm saying is that we as Americans shouldn't allow our defenses to slide like this,'' Hardcastle said. ''Everyone thinks,

'There's no threat, why spend the money to prevent something that may never happen?' I'm telling you, based on all my years in the field of border security and national defense, that the threat *exists*. I'm not talking about Saddam Hussein invading Washington—I'm talking about drug smugglers owning American banks, arms merchants shipping black-market weapons on our highways and through our airspace, and government buildings open to direct assault from relatively low-tech, easily concealable terrorists. We don't have to put up with it."

"Yeah," a young college-age caller said. "I heard you got fired because of alcoholism and because of getting stressed-out from your time in Vietnam and family problems and all. Frankly, old man, I don't think you got what it takes to go around tellin' the President how to run the military."

There was a smattering of applause from the audience.

"Making assumptions without all the facts is like trying to shoot a gun without bullets, son," Hardcastle said. "First of all, it's true: I suffered from a stress disorder brought on by my years in Vietnam and by alcohol. I've never shied away from admitting my faults. But I've also got almost thirty years of military service, most of it dealing with the difficulties this country faces when we fail to enforce our sovereignty and protect our borders. More importantly, I'm an American, and I've got something to say about how our country's being defended. I've got the facts and I've got the experience, so I know what I'm talking about. Question is, who's willing to listen?"

There was another round of applause, this time a little louder than before.

"Not me, man," the caller said. "I think you're crazy," and he hung up.

"And we'll be right back," Donahue said. The music rose, and they cut away for another commercial.

PART 1

Chico Municipal Airport, California
2108 hours, PT, August 1995

"Get your butts in gear," Henri Cazaux ordered, swinging the AK-47 assault rifle on its sling from behind his back, holding it high so everyone in the hangar could clearly see it. He noisily jacked the cocking lever back, allowing a cartridge to spin through the air. The spinning brass glinting against the overhead lights made heads jerk all around the hangar. The sound of the cartridge hitting the polished concrete floor seemed as loud as if he had pulled the trigger. "*Move,* or I'll end your miserable lives right *now.*"

Cazaux was perfectly capable of threatening any one of the burly workers before him even without the antiquated Soviet-made assault rifle. Born in the Netherlands of French and English parents who were residing in Belgium, Cazaux was a former commando in the elite First Para, the "Red Berets," of the Belgian Army. During his youth he was in and out of trouble. At age fifteen he was caught smuggling drugs into the U.S. Army barracks near Antwerp, Belgium; he was incarcerated and abused by U.S. Army soldiers for two days before his identity was established and he was turned over to Belgian authorities. At that time he was offered a choice between a sentence of ten years in the Belgian Army or ten years in prison. He enlisted. He had some expeditionary assignments in Africa and Asia, but got in trouble with the authorities, again, and spent two years in a Belgian stockade until he was given a dishonorable discharge in

1987. He entered the drug trade in Germany, graduating to black market weapon sales, mercenary activities, and terrorism.

His shaved head, tanned to a deep leathery brown by years in innumerable jungles, desert training camps, and killing grounds, revealed scores of scratches, dents, and blemishes that he hadn't obviously been born with. The face was ruggedly handsome, with bright, quick green eyes, a masculine, oft-broken nose, prominent cheekbones, and a thin mouth that clamped down hard on the stub of a cheroot. His baggy flight suit could not hide a well-muscled body. Thick forearms and deeply callused hands gripped the AK-47 as if it weighed only a few ounces. He could have been a model for a cologne or cigarette ad, except for the scars and punctures, most never properly sutured or dressed, that spoiled an otherwise photo-perfect physique. The ex–Belgian Special Forces warrior kept his body tense and his eyes darting to any face that might dare to turn on him, but inwardly Cazaux relaxed.

Cazaux had been an infantry soldier for almost all of his adult life. That was his profession, but his first love was flying. Basic fixed- and rotary-wing pilot training was standard for most Belgian Special Forces cadre, and Cazaux found he had a real aptitude for it. Once out of the Special Forces and into the dark world of the professional soldier, *le mercenaire,* he became a pilot who could handle a gun and who knew explosives, assault tactics, and the other arcane arts of killing—a very valuable commodity. Cazaux held an American Federal Aviation Administration commercial pilot's license, kept current as part of his "aboveground" life, but he had thousands of hours in hundreds of different aircraft, with landings all over the world that would never see the inside of any pilot's logbook or FAA computer database.

The plane was almost loaded; they would be airborne in less than a half-hour. The workers were just about finished loading three narrow wooden pallets aboard the rear cargo ramp of a Czechoslovakian-made LET L-600 twin-turboprop transport. The L-600 was one of the thousands of old aircraft bought on the open market after the collapse of the Soviet Union, when anyone could get an old Soviet military transport, spare engines and parts, and even experienced pilots for a song. This thirty-year-old bird had been purchased from a Greek broker for only five hundred thousand dollars, including a spare Motorlet engine, some other miscellaneous spare parts, and even a ferry pilot. The LET was in good condition—unlike the ferry pilot, who was an old alcoholic ex-Romanian Air Force colonel who flew this beast from Prague to the United States. The Romanian was overheard discussing his boss, Cazaux, with some bar bimbo one night—a fatal error in judgment. Henri Cazaux used the old fart and his new American girlfriend as a moving target when he was zeroing in a new sniper rifle several weeks ago, then buried them both under five thousand tons of gravel at a quarry near Oakland. Cazaux was in the weapons business, and the first standing order for all of his employees was strict secrecy.

Henri Cazaux was the LET L-600's one and only pilot, as well as its loadmaster, engineer, crew chief, and security officer. Cazaux entrusted the duties of copilot to a young Cuban-trained Ethiopian pilot named Taddele Korhonen, whom Cazaux called "the Stork," because of his very tall, thin body and his ability to sit still for an incredible length of time. Cazaux had even seen Korhonen standing on one leg once, like some large dark swamp bird.

Satisfied that the six loaders were sufficiently cowed and working as hard as they could, Cazaux stepped through the L-600's forward port doorway into the cargo bay to inspect the goods. He had just a few inches to squeeze through between the fuselage and the three cargo pallets that occupied the bay—no fat boys on this crew—and Cazaux had to be careful to step over the thick canvas anchor straps securing each pallet to the deck.

The cargo hold smelled like gun oil and machined metal, like sulfur and gunpowder, like terror and death—and money, of course. Lots of money.

The first pallet was just forward of the cargo ramp, and it held the big prize, a cargo worth more than the aircraft that carried them and probably all the humans nearby—three "coffins" of Stinger shoulder-fired heat-seeking antiair missiles stacked aboard, with nine cases to go. Nine coffin-shaped cases each held two Stinger missiles, preloaded into disposable fiberglass launch tubes, and four cylindrical "bean can" battery units. The other three cases held two launcher grip/sight assemblies and four battery units. The missiles had been stolen from a National Guard unit in Tennessee shortly after the unit returned from Desert Storm, and scattered in various hiding places across the country while the sales deals were cut. Cazaux had managed to stay well ahead of the authorities as long as the missiles were hidden and off the market. But as soon as the missiles came out of hiding—which meant hiring loaders, truckers, middlemen, guards, and bankers—the U.S. Alcohol, Tobacco, and Firearms agency, the Army Special Investigations Unit, and the FBI were howling at his heels. Cazaux was certain there was an informant in his operation, and he would ferret him or her out soon. Killing the informant would be his pleasure.

The next forward wooden pallet contained shipment crates of various military field items, ranging from fatigues and boots to U.S. Army MREs (Meals Ready-to-Eat, or more popularly known as Meals Rejected by Everyone), from medical supplies to tents, from power generators to five-pound bundles of cash worth at least two thousand dollars a bundle. When it came time to bribe a customs official in Mexico, the Bahamas, Bermuda, or at the cargo's destination in Haiti, just one discreet toss, and the plane, five pounds lighter, would be on its way within moments. Each bundle of cash was worth about ten times what a Haitian Customs officer legitimately earned in a year, and Cazaux rarely encountered anyone who would turn down a bribe.

The third pallet, secured closest to the front of the cargo bay, held the really nasty stuff—almost five thousand pounds of ammunition, high explosives, detonators, claymore mines, demolition gear, and primacord. Most of the stuff was stable and fairly safe to ship, except for the stuff in the center of the pallet, surrounded by Styrofoam shock absorbers—five hundred pounds of pentaerythritol tetranitrate, or PETN, the primary component of detonating cord and used as a booster in large demolition charges. For the flight, the crystalline PETN was mixed with water to form a gray sludge, then packed in cases surrounded by wet sponges to keep it cool and protect it from shock—it had a detonation temperature of only 350 degrees Fahrenheit. PETN was the most sensitive of the primary military explosives, almost as bad as nitroglycerin—the friction of two crystals rubbing against each other could be enough to set it off.

The explosives-laden pallet was placed toward the front of the plane to keep it closer to the L-600's center of pressure, where aerodynamic forces were more balanced—no use whipping the pallet around unnecessarily. Cazaux was not the best pilot in the world, but he had not lost a shipment of weapons yet in over ten years. Although his copilot, the Stork, always checked the security of each holddown strap in his cargo bay several times before and during each flight, Cazaux himself triple-checked the security of all the straps on the third pallet, then double-checked the security of the middle pallet.

A few moments later, one of the beefy loaders came up to the entry hatch nearest Cazaux. "All cargo loaded aboard as ordered," he reported.

Cazaux maneuvered his way aft to the third pallet and inspected the Stinger coffins. He had placed an almost invisible pencil line on each crate lid that would clearly not be aligned if the lids had been opened—none had been touched. Cazaux made a few tugs on the straps and several hard pushes on the stacks of crates and found them secure. He reached over to the second pallet and extracted three packets of cash. "Good job, gentlemen," Cazaux said. "Your work here is finished. That buys your silence as well as rewards you for your labor. See to it that silence remains golden."

The loader's eyes flashed with delight when he saw the bundles, but they just as quickly blinked in surprise when a large switchblade stiletto suddenly appeared in Cazaux's hand out of nowhere. Cazaux's eyes registered the loader's surprised expression, and his handsome face smiled, if only for a brief moment. Then he dropped the packets into the loader's arms and drew the stiletto's razor-sharp edge across one of the packets. The loader's greedy hold on the money packets allowed waves of one-hundred-dollar bills to ooze out of the incision. "Count it," Cazaux said casually as he folded the switchblade and instantly returned it to whatever secret place he had drawn it from.

"Not necessary, sir," the loader said breathlessly, turning to leave. Cazaux looked a bit perturbed at first, then shrugged and nodded as if silently acknowledging the man's offhanded compliment. "Call on us anytime, sir."

"I could use some men like you in my operation," Cazaux said to the back of the man's head. "Join my team now, and you'll make that much cash, and more, on every mission."

The loaders stopped, looking at each other—obviously none of them wanted to accept, but they were afraid of the consequences of saying no to Henri Cazaux. But one black man turned toward Cazaux. "Yo, man, I'll take it, right here." The other loaders, all white, looked relieved that the lone black had left them.

The black guy was big, with beefy shoulders and arms and a broad, massive chest, but with a bit of a roll of fat around his middle and a spread in his ass, like a veteran truck driver, a played-out boxer, or an ex–artillery loader turned couch potato. His eyes were clear, with no hint of dullness from drugs or too much alcohol, although the flabby waist and chest said this guy downed at least a case of beer a week. "Do you have a passport?" Cazaux asked him.

"Uh-uh . . . Captain," the loader said in a dark, cave-deep voice.

"It will cost you one thousand dollars, in advance," Cazaux said. He extended his hands toward the bundles of cash held by the head loader, motioning for the man to toss him the money.

"That ain't the deal," the head loader said. "We split the money later." But Cazaux hefted the AK-47—not aiming it at them, but the threat was clear—and the loader counted out a thousand dollars in one-hundred-American-dollar bills from the sliced-open packet and handed it to the black man.

"Work hard, and it will be returned to you with substantial interest," Cazaux said, holding out his hand.

The black man scowled at Cazaux, clutching the cash in his big hands. "I ain't paying you nuthin,' man," he said. "You got your own damned plane, man, you can get me in."

"Just stick the nigger in with the rest of the baggage," one of the other loaders suggested with a laugh.

A stern glare from the Belgian mercenary silenced the loader. "You will need a passport for some of our destinations," Cazaux said, "and it costs a lot to get a good document." He shrugged. "Part of the price of doing business."

The anger rising in the black man's chest was enough to raise the air temperature in the hangar several degrees.

"*Trust* me," Cazaux said reassuringly.

The guy finally relented, handing Cazaux the money and hopping aboard the L-600. The others were hustling toward the side hangar door as fast as they could. They were sure the big black guy was going to turn up dead in a very short period of time, like as soon as he closed the hangar doors.

"You are the one they called Krull?" Cazaux asked the one remaining loader.

"Yeah," the black man replied.

"Is that your real name?"

The man hesitated, but only for a second: "Hell no, Captain. And I'll bet you ain't no *captain,* either."

Cazaux knew the man's real name was Jefferson Jones, that he was just paroled from a Florida state penitentiary, serving three of seven years for armed robbery, and that he had a common-law wife and two kids. An arrest for dealing drugs, no conviction, and an arrest for selling guns, again no conviction. A small-time hood, dabbling in crime and so far not demonstrating any real aptitude for it. Cazaux's sources described this one as a good worker, good with a gun, more intelligent than most foot soldiers, a quick temper when provoked but otherwise quiet. "Good answer, my friend," Cazaux said. "I saw your dossier."

"Say what?" Big eyes growing wide with surprise.

"Your records. I know you are telling the truth. Lying to me is fatal, I assure you."

"You're the boss," Krull said. "I ain't lying to you."

"Very well." Cazaux knew that Jones had used a variety of weapons in his years as an armed thug, and Cazaux had chosen him, whether Krull knew it or not, over all the other hirelings as a possible recruit. "You begin work immediately. Open those hangar doors, close them after we taxi clear, hop aboard, then close this door like so." Cazaux showed him how to close and latch the large rear cargo door, and Krull left to see to the hangar door. He had no trouble opening the manually operated steel doors, and soon the warm California night air was seeping into the hangar. Time to get moving.

"Prepare to start engines," Cazaux shouted forward to the Stork. "I want taxi clearance right now. Report our position on the field as the Avgroup cargo terminal, not this location. Let's go." He bent to make one last check of the cargo straps before heading up to the cockpit.

**Aboard an Army UH-60 Assault Helicopter
That Same Time**

The image on the nine-inch color monitor wavered as the helicopter passed by some electrical transmission lines, but the picture steadied as soon as they were clear. "I didn't hear you that time, Marshal Lassen," Federal District Court Judge Joseph Wyman, Eastern District of California, said. "Repeat what you just said."

"Your Honor, I said that because Henri Cazaux is extremely dangerous, I must be granted extraordinary latitude for this capture," Chief Deputy Marshal Timothy Lassen said into the videophone, a suitcase-sized unit strapped into the UH-60 Black Hawk's helicopter seat across from Lassen. Lassen, age forty-eight, was the number-two man in charge of the Sacramento office of the U.S. Marshals Service, Eastern District of California. He was speaking on a secure voice/video/data microwave link to the federal courthouse in

Sacramento while speeding southward only one thousand feet above ground toward Chico Municipal Airport. Lassen's lean frame was now artificially beefed out with a thick Kevlar body armor vest over a loose-fitting black flight suit, recently purchased from a mail-order catalog for this particular mission; a black vest with the words U.S. MARSHAL in green covered the bulletproof vest. His boots were scuffed-out survivors of the Marshals Service Academy Training Course at Quantico, Virginia, and used since then only for duck hunting. He wore a plain black baseball cap backwards and a headset to speak on the videophone over the roar of the helicopter's twin turboshaft engines.

Judge Wyman had been summoned to his desk at midnight to issue an arrest and search warrant for Lassen's operation. Even distorted by the scrambled microwave linkup and the occasional interference, it was obvious that the judge was not happy. " 'Latitude' is one thing, Deputy," Wyman said irritably, "but your warrant justification reads like something out of the frontier West."

"I think that's a slight exaggeration, Your Honor."

The videophone system was full duplex, like a regular telephone, but it would not easily tolerate interruptions—Lassen's interjection went unheard: "I'll buy a no-knock and use of military *transport* aircraft for the raid, Deputy, but the gunship is out."

"Your Honor . . . Your Honor, excuse me," Lassen said, repeating himself to successfully interrupt the judge, "Henri Cazaux is the number-one fugitive on our most-wanted list, with fifty-seven federal warrants issued for him to date. He is an internationally known terrorist and arms dealer. He's the biggest gunrunner in southwestern Europe, his efficiency and ruthlessness is putting the Italian Mafia to shame in southern Europe, and now he's in the United States, where he's been connected to several attacks against military arsenals. He has stolen everything from Band-Aids to glide bombs, and he knows how to use them all—he's ex–Belgian Special Forces and an accomplished pilot. He has the Marshals, the FBI, ATF, and the state police outgunned in every category. We have to use military air just to even the odds."

Judge Wyman shook his head at the videophone unit's camera lens on his desk and continued: "Use of deadly force? Use of military aircraft and weapons? *Dead or alive?* What is this, a vendetta? I will *not* sign a 'dead or alive' warrant, Deputy."

"Your Honor, Cazaux is known to have killed four federal officers this year," Lassen said. "He hasn't used anything smaller than an M-16 or AK-47 infantry rifle on any of his victims, and one marshal was believed to be killed by a direct hit by a forty-millimeter grenade, a weapon used for punching holes in walls and bunkers. We identified the dead agent by recovering one of his fingers that had been blown nearly a hundred yards away."

It was the judge's turn to interrupt—Lassen stopped talking when he saw Wyman talking, and the judge's stern voice came through as soon as Lassen stopped talking: ". . . have to remind me of any of that, Deputy," Wyman said, "and I'm very familiar with an M206 grenade launcher and its effects, thank you. I fully understand how dangerous Henri Cazaux is. But the objective of a warrant issued by this court is to grant legal permission to *arrest* a fugitive suspect, not carry out an assault—or an execution."

"I assure you, Your Honor, my objective is to capture Cazaux and bring him to trial," Lassen said. "But I cannot accomplish this mission safely without substantial firepower. Cazaux is a killer, Your Honor. He has demonstrated that he will fight it out, kill any law-enforcement agents nearby, use the weapons he smuggles for his own defense, even kill his own workers, rather than be captured. He's like a raccoon caught in a trap, Your Honor, except he won't hesitate to chew off someone *else's* leg to escape. I need extraordinary powers if I'm to try to apprehend him. If I don't get them, I *will not* send my men in."

"Don't you give me ultimatums, Deputy Lassen," Wyman said angrily.

"I'm trying to emphasize how dangerous Henri Cazaux is, Your Honor," Lassen continued quickly. "I attached an FBI psychological profile. Cazaux was imprisoned and abused by GIs when he was a child, and he turned to violence ever—"

"Say again, Deputy Lassen?" Wyman interrupted. "I thought Cazaux had never been in prison?"

"As a minor, he was caught on a U.S. Air Force cruise missile base in Belgium, selling hashish to U.S. security policemen," Lassen explained. "He was turned over to the Belgian authorities, but not before being imprisoned and repeatedly raped by the guards for two days. I heard they even shoved nightsticks up him. And he was only fifteen years old. He kills foreign servicemen on sight, Judge—he always has. I think he'll target my SOG troops the same—"

"I understand what you're telling me, Deputy," Wyman interrupted, "but even though he may seem like one, I want him brought to justice, not killed like a rabid dog. Don't ask this court for the power of life and death, then refuse to carry out your duties if you don't get it. You want my signature on a warrant, mister, you follow by my rules.

"I'm deleting the 'dead or alive' condition—you *will* bring Cazaux and his men in alive, or you will explain to me and the Attorney General of the United States why you failed to do so, and I assure you, Deputy, your career and where you spend the night—at home, or in a federal prison cell—will hang on your response. And you may use any military aircraft to transport your agents and for *observation*, but they may not approach closer than five hundred meters from the suspects, and they may not use their weapons unless fired upon by the suspects. Now, are you going to abide by my orders, Deputy Lassen?"

He had no choice. Wyman was the most cold-blooded of the federal judges and magistrates in the District, and if *he* had objections to any aspect of a warrant, it was best not to argue. The way was still clear to do whatever it might take to put Cazaux out of business, but an unwarranted death would mean the end of Lassen's career. It might be worth a twenty-year career for the chance to end Cazaux's miserable life, but playing by the rules was important to Timothy Lassen. Carrying a gun, a badge, and a federal warrant made a man pretty big in some people's eyes, and it was easy to start believing that justice was whatever you chose to make it, especially with sociopathic killers like Cazaux. Lassen was determined not to let his Constitutionally mandated power corrupt him. Lassen was also determined not to fuck up his career at this point, no matter who they were pursuing. Tall, with an athletically lean frame and dark hair and brown eyes, Timothy Lassen had been with the Marshals Service since 1970, and had several assignments in both California and Oregon. For eight of those years (from 1980 to 1988) he had served in the Special Operations Group (SOG). He was the SOG deputy commander from 1988 to 1990 and then reassigned to the Sacramento office as Deputy U.S. Marshal in 1991. "Yes, Your Honor," Lassen replied.

"Good. I want Cazaux as bad as you do, Lassen, but you've got to do this one by the book or the circuit court will put us *both* out of business." Wyman raised his right hand, and in the passenger section of the Black Hawk helicopter, Lassen did likewise. "Do you swear," Wyman recited, "that all the information in these warrants are the truth, the whole truth, and nothing but the truth, and do you swear to abide by the regulations and restrictions contained herein and execute these warrants to the best of your ability?"

"I swear, Your Honor."

Wyman signed three documents and handed them to an assistant, who unclipped the pages and sent the pages one by one into a fax machine connected to the same secure communications link. Seconds later, the warrants appeared in the plain-paper fax machine on board the Black Hawk assault helicopter. A recent Supreme Court decision ruled that the faxed copy of a warrant sent via a secure datalink was as good as the original. "I'll be standing by here in case you need me, Lassen. I'm with you all the way."

"Thank you, Your Honor," Lassen said.

"My clerk tells me that Judge Seymour signed a series of warrants for ATF the same time period," Wyman said. ATF, the Bureau of Alcohol, Tobacco, and Firearms, a division of the Department of the Treasury, was involved with the regulation of restricted, high-value goods such as liquor and weapons. "Since I wasn't briefed on their involvement, I assume you're not working with ATF on this one."

"I didn't know ATF was involved, Your Honor," Lassen said. "We got the information that Cazaux had surfaced only a few hours ago. Can you give me any details on the warrant, sir? Is Agent Fortuna in charge?"

"Your old friend," Wyman said with a wry smile—the sarcasm in his voice came through loud and clear, even via the wavering secure datalink. "I see you have your Kevlar on—I think you'll need it, and not just against Cazaux."

"I'd better try to raise Fortuna on the secure phone, then, Your Honor," Lassen said. "Thanks again for your help."

"I have a feeling the shooting is going to start long before you encounter Cazaux," Wyman said, trying to interject a bit of humor into what promised to be a very humorless scene coming up. "Good luck." The encrypted datalink buzzed when Wyman hung up, then beeped to indicate the channel was autochecked for security and was clear.

Lassen keyed in a user address key into the transceiver's keypad, listened for the autocheck tone again, and waited. Seconds later, he heard a cryptic "Tiger One, go."

Even on an ultrasecure microwave datalink that was virtually untraceable and eavesdrop-proof, Special Agent Russell V. Fortuna still liked using his old Vietnam Recondo code name. "This is Sweeper One, on channel seventeen-bravo," Lassen replied. Although he disliked using all this code crap, he knew Fortuna would not respond, especially during an operation, unless he used his code name and confirmed the secure datalink channel in use. "What's your location and status, Russ? Over."

There was a slight pause, and Lassen could easily envision Fortuna, dressed in his *Star Wars* semirigid body armor that made him look like an Imperial storm trooper from the movie, shaking his armored head in complete exasperation. "Lassen, what the fuck do you want?" Fortuna finally said. "You may have just blown this operation. You ever hear of communications *security?*"

"We're on a secure datalink, Russ. Get off it. I need to know your status. Are you moving against Fugitive Number One? Over."

"Jesus, Lassen, why don't you just get on the PA and tell the creeps we're coming?" There was another short pause, then: "Yeah, we're ten minutes out. We zeroed in on his operation at Chico, and we're moving in. Since we didn't have time to coordinate this strike, do me a favor, get hold of the administrator of the airport and the sheriff's department, and cordon off the airport. Stay on the outside until I give you the word. Over."

"Russ, we've got word that Cazaux has got heavy weapons and high explosives at his location, enough to take out half the airport. SOG is about fifteen minutes out, and we've got some Apaches and Black Hawk assault helicopters from the California Air National Guard with us. We'll back you up."

"Assault helicopters? Are you nuts?" Fortuna asked. "Cazaux will start shooting the minute he hears one of those things overhead. Keep them away from the airport. Who the hell gave you a warrant authorizing attack helicopters, anyway? Are you going to seal off the airport for me or not?"

"Affirmative, Russ, I'll take care of that," Lassen said, pointing to the VHF radio and motioning for the chief of the Special Operations Group, Deputy Marshal Kelly Peltier, to make the initial calls for him. SOG was the Marshals Service's assault and special weapons team, organized to capture the most violent and heavily armed fugitives. "But hold off on your operation until we get closer, and brief me on your plan of attack."

"I don't have time for that shit," Fortuna snapped. "You can monitor our tactical frequency if you want, but do not, I repeat, *do not* overfly the airport. We might mistake your choppers as one of Cazaux's escorts and take a shot at it."

Special Agent Fortuna was director of the southeast district of the Bureau of Alcohol, Tobacco, and Firearms. Ex–Marine Corps, all-around weapons expert, and a human dynamo, as gung-ho as any man in the Treasury Department, Fortuna was an expert in small-unit assault tactics—at least in his own mind. He relied on the elements of shock and surprise to overwhelm the bad guys. However, the shock and devastation of his attacks, in Lassen's view, made up for a lot of sloppy investigative work. Judges gave him warrants regularly because he got results. Lassen liked to gather his deputies, surround a suspect, and wait him out. Although these standoffs took time and manpower, this substantially reduced the risk to his deputies. Fortuna liked to form a strike team, plan an assault, and attack head-on at night with heavy weapons blazing. The result was usually a lot of wounded agents and dead suspects, but the shooting was over long before the TV camera crews arrived. Because of this fundamental difference in tactical style, the two organizations sometimes moved without coordinating with the other.

"Jesus, Fortuna's gonna play Rambo again," Lassen said on the helicopter's intercom so the pilots and the rest of the crew could hear. "Paul, you better plan on setting down on the far side of the runway opposite the action, off-loading the crew, then evacuating the area," Lassen told his pilot. To his SOG strike team leader he said, "Kel, get on the phone to the chief of the Oakland Flight Service Station and have them issue an emergency airspace restriction in a five-mile radius of the airport. I'll be the point of contact in charge of placing the restriction. If you hit any delays after nine minutes from now, just get on VHF GUARD on 121.5 and UHF GUARD on 243.0 and broadcast the warning in the blind for all aircraft to avoid the airport. Christ, what a mess."

"The TV stations will pick up the news if I broadcast on the GUARD channel, Tim."

"I'm not worried about that—I'm worried about Fortuna taking a shot at us or at some commercial job who wants to land," Lassen said. "Do it."

Chico Municipal Airport, California
That Same Time

"Chico ground, LET Victor Mike Two Juliett, ready to taxi from Avgroup Airport Services with information uniform," Cazaux radioed.

"LET Victor Mike Two Juliett, Chico ground, taxi to runway one-three left via alpha taxiway, wind one-eight-zero at one-three," came the response from ground control.

"LET Two Juliett," Cazaux replied.

Russ Fortuna, sitting in the front of the "six-pack" pickup truck, lowered the handheld VHF radio and turned to his deputy strike leader beside him. "Right on time and right where he's supposed to be," he said. The six-passenger pickup truck they were riding in cut a corner and sped toward an open gate guarded by an ATF agent and a sheriff's deputy. The three ATF agents sitting in the back of the truck clattered as their armored shoulders bumped against each other. The semirigid Kevlar armor they wore resembled a hockey player's pads, with thick face, neck, arm, torso, groin, and leg plates that would protect them against heavy machine-gun fire with reasonable mobility. Their helmets were one-piece bulletproof Kevlar shells with built-in microphones, headphones, and flip-up night-vision goggles, powered by a lithium battery pack mounted on the back of the helmet. They wore thickly padded ALICE vests over the armor, with spare ammunition magazines, flash-bang grenades, and .45 caliber automatic pistols in black nylon holsters. The agents carried no handcuffs or restraining devices—this was a hard-target assault all the way. If the suspects weren't restrained by the sight of pistols and assault rifles, they were going to be suppressed by a bullet in the head. Their main weapons were Heckler & Koch MP5 submachine guns with flash suppressors; the driver of the truck would man a .50 caliber heavy sniper rifle with a 30× nightscope that was big enough to destroy an aircraft engine with one shot.

Once through the gate, the truck headed along rows of small-aircraft hangars on their right. A high-wing Cessna was taxiing toward them, flashing its landing light, and the driver of the truck turned on emergency flashers to warn the plane's pilot to stay away. Another truck, an eight-passenger van with smoked windows, was directly behind them, loaded with six more ATF agents in full ballistic armor and combat gear. This van, and another one heading across the airport to encircle Cazaux, each carried six fully equipped agents.

"Give me a rundown of the location."

The deputy strike leader opened an airport guide to the paper-clipped pages. "Avgroup Airport Services is the large parking area southeast of the control tower, closest to the departure end of runway thirteen left," he replied. "One large hangar east, one more southeast, one more north. Pretty open otherwise. From the northwest gate, we'll have to come in from the north between this hangar and the tower. That way we can cut off his taxi route."

"But he could use the parallel runway instead of the longer one, right? We should cover both runways."

"Runway thirteen right is only three thousand feet," the deputy strike leader said. "The LET L-600 needs a good five thousand feet even for a best-angle takeoff, and more if Cazaux's got it loaded down with fuel and cargo. In addition, he's got a strong crosswind—that'll cut down his takeoff capability even more. I think he'll have to take the long runway."

"All the same, I want unit three to go around east of the tower, down taxiway delta, and take up a position on the east side of runway one-three right in this intersection," Fortuna said. "That way he can cover the departure end of runway thirteen right and block the long runway if we need to."

"That'll only leave two units on Cazaux," the deputy strike leader said. "The airport's pretty big—if he rabbits, we might lose him. If they got choppers, we might want to bring the Marshals in on this after all."

"It's too late to bring them in now," Fortuna decided. "Once we get Cazaux's plane stopped, we'll have the Marshals move in, but I want to move into position before anyone else appears in the line of fire." The deputy strike leader got on the tactical radio to issue his instructions.

The intersection up ahead near the control tower appeared deserted, with no aircraft or vehicle movement at all. Floodlights were on around and inside the Avgroup Aviation Services hangar. Cazaux's plane was just visible, taxiing away from the front of the hangar. Fortuna clicked on his radio: "I've got the plane in sight. I'm moving in."

"Unit one, this is two," the driver in Fortuna's van radioed. "I've got five individuals walking west along the taxiway away from the Avgroup hangar. Some of the people are definitely suspects. They're carrying packages, but I can't tell what they might be. I don't see any weapons or radios. I can take them with two of the security team and position the others to flank the target and block him from the west."

"Do it," Fortuna radioed.

Two ATF agents dismounted from the van and silently trotted into position, taking cover near some parked airplanes. The five men practically walked right up to them, never noticing them or the van just a few dozen yards in front of them in the darkness. As soon as the driver of the van saw the five men's hands go up—they were carrying small bundles, and through their night-vision goggles they could clearly see they were bundles of cash—the van sped forward to take up its position to surround Cazaux's plane.

"Drop those packages," one of the ATF agents shouted. *"Now!"* The bundles of money spilled from their hands and hit the ground—and then the whole world seemed to erupt in a flash of light and a huge ear-shattering explosion.

"I told them to count the money," Henri Cazaux mused as he put the tiny remote detonator transmitter in his flight bag beside his seat. Off in the distance, they could see a truck burning brightly alongside the Avgroup Aviation Services hangar. Krull, squatting between the pilots' seats to watch the takeoff, stared out the forward windscreen in horror. "Joining my outfit is looking like a better idea all the time, isn't it, Mr. Krull?"

"No shit . . . Captain," he responded. The Stork grinned, showing the newcomer his few remaining tobacco-stained teeth. Cazaux turned off the telescopic nightscope he had been using to monitor the ATF agents' approach, then handed it to Krull, who placed it carefully into a padded case. "I never did care for them white boys anyway. Fuck 'em."

"You work hard and keep your mouth shut, Mr. Krull," Cazaux said, shoving the throttles forward and picking up speed along the north terminal buildings, "and we will enjoy a long and profitable relationship. I don't care what color your skin is. Cross me, inform on me, or speak to anyone about my operation or myself, and you'll be crow food too. That I promise."

"I get the message."

"Aircraft on taxiway bravo near the tower, this is Chico ground, hold your position and acknowledge. Orders from the sheriff's department. Say your call sign," the ground controller radioed.

"Checklists, Stork, checklists," Cazaux shouted cross-cockpit. He reached across the cockpit and flipped on the engine ignition switches—if the engines faltered during takeoff, leaving the igniters on would help to restart them quickly. "Mr. Krull, your job is to watch this indicator. When it hits sixty, punch this button to start the stopwatch. You will count down precisely twelve seconds and give me a warning beginning five seconds before the sweep hand reaches twelve seconds, using the words 'ready, ready,' then 'now' in a loud voice when the clock reads twelve seconds. Do you understand?''

''What the hell for, man?''

''I told you, keep your mouth shut and pay attention, Mr. Krull, and you'll do fine in my organization,'' Cazaux said. ''Do you understand what I just told you?''

''Yeah, yeah, I got it.''

''Very good. This is an acceleration test, Mr. Krull. You see, we're not going to take the long runway—we're taking the short runway, one-three right. The twelve seconds is our safety margin—we have twelve seconds to go from sixty knots to one-twenty. If we don't do it, we won't take off. Simple enough.''

''Then we better make it, man,'' Krull said, ''because whoever's chasin' us ain't gonna be too happy about us settin' off a stick of dynamite in their faces.''

''True enough. Oh—hit that button for me right there, if you would.'' Krull reached over to a small aluminum box mounted atop the glareshield above the instrument panel, took a look at Cazaux, who was busy with the checklists, and at the Stork, who was grinning with complete mirth at him. Krull hit the button . . .

. . . and a ring of volcanoes appeared to erupt all around them, with huge thick geysers of fire shooting into the sky, obscuring the buildings on the east ramp near the control tower. One by one, private airplanes and crop dusters were sent spinning into the air by the explosions. The explosions were set in precise patterns, causing a rippling effect across the airport—as soon as the L-600 taxied past a spot, the explosions would cut off the taxiway and obscure them with fire and smoke. ''Jesus Christ, what in hell . . . ?''

''It is so pitifully easy to set explosives on airports in America,'' Cazaux said. ''Offer to wash a windshield or paint a few stripes on the ground, and pilots in this country will let you do anything you want around their planes. But I am disappointed—only about half of my detonators are going off. I think I'll have a talk with those Mexican dealers. They owe me a refund.'' Krull felt as if he was in some kind of hellish nightmare—the airport was systematically being destroyed all around them, and Henri Cazaux was chatting on about business matters as if the explosions were just the twinkling of fireflies. Krull saw one explosion erupt under the control tower, but the darkness and smoke obscured his view and he couldn't see if the concrete and steel structure hit the earth.

"Rather like setting up dominoes in a row and watching to see if the pattern completes itself, no?" Cazaux asked Krull. "You cannot help but watch. The disaster is magnetic."

Sixty seconds ago, Special Agent Russell Fortuna was in command of three trucks filled with seventeen heavily armed ATF agents—now, two trucks had disappeared in balloons of fire, and his own truck was abandoned and they were taking cover behind it. Like a freight train out of control, the six agents were helpless as the columns of fire erupted all around them. A small single-engine Cessna with a Playboy bunny painted on the tail disappeared in a flash of light and an ear-splitting sound only twenty yards away, shattering the windshield in the truck and blowing out two tires. Two agents were dazed, one finding blood oozing from a ruptured eardrum in one ear. All the rest appeared unhurt—four out of a strike team of eighteen. Aftermath of a typical Henri Cazaux ambush.

"Team two, check in . . . team two, check in," Fortuna tried on the portable radio. Nothing. "Team three . . ." He didn't try team three anymore, because he *saw* those poor bastards get blown away when the booby traps Cazaux's thugs were carrying went up. "Damn it, somebody answer me!"

"Russ, this is Tim," Chief Deputy Marshal Lassen radioed. "I've been monitoring your frequency. What's your situation?"

"The target booby-trapped this entire airport," Fortuna replied. "No reply from my two support units." He was not about to say on an open frequency, scrambled or not, that both his assault trucks had been blown sky-high. "Suspect is taxiing to the northwest for takeoff on runway one-three left. What's your position?"

"We're five minutes out, Russ," Lassen replied. "We'll try to block the runways."

Lassen's three-helicopter SOG team was less than five minutes out—they were close enough to see the burning aircraft, like large bonfires, dotting the darkness around the airport. The runway lights, taxiway lights, and tower rotating beacon were all out. The flight crew of the Black Hawk had to lower night-vision goggles in place to find the airport. The moving shape of the large cargo plane was now visible, moving rapidly down the inner taxiway. Only a few dozen yards and Cazaux would be at the end of runway one-three left, lined up for takeoff. "I want one Black Hawk in the middle of one-three left," Lassen radioed to his other helicopters, "and the Apache hovering at the southeast end to cover. We'll fly overhead and take one-three right in case he tries to use the shorter runway. I want—"

Suddenly a bright flash of light erupted on the ground ahead of them, and a streak of light arced out across the sky, heading right for them. Lassen's Black Hawk banked hard left, away from the second Black Hawk, which was flying along in formation on their right. The streak disappeared immediately, and Lassen was about to ask what it was when a brilliant burst of light flashed off to their right. The second helicopter was illuminated by an orange-blue sheet of fire on its left side. "Mayday! Mayday! Mayday!" the pilot of the second Black Hawk radioed. "Hunter Two has taken some ground fire. One engine on fire, losing oil pressure. We're going down!"

"Hunter One, this is Wasp," the pilot of the Apache attack helicopter radioed. "I have a vehicle at the spot where that missile came from. Three men. They appear to have another man-portable missile and are preparing to fire. Request permission to engage."

Lassen didn't hesitate—he had run this very scenario in his head a dozen times since putting the request for the AH-64 Apache helicopter into the California Air National Guard. His warrant, signed by Judge Wyman, specifically said that he could not use the Apache's weapons unless they were under attack—well, they were definitely under attack. "Request granted, Wasp," Lassen radioed immediately. "Clear to fire."

He was about to ask his pilot where the Apache was, but he found out himself a moment later as several bursts of rocket fire flashed just a few yards away, the strobe light–like flashes freezing the rotors of the deadly Apache gunship. The Apache launched at least two missiles, and both hit the same spot on the ground ahead, creating a mushroom of fire. Lassen saw a swirl of light on the ground, jumping and looping and cartwheeling in the air like a comet gone crazy—an unfired Stinger or Redeye missile round cooking off, he guessed.

"Target suppressed, two secondary explosions, target destroyed," the Apache pilot reported.

"Good shooting, Wasp," Lassen radioed. "Take the end of runway one-three left, keep the suspect aircraft in sight, and attempt to block its taxi path."

"Wasp copies." But a moment later, the pilot came back: "Hunter, this is Wasp, suspect aircraft is lined up on runway one-three right, repeat, one-three *right,* and he appears to be on his take-off roll. Am I clear to fire?"

Lassen put his night-vision goggles back in place and searched the airport, now less than a mile away. Sure enough, Cazaux had decided not to taxi all the way to the long runway—he was on the short runway and already starting his takeoff run. It would be impossible to block his path now. But he could still stop him—the Apache gunship had a 20-millimeter cannon that could shred Cazaux's plane in two seconds, plus at least two more wire-guided TOW (Tube-launched, Optically-tracked, Wire-guided) missiles that would rid the earth of Henri Cazaux once and for all. One word from him, and Cazaux would be a flaming hole in the earth.

"Hunter, this is Wasp, am I clear to engage? Over."

Henri Cazaux had killed a handful of ATF agents that night alone, plus killed or injured his deputy marshals on the second helicopter, plus any unlucky civilians who were on that airport when Cazaux decided to destroy it to cover his escape. Add all those souls to the list of his victims in the past several years. And those were only the ones Cazaux *himself* had killed that were known to the Justice Department—he was undoubtedly responsible for hundreds, perhaps thousands of other deaths because of his gun-smuggling and terrorist activities.

Henri Cazaux *deserved* to die.

Unfortunately, Chief Deputy Marshal Timothy Lassen didn't have the legal or moral authority to kill him. Would Judge Wyman or any other federal judge throw the book at him for putting a TOW missile into Cazaux's filthy hide? Probably not, Lassen decided . . .

"Hunter, the target is reaching my max tracking speed. I need authority to shoot. Am I clear to engage?"

. . . but his own conscience would prosecute him, find him guilty of selling himself out, and sentence him to a life of remorse and guilt for betraying his badge, his sworn oath, and himself.

"Negative," Lassen said on the radio. "Do not engage, repeat, do not engage. Stay clear of the suspect aircraft, tail him as long as you can, report his position. Hunter out."

Cazaux taxied the LET to the end of runway 13 Right, rapidly performing last-second checklist items as he aligned himself with the runway centerline. Then he stomped hard on the brakes and held them. The Stork was intently watching the engine instruments as Cazaux pushed the throttles up. The LET rumbled and rattled like a freight train out of control as the two sets of engine needles began to move. They heard a few loud coughs and bangs from the engines, and out the corner of an eye Krull could see long tongues of flame occasionally bursting from the exhausts and lighting up the tarmac.

"Attention aircraft on runway one-three right, warning, shut down your engines immediately."

The Stork yelled something and pointed to one of the instruments, but Cazaux shook his head. Krull saw several gauges with their needles in the red arcs, but Cazaux was ignoring them all. It seemed to take forever, but finally the power needle made it up past 90 percent, and Cazaux released the brakes. The Stork kept his hand on the throttles to make sure they were full forward, jabbering away unintelligibly about something. The engines still didn't sound right, were obviously not putting out full power yet.

"Hey, Captain," Krull said, "this looks bad."

"Sixty knots . . . *now!*" Cazaux shouted. Krull hit the stopwatch. "Just be quiet and give me a countdown."

"Five seconds!" Krull shouted. It looked as if the airspeed needle had barely moved. "Eight seconds . . ." The needle was just over ninety knots, bouncing back and forth wildly in its case. "Ready, ready . . . *now!*"

Cazaux did nothing but continue to watch the instruments, both hands on the yoke, feet dancing on the rudder pedals, trying to keep the plane on the centerline.

"I said twelve seconds, Cazaux, twelve seconds! We're only at one-ten. Aren't you going to abort the takeoff?"

"Not likely," Cazaux said. He waited until the runway end-identifier lights had flashed under the nose, then hauled back on the control yoke with all his might. The nose of the LET L-600 hung in the air precariously. The Stork's eyes were wide with fear as the white chevrons of the runway overrun area became visible—and then the cargo plane lifted off. But it was as if the Belgian mercenary wanted to commit suicide, because he immediately pushed the control yoke away from his body, forcing the nose of the LET *down.*

"What the hell are you doin'?"

"Shut up, goddammit!" Cazaux shouted. "We lifted off the runway in ground effect—we aren't at flying speed yet." His eyes were glued to the airspeed and vertical-speed indicators. Airspeed was pegged at one-ten, still ten knots below flying speed. Krull could do nothing but watch the trees at the departure end of the runway get closer and closer by the second. A lighted windsock whizzed by, the orange, cone-shaped flag not far below eye level. They were still too low.

"Pull up!" Krull shouted. "We're gonna hit!"

Cazaux watched, and in a few seconds the airspeed indicator crept up to one-twenty and the vertical speed indicator nudged upwards. As soon as it did, Cazaux raised the landing-gear handle. The cockpit occupants heard a loud *swiissssh!* outside the windows as the tops of a stand of trees were chewed apart by the propellers. Krull could see the lights of homes atop the nearby hills getting larger and larger by the second. But as soon as the red landing gear warning lights were out, Krull felt pressure on the bottom of his feet, the LET behaved more like an airplane and less like a ballistic sausage, and the homes disappeared safely under the nose—close enough to rattle the windows, but there was no impact.

"Jesus . . . man, I thought we were goners," Krull exhaled. "You either crazy or you got big brass balls. What was all that bullshit about acceleration timing? I thought you said you were gonna abort the damn takeoff."

"Mr. Krull, there is only one thing worse than dying in a massive fireball in Chico, California, and not making the delivery as promised," Cazaux said as he slowly, incrementally raised the flaps, carefully watching the airspeed to make sure it didn't decay, "and that is surrendering to the police or to the military. I will never surrender. They will have to take my bullet-riddled body away before I will give up, and I will take as many with me as possible before I go. If I'm awake I will try to escape, because capture is worse than death to me. I was in a prison once. It will never happen again."

"Well, you crazy motherfucker, you did it," Krull said with undisguised glee and relief. "Those pricks ain't gonna catch us now." The Stork looked at Krull with wide, white, disbelieving eyes, then began to laugh loud enough to be heard over the thunder of the LET's turboprops. "What's this brother laughin' at?"

"He's laughing because we're not out of danger yet, Mr. Krull," Cazaux said. "If the authorities want me as badly as I think they do, they have one more card they can play."

Southwest Air Defense Sector Operations Command Center (SOCC)
March AFB, Riverside, California

The night crew had just finished a grueling three-hour-long exercise in which a flight of ten Sukhoi-25 attack bombers from Mexico had tried to penetrate the air defense screen around the United States and bomb the Coast Guard base at San Diego and the U.S. Customs base at March Air Force Base so all drug smugglers could enter the United States easier. They had gotten that idea from a series of actual attacks a group of Cuban terrorists had made a few years back, when sophisticated drug cartels used military weapons to protect their drug shipments from American interdiction forces. That was good for about a dozen different air defense scenarios built into the computer system at the Southwest Air Defense Sector.

Lieutenant Colonel John Berrell, the Senior Director on the floor that evening, made the last few remarks in his shift exercise critique sheet. Overall, it was a very good exercise. His shift was young and inexperienced, but they performed well. There were usually no instructors around at night, so every console operator had to be on his toes and be prepared to carry his or her load alone. A few coordination items had been missed by overzealous operators in one of the Weapons Control Teams who thought they knew their procedures down cold and didn't use their checklists. The plastic-covered pages in the red folders before each operator had been built over decades of experience and covered every known contingency in the air defense game. It was almost guaranteed to keep the operators out of trouble when the fur started flying.

His crew had accomplished the most important aspect of the job: detect, track, and identify.

Berrell clicked on his master intercom button: "Ops to all stations, well done." No use pointing out the ones that screwed up—they still had a long night ahead of them, and he wanted everyone's mind clear and sharp. "Run your postexercise checklists and check your switches are back in real-world mode. Repeat, check switches back in real-world mode." Several years ago in Europe, an American air defense unit had been running a computer simulation in which a large stream of Soviet bombers invaded West Germany. The exercise was a success and the computer-generated bad guys driven off—unfortunately, after the exercise, one operator forgot to turn off the simulation. An hour later, the "second wave" of Soviet bombers "appeared" on radar, and the panicked operator scrambled dozens of very real, very expensive American, West German, Belgian, Norwegian, and Danish fighters against the phantom bombers before someone realized it was not happening.

Those were the good ol' days, Berrell thought. Before the sweeping world political changes in 1991 and 1992, air defense units were the spearhead of national defense and deterrence. Radar constantly sweeping the horizon, young faces staring at green cathode ray tube radarscopes, picking out the enemy from within the friendly targets; determined, daring men sitting by their planes ready to launch at a moment's notice to track down and destroy any intruder. Before 1992, before the collapse of the Soviet bloc, the threat was deadly real. A Soviet Backfire bomber that appeared on radar five hundred miles off the coast was already in position to launch a large AS-12 nuclear cruise missile—one such missile could destroy Washington, D.C., or any major city on the eastern seaboard.

Now, in 1994, the Soviet Union was gone; the Russian long-range bomber threat was nonexistent. The Russians were still flying their heavy bombers, but now they were *selling* rides to wealthy Westerners in mock bomb runs out in Nevada, for God's sake! The air defense forces of the United States had been cut down to only eighteen locations across the contiguous United States, Alaska, Hawaii, and Puerto Rico. With only two alert aircraft per location, that meant a total of thirty-six aircraft were defending approximately forty *million* cubic miles of airspace. True, many countries, including Russia, China, Iran, and North Korea, still had bombers and cruise missiles aimed at the United States, but the real day-to-day threat had all but disappeared. Air defense had all but gone away as a mission.

America still had a need to protect and patrol its borders and maintain the capability to hunt down and identify intruders, but now the intruders were terrorists, hijackers, criminals, drug smugglers, and lawbreakers. In order to prove to the world that the United States was not becoming lax about national defense and readiness, it was important for America to demonstrate its capability to patrol its frontiers. The remaining air defense units were clustered in the south and the southeast instead of the north so that the fighters could better cover the Mexican and Caribbean regions, where drug smugglers, illegal alien movements, and fugitive flights were clustered.

Berrell was busy reviewing the postexercise checklist cleanup and working on the after-action critique when the deputy sector commander, Navy Captain Francine Tellman, came over and sat beside him. As part of NORAD, the North American Air Defense Command, the individual air defense sectors were under joint services command, representing all the branches of the U.S. military as well as the air defense forces of Canada. Tellman, a twenty-year Navy veteran of air traffic control and air defense operations, was the Navy's representative at the Southwest sector. The fifty-two-year-old Navy veteran was not due to come on duty for another three or four hours, but it was typical of her to come in early when a big exercise or some other unusual event was underway. Divorced twice and currently unattached, the sector was the big part of her life now. "Evening, John," she said to Berrell. "How did the Hammerheads-7 surge exercise go?"

"It went fine, Francine. I need to schedule George on WCT three for a refresher on checklist discipline—he missed a couple coordination calls. Other than that . . ." The phone rang at Berrell's console—the flashing button was the direct line between the sector and the chief of the Oakland Air Route Traffic Control Center. Oakland ARTCC, or Oakland Center, was one of the busiest and most diverse air traffic regions in the world, covering northern and central California and Nevada. "Southwest Air Defense Sector, Senior Director, Lieutenant Colonel Berrell."

"John, this is Mike Leahy," the deputy director of Oakland Center replied. "I just got a call from a Special Agent Fortuna of ATF. They have a fugitive smuggling suspect that just launched out of Chico Airport, and they're asking for assistance. He's southwest-bound, not squawking. His ID code is seven-delta-four-zero-four."

"Sure, Mike," Berrell replied. "Stand by one." Berrell put Leahy on hold and turned to his SD tech, Master Sergeant Thomas Bidwell. It was not unusual at all to get calls like that from the FAA—that's what the hot line was for—but to get it directly from the deputy director of the Center was a bit unusual. "Tom, Oakland Center has a recent fugitive departure from Chico airport, ID number seven-delta-four-zero-four. Zero in on him for us. Don't make him a pending yet, just an item of interest. Request for support from ATF."

"Yes, sir," Bidwell replied. He opened his checklist to the proper page, logged the time of the request in the correct block, and passed the information to the Surveillance and Identification sections—since this was a target already over land, and the Sector Operations Command Center usually only tracked targets penetrating the air defense identification zones, Bidwell had to get his technicians to break out the new target from the hundreds of others on the scope and display it to each section. On the phone, Berrell said, "Mike, I got your slimeball on radar. Do you want to make him a pending or just monitor him for you?"

"Monitor him for now," Leahy said. "I don't know what Treasury wants to do. You might want to get your flyboys up out of bed and thinking about heading toward their jets, though."

"Is this an exercise, Mike?"

" 'Fraid not, Colonel," Leahy said. "The pilot of this one is apparently some hotshot gun smuggler. The suspect killed some ATF agents at Chico a few minutes ago. He's got several tons of explosives on board his plane."

Berrell rose out of his seat, pointed to an extra phone for Tellman to listen in on the call, and rang a small desk-clerk bell on top of his console with a slap of his left hand. Serious shit was going down. Technicians who were chatting and taking a breather hurried to their stations and began scanning their instruments. "What kind of plane is it, Mike?" Berrell asked.

"A Czechoslovakian LET L-600," Leahy replied after retrieving some notes. "Twin-turboprop medium transport. Gross weight about thirty thousand pounds, payload with full fuel about six thousand."

"What kind of explosives is he carrying?"

"You name it," Leahy replied. "Ammunition, demolition stuff, pyrotechnics. Suspect might be connected with a National Guard armory heist a few years ago. You heard of the name Henri Cazaux before?"

"Oh, shit," Berrell said, cursing under his breath. Had the world heard about Carlos the Jackal? The IRA? Abu Nidal? "I understand," Berrell said. "Stand by one." *Fuck,* he thought, *this one's going to happen.* A night intercept, over a heavily populated area, with dangerous fugitives and someone like Cazaux on board. Berrell never wanted to see his sector's pilots or anyone on the ground put in harm's way, but if there was a way to gun down Henri Cazaux, Berrell wanted to do it.

Berrell turned to his SD technician, but Bidwell had been listening in and was ready with the information Berrell wanted: "Sir, I recommend we put Fresno in battle stations," he said. "I'm betting he'll make a run for Mexico, but we'll have to wait and see. A cargo plane like an L-600 has plenty of legs—he can go either to Canada or Mexico. But I'll put my money on Mexico."

Sergeant Bidwell was seldom wrong—in fact, Berrell couldn't recall when one of his predictions was off the mark. Bidwell was always tuned toward economizing their forces—predicting the flight path of the target and putting the closest interceptors on the target. But Berrell had a feeling that the Treasury Department and ATF weren't going to care about economy on this one. They wanted every throttle jockey in the Air Force ready to jump the bastard that killed their agents. Cazaux was supposed to be as wily as he was psychotic, and Berrell didn't want anyone in his sector to drop the ball if they had a chance to catch him. "All the same, get Kingsley and March suited up, too," Berrell said. "I got a feeling Treasury or the ATF won't want to let this guy go as long as he's within radar range of the States. Let's get Northwest sector geared up in case this turns out to be a relay marathon, too." The Oakland Center phone rang again. "Senior Director Berrell."

"We just got word from the Treasury Department," Leahy said. "They want you to intercept the target, accomplish a covert shadow, and stand by for further instructions. It sounds like Treasury is leaning toward an intercept and force-down. Treasury would like to try to force him away from populated areas if possible, and then attempt to force him down at a less populated airport or over water."

"Mike, I have Captain Tellman, the deputy sector commander, on the line. Repeat what you just said." The FAA Center deputy repeated his message. "Mike, we need to talk to Justice and Treasury right away and straighten those boys out," Tellman said, "because you know we don't have any procedures for trying to force an aircraft down."

"You can't fire some shots across his bow, crowd him a little on one side to make him turn?"

"You been watching too much TV. We have no procedures for anything like that, and I wouldn't want to free-lance something like that at night over populated areas with a terrorist like Cazaux at the controls of a plane full of explosives. The potential for disaster is too high, especially compared with the option of just letting him go and shadowing him. But even if Air Combat Command approved a maneuver like that, I don't think it would work. If the target doesn't comply with visual, light, or radio signals to follow or turn, we either shadow him or shoot him down. Period. Our procedures say we can't get any closer than searchlight range of a known armed aircraft, and I'm sure as hell not going to have them try to turn a plane loaded with explosives—especially one piloted by an operator like Cazaux."

"All right, Captain, I hear you," Leahy said. "I'm just passing on this ATF agent's requests. Obviously he doesn't know your procedures, and he thinks you'll do whatever he asks because of his dead agents. We'll have to conference-call this one with Justice. What's your recommendation?''

''I'd gladly give the order to blow this scumbag out of the sky,'' Berrell said, ''but your best option is to have us do a covert shadow on the target, find out where he goes. Does ATF know his destination?''

''I don't think so,'' Leahy replied. ''He's filed a VFR flight plan to Mesa, Arizona, but I don't think anyone expects him to land there.''

''If he goes away from the mainland, then we can talk about trying some heroics, if you want to catch him so bad—and I think we'd all like to bring that bastard down,'' Berrell suggested. ''But if he stays over U.S. soil, I recommend a covert shadow. My fighters can follow him easily, and with our night-vision gear, Cazaux won't even know he's being tailed by an F-16 Fighting Falcon. Have ATF agents leapfrog after us in jets or helicopters, land when he lands, then nail him.''

''Stand by, Colonel, and I'll pass that along to Treasury,'' Leahy said. The reply did not take long: ''ATF didn't see anything wrong with just putting a missile into him,'' Leahy said, ''but the Treasury Department okayed the shadow. They'll be putting the official request for support through channels, but I'm authorized to request assistance now.''

''You got it, Mike. I concur and agree. Stand by.'' He turned to Captain Tellman, who had been listening in on a companion phone at Berrell's console. ''What do you think, Francine?''

''Well, I'm with the covert ID and shadow also,'' the Navy captain replied. ''What's his track?''

Berrell checked the radar once again. ''Still heading southeast, away from San Francisco Class B airspace,'' he said. ''Class B airspace,'' what was once called a Terminal Control Area, was the high-density air traffic airspace over San Francisco airport, the fifth-busiest airport in the United States. The target was approaching the ''upside-down wedding cake'' of the class B airspace, so technically he was clear, but San Francisco International averaged one landing and one departure every sixty seconds all day long, and the target with fighters in pursuit was definitely going to mess up air traffic if he decided to veer back toward San Francisco.

''I agree with Sergeant Bidwell, except I think we ought to move on the target as soon as possible in case he heads for the Sierras and we lose him,'' Tellman said. ''Scramble Fresno, put Kingsley at battle stations, and suit up March. We should also get the alert AWACS airborne from Tinker in case he tries to hide in the mountains.'' The Air Force E-3 Sentry AWACS (Airborne Warning and Communications System) was a radar plane designed to look down and track aircraft at all altitudes from long range—if their target made it over the Sierra Nevada Mountains before a fighter found it, ground-based radars could lose it. ''I'll get on the horn to the commander.''

''Roger,'' Berrell said. He opened his checklist binder, got out his grease pencil, then turned to Sergeant Bidwell and said, ''Okay, Tom, make the target a Special-9, covert ID and covert shadow.''

''Yes, sir,'' Bidwell said. He opened up his own checklist, filled out the first few squares, then announced over the building-wide intercom, ''Attention in the facility, attention in the facility, target ID number seven-delta-four-zero-four, designate a Special-9, repeat, Special-9 covert intercept, stand by for active alert scramble Fresno. All duty controllers report to your stations. All duty controllers report to your stations.''

''SD, this is the WAO, we have positive contact on target ID seven-delta-four-zero-four, confirm ID.'' The WAO, or Weapons Assignment Officer, was the overall supervisor of the section of the command center that controlled the fighters from takeoff to landing and monitored the entire intercept.

''Target ID seven-delta-four-zero-four, confirmed, WAO, you have the intercept.''

''Roger, SD, WAO has the intercept,'' the senior Weapons Assignment Officer replied. He made an entry in his checklist log, then turned to the WAT, or weapons assignment technician, seated next to him. ''Active alert scramble, Fresno, hold for confirmation. Put WCT One on this one.''

''Copy, sir,'' the WAT replied. He checked the status readout of the four Weapons Control Teams (WCT) on his panel to be sure the team the Assignment Officer wanted was free and were ready to go to work. The WCT, consisting of one Weapons Director and a Weapons Technician, would be the persons in contact with the interceptor throughout its mission. WCT One was the most experienced of the young shift on that night. The WAT clicked open his intercom after seeing that all four WCTs were ready to go: ''WCT One, your target ID is seven-delta-four-zero-four, a Special-9 covert intercept, repeat, Special-9 covert intercept. Clear for active air scramble Fresno.''

''WCT One copies all,'' the Weapons Director of Control Team

One responded. "We have the intercept. All stations, this is WCT One, stand by for active alert scramble Fresno, target ID seven-delta-four-zero-four."

The weapons technician opened his checklist to the proper page, cleared his throat, then ran his hand along a row of switches guarded by clear plastic covers, selected the one marked FRESNO, opened the cover, and stopped. "Sir, I have Fresno, active alert scramble. Ready."

The Weapons Director checked to be sure that the technician had his finger on the right button, then tapped him on the shoulder and pointed at the button, and the communications technician pressed the button. Silently, he said, *Sorry to get you up like this, boys,* apologizing to the crews up in Fresno for what he knew was going to be a rude awakening.

Interceptor Alert Facility, 94th Fighter Squadron (California Air National Guard) Fresno Air Terminal, California

The Navy called it "channel fever," describing the excitement of the last full night at sea before pulling into port. Back in the days of the Strategic Air Command, when most alert units changed over on Thursdays, it was called "Woody Wednesday," describing the almost unbearable anticipation most crewmen felt about going home and greeting the wife or girlfriend after seven days on 'round-the-clock alert. Whatever it was called, the feeling was the same—you were so excited about getting off alert and going home that you stayed up late, ate every piece of food in sight, watched every movie available, played poker all night, and generally burned yourself out.

Major Linda McKenzie, one of the two F-16A ADF (Air Defense Fighter) pilots on duty at Fresno Air Terminal in central California, pushed herself away from the all-night poker game table at ten-thirty P.M. Channel fever was not too bad here at Fresno—alert was only three days, and families spent a lot of time with the crews at the alert facility. The anticipation was still real, however, and it usually manifested itself as an all-night poker game, attended by every available crewman at the facility. McKenzie had been playing for the past five hours, and she had finally gotten to the point where the need for sleep was numbing the excitement of getting off alert. "I'm out," she said after the last hand had finished. She steeled herself for the simultaneous moans of disappointment from the crew chiefs and security guards around the table, gave everyone a tired and slightly irritated smile, then reached out to scoop up the small pile of coins and dollar bills on the table before her.

"C'mon, Linda, one more hand," her flight leader, Lieutenant Colonel Al "Rattler" Vincenti, pleaded. But even he could not stifle a yawn. Vincenti was a longtime veteran of air defense, flying with the 194th Fighter Squadron "Black Griffins" since 1978. He was a veteran command pilot with over seven thousand hours' flying time, all in tactical fighters.

"Hey, I'm on a three-hop to Seattle in thirteen hours. You get to sleep in. Don't give me this bull." Like many Air National Guard pilots, McKenzie was an airline pilot, a first officer with American Airlines based out of San Francisco. Because of monthly flight duty day restrictions, the airlines gave each Guardsman plenty of time to spend on UTA, unit training assembly.

"Is this the same person who threatened to emasculate us all if we got up and left the game last week?" one of the crew chiefs asked. "Little bit different if you're winning, isn't it, Linda?"

"Damn right it is," McKenzie said. "I'm outta here. See you clowns in the morning." She traded in coins for bills, stuffed her winning into her left breast pocket, and headed for her quarters.

Once there, Linda McKenzie got undressed, taking the unusual risk of piling her clothes and survival gear in a heap rather than laying it out so she could easily find it all and dress quickly. The last scramble exercise was early that morning, which meant the odds of getting another one in the middle of the night on the night before changeover were slim, so she decided to risk a quick shower. No luxuriating in the shower while on alert—get in, get clean, and get out—but she was relaxed as she did so, confident that there would be no interruptions. Her shower took less than five minutes.

Perfect timing.

She heard voices in the hallway, then the door next to hers open. Wrapping a towel around herself, she peeked out her door just as Al Vincenti was closing his. "Al? Come here a second." He stepped over to her, and when he was in range she grasped the front of his flight suit and pulled him into her room.

"Linda, what in hell are you—" But he was interrupted as she wrapped her arms around him and gave him a kiss. He resisted at first, then relented. That only spurred her on, and she held him in her grasp even longer. She finally released him, but began kissing his neck and unzipping his flight suit. "Linda, it's late."

"Nobody will hear us, Al. The game will go on for another hour at least, and the crew chiefs all like to sleep in front of the TV."

"Linda, I'm not going to do anything with you," he said. His flight suit zipper was down to the top of his G-suit waistband, and she was reaching for the zippers on the sides of the device. He was not helping her, but he was not stopping her either. "Linda . . ."

"You don't have to do anything," McKenzie said in a whisper. "I'm doing the driving on this trip." She stepped back from him, removed her towel, grasped his hands, and brought them to her breasts.

"Linda, this isn't a good idea."

"I won't argue with that," McKenzie said with a teasing smile, "but I should tell you, Colonel, that you have more animal sex appeal in your little finger than most guys half your age have in their entire bodies."

"That include your husband Carl?"

"I'm *referring* to my husband Carl." McKenzie laughed, running her hands inside his flight suit against his chest.

"You think just because I made a stupid mistake by screwing you at SENTRY EAGLE in Klamath Falls last summer that I think this is right or justified? I'm not going to sleep with you, Linda."

Suddenly, the PA system blared, *"For the alert force, for the alert force, active air scramble, active air scramble! All crews report to your combat stations!"* and an impossibly loud klaxon split the late-night quiet. Vincenti was zipped and out the door in seconds, leaving McKenzie cursing as she hurried to get into her flight suit and G-suit.

Al Vincenti had a fleeting vision of McKenzie's flowing, wet red hair and big, round, firm breasts float in his mind's eye as he made the dash to his plane, but the thought quickly disappeared as he automatically ran down the alert scramble checklists and procedures in his head. She was nothing more than a wingman to him now, his backup, someone to watch his rear quadrant as they hunted down whatever was out there. Vincenti sprinted for the alert hangar. His crew chief, who had just come around a corner, had no chance to catch up. Vincenti reached the hangar first.

On the wall to the right of the small entry door were two large handles. Vincenti yelled, "Hangar doors coming open!" and pulled both handles down. The handles unlocked two sets of huge counterweights, whose weight began swinging both the front and rear hangar doors open. His backpack parachute was in a rack near the hangar door handles. Vincenti stepped into the parachute harness and fastened the crotch and chest clips, leaving the straps loose so he could run up the ladder and into his F-16 ADF Fighting Falcon fighter jet. Gloves went on, sleeves rolled down, zippers zipped, and collars turned up as Vincenti trotted toward his fighter.

Six steps up the ladder and a quick leap into the cockpit, and Lieutenant Colonel Al Vincenti was in his office and ready for work.

As soon as his helmet was on and fastened, he flipped the MAIN PWR switch to BATT, the JFS (Jet Fuel Starter) switch to START 1, cracked the throttle on the left side of the cockpit from its cutoff detent forward a bit to give the engine a good shot of gas, then moved it back into idle when the rpms reached 15 percent.

Sixty seconds later, the engine was at idle power and his crew chief had his seat belt, parachute, and G-suit hoses connected and tightened. The GPS system was feeding navigation information to the inertial navigation set, and he performed a flight control system and emergency power system check. He made a quick flight control check by moving the control stick in a circle, or "stirring the pot," and his crew chief was standing in front of the hangar, ready to marshal him forward. He saw Major Linda McKenzie running past his open hangar door, carrying her boots and wearing nothing on her feet but white athletic socks, still zipping her G-suit zippers. She flashed her middle finger at him as she sprinted by.

"Should've showed me your tits *after* you put your gear on, Linda," Vincenti said, chuckling. He completed his checklists, flipping through the radios as he waited for McKenzie to start engines and check in. His VHF radio, secondary UHF radio, and HF radios were set to the GUARD emergency frequencies, but there was dead silence. The silence meant that this was going to be a covert intercept—they were going to try to approach the unidentified aircraft without being detected.

Vincenti unstowed a canvas box from behind his ejection seat, opened it, and checked the contents. It was a set of AN/NVG-11 night-vision goggles which clipped onto his flight helmet and would provide near daytime-like vision with just a few ground lights, moonlight, or even starlight.

Vincenti saw McKenzie's crew chief trot out to his marshaling position outside the hangar, and a second later he saw her fighter's taxi light flash on and off, so he clicked on the microphone of his primary radio: "Foxtrot Romeo flight, check."

"Two," McKenzie replied breathlessly from exertion and excitement. "Foxtrot Romeo" was their unit call sign for their three-day tour; interceptor call signs were always a combination of two letters and a two-digit number, changed regularly by North American Air Defense Command.

"Fresno ground, Foxtrot Romeo flight ready to taxi, active air scramble."

"Foxtrot Romeo flight, Fresno ground, taxi runway three-two, wind calm, altimeter three-zero-zero-six." The traffic signal on the fence changed from a flashing red to green, Vincenti flipped the flight control/nav function knob to NAV, armed his ejection seat, turned on the taxi light and released brakes, received final clearance from his crew chief, and shot out of the alert hangar, snapping a return salute and a thumbs-up to his crew chief. As soon as he was on the throat leading to the end of the runway, he radioed, "Foxtrot Romeo flight, button two, go."

"Two."

He switched to the tower frequency: "Foxtrot Romeo flight, check."

"Two."

"Fresno tower, Foxtrot Romeo flight, active alert scramble."

"Foxtrot Romeo flight, Fresno tower, wind calm, runway three-two, cleared for takeoff, contact Fresno Approach."

"Foxtrot Romeo flight cleared for takeoff, Foxtrot Romeo flight, button three, go."

"Two."

Vincenti switched to the next preset channel, checked in McKenzie; then: "Fresno Approach, Foxtrot Romeo flight of two, takeoff roll Fresno, active air scramble."

"Foxtrot Romeo flight, Fresno Approach, air scramble departure, climb unrestricted, contact Oakland Center passing ten thousand."

"Foxtrot Romeo flight, wilco." Without stopping or looking for McKenzie, he taxied quickly to the runway, lined up, gave his control stick one more experimental "stir," moved the throttle to military power, twisted the throttle grip, and shoved it forward to full afterburner. At seventy knots he clicked off nosewheel steering, at ninety knots he rotated the nose to liftoff attitude, and at one hundred and twenty knots the F-16 Fighting Falcon lifted into the sky. He immediately lowered the nose to build up airspeed, retracted landing gear, made sure the trailing-edge flaps were up, accelerated to two hundred and fifty knots, then pulled the nose skyward. By the time he was over the end of the runway, he was two thousand feet above the ground. At four hundred and fifty knots he pulled the throttle out of afterburner and into military power, then clicked on his radio: "Foxtrot Romeo flight, button four, go."

"Two."

He switched radio frequencies. By that time he was passing ten thousand feet. "Foxtrot Romeo flight, check."

"Two."

"Oakland Center, Foxtrot Romeo flight of two with you out of ten thousand, active alert scramble."

"Foxtrot Romeo flight, radar contact seven miles northwest of Fresno Air Terminal passing ten thousand feet, have your wingman squawk standby, cleared to tactical control frequency."

"Foxtrot Romeo flight, squawk standby, button five, go."

"Two."

On March Air Force Base's SIERRA PETE's frequency now, Vincenti checked in McKenzie, then: "SIERRA PETE, Foxtrot Romeo flight is with you, passing sixteen thousand."

"Foxtrot Romeo flight, radar contact, check noses cold, turn left heading three-zero-zero, climb and maintain angels two-four block two-five."

"Copy, heading three-zero-zero, climbing to two-four block two-five, Foxtrot Romeo flight, check." Vincenti had to push the nose down to level off at twenty-four thousand feet—usually he was sent to thirty thousand feet or higher. He quickly accomplished his "After Takeoff" and "Level-Off" checklists, checking his oxygen, cabin pressurization, fuel feed, and all gauges and switches, especially checking that the arming switches for the 20-millimeter cannon were off—that was the "noses cold" check. The external tanks were empty, and he was already feeding from his wing tanks—about two hours of fuel remaining.

"Two's in the green, twenty point nine, nose is cold," McKenzie reported after her cockpit checks were completed, including her fuel and weapons status with her report.

"Copy. Lead's in the green with nineteen, nose is cold."

"Roger, Foxtrot Romeo flight, copy you are in the green and noses cold," the Weapons Control Technician at March Air Force

Base, call sign SIERRA PETE, replied. "Your bogey is now at your eleven o'clock, one hundred and fifty miles, a Czechoslovakian L-600 cargo plane at six thousand feet and climbing. These are vectors for a Special-9 intercept."

"Foxtrot Romeo copies," Vincenti replied. *Pretty good guess,* he thought, congratulating himself—a Special-9 intercept was a covert shadow, where the SOCC controller would put him on a one-mile rear-quartering vector on the bogey. From there, he would use his night-vision goggles to close in on the bogey. If they needed a tail number or other such positive identification, they could close in more—Vincenti had flown as close as ten meters to another plane, in total darkness, without the other plane ever knowing he was there—but normally they would stay within fifty to one hundred meters of the target and shadow him while the brass on the ground figured out what to do. "Foxtrot Romeo flight, take spacing and configure for Special-9."

"Two." McKenzie would now move out to about five miles in trail, keeping her flight leader locked on radar, and put on and test her night-vision goggles. Vincenti turned off all the cockpit and external lights, reached into the canvas case for the AN/NVG-11 goggles, slid them into place entirely by feel, and snapped them into the slot on his helmet.

But when Vincenti lowered the goggles into place, all he got was black. He flipped the on-off switch, made sure they were turned on, and looked for the telltale green spot of light behind the lenses. Nothing. The battery was in place, and they were tested and replaced after every use and at the beginning of every three-day shift. These were dead. He clicked open his mike button in frustration: "Hey, Two," Vincenti radioed to McKenzie, "did you check your NVGs yet?"

"Affirmative," McKenzie replied. "They're in the green."

"My NVGs are bent. You got the lead and the intercept."

"Roger that, Rattler." The excitement in McKenzie's voice was obvious. Except during exercises or when McKenzie was paired with a less experienced wingman, Vincenti was always the flight lead and always did the intercepts. "Take the bottom of the block, I got the top, and I got the radios. Take spacing. I have the lead."

"Roger, you have the lead," Vincenti replied, descending to twenty-four thousand feet and pulling power back to 80 percent. He tuned up his radar, preparing to lock on to her when she passed by.

"Foxtrot Romeo, your bogey is at eleven o'clock, ninety miles, turn right heading three-three-zero, maintain angels twenty,'' the weapons controller at SIERRA PETE directed.

McKenzie acknowledged the call. She had pushed the power up to nearly full military power, anxious to get the intercept going, and Vincenti had to hit the afterburner to catch up once her fighter passed by and assumed the lead.

''Foxtrot Romeo, your bogey is heading southwestbound, altitude nine thousand five hundred, airspeed two-two-five knots, squawking VFR, call when tied on.''

That was the ''setup'' call, probably the last radio call before the F-16's AN/APG-66 radar would pick up the target, helping to get the pilots oriented. Once the radar locked on and the proper target identified, the fire control computer would present steering cues on the HUD, or heads-up display, a transparent electronic screen in front of the pilot that allowed the pilot to read flight, radar, and weapon information without looking down into the cockpit.

McKenzie's radar was picking up several air targets at altitudes between five to twenty thousand feet, but there were not many aircraft flying around at eleven o'clock at night. About two minutes later, at a range of about forty miles, McKenzie locked on to an aircraft that met the last reported radar track information perfectly: ''SIERRA PETE, Foxtrot Romeo has radar contact on a bogey at thirty-eight miles, angels nine-point-five, bearing zero-one-zero.''

''Foxtrot Romeo, that's your bogey.''

''Roger. Foxtrot Romeo is judy, request clearance for the Special-9.''

''Foxtrot Romeo, this is SIERRA PETE, you are cleared for Special-9 procedures.''

''Foxtrot Romeo copies,'' McKenzie said, the excitement spilling over in her voice. Vincenti had to smile to himself. This was certainly not McKenzie's first intercept, or even her first night intercept, but it was one of her most important. He remembered his first no-shit real-world night intercept well, a Chinese airliner suspected of being a spy plane that was ''drifting off course'' and trying to fly over the Alameda Naval Base near Oakland. That was over fifteen years ago.

That was just one of the things Vincenti remembered in what had been, for him, a pretty good career. He got into flying back in the 1960s, after receiving his bachelor of arts degree in political science from West Virginia State University in 1967. He'd attended college on a football scholarship. The typical jock. But unlike a lot of jocks who went on to illustrious jobs like selling cars and getting flabby, Vincenti was unable to avoid the draft and ended up in Officer Candidate School, where he received a commission and attended pilot training in 1968. He flew 113 missions in Vietnam in the F-100 Super Sabre fighter-bomber and the F-4D Phantom II fighter-bomber from 1969 to 1973, as well as holding command positions in various tactical units.

Vincenti went on to the Air Command and Staff College upon returning from Vietnam and joined tactical and training units in New Jersey and Arizona, but was later involuntarily separated from the active-duty Air Force, after his second divorce. He got a position with the California Air National Guard in 1978. Except for a brief deployment to Germany in 1986 and 1987, Vincenti had been flying F-106s, F-4Ds and F-16 fighters from the Fresno Air Terminal for seventeen years.

And speaking of flying . . . his mind immediately returned to the situation at hand. In this intercept, McKenzie still had to remember her procedures and not get caught up in the excitement. Vincenti checked a plastic-covered decoder device strapped to his left leg, sliding a yellow plastic marker to the fifth row of characters, then keyed his mike button: "SIERRA PETE, Foxtrot Romeo flight, authenticate echo-echo."

"SIERRA PETE authenticates india," came the reply. It was the correct reply. All intercept instructions that might place a fighter within close proximity of another aircraft in a potentially unsafe manner had to be authenticated, whether or not weapons were expected to be employed, using the daily authenticator cards issued to every pilot. Hopefully, this one omission was going to be the last one for Linda McKenzie tonight, Vincenti thought ruefully. Well, that's what wingmen were for—back up the leader at all times.

Unfortunately, there was one switch McKenzie did forget.

On a normal intercept, the 150,000-candlepower identification light on the left side of the nose was used to illuminate the target—on a Special-9 covert intercept, the light was supposed to be out. The large, bright beam, twice as bright as an airliner's landing lights, was on full bright as McKenzie made her approach toward the target, and, because it was a crystal-clear night and he was flying five miles behind and to his leader's right side, Vincenti didn't notice the light was on.

* * *

It was the Stork who saw it first, high and far off in the distance, to the right rear of the LET L-600 and almost blocked from view by the right wing and engine nacelle. The horizon was dark, and the single, unblinking light was like a laser beam aimed right at them. He grasped Cazaux's right sleeve and pointed. The Belgian mercenary had to get up out of his seat to get a glimpse of the light. "I see it," Cazaux acknowledged. It was hard to judge distances at night, but the brightness of the light could mean that the aircraft, if it was an airliner, was pretty far off in both distance and altitude.

But it wasn't an airliner—Cazaux knew it right away.

It was moving fast and turning with them, not crossing their path. It was *intercepting* them, no doubt about it. *"Puta,* Stork," he said, "they found us already, the fuckers. I think they zeroed the Air Force in on us."

The Stork pointed to the San Francisco sectional chart and chattered away in a strange mixture of Ethiopian, English, and Spanish.

"Relax. There is nothing they can do to us."

"Say what?" Jefferson "Krull" Jones asked, staring out the windows with eyes so wide that the whites could be seen in the dark cockpit. "There's an Air Force jet out there? Is it gonna gun us down?"

"Relax," Cazaux said casually. "I have been intercepted dozens of times by the American Customs Service, the Coast Guard, and the Drug Enforcement Agency—even an Army helicopter. I have *never* been fired upon. I do not think they have the authority to kill anyone in peacetime without due process."

"Was that before or after you blew up a bunch of cops and an entire airport, my man?" Krull asked. "Maybe this might be the time they let those flyboys 'accidentally' let a few missiles fly." Krull motioned out the cockpit windscreen to the inky blackness of eastern California and the Sierra Nevada mountain range ahead. "Looks pretty black out there, Captain. A pretty good place to splash a bunch of gunrunners."

"Shut the fuck up. You don't know a damn thing." The big black hoodlum had vocalized Cazaux's own fear—this time, after so many close calls and so much death, the authorities might want Henri Cazaux out of the way for good. There was no one better to do it than the U.S. Air Force. Who would mourn his loss or condemn the United States for such an act? He had enemies all over the world, of every religion and nationality. The only ones to be sorry might be the bounty hunters who would be cheated out of the reward money.

No, he was *not* sure that the fighters would not open fire.

He thought about their route of flight. To try to stay away from ground radar, Cazaux had chosen to fly on the eastern slopes of the Sierra Nevadas, as low as he dared to go. The sectional aeronautical charts gave maximum elevation figures for each thirty-by-thirty-mile block of land, and he would simply add five hundred feet to each quadrangle elevation—that would put his plane well below radar coverage but safely above the terrain. But that wouldn't faze an airborne radar, such as from a fighter. Without extensive jamming equipment or fancy flying, Cazaux had no hope of trying to break a radar lock. If ordered to fire, the fighters would have a clear shot—and flying along the California-Nevada border, the area was desolate enough so as not to threaten citizens on the ground. They could simply pick their moment, and shoot.

"They will *not* open fire on us," Cazaux decided. "This is America, and they are the military—the military is forbidden to actively get involved in law-enforcement activities, except to assist in surveillance and to provide transportation. They cannot act as judge, jury, and executioner. Period."

"I sure hope you're right, Captain," Jones said, sitting back into the spot he had picked out in a corner of the cockpit. "And if you ain't, I don't want to know about it. I just hope it's over fast."

When the target's altitude dipped below the hemispheric altitude for his direction of flight, Vincenti became concerned. When his altitude dipped below the IFR (Instrument Flight Rules) minimum safe altitude in this area, he was more concerned—and when it drifted to within a few hundred feet of the rapidly rising terrain ahead, Vincenti was positive that they had been discovered. A quick S-turn to McKenzie's portside confirmed it: her big ID light was on full bright. The target must've seen the light and was attempting to descend into the mountainous terrain ahead. Their Special-9 covert intercept was blown. Well, no use in embarrassing McKenzie. Vincenti keyed his mike button: "Foxtrot Romeo, station check."

"I'll make the call when I'm ready, Two, just stand by."

"Foxtrot Romeo lead, I recommend a station check. I'm complete."

"Later, Al. Stand by."

She wasn't taking the hint. He had no choice: "Lead, I'm on your *left* wing. Check your damn switches!"

The ID light went out immediately this time—Vincenti could

almost feel her exasperation at her mistake, now that she realized what the target was doing and why. A few moments later, just as Vincenti was worrying about whether or not she was going to do something about the new development, he heard McKenzie on the command radio. "SIERRA PETE, this is Foxtrot Romeo. I believe the target aircraft got a visual on us. He has descended very close to the terrain in this area. Request further instructions." The weapons controller replied with a simple "Stand by, Foxtrot Romeo," and McKenzie and Vincenti were left with their thoughts and doubts as they closed in on the target.

"How in hell did they see the fighters closing in on them in the middle of the night?" Charles Lofstrom, Deputy Director and Chief of Operations for the Bureau of Alcohol, Tobacco, and Firearms, thundered over the phone. In the fifteen minutes since the F-16 fighters had been scrambled against Cazaux, the BATF, the Marshals Service, the Air Force, and the FAA were on a conference call, and Colonel Berrell had just finished briefing the conference members on the status of the chase. "I've worked with night intercepts before—done properly, the pursuer can close to within a few dozen yards without the suspect realizing a thing."

"It doesn't matter how it happened—it happened," U.S. Marshal Collins Baxter of the Eastern District of California interjected. "The problem is, the possibility exists that Cazaux knows he's being tailed."

"Let's shoot the bastard down, then," Agent Lofstrom said irritably. "I can get a warrant."

"We *can't* shoot him down, and that's that," Captain Tellman said. "I thought this was explained to you, Lofstrom."

"I know what you said, Captain, but I also know that I got a federal judge that will give me a warrant ordering you to take all necessary actions to stop Cazaux from escaping."

"A federal judge can't compel the Air Force to do anything, especially kill someone. If such a warrant existed, and if you asked me to follow its instructions, I would turn it over to my superior officer for evaluation, who I'm sure would turn it over to *his* superior . . . you get my drift, Lofstrom? I suggest you try a different approach."

Tellman's statement of the obvious infuriated Lofstrom, but he decided that trying a different approach might not be a bad idea: "I don't mean shoot him down, as in terminate him," Lofstrom said.

"What I meant was, scare him. Fire across his flight path, something like that."

"Agent Lofstrom, as I explained to you earlier, the only way our pilots are authorized to fire their weapons is to kill someone," Tellman said, shaking her head in exasperation. "We don't try to scare anyone by spraying the skies with twenty-millimeter shells."

"You do it in the Navy—you know, a shot across the bow."

"Only when we know precisely and absolutely that no one is in the way when the shell splashes down," Tellman explained. "Racing across north-central California at three hundred miles an hour and ten thousand feet in the air, there's no way of knowing who's under those rounds. And this would be done at night, at close quarters. We can't take the risk."

"*You* can't take the risk? What about my agents? What about the innocent victims at that airport? Christ, it's not Santa Claus we're chasing!" Lofstrom exclaimed. "Lady, Henri Cazaux is probably responsible for killing more human beings in the past three years than your precious Navy has since Vietnam."

"All the same, Lofstrom," Tellman said, "I won't put my forces in a situation where they may have to do that. Law enforcement should have gotten the suspect on the ground, alive. My interceptors can't do the job for you in the air."

"Then the suspect gets away with murder," Lofstrom said angrily, "and I won't allow that to happen. Six of my best agents died tonight, Captain Tellman, and I want Cazaux to pay for what he did. Your planes are in a position to do that—and I want some action!"

"Look, this argument is getting us nowhere," Timothy Lassen said via his portable scrambled phone from the parking ramp at Chico Airport, where his Black Hawk helicopter had set down—the open ramp was the only part of the airport not substantially damaged. "We've got the Air Force interceptors trailing the suspect, and he's got to come down sometime. It's doubtful if he has the fuel reserves to make it all the way into Mexico, but if he does, let's get DEA and the State Department on the horn and get permission to do a joint capture. We set up a helicopter relay for his route of flight, and we keep the Air Force fighters on the suspect's tail, augmented with Customs trackers and anyone else that can help. We send the helicopters down to recover the guns if he tries to drop them, and we'll know his exact location if he tries to land."

"We don't have time for that," Lofstrom said. "It takes time to set up a relay system, and days to coordinate with the Mexican government for law-enforcement support.''

''Cazaux will be airborne for at least two, and more likely three hours,'' Lassen said. ''I've already got the California Air National Guard alerted, and I've got access to all the helicopter support I need. We can get permission for the choppers to cross state lines.''

''So how in hell are your choppers in California going to chase down a fixed-wing flying over Nevada, Arizona, and New Mexico?'' Lofstrom asked. ''Unless they're right in Cazaux's flight path, they won't be able to catch up, even if they launched right this second. We've got to get Cazaux turned away from Mexico if we want any chance of nailing him—and the best thing we've got right now is the Air Force. Those pilots have got to turn Cazaux westbound. Even if he just slows him down or gets him to make a few turns or descend, it'll disorient him and may give us a chance to surround him. If he tries to fight out of the trap, we can legally blast him out of the sky and be done with all this nonsense,'' Lofstrom said to Tellman. ''So how about it, Captain? Can your hotshot pilots force Cazaux to turn or descend? You say your pilots can't safely fire a few shots across his bow—I say they can. Crowd him so he's forced to turn away . . . ?''

''We don't have procedures for any of that, Agent Lofstrom,'' Tellman replied. She thought about it for a moment, checking the aircraft's position, then: ''However, at the target's present position, I think our crews may be able to safely fire their cannon without endangering themselves, the suspect, or anyone on the ground. I can pitch the idea to NORAD and Air Combat Command and get a response in a few minutes.''

''Now you're talking, lady,'' Lofstrom said on the scrambled phone link. ''Lassen, get your choppers airborne and spread out across his flight path. If this works, he'll be forced to head westbound and eat up more fuel, and we can nail him in California.''

''Agent Lofstrom, the suspect is carrying a planeload of explosives, and I think the *last* thing you want to do is steer him over any populated areas,'' Agent Lassen radioed in. ''I recommend either getting him to land at an isolated airfield in the Sierras or shooting him down over the Sierras. If he flies over Sacramento, or Stockton, or San Jose, or San Francisco, there's no telling what he might do.''

''I agree,'' Captain Tellman said. ''Tactically, keeping him over sparsely populated areas is better because it gives our pilots more options.''

"Listen, I'm all in favor of seeing the man blown out of the sky," Lofstrom said. "I'll throw a fucking party for you if you do it. But just letting him orbit over the Sierras, hoping he'll dump his cargo, or forcing him to crash-land in the Sierras, means he'll have a chance to get away. It'll take a half a day to send our search teams up into the hills to be ready to pick him up—there's no time for that. Cazaux's an expert in mountain survival—he could survive for weeks up there. Have the fighters corral him into the hands of our choppers and SOG units in the valley. In case he jumps I'll get State working on a cross-border or joint capture with Mexico—the taco-crunchers owe Cazaux plenty over the years. You know, I think we *got* the bastard now."

Cazaux completed a steep right bank as the Stork searched out the cockpit windows in the direction of the turn. Krull searched out the windows in the entry door for any sign of pursuit. Instead of turning left back to course, Cazaux made another unexpected bank to the right, hoping to catch their pursuers. But the darkness was absolute—not even the stars were shining anymore. Cazaux eased the L-600 back on course, then accomplished another fast turning maneuver. "I don't see them anymore," Taddele "Stork" Korhonen said cross-cockpit to Cazaux. "The light has disappeared."

"They obviously discovered their error," Cazaux said. "Whoever it was, they could be heading back to base."

"Or they could be right on our butts," Jefferson "Krull" Jones observed. "What are you gonna do, man?"

"I need not do anything," Cazaux said. "We will either die when they open fire on us or we will be allowed to continue. But I don't think they have the stomach for a fight. They will follow us and try to capture us when we land."

"So you got something planned for them at the landing zone, Captain?" Krull asked.

"That will be a surprise, Krull," Cazaux said. "Right now, I want you to—"

Suddenly a flash of blue-orange light erupted just a few feet away from the right side of the LET L-600, and the loud, unmistakable *brrrrrr!* of a high-speed, heavy-caliber cannon could be heard over the roar of the engines. They saw another tongue of fire flash, causing a stroboscopic effect that froze the L-600's right propellers; then, an impossibly bright white searchlight flashed directly into Cazaux's face. All three men on the flight deck of the L-600 were instantly blinded. The searchlight began to blink in rapid flashes of three, followed by a pause, then another group of three flashes, a pause, then a third group of three—the ICAO (International Civil Aviation Organization) signal that an armed interceptor aircraft is following you.

"Attention on the aircraft under my searchlight, this is the United States Air Force," a female voice came over the radio on the emergency GUARD channel. "You are surrounded by two armed U.S. military fighter aircraft. By order of the U.S. Department of the Treasury and the U.S. Justice Department, immediately turn right to a heading of two-four-zero and lower your landing gear. If you do not comply, you will be fired upon. Acknowledge immediately. Over."

"They were on our tail the whole time!" the Stork yelled. He instinctively tried to bank away from the F-16 that was so close to his front windscreen, but Cazaux held the controls firm. "What do we do? What should we do?"

"Get a grip, Stork," Cazaux ordered, pushing the Ethiopian's hands away from the control yoke. He quickly shut off the aircraft's transponder, the radio device that transmitted standard identification and tracking data to FAA air traffic control—no use in trying to pretend they were a regular flight anymore. "We are not going to surrender to the authorities. *Never!* I will not give them the satisfaction." The cannon on the F-16 flashed again near the right windscreen, and the searchlight pierced the darkness of the L-600's cockpit. Cazaux's eyes had just gotten readjusted to the darkness, and the hot white light was painful this time. "Attention on the L-600, this is your last warning."

"No!" Cazaux shouted. "Fuck you, bitch!"

"Lower your landing gear immediately!" the female voice shouted once again on the GUARD radio channel. "This is your final warning!"

"Look out!" Korhonen shouted. The glare of the F-16's searchlight revealed how close they were getting to the mountains ahead—they could see the tops of trees in the glare of the fighter's position and anticollision lights. They had been forcing him lower and lower toward the rising terrain, he realized. He would be forced to use more power, and more fuel, to climb over the terrain, or be diverted left or right around it. Every minute he wasted on these unplanned maneuvers was another minute farther from his objective.

"Bastards!" Cazaux shouted. "You want me, you take me—but I

will take you to hell with me!'' And at that, Cazaux threw the LET L-600 into a steep right turn into the F-16 fighter.

Not surprisingly, the F-16 effortlessly dodged away—his maneuver was totally expected. They were toying with him, Cazaux realized, a very real cat-and-mouse game. That hard turn probably cost him his scheduled landing in Mexico. If Cazaux was correct about their position, he knew that the terrain was rising much faster to the left, and a turn in that direction might be fatal. He had no choice—he had to turn right and climb.

''You are not going to make it to your destination, mister!'' the female Air Force pilot radioed. ''Federal agents are in helicopters all the way from here to the Mexican border waiting to pick you up when you land, and there are more fighters and radar planes on their way to track you, so flying low won't help you. Your best option is to follow me and surrender.''

Korhonen and Jones were staring at Cazaux, worried. The powerful searchlight on the F-16 revealed every tension line, every quivering muscle in the terrorist's face. For the first time, they saw real despair in that face, like a wild animal caught in a trap. ''What you gonna do, Captain?'' Jones asked him.

''What can I do? I need time to think!'' Cazaux snapped. ''I try to tell myself that they will not open fire, that they will not shoot this plane down, but I am not so sure now. It'd be too easy for them to make a convenient 'mistake,' and this countryside is sparse enough that they wouldn't endanger anyone if they send this plane crashing into the ground. I need time to think.'' He paused for a few moments, his fingers nervously massaging the well-worn horns of the control yoke; then he turned the LET L-600 farther right, pulled off a notch of power and, to the Stork's surprise, lowered the landing gear and turned on all the exterior lights.

''What are you doing, Captain?'' the Stork shouted over the roar of the gear in the slipstream.

''I am buying time, Stork,'' Cazaux said. ''With the gear down, their fingers will stay off the cannon trigger—I hope. Keep this plane headed toward Sacramento or Stockton—any population center you can see. The longer we stay over populated areas, the less likely they will shoot.''

''Fly a heading of three-zero-zero for Mather Jetport,'' the female Air Force pilot radioed. Mather Jetport was a former Air Force base that had been taken over by the county of Sacramento and turned into a commercial cargo and airliner maintenance facility. It had a long two-mile-long runway and was an Air National Guard helicopter gunship base. They would have plenty of firepower support to help capture Cazaux and secure the cargo plane. "You have two F-16 fighters on you now, both within one mile. Do not deviate from course unless instructed. Do you understand? Over."

Cazaux keyed the microphone button: *"Mais oui, mademoiselle.* I understand. I do not know why you are doing this. You obviously have confused me with someone else. I have done nothing wrong. But I will follow your instructions. Can you activate your position lights, *mademoiselle?* I cannot see you."

"I have visual contact on you just fine," the Air Force pilot replied. "Stay off this frequency unless instructed to reply."

It was the reply he was hoping for: "Mr. Krull, in the second pallet, gray metal case, a pair of night-vision goggles. Get them quickly." On the radio, Cazaux continued: "Obviously you accuse me of doing something so wrong as to threaten to shoot me down—I think a relatively minor crime such as talking too much cannot be any worse," Cazaux said, using his best, most urbane, most lighthearted voice. "You sound like a very young and pretty woman, *mademoiselle.* Please tell me your name. Over." There was no response—Cazaux did not expect one. He pulled back another notch of power and lowered five degrees of flaps—not enough to be noticed by the fighter, but enough so he could safely slow down another ten to twenty knots. As he fed in some elevator trim to maintain altitude at the slower airspeed, he said cross-cockpit, "Let's see how slow the F-16 fighter can fly, shall we?"

"I got 'em," he heard Krull say behind him. The "goggles" were actually older NVG-3 model monocular night-vision scopes, bulky and heavy, with a separate battery pack and a head mounting harness kit.

"Plug them in, search out the windows for the fighter on our right wing," Cazaux said. "Tell me the approximate angle of attack of the fighter."

"The what?"

"Tell me how high the fighter's nose is from the horizon, and whether she has deployed flaps—the control surfaces on the front and back edges of the wings. Do it."

It took a long time for Krull to figure out how to use the night-vision goggles and to study the F-16 fighter beside them. In that time, Cazaux had slowed the LET down to below 160 knots and had fed in ten degrees of flaps. They were also much closer to the central part of the Sacramento Valley, with the city lights of central California's megalopolis stretching from Modesto to the south all the way up to Marysville to the north, and the bright glow of San Francisco to the west, visible to them. In a few minutes they would be flying over the Route 99 corridor, a two-hundred-mile-long string of cities and towns with over two million residents. Cazaux felt safe from attack by the Air Force fighter now—they would probably kill hundreds of persons on the ground if they were shot down.

"You still have not told me your name, *mademoiselle,*" Cazaux said on the radio. "You know we shall never meet, so indulge me this simple pleasure."

"Stay *off* the frequency," the female Air Force pilot replied angrily. The terrorist smiled—he could easily hear the tension in the woman's voice. At only one hundred and sixty knots, the F-16 must be getting extremely difficult to control.

"I can't tell shit, man," Krull said as he came back into the cockpit and knelt beside the pilots' seats. "I can see the tail thingamabobs movin' like crazy."

"The horizontal tail surfaces."

"What-the-fuck-ever. I think I see the front part of the wings curled downwards a bit. I can't see nothin' else."

"What about the landing gear? Did you see the wheels down?"

"Oh, yeah, man, I saw them. They was down."

"Good." Cazaux didn't know much about the F-16 Fighting Falcon, but he did know that they must be close to its approach speed. At the very least, the F-16 pilots would have their hands full trying to keep up with the slow-flying L-600—and if he was lucky, they wouldn't be able to keep up, and they'd be forced to break off the intercept or turn it over to someone else. Either way might provide an opportunity to escape.

"Lead, go ahead and accelerate out," Vincenti radioed to McKenzie on the command channel. He was one thousand feet above the LET L-600 cargo plane, in a tight orbit over Cazaux and McKenzie. Since he put his landing gear down, Cazaux's airspeed had bled off to the point where he could no longer safely shadow the target, so he had to orbit. Soon, McKenzie would have no choice but to orbit as well—the sooner she transitioned to an orbit, the better. "I've got a lock on him. Transition to your racetrack."

McKenzie wasn't listening.

With her landing gear down, her leading-edge and trailing-edge flaps extended, and the flight control system in takeoff/land, the angle-of-attack indexers were beginning to hit the stops, and the low-speed warning tone would intermittently sound, which meant she had to take her hand off the throttle to silence the horn. Flying at such low airspeeds was common for landing, but she wasn't accustomed to doing it in level flight, at night, flying close to a strange aircraft that had already tried to turn into her. But she didn't want to break off the intercept—Henri Cazaux wasn't going to get the satisfaction of watching her fly away.

"Lead, you copy?" Vincenti radioed to her again. "Clean up and I'll take over. Transition to radar pursuit."

"I got it, Al," she radioed back. But she didn't have it, and couldn't keep it, and she knew it. When pursuing a slow-speed target like this, the normal procedure was to begin a racetrack pattern around the target, keeping the speed up in safe limits. A racetrack was dangerous at night, since radar contact could not be maintained on the wingman while in the racetrack, and Vincenti had no night-vision goggles.

But she had no choice. The low-speed warning tone came on for the seventh time. The target had slowed down below 150 knots, and there was no way McKenzie could hold that speed in an F-16. "Correction. Lead's entering the racetrack. Two, you have the intercept. Break. SIERRA PETE, this is Foxtrot Romeo flight, the target has decelerated—we are transitioning to radar pursuit."

"Two's in," Vincenti replied. McKenzie smoothly advanced the throttle to military power, raised the landing gear before passing 80 percent power, and began a right turn away from the LET L-600.

"The fighter's leavin'!" Jones crowed. "Landin' gear's up . . . it's turnin' away!"

"They won't be leaving, only setting up an orbit over us so they can keep us in sight and keep their airspeed up," Cazaux said. "But they'll give us some breathing room now, and the lower airspeed gives us some more time."

"To do what, man?" Jones asked. "We still got two jets on our tail, and sure as shit they're callin' their buddies to help out. With the gear hangin', we'll be runnin' on fumes in an hour."

"I know all that, Mr. Krull," Cazaux said in exasperation. "Shut up and let me think."

He didn't have much time to think, because soon the line of lights along the Route 99 corridor reached its largest expanse at the capital city of Sacramento. There were four major airports around Sacramento, all surrounded by housing subdivisions, offices, and light-industrial facilities; Mather Jetport was the largest airport east of the city. Already the rotating beacon and runway lights were visible—they were less than thirty miles out, about fifteen minutes from touchdown. Their flight path was taking them northwestbound toward Highway 50, a busy freeway linking Sacramento with the Sierra Nevada foothills; once reaching that freeway, a turn to the west would put them on a five-mile final approach to Mather Jetport. The lights of the sprawling city were breathtaking, but Cazaux hardly noticed them—all he saw was his plane surrounded by federal agents, a shootout, an explosion, a fireball . . .

Explosion . . .

Fireball . . .

He certainly had enough ingredients on board to create plenty of very big explosions and fireballs. "Take the aircraft," he told the Stork as he unfastened his lap and shoulder belts. "Do whatever they say, follow any vectors they give you, until I give the word."

"We are *landing?*" the Stork asked incredulously. "We will *land?*"

"Not unless they shoot out the engines, Stork, and then they will still have a fight on their hands. Mr. Krull, give your night-vision goggles to Stork and follow me." He stepped out of his seat and hurried aft.

There was not much room, and the two men had difficulty squeezing themselves between the cargo on the pallets and the cold aluminum aircraft fuselage. Krull thought he couldn't make the tight squeeze, but as if by magic he sucked it all in when it came time to squeeze around the forward pallet—he didn't want one unnecessary bit of clothing or skin to touch the crates of high explosives stacked atop that pallet. Krull didn't have any fear of those explosives when they were on the ground or being loaded, but now up there in the air, being swayed and bounced around, it seemed as if they were tiny thin eggshells waiting to . . .

"Grab two cases of grenades from that pallet and bring them to me, Mr. Krull," Cazaux shouted over the roar of the engines.

Krull's eyes widened in absolute horror. "Say *what* . . . ?"

"Damn it, stop stalling! Loosen those straps and bring two crates of grenades back here on the double."

Loosening the cargo netting and withdrawing those two cases was one of the most terrifying things Krull had ever done—all he could see was the Styrofoam-shrouded canister of PETN in the center of the pallet. Every inch he moved the two grenade cases meant loosening the white foam blocks, and in his mind's eye he could visualize the explosive crystals sloshing around, the molecular heat building, the blinding flash of light as the unstable chemicals exploded, detonating the rest of the explosives they carried, then destroying the aircraft in a big jet fuel fireball. His own strength amazed him—he held one thirty-pound case of grenades securely in one hand while maneuvering other crates and bags around to fill the gap and secure the PETN canister, while keeping his balance against the occasional turbulence and swaying. Cazaux offered him no help except to take the first crate of grenades and begin working.

When Krull brought the second case of grenades back to Cazaux, he couldn't believe what the terrorist was doing—he had released all of the cargo straps on the entire pallet of Stinger missiles and was placing the grenades in between the missile coffins, with the safety pins removed and the arming handles held in place—barely—by the loosened crates! "What the fuck are you doin,' man?" Krull shouted.

"Doing a little creative mine-laying, Mr. Krull," Cazaux said, wearing a twisted smile. "I am going to attack the law enforcement officers on the airport below us."

"You gonna *what?*"

"The Stinger missile motors will explode, but they need a booster," Cazaux said calmly. "The grenades will do, but I don't have time to rig up a contact fuse. But if we push this pallet outside while we're above one hundred and twenty-eight feet aboveground, the grenades will explode before the pallet hits the ground. The results should be most rewarding."

"You're really fuckin' crazy, man."

But Cazaux ignored him. He put on a headset and clicked open the intercom button: "Stork, I want you to make a normal approach to the runway they designate. Let me know when we're one mile from the runway. Just before touchdown I want you to maneuver over the vehicles that will undoubtedly be parked on the side of the runway. Then I want you to go to full throttle and climb over them. When we pass two hundred feet, signal me. Do you understand?" Cazaux didn't wait for a response—they would have only one shot at this, so either Korhonen would do it or he wouldn't. "After that maneuver, I want you to fly as low as you can go westbound. Stay over the interstate and keep the power up. Low altitude and speed is the only protection we'll have when they come after us."

Linda McKenzie had never felt such an overwhelming sense of accomplishment as she did that night as they approached Mather Jetport. They had just assisted in the capture of one of the world's most wanted terrorists—and *she* led the intercept! Her minor switch slipup at the beginning of the intercept would certainly be forgotten. In fact, this seemed to be having a better result than a covert Special-9 intercept would have had.

The feds and the cops were certainly out in force to put the suspect on ice. Both sides of Mather's two-mile-long runway were choked with flashing lights, and more were pouring onto the former military base—the entire parking ramp in front of the old base-operations building was bumper-to-bumper emergency vehicles. Streets were being cordoned off all around the facility. The five-mile exclusion zone around Mather had been breached years ago, but residential sprawl had not yet totally closed in on the base, so the area around the airport was only sparsely dotted with residences.

"You're cleared to land on two-two left, Cazaux," McKenzie radioed to the L-600. "Stop straight ahead on the runway and don't try to turn off."

"I understand," a strange voice replied. It wasn't Cazaux—probably the copilot. Could Cazaux have escaped? Once they went to radar tracking instead of visual tracking, someone could have parachuted from the aircraft without their noticing. Capturing the plane and the weapons on board was good, but Cazaux himself was the big prize.

"Henri Cazaux, this is Special Agent Fortuna of the Bureau of Alcohol, Tobacco, and Firearms, U.S. Treasury Department," a voice cut in on the channel. "I'm the on-scene commander. We are tracking you with Stinger missiles and helicopter gunships. If you try to evade capture, we are authorized to open fire on your aircraft. Do you understand, Cazaux?"

"Russ? Is that you? *Ca va bien, mon ami?*" a thick, French-accented voice came on over the channel. "How is America's famous Nazi storm trooper doing?" It was Henri Cazaux's voice—he was still on the plane. This was going to be one sweet evening, McKenzie thought.

"You wouldn't be so cheerful if you knew how many guns and missiles we got on you right now, Henri," Fortuna radioed back. "Make a nice pretty landing. You're on the news from coast to coast."

"I would not want any of your gunners' fingers to twitch on the triggers, Russell," Cazaux said. "Would you please ask them to lower their weapons? I have decided to surrender—I will take my chances with the American justice system."

"You might as well get used to the sight of guns pointed at you, Cazaux," Fortuna said, "because that's what you're going to see every waking minute of your life from now on. Now get off my radio frequency and do as you're ordered. We've got this entire area closed off, and we've got the green light to blow your ass out of the sky. Don't screw it up."

"It will be good to see you again too, *mon ami.*" Cazaux laughed.

They were now less than two miles from the runway. McKenzie had made the decision to stay with the cargo plane for the entire approach, flying to the left and slightly behind the L-600—and she kept her 20-millimeter cannon armed and the pipper within a few mils of Cazaux's plane. If given the signal, she could squeeze off a one-second burst that would certainly shear off the L-600's left engine nacelle and propeller and send the cargo plane spiraling into the ground, away from the more populated areas of the town of Rancho Cordova north of the airfield and into the vacant tracts of land to the south. She was not sure where Vincenti was, but she assumed he would keep both aircraft in sight at all times and be ready to assist, track, or attack if something went wrong.

"Keep it coming, Cazaux," Fortuna radioed again. "Keep that airspeed down—and if we hear the power come up on those engines, that'll be our signal to open fire."

"I understand, Russ," Cazaux radioed. He switched quickly to intercom: "Stork—how far?"

"One mile now, sir."

Cazaux hit a switch on the aft cargo-bay bulkhead, and the cargo ramp began to lower and the upper ramp door began to retract upward into the cargo bay. The electrically actuated upper door was fully raised in just a few seconds; the ramp, powered by large hydraulic arms, took considerably longer. "Get on the front of that pallet,

Mr. Krull,'' Cazaux said, wearing an evil grin, ''and stand by on that last toucan clamp.''

Krull had just barely made his way forward to the front of the pallet when he heard the engines rapidly spooling up to full power. ''Get ready!'' Cazaux shouted. He switched to the comm channel on the intercom and shouted into the microphone, ''Russell, my friend, hold out your hands and close your eyes—I'm going to give you a *big* surprise!'' then dropped the microphone and grasped a bulkhead handhold.

At that instant, the cargo plane heeled sharply upward. Korhonen's timing was perfect: when Cazaux looked out of the open cargo doors, all he saw was dozens of emergency vehicles clustered near the intersection of the main runway and the large midfield taxiway.

''Now!'' Cazaux shouted. ''Release!''

Krull pulled on the clamp lever, but nothing happened—it was jammed. He struggled with it, but the steeply angled deck had pulled the straps tight, and the curled toucan clamp would not budge. ''It ain't goin,' man!'' Krull shouted.

But Cazaux was already moving. Struggling against the steeply sloped deck, Cazaux reached across the pallet, his large switchblade knife in his hands, and cut the remaining strap. The pallet did not need a push by anyone—sliding on the rollers embedded in the floor of the self-loading cargo hold, the pallet picked up speed rapidly and actually seemed to fly for several feet before it disappeared from view.

Just as McKenzie thought it was all coming to an end, when she could fly her F-16 back to Fresno and receive the warm congratulations of her friends and commanders, all hell broke loose.

The LET L-600 heeled sharply right just a few feet from the ground, right over the biggest cluster of emergency vehicles lining the north side of the runway. The move took her by surprise—she was concentrating more on lining up with the south edge of the runway and keeping the Fighting Falcon in control as she followed the L-600 down the glide path. She applied right stick to follow, but the fighter wallowed and started to sink, and she goosed the power back up to 80 percent. Her next responsibility was to get the gunsight back on target, but at her present speed and angle of attack, that was impossible. Then the L-600 went into a steep climb, passing virtually directly in front of the pipper. "Control, this is Foxtrot Romeo Two, do I have permission to fire?" she radioed.

"No!" a frantic voice shouted. "Don't fire! Hold your fire!" But McKenzie realized that the voice didn't identify himself, and it could be anyone giving that order—even Cazaux himself. She brought the landing gear handle up, then put the aux flap switch to EXTEND, which would keep the trailing-edge flaps down while the gear was up and allow her to fly slower and stay in control.

"Control, do you want Foxtrot Romeo to attack? The target appears to be evading—do I have permission to attack?"

"Linda, this is Al," she heard on the interplane frequency, *"break left!"*

She could hear Vincenti's sudden warning, but she didn't dare try to look down into the cockpit to change radios—she was less than three hundred yards from the L-600. She had a momentary thought about turning—an order to "break" was not just a turn, it was a command to get the hell out of there. Instead, she stayed lined up on the left wing of the L-600 and said on the command channel, "I'm staying on the target! Control, what are your instructions? Do you want me to attack? Control, respond . . ."

McKenzie caught a glimpse of a bright flash of light off to her right, but it was near the ground and she assumed it was one of the emergency vehicles' rotating lights or a photographer's flash.

Then she saw a huge ripple of lights erupt all around her jet, heard a thunderous *bang!* and felt a gigantic ramming force smack her F-16's fuselage.

The thirteen grenades shoved between the cases of Stinger missiles exploded well before the pallet hit the ground, which only served to increase the devastation. The chain reaction created by the exploding grenades was quick and furious—the shrapnel from the grenades tore through the battery unit cases, blowing apart the high-pressure nitrogen-gas canisters, rupturing the battery cells, cooking off the chemicals and spraying superheated chemicals inside the missile coffins. The rocket motors went next. Normally they would slowly burn inside their cases, but the shock and hot chemicals caused them to explode instead. Some of the missiles did cook off, sending white-hot spears of fire into nearby buildings and vehicles. The fragmenting pallet erupted into a blossom of fire when it hit the emergency vehicles on the ground, throwing petals of fire and explosive Stinger warheads out in all directions. The Stinger missiles seemed to have eyes, or active seeker heads—it seemed as if every one of the missiles that cooked off slammed right into a building or vehicle.

"Oh, shit . . ." was all Jefferson Jones could say as he and Cazaux watched the maddening scene unfold below them. It was like watching a fireworks show's finale from above—the big explosion, followed by numerous smaller explosions, then ripple after ripple of side explosions, and then the twinkling of burning debris scattered all across the airfield.

"That . . . was . . . magnificent," Cazaux muttered. "That was . . . incredible. Absolutely incredible . . ."

As the L-600 began to level off, then point earthward to regain speed and begin evading pursuit, Krull moved aft and began motoring the ramp and upper cargo doors closed.

Cazaux stumbled around on the right side of the cargo bay, leaning against the second pallet. He then eyed the forward pallet, the one containing the *real* explosives.

"Move that second pallet aft to the edge of the ramp," he told Krull as he located the microphone, "and help me move that third pallet aft. I am going to deliver that last pallet on a target that no one will forget for a very long time." He clicked open the mike: "Stork, do exactly as I say, and your navigation had better be dead on."

The large MASTER CAUTION light on the left eyebrow panel came on, along with the HYD/OIL PRESS warning light on the right eyebrow panel. It seemed as if the entire caution-light panel was illuminated—ELEC SYS, CADC, STBY GAINS, FUEL HOT, those were the biggies—and the oil and hydraulic pressure gauges were bouncing all over the place.

It was time to jump out, she decided.

She had never even come close to ejecting out of any aircraft before, not in ten years of flying the F-16. Air Force training always said, "Don't hesitate. Trust your equipment," and she was perfectly willing and ready to do so. McKenzie reached for her ejection seat lever and . . .

"Linda! This is Al! How do you hear? It looks like you've been fragged, but there is no fire, repeat, *negative fire.* How do you hear? Over?"

She was surprised to hear Vincenti on the radio—she had assumed, incorrectly, that everything in her stricken ship was out. She moved the throttle—no response, with FTIT and fuel flow in the red but rpms below idle power. She moved the stick—aha, the controls were stiff but responding. Emergency power unit had turned on automatically. She raised the nose, and the jet responded by climbing. If nothing else, she was able to trade airspeed for altitude and get a little higher before ejecting, but she had a few seconds to try to work the problem.

McKenzie took her hands off the ejection lever and back on the stick and throttle, then started to work on her caution-light analysis. The engine was stalled from a massive disruption of airflow through the engine, so she immediately pulled the throttle to idle, waited a few excruciating seconds as the airspeed bled off below safe engine-restart speed, then slowly advanced the throttle again. Just as she was convinced the engine was not going to come back, the rpms eased from 55 percent to 65 percent and the fan-turbine inlet temperatures subsided out of the red zone. Quickly but carefully she advanced the throttle, and the rpms responded. Airspeed climbed above 170 knots. She was safely flying again.

She set the throttles to 80 percent and, one by one, began working on the other malfunctions. As soon as she could, she tried to reset the generators with the ELEC CAUTION RESET button—no go, it kept on tripping off. She placed the emergency power unit to ON, and checked the power-distribution lights. With only the emergency power unit providing power to the essential bus, she had the barest minimum equipment running—but she was still flying. Only the UHF radio on the interplane frequency was operating—that's how she could still hear Vincenti. "Al, how do you hear me?"

"Fine, Linda," Vincenti said. "Roll out of your turn and get your nose down. I've got you at five thousand feet. How's your controllability? Check your engines."

"I cleared a stall, and I've got partial generators and EPU on line," McKenzie said. She straightened her F-16's wings and found the controls very sluggish. "Looks like I lost my hydraulics—the EPU is the only hydraulics and power I got left." The EPU, or emergency power unit, used bleed air from the engine or hydrazine to power a simple power unit that supplied backup hydraulic and electrical power for about fifteen minutes. "System A pressure is good, and my essential bus is energized. What the hell happened?"

"Cazaux," Vincenti replied simply. "He dropped something out the back end, a bomb or something. I can still see explosions.

Just hold your heading. I'll come around on your left side. Hang tight, we'll be OK. Let's start a slow climb to ten thousand and start working out what we got. What's your fuel state?''

''I can't tell—gauge is inop,'' McKenzie said. ''Fuel low and fuel hot lights came on right away, and I think one of my wing tanks is gone.''

''That's confirmed, you lost one. You still got your right tank, and it's pretty beat-up,'' Vincenti said as he checked out McKenzie's fighter with his ID searchlight. ''I don't think it'll do a normal jettison because of the damage, so you're going to have to land with it.''

It took Vincenti a few minutes to fly around McKenzie's jet and look her over. In that time, they had climbed up to ten thousand feet over the sparsely settled ranches and farms south of Sacramento. ''I see lots of damage to your underside, Linda. You may or may not get a good landing gear. What do you think, Linda? How does she feel to you?''

McKenzie knew what that question meant: did she want to eject or did she want to try for a landing? ''I'm not jumping out of this plane, Al,'' McKenzie said. ''Lead me over to McClellan.'' McClellan Air Force Base, just north of Sacramento, was a large military aircraft maintenance depot with lots of runways and crash equipment—McKenzie was going to need all the help she could get.

It was only twenty miles across the top of the city of Sacramento to get to McClellan, but for McKenzie it was the longest flight of her entire life. Her approach speed when starting her descent into McClellan's north-south runway was 220 knots, much faster than normal, and it was nearly impossible to maintain it without considerable control problems. Several times the engine did not respond to throttle movements. ''Better get ready for a flameout landing, Linda,'' Vincenti told her. ''We're looking for two hundred knots landing speed—it's gonna happen fast.''

''Just lost the engine, Al,'' McKenzie said. Her voice was wooden, as if she were talking inside a bucket.

Vincenti knew that calm wouldn't last too long. The toughest fighter pilots in the world get high, squeaky voices when their air machines start to crap out on them. ''Okay, Linda, forget it,'' Vincenti said. ''We're committed for a flameout approach. Check your JFS switch on START 2. Turn off your FUEL MASTER switch.''

''Got it . . . negative JFS RUN light, Al.''

''Okay, forget it. Turn the starter off—we'll try it again in a minute or so. We're six miles out.'' They were surrounded by the city of Sacramento, a vast shimmering expanse of lights below them. McClellan was dead ahead, its rotating beacon and runway lights plainly visible. They had it made, but they still had a long way to go. ''Check your air source knob on RAM and your defog lever forward. Keep your touchdown point eleven to seventeen degrees below the horizon. Stand by on the gear.''

''I'm ready, Al.'' Her glide path was steady, right on Vincenti's left wing. Her jet was a heavy toy glider right now. Actually, ''glider'' was a misnomer for the F-16 Fighting Falcon—with its short supercritical wings, the F-16 made a lousy glider. But as long as you had airspeed and a working EPU, though, a flameout landing was very doable. Her HUD, or heads-up display, was still operable, and the flight-path pipper was directly on the end of the runway—all she had to do was keep the pipper on the touchdown point and maneuver the fighter to keep the pipper within 11 to 17 of the horizon. So far it was going smoothly.

''Five miles, Linda, lower the gear when you're ready.''

''Coming down.'' She pressed the gear-permission button and tried to move the gear lever downward—nothing. ''Gear handle won't move,'' she radioed. She hit the DN LOCK REL button, which mechanically allows the handle to be lowered—and she got no safe gear indications. ''No green lights, Al.''

''I see your right gear, and a partial nose gear,'' Vincenti said. ''Cycle the gear handle.''

McKenzie raised the gear handle, waited a few seconds, pressed the DN LOCK REL button, and lowered the handle. ''Did it,'' she radioed. ''No red light, no green lights.''

''Four miles out. Use alternate extension. Watch your airspeed, Linda, you're sinking. Drop your nose a bit.''

''Copy.'' She made the proper attitude correction. Three miles out—and the left landing gear came into view. ''What's it look like, Al?''

''I got two main gear, no nose gear,'' he said. ''Your nose gear might come down below 190. Let's go to thirteen AOA and get ready for touchdown. Try your JFS to START 2 once more, and secure your throttle. Glide path looks good, and you're cleared to land. Nice job, Linda. Little bit more nose up, you're at eleven AOA.''

''She starts to get squirrelly below two hundred,'' McKenzie said. ''I want to keep my speed up until I'm over the threshold.''

"Okay, but remember you might not have all your brakes, and you have no speedbrakes," Vincenti said. "Use aerodynamic braking all you can, and use every inch of the runway. Go get 'em, babe."

"Thanks, Al," McKenzie said; then she added, "We should've done it, Al, you know that, don't you? It would've been *sooo* good."

Leave it to Linda McKenzie to think about sex just seconds before making a 220-mile-per-hour flameout approach in the dark to a strange airfield in a damaged F-16 fighter, Vincenti thought grimly.

He did not reply, because there was no time. With Vincenti flying just a few feet above the right edge of the runway, McKenzie hit the pavement, traveling at 210 knots.

. . . and the worst-case scenario happened.

The nose gear never came down, but McKenzie held the fighter's nose high in the air to let the jet's fuselage create enough drag to slow down. A stream of fire trucks began their chase after her down the runway. Suddenly, Vincenti saw a flash of light—sparks caused by the damaged right fuel tank separating from the wing and dragging the runway. The fighter's nose slammed hard into the runway, then began to spin clockwise. Fire erupted in the engine compartment and right wing—and then McKenzie ejected. Vincenti caught a glimpse of two full burns of her seat's ejection motors before he passed the runway and began his climbout.

"Foxtrot Romeo Zero One, this is McClellan Tower, say your intentions."

Vincenti knew the runways would be closed at McClellan and Mather, the two large military-capable airports in Sacramento. Metro Airport was just a few miles away—they might send him there, although the Air Force didn't like to send armed combat aircraft to civil airports. Beale and Travis Air Force Bases were both less than fifty miles away, and he had plenty of fuel to make it all the way back to Fresno Air Terminal. He wanted to see Linda, wanted to stay with his flying partner. No doubt they'd be convening an accident board, and as the original flight leader and close chase plane he'd be the star witness.

Screw 'em, Vincent thought angrily. He jammed the throttle to MIL power and keyed the radio button: "Tower, Foxtrot Romeo-01 requesting handoff to Approach and vectors to the suspect aircraft that just overflew Mather."

"Roger, Foxtrot Romeo, stand by." The wait did not last long: "Foxtrot Romeo-01, your control requests you land at Beale as soon as possible. You can contact Sacramento Approach on one-one-nine point one."

Vincenti turned his aircraft southwestbound, not northbound, and began searching the skies with radar for a target.

"Foxtrot Romeo-01, did you copy? You are requested to land at Beale. Over."

Vincenti cut off the tower controller's insistent orders by tuning the radio to Sacramento Approach Control's western sector frequency. "Sacramento Approach, Foxtrot Romeo-01 with you climbing to six thousand, active air scramble, requesting vectors to the suspect aircraft that overflew Mather, over."

"Foxtrot Romeo-01, Sacramento Approach, roger, last reported position of your target is at one o'clock, approximately fifty-three miles, altitude unknown. You are leaving my airspace, contact Travis Approach on one-two-seven point one-five."

That wasn't much of a vector, but it was enough. A minute later Vincenti picked up a low-flying aircraft thirty-two miles to the west, at the foot of the coastal mountains between Sacramento and San Francisco, traveling at two hundred knots at only a few hundred feet above the terrain.

That had to be Cazaux.

He was trying to sneak away under local radar, avoiding the TRACON (Terminal Radar Approach Control) center near Travis Air Force Base. "Travis Approach, Foxtrot Romeo-01 requesting clearance to intercept the aircraft at my twelve o'clock, thirty-one miles, with a three-hundred-knot closure rate. Over."

Henri Cazaux's characteristically ice-cold heart started to pump superheated lava through his veins as he listened in on the exchange between the Air Force fighter and the civilian radar controllers: "Foxtrot Romeo-01, Travis Approach, maintain two-fifty maximum airspeed, stay clear of Travis class D airspace, and stand by on your request."

"The wingman is after us," Cazaux said to the Stork. "I thought they'd both land after the bitch was hit." He shrugged. "I was wrong."

"He was ordered to land," the Stork said incredulously. "He was ordered to land! Why is he disobeying orders?"

"Revenge," Cazaux said simply. "Something I know all about.

And this fighter jock, he smells revenge. This pilot is the real leader, not the other. She was the inexperienced one. This one . . . will not let us live. He will try to kill us."

"Oh, great!" Jones moaned. "You mean that Air Force jet's gonna flame us? What the hell we gonna do?"

"Foxtrot Romeo-01, Travis Approach, sir, reduce speed and do not exceed two-five-zero knots indicated, do you copy?" they heard once again on the radio. "Reduce speed *now* . . . leaving my airspace, Foxtrot Romeo-01, contact Bay Approach on one-two-seven point zero. How do you copy, Foxtrot Romeo-01?"

"He ain't answerin' back," Jones said. "What's he doin'?"

Cazaux switched the radio to the same frequency, which was the terminal radar controller for the dozens of major airports in the San Francisco Bay Area. Still no response, no check-in. "This man, he is no longer taking orders from either his superiors or the federal aviation authorities," Cazaux said. "He is going to pursue us until . . . the end game."

"What the hell does *that* mean?" Jones shouted.

"It means he's a renegade, you idiot. He will put a two-second burst of cannon fire into this aircraft, whether or not he receives orders to the contrary," Cazaux said calmly. "That will be approximately one hundred depleted uranium shells about twice the size of your thumb, weighing approximately one pound, hitting us with supersonic force. He will blow this plane apart as easily as a baby bursting a soap bubble . . . get it?"

His eyes scanned out the window to the south, toward San Francisco, Oakland, Alameda Naval Air Station, Hayward, and San Jose—the San Francisco Bay region, busy even late at night. The landing lights of dozens of aircraft filled the skies. Like gigantic strings of Christmas lights, the airliners formed long sparking lines of light in the sky, strung out for nearly a hundred miles in all directions, all sequenced to land at their various air terminals. Finally Cazaux said, "That way," and moved the control yoke hard left and pushed, descending even farther toward the dark, light-sparkled earth below.

"What now, man?"

"We cannot escape the pilot who pursues us," Cazaux said. "So perhaps we can force him to retreat—if he will."

"How you gonna do that?" But Krull soon realized how. In just a few minutes, the answer was obvious—they were heading right for San Francisco International Airport, the locus of the greatest number of those strings of light in the sky.

He was heading directly into the airspace of one of the busiest airports in the United States.

"Oh, shit . . . you're gonna fly into the middle of all *that?*"

"It is the ultimate game of chicken," Cazaux said with a grin on his face, "the ultimate game of Russian roulette." He changed his radio frequency to Bay Approach, listening in as the busy controllers vectored aircraft for landings into Oakland, Martinez, Alameda, Hayward, and San Francisco International. They were already approaching the northern shore of San Pablo Bay, with the city of Vallejo on their left and the dark forested expanse of Marin County on their right, illuminated by the lights of small communities along Highway 101. Soon they were over San Pablo Bay at one thousand feet, traveling three miles per minute through the wispy fog and haze.

"Cactus Niner-Seventy-Three, traffic alert, pop-up target, ten o'clock, three miles, no altitude readout," they heard the controller at Bay Approach call to another aircraft.

"Nine-Seventy-Three, searching, no joy," the pilot of the Southwest Airlines commuter, a Boeing 737 airliner out of Oakland International, responded. The pilot sounded bored. Spurious radar targets caused by birds, fog, smog, or high humidity were common in this area. At night, airplanes had their lights on, and if it didn't have lights on, it wasn't an airplane. After all, who *wanted* to hit another plane in midair?

"There he is," Cazaux said, pointing out the window, high and slightly to the right. The aircraft could not be identified as to type, but there was no missing it—it was ablaze in landing, recognition, position, and anticollision lights. The turbofan-powered airliner was much faster than Cazaux's L-600, but he had the cutoff angle. Cazaux pulled back on the yoke and turned left, putting the LET L-600 directly on an intercept course, climbing above three thousand feet.

"Niner-Seven-Three, Bay Approach, traffic appears to be maneuvering, now at eleven o'clock, two miles."

"Nine-Seventy-Three, still searching, no joy," came the reply.

"He cannot see us," Cazaux said. He reached down and flicked on his landing lights. "How about now?"

"Nine-Seventy-Three has contact on the traffic," the commuter pilot radioed. "Say his altitude again?"

"Still no Mode C on your traffic," the air traffic controller responded. "You should be passing in front of him."

"Not so fast," Cazaux said. He turned farther left to increase the cutoff angle, maintaining his climb rate. "How about now?"

"Collision alert, Cactus Niner-Seven-Three, turn thirty degrees right immediately!" the air traffic controller shouted over the radio. The commuter plane's lights altered shape as the plane turned. Cazaux laughed as he imagined what the occupants on board that red-eye flight were experiencing—heads banging off shoulders and windows, necks creaking in pain, coffee splashing, flight attendants scrambling for balance.

"That bastard turned right into me!" the pilot of the commuter plane shouted, forgetting proper radio discipline. "Bay Approach, be advised, that guy turned right into me. I want his tail number and controller tapes!"

"Roger, Cactus Niner-Seven-Three, I have your request, contact Bay Approach now on one-three-five point four. Break. Aircraft on the three-zero-zero degree radial, twelve DME fix from Oakland VOR, be advised, you are entering San Francisco Class B and Oakland Class C airspace without a clearance, and you have entered the thirty-mile Mode C veil without a Mode C readout. Remain clear of Class B and C airspace and contact Bay Approach on one-two-seven point zero. Acknowledge."

Henri Cazaux laughed. "Oh, this is *perfect,* perfect!" he cackled.

"We coulda gotten killed, you crazy motherfucker," Krull said, shaking his head.

"Mr. Krull, our death warrants were signed the second I heard that Air Force pilot's voice on the radio," Cazaux said, stone-serious. "He wants revenge, and he is willing to ruin his career in order to get it. We are fighting for our lives." Then, just as quickly as it had gone away, the broad smile was back. "And if I am fortunate, I will take a few American citizens out with me before we die."

With that, he turned the LET L-600 back toward San Francisco and began another descent, aiming right for the international airport itself.

"Foxtrot Romeo-01, radar contact, ten miles southwest of Travis Air Force Base," the military air defense controller SIERRA PETE reported. Through a massive communications and radar relay network, military controllers from southern California could talk to and track on radar all military interceptors anywhere. "You should have been relayed instructions for landing at Beale, sir. Are you experiencing difficulty?"

"Negative, SIERRA PETE," Vincenti replied. "Who's the senior director tonight? John? Marie?"

"This is Colonel Berrell, Al," John Berrell responded, cutting in on the Weapon Control Team channel. "I'm the SD, and Bravo is on the floor as well." Bravo was the code name for the deputy director of the Southwest Air Defense Sector, Navy Captain Francine Tellman. "What in hell are you doing? I ordered you to land at Beale for a debriefing."

"John, I want permission to engage Cazaux's plane over the bay," Vincenti said.

"Say again, Foxtrot Romeo?"

"You heard me, John," Vincenti said in a calm, even voice. "Cazaux's driving directly at San Francisco International. He's flying right into the path of the arriving and departing traffic—he made one airliner almost do a backflip trying to avoid a midair. I believe he's got another load of explosives on board that cargo plane, and that he's going to drop them somewhere—on the city, on the airport, I don't know where. I've got a judy on him, about thirteen miles north of SFO. He crosses the Bay Bridge into San Francisco Bay in about one minute. I want permission to bring him down as soon as he crosses the Bay Bridge. Over."

"Al, I can't upchannel that," Berrell said. "I know how much you want Cazaux . . ."

There was silence for a moment; then, a woman's voice came on the channel: "Foxtrot Romeo-01, this is Bravo." Vincenti recognized Francine Tellman's cutting, no-nonsense voice immediately. "I'm *ordering* you to land at Beale Air Force Base immediately. Acknowledge and comply. Over."

"If you want Henri Cazaux, Francine, I can take him. Just give me permission."

"You've got your *orders,* Foxtrot Romeo-01. Comply with them or I'll court-martial you the minute you step off that plane. And you had better start using proper radio procedures."

"Francine," Vincenti said, ignoring her last request, "he tried to ram an airliner, and now he's headed right for the stream of arrivals into SFO."

"I can *see* that, Vincenti, we're tracking him as well," Tellman said. Obviously she gave up trying to use proper radio discipline as well. "I also know that *you've* violated almost as many federal air regulations as Cazaux has. Bay and Travis TRACON and Oakland Center are screaming bloody murder about you blasting through their airspace. Now get the hell out of there and land at Beale.'' There was a slight pause, then she added, *"Please."*

Vincenti alternately loosened and tightened his grip on the control stick. This was the turning point, he thought. He was still outside San Francisco Class B airspace, and he could easily climb above eight thousand feet to get above the airspace to stay legal. If Cazaux tried something, he'd still be in a position to act. He considered doing the old ''radio-out'' routine—go radio-out, squawk emergency, then turn everything back on when Cazaux was safely away from traffic—and as long as he stuck to his story they'd have to believe him. But either way, Henri Cazaux would be getting away with murder. ''I can't do it, Francine,'' Vincenti said.

''Cut the crap, Vincenti,'' Tellman hissed angrily. ''Stay out of the Class B airspace. That's an *order.* Don't trash a long and successful career because of Cazaux. You did your job. Break off your pursuit, *now.* If there's another incident because of you busting into B airspace, I won't be able to keep you out of Leavenworth.''

Vincenti swore loudly into his oxygen mask. Cazaux was about twenty miles ahead of him, flying just north of Treasure Island. In less than a minute he'd be over the San Francisco Bay Bridge. He could turn right and be over the city of San Francisco in another minute, or over the Golden Gate Bridge in three minutes; or continue straight ahead for four minutes and be over San Francisco International Airport. It was like watching a tornado move across a prairie, not knowing which way it was going to go, praying it would go one way but not the other.

''Vincenti . . . Al,'' Tellman tried once more, ''break off your pursuit, *now.*''

''Damn you all to *hell,*'' Vincenti muttered as he shoved in full afterburner and pulled the nose skyward. In sixty seconds, he was level at eighty-five hundred feet, above the San Francisco Class B airspace and on the proper hemispheric altitude for his direction of flight. He was flying above the city of Richmond and barreling toward Oakland when Cazaux crossed the Bay Bridge, heading directly for San Francisco. On his backup VHF radio, he called, ''Bay Approach, Foxtrot Romeo-01 on one-two-seven point zero, F-16 active air intercept, level eight thousand five hundred, ten miles north of Oakland VOR, requesting Class B clearance, vectors to intercept unidentified aircraft crossing west of the Bay Bridge, and requesting speed to four-zero-zero knots, over.''

"Foxtrot Romeo-01, Bay Approach, unable your request," the air traffic controller responded. "I don't show you as an active air intercept—I'll have to check with your air defense sector people. Squawk four-three-zero-zero, maintain present course and altitude, remain clear of San Francisco Class B airspace. Break. United Three-Seventy-Two, turn left heading one-five-zero and slow to your approach speed for separation. Amflight Two-Zero-Niner-Niner, keep your speed up, sir, traffic at your seven o'clock, three miles, an unidentified aircraft, altitude unknown . . ."

The stress in the controller's voice was painfully obvious, and Vincenti knew why. As soon as he heard a break, Cazaux interjected, "Approach, my target is that unidentified aircraft, and I've got him tied on radar. Let me intercept him and I'll try to get him out of your arrival pattern, over."

"Several aircraft talking at once, everyone please *shut up* and listen," the irritated controller said. "Foxtrot Romeo-01, I said *unable,* maintain your present course and stay clear of the Class B airspace. Delta Fourteen, turn left heading two-zero-zero, descend to five thousand, vectors for VOR runway one-niner left arrival. United Eight-Twenty-Two, descend and maintain six thousand . . ."

It was impossible to cut through the rapid-fire controller's instructions. Vincenti thought about doing a rapid descent and dropping right on Cazaux's tail, but now it was far too dangerous—the closer Cazaux was to San Francisco International, the more aircraft he was mixing around, and the harder it would be to stay away from the traffic.

Well, he had done at least part of what he was ordered to do—stop the pursuit—but he wasn't ready to give up on Henri Cazaux. Vincenti still had an hour of fuel to burn, and plenty of suitable bases nearby to choose from. Better wait up here, clear of all the traffic and confusion, and watch to see what the maniac Cazaux had in mind.

On his backup radio—no use in listening to Francine Tellman and the rest of the Southwest Air Defense Sector yell at him—he switched over to San Francisco Tower and set up an orbit above the Class B airspace so he could watch Cazaux on radar. He felt completely useless, orbiting thousands of feet above his prey, but there was absolutely nothing he could do except listen to the horrible tragedy unfold below him.

* * *

"Unidentified aircraft over the port of San Francisco, this is San Francisco Tower on GUARD," the frantic tower controller radioed on the VHF emergency frequency. "You have entered Oakland Class C airspace without proper radio callup, and you are on course to enter San Francisco Class B airspace without a clearance. There are numerous aircraft departing San Francisco at your twelve o'clock position."

The controller tried a different tactic: he decided to assume that the pilot of the aircraft was in trouble—perhaps it was the wife flying after her husband had a heart attack, or a kid had stolen a plane to go for a joyride and was aiming for the biggest airport he could see. No use trying to threaten him or her—better to offer plenty of options while protecting the airspace and the legitimate aircraft already in it.

"You must execute a one-hundred-and-eighty-degree turn and fly away from San Francisco because there are a lot of very big airliners in your vicinity and you could get hurt," the controller said, trying hard to control his anxiety and anger. "If you can hear me, it is important that you turn around and head back towards the north bay or toward Sacramento, right now. You don't have to reply, just turn away from San Francisco until we can get some of these planes out of your way, and then we can help you get oriented . . . TWA Five-Eighty-One, roger, report the outer marker . . . Unidentified aircraft flying over the Seagram's sign heading towards San Francisco Airport, you *must* turn away right now . . . American Three-Seventy-Two, traffic alert, two o'clock, altitude unknown, NORDO aircraft in Class B airspace, stay with me until you're clear and be prepared to maneuver . . . Delta Four-Twenty-Two, I can't give you that, we've got NORDO VFR traffic in the area, unless you declare an emergency I'm going to have to send you back to FAITH intersection for the ILS . . ."

Vincenti dropped his oxygen mask in absolute frustration. The air traffic situation around San Francisco and Oakland was going haywire, all because of one madman.

He had to do something!

He refastened his mask and keyed his mike: "San Francisco Tower, Foxtrot Romeo-01, over the Bay Bridge at eight thousand five hundred, be advised that VFR NORDO aircraft is at one thousand feet. He is a LET L-600 cargo plane piloted by a suspected terrorist. I strongly suggest you hold all departures on the ground, divert all arrivals, and let me take care of the bastard. Over."

The radios were completely, utterly silent after that—it was as if all the air had been sucked out of the San Francisco Bay area. The word "terrorist" had that effect on people, and now his reign of terror was being felt here, now.

Finally, after what seemed like a very long time, the tower controller radioed, "Roger, Foxtrot Romeo-01, San Francisco Tower copies, stand by." It was not the same "stand by" issued by the other controllers, which in effect meant "don't bother me"—this "stand by" meant "wait while I clear a path for you." "United Twelve-Oh-Four, cancel takeoff clearance. Delta Five-Niner-Eight, hold your position. TWA Five-Eighty-One, go around, contact Bay Approach. Delta Fourteen, go around, stay with me until advised. Attention all aircraft, emergency air traffic operations in effect, expect delays. Amflight Two-Zero-Niner-Niner, clear to land, keep your speed up on final and land past the intersection of runway one-niner right. Foxtrot Romeo-01, you are radar contact, one-one miles north of the San Francisco VOR at eight thousand five hundred, what are your intentions?"

"Foxtrot Romeo-01 requesting emergency descent through Class B airspace at five-zero-zero knots and MARSA operations with the suspect aircraft," Vincenti replied. "MARSA" stood for "military accepts responsibility for separation of aircraft," and although it usually applied only to military formation flights or aerial refueling, Vincenti wanted to use it to intercept Cazaux.

"Roger, Foxtrot Romeo-01," the tower controller said. Although air traffic control tower controllers rarely issued clearances other than "cleared for takeoff" and "cleared to land," this was obviously an unusual and dangerous situation. "You are cleared to descend through Class B airspace at your most expeditious airspeed to the block surface to two thousand feet within five nautical mile radius of San Francisco VOR, and you are cleared MARSA with the NORDO aircraft. Stay on this frequency."

"Roger," Vincenti replied—just before he pulled hard on his control stick in a tight loop. When he emerged from the loop, he was just south of the Bay Bridge in a fifteen-thousand-foot-per-minute descent, heading "down the ramp" right at San Francisco International Airport. There were very few aircraft on his radarscope, and only one aircraft near San Francisco International was not transmitting any air traffic transponder codes—that had to be Cazaux. "Foxtrot Romeo-01 is tied on radar and accepts MARSA with unidentified aircraft," Vincenti radioed. "I suggest you get on the radio and try to get Oakland to keep its planes on the ground, too. I don't think it'll be safe for any other planes to be flying around over San Francisco Bay right about now."

"Say that last transmission again, Foxtrot Romeo-01 . . . ?" San Francisco Tower called. But there was no reply.

Taddele Korhonen, at the controls of the LET L-600, had pushed the throttles up to full power, and they were skimming across the top of the piers, docks, and warehouses of the Port of San Francisco, west and south of the Bay Bridge. "Why the hell we flyin' so low to the city?" Jefferson "Krull" Jones asked. He and Henri Cazaux were in the cargo bay of the L-600, removing some of the packets of money and cocaine from the second pallet. "You gonna drop all those explosives on San Francisco, too?"

"Of course not," Cazaux replied. "The loss of the Stinger missiles was regrettable and will dearly affect my business, but all is not lost if I can salvage the explosives and ammunition. Besides, we are still flying. As long as we're airborne, there is hope."

Suddenly, the chatter on the air traffic control channel seemed to cease. The quiet caught Cazaux's attention as easily as a loud gunshot. Then he heard, "Roger, Foxtrot Romeo-01, San Francisco Tower copies, stand by . . . United Twelve-Oh-Four, cancel takeoff clearance. Delta Five-Niner-Eight, hold your position. TWA Five-Eighty-One, go around, contact Bay Approach . . ."

"What the hell is goin' on?" Jones asked. "Sounds like they're clearin' everybody out."

"That is exactly what they're doing," Cazaux said. "But why?"

"Attention all aircraft, emergency air traffic operations in effect, expect delays. Amflight Two-Zero-Niner-Niner, clear to land, keep your speed up on final and land past the intersection of runway one-niner right. Foxtrot Romeo-01, you are radar contact, one-one miles north of the San Francisco VOR at eight thousand five hundred, what are your intentions?"

"Foxtrot Romeo-01 requesting emergency descent through Class B airspace at five-zero-zero knots and MARSA operations with the suspect aircraft," came the reply.

"Foxtrot Romeo Zero One . . . that's the damn fighter again!" Jones said. "Man, he's back on our tail!"

"They will never give him a clearance to descend at five hundred knots through dense airspace like this,'' Cazaux said. ''Impossible.''

''Roger, Foxtrot Romeo-01, you are cleared to descend through Class B airspace at your most expeditious airspeed to the block surface to two thousand feet within five nautical mile radius of San Francisco VOR, and you are cleared MARSA with the NORDO aircraft. Stay on this frequency.''

''Jesus, they just gave him carte blanche,'' Cazaux said, stunned. ''A tower controller is not authorized to give such a clearance!''

''Well, he just did it,'' Jones sneered. ''And now he's gonna be gunnin' for our asses. What the hell we gonna do now?''

Cazaux looked like a balloon that was pricked with a pin and was slowly losing air.

For the first time, Jones saw real depression, real defeat in his face. He stared out the open end of the L-600 as if he could see the F-16 diving down on them, could see the cannon muzzle flashing, could see the heavy 20-millimeter shells peppering him and his plane. ''We can surrender, man,'' Jones continued. ''Tell him we give up. It's better than dyin,' man.''

''I will *never* give up!'' Cazaux said emphatically. ''I will never surrender!'' He went over to the intercom panel and hit the mike button: ''Stork, fly over San Francisco International Airport, right over the terminal buildings.'' The L-600 banked left and descended in response. Cazaux switched the intercom switch to the VHF radio: ''Attention, F-16 fighter, this is Henri Cazaux. I have several thousand pounds of explosives on board this aircraft, and I will release them on San Francisco International Airport unless you depart this area.''

''You'll be dead long before you reach the airport, Cazaux,'' a voice said over the frequency. ''I show you two minutes to the airport, and I'm in missile range right now.'' Vincenti hoped the bluff would work—he wasn't carrying any missiles at all, and he wouldn't be in optimum gun range for another thirty to forty seconds. ''Jettison the explosives right now, into the bay, and then fly away from the airport straight down the bay. After that, I'll direct you to make a turn over the bay north, and we'll land at Alameda Naval Air Station.''

To Jones, Cazaux shouted, ''Get that second pallet ready to drop.'' On the radio, he asked, ''How do I know you will not kill me after I do all that you order?''

"I'm not giving you any guarantees, you sonofabitch, except this—if I don't see your course altered away from land, you'll be dead in three seconds. What's it going to be?"

"Very well, I am dumping the explosives overboard right now. Do not fire your missiles." He motioned to Krull, and he and the big loader pushed the second pallet of military gear out the cargo ramp, just a few hundred yards east of Fullers Point, north of the airport. Cazaux then picked up the microphone and switched to intercom: "Stork, decrease speed and execute a turn back to the north . . . and then turn directly towards San Francisco International again and go to full throttle." Back on VHF: "All right, I have done as you asked. I have dropped the explosives, and I am turning north. Hold your fire. I broadcast my surrender to all who can hear my voice on this frequency. I am surrendering to the United States Air Force, for assurances that I will not be fired upon. You are all my witnesses in case there is a so-called unfortunate accident."

"You gonna do it?" Jones shouted over the windblast and the roar of the engines through the open cargo ramp. "You gonna drop the last pallet on San Francisco International? Holy shit! He'll put a missile up our asses for sure . . . Jesus, mother of god . . ."

"If he had missiles, he would have killed us long ago," Cazaux decided. "He has only guns, like the first fighter. I believe he will wait until we fly down the center of San Francisco Bay, then open fire. I am hoping he cannot follow us if we slow down and turn. No one threatens me and gets away with it." He dropped the microphone, then went over to a rack with several backpack-style parachutes and pulled one off. "We'll drop the explosives on San Francisco International, then parachute to safety. The Stork will put the plane on autopilot and join us."

"We're not dropping anything," Jones said. As Cazaux began fastening his parachute harness, Jones reached down and pulled a small automatic pistol from an ankle holster. "Hold your hands straight out from your sides and turn around."

"What is this?" Cazaux asked, a trace of amusement in his eyes.

"U.S. Marshal, Cazaux," Jones said. He retrieved a wallet from a back pocket, flipped it open to reveal a five-pointed star, and tucked the wallet in his belt. "You're under arrest, motherfucker. I said turn around."

"If you fire that gun in here, Marshal Jones, you will blow us all to hell."

"It would be worth it to watch you die, Cazaux," Jones said.

"Step away from there, across the plane, facing the wall. Move." As Cazaux moved slowly in front of the third pallet toward the left side of the cargo bay, Jones reached the intercom panel: "Stork, this is Jones. Don't turn back towards San Francisco. Fly north down the middle of the bay. I'm a federal marshal, and you're under arrest. If you turn towards land, I'll—"

Suddenly the LET L-600 seemed as if it flipped completely upside down. Korhonen had thrown the plane into a steep left bank, causing Jones to lose his balance for just a few seconds—but that was more than enough time for Cazaux. With incredible speed, Cazaux knelt under Jones's first bullet, withdrew a Walther PPK automatic pistol from his right boot, dodged a second shot fired at him by throwing himself aft toward the open cargo ramp, then opened fire on Jones. He missed his intended target—Jones's heart—but he managed several shots into the big man's chest and one in the head. The undercover U.S. marshal fired several more shots at Cazaux before he dropped, still fighting even as he was dying.

"I have got to get out of this damned business. The authorities are practically in bed with me." Cazaux tried to clear his head and get to his feet. One bullet had hit him in the left leg, creasing across his calf and ankle. Walking on it was difficult, but he ignored the burning pain, made his way forward and said to Korhonen, "Good job, Stork. I knew I could depend on you. You're one of the few in my organization I can trust."

"Thank you, sir," the Stork said, showing two grimy rows of teeth. "I am getting a fluctuating oil pressure on the number two engine, sir. I think one of your shots hit the right engine. We have perhaps ten minutes' time before I have to shut down. What are your orders?"

"One last act of revenge, and we will get out of this place, take the money, and go into hiding in Mexico," Cazaux said. He pointed at San Francisco International and said, "Fly right over the main terminal building, Stork. Dive right for it, then pitch up at the last moment. I will get the pallet ready to drop. After that, fly her south along the coast at medium altitude, set the autopilot, and we'll bail out together. We will make our way to the central valley and make contact with our Mexican agents. Thank you again, old friend." He clasped Korhonen on the shoulder once again, then returned to the cargo bay.

But it wasn't going to happen, Cazaux realized. Jones's body was lying across the rear deck, directly in the path of the one remaining pallet, blocking the cargo ramp opening, and as hard as he tried, he couldn't move the three-hundred-plus-pound corpse. The explosives weren't going anywhere.

He shrugged, checked that his PPK was secure in its boot holster, stuffed a few bundles of cash into his fatigue shirt, tightened up his parachute straps, and hefted two of the remaining hand grenades. "Thanks again, Stork," he said to no one. "You were a good pilot." He then popped the safety pins off the grenades, tossed them atop the last pallet filled with explosives, and ran out the open cargo ramp, pulling his parachute D-ring as he cleared the ramp.

Taddele Korhonen was well above redline on both engines and at the plane's structural redline as he careened through three hundred feet, aiming right for the main commercial terminal at San Francisco International—what was the worry about overstressing the plane, he reasoned, when they were apparently going to ditch it? Coming in from the northeast, he was lined up with runways 19L and 19R and offset a bit to the north. The taxiways on the X-shaped airport were dotted with airliners waiting to depart, and the entire circular main terminal building was choked with airliners and service trucks. As the center of the largest part of the main terminal building almost touched the cargo plane's nose, the Stork clicked twice on the intercom to let his master know they had arrived, then began to pull up into a steep climb . . .

The first explosion did not seem too loud, and since Korhonen was concentrating on the pullout, he ignored it.

Then his ears registered a second loud *bang!* and then another explosion a hundred times louder and more powerful.

He had a brief sensation of intense heat on the back of his head before his body, and the rest of the LET L-600 cargo plane, was blasted apart by the sheer force of over two tons of high-explosives detonating at once.

Damn it, Vincenti cursed, he *knew* Cazaux was going to pull something like this. Shit! It was the same act he pulled with McKenzie: beg for surrender, then turn, attack, and run. Well, he wasn't going to get away with it. He was determined to kill Henri Cazaux. Vincenti had bluffed a bit about how far away he was and about carrying missiles, but he wasn't bluffing about wanting to see Cazaux dead. *That* was real.

Unfortunately, he wasn't in the best position to attack.

When Cazaux turned away from San Francisco International, Vincenti found himself relaxing, momentarily confident that he'd won—and then he found himself high and fast, unable to stay with Cazaux's slow-flying cargo plane without burying the nose and risking a crash into San Francisco Bay. He had no choice but to pull the throttle to idle, pop speedbrakes, and widen his turn beyond radar lock-on. Cazaux had turned his lights on when he dumped the cargo overboard—Vincenti did not believe for a moment that Cazaux had willingly dumped *all* his deadly cargo—so it was easy to keep him in sight as he closed in on him. But when Cazaux tightened his turn, shut off his lights, and headed back for San Francisco International again, Vincenti found himself ten seconds out of position and without a solid contact. He reacquired Cazaux's plane a few seconds later, but by then Cazaux was over the airport at high speed. Just as Vincenti put his gun pipper on the radar return and got an IN RANGE readout on his heads-up display, the cargo plane's nose began to pitch up, and . . .

And then the LET L-600 disappeared in an immense blinding ball of fire. Vincenti had a brief glimpse of a small flash of light inside the cargo bay, like a flashbulb or the muzzle blast of a rifle, followed immediately by a huge explosion that completely obscured the main airport terminal and effectively blinded the veteran fighter pilot. Vincenti shoved in full military power, retracted speedbrakes, pulled the nose of his F-16 ADF up, fed in afterburner power, and climbed away from the fireball. He had no way of knowing in what direction he was headed or what his airspeed was, but altitude was life right now.

When Vincenti's vision cleared a few moments later, he leveled off and set up an orbit over San Francisco International. He couldn't believe the carnage. The flaming wreckage of the L-600 had hit the central terminal, showering the control tower and the entire western half of the terminal with fire and debris. The entire multistory central terminal looked as if it was on fire, just seconds after the impact. The wreckage had spread across the center of the circular terminal, engulfing hundreds of cars and buses in the inner departure and arrival area. The impact pattern formed a gigantic fiery teardrop covering several hundred feet, all the way across the inner-terminal circle to the south terminal. Burning aircraft at the gates were setting other nearby planes on fire with incredible speed, like a candle flame being passed from person to person by touching wicks. Soon Vincenti could count about a dozen planes on fire near the impact point. Several explosions could be seen through the dense jet-fuel smoke, with great mushrooms of fire billowing into the sky very close to Vincenti's altitude over the airport . . .

And then he saw it, plainly illuminated by the intense fire below—a parachute, less than half a mile away and no more than a few hundred feet below his altitude.

Incredibly, someone had bailed out of that cargo plane seconds before it exploded . . .

Henri Cazaux! Without thinking, Vincenti turned toward the rapidly falling white dot, nearly going inverted to keep the parachute in sight. Cazaux obviously heard the fighter fly nearby, could probably see the position and anticollision lights, because the 'chute started falling even faster. Cazaux had grabbed the two right risers of his parachute and pulled them down, spilling air out the left side of his canopy, increasing his descent rate, and sending him into a wide, violent left spin.

Vincenti didn't know if it was planned or not, but Cazaux was too late. The intense fire at the terminal, less than a thousand feet away, was buoying his parachute up in the air—he was a sitting duck. Vincenti had to shove his fighter's nose to the ground to get lined up . . . and just as he did line up his shot, a rescue or news helicopter popped up in the middle of his HUD, less than two hundred feet away. He had to bank hard left and pull to miss the helicopter, and he lost sight of Cazaux immediately. By the time Vincenti could roll out and look for Cazaux's 'chute, the terrorist was on the ground and moving. Vincenti had a brief thought about trying a strafing run, but now the entire area near the crash site was choked with rescue aircraft and vehicles. Flying down into that melee would be very dangerous. He could do nothing else but climb above the San Francisco Class B airspace and head back to Beale Air Force Base, and the inquisition that he knew would face him there.

The two crewmen from the Coast Guard Air Station just north of San Francisco International Airport couldn't believe their eyes as they watched the medium cargo plane plow into the central terminal—it looked like the aftermath of an oil-refinery explosion or a replay of a successful bomb strike during the Persian Gulf War. They heard the low-flying cargo plane as it buzzed their hangar, and they saw it explode and crash into the terminal as they watched. The entire airport seemed to be waist-deep in fire so hot that it could be felt from inside their pickup truck nearly a half-mile away.

But even the explosion and devastation itself were nothing compared to their surprise as a lone parachutist dropped into the grassy field bordering the airport's outer security fence. "Jesus Christ . . . did that guy jump out of that cargo plane?" one of the Coast Guardsmen asked.

"He's gotta be the luckiest sonofabitch in the world," the other said. "He got out of the plane in time, and he missed that fence by inches. He looks pretty bad." They drove over, found the man lying faceup in the grass, just a few feet from the security fence. One seaman went over to him while the other set to work deflating the parachute so it wouldn't drag him into the bay. "Hey, Todd," the first seaman shouted over the roar of the nearby explosions and fire, "we got a radio in the—"

The second seaman couldn't hear his buddy over the sounds of sheer devastation at the airport. A few fire trucks from the Coast Guard base were racing toward the terminal, but they were too far away and moving too fast to flag down. "Say again, Will?" No reply. He managed to collapse the billowing parachute, then turned to his partner: "What did you say?"

His buddy Will was lying on the ground just a few feet away, the entire top of his head blown off. The parachutist was standing beside the second seaman, a gun pointed at his face. He saw a bright flash of light and barely registered a loud *bang!*, then nothing.

Henri Cazaux unbuckled his parachute harness, rolled up the parachute, and threw it into the storage area behind the seat of the pickup truck so it wouldn't be easily spotted. He then collected the Coast Guardsmen's ID cards, found a jacket and cap that fit him, and started up the pickup truck. He followed the line of emergency vehicles heading toward San Francisco International via the parallel taxiways. Then, when he saw it was clear, he drove away off the airport. He was challenged once by an airport security guard who enlisted his help in trying to control traffic as thousands of persons tried to flee the carnage. The security guard was shot in the face as well.

Henri Cazaux's killing spree did not stop at San Francisco Airport. He killed two more persons, stole two more cars, made his way undetected through central California, then risked taking an early-morning plane from Stockton to Phoenix. Sensing that federal marshals and security patrols would be screening everyone coming off the plane, Cazaux told the flight attendants he had lost some jewelry under the seats, waited until the airliner cleaning service workers arrived at the plane, executed two workers and slipped away out the rear exit dressed in their overalls and using their ID badges.

A few hours after sunrise, after stealing another car, he was safely across the border in Nogales. Shortly after that he could be in one of his many hideouts in Mexico, safe from all but a determined paramilitary assault—but he did not want to stop. Each time, the vision of his cargo plane crashing into San Francisco International's central terminal flashed in his mind, and he smiled a sort of twisted, pathological smile. He knew he wanted to see that kind of pure destruction again very, very soon. It was one way to get even with the U.S. Air Force, the Marshals, the Bureau of Alcohol, Tobacco, and Firearms, the entire United States fucking government. There was so much the Americans had to pay for: torture, false imprisonment, rape, assault, robbery, perjury—those were just the least of their crimes against Henri Cazaux over the years. And as those years went by, Cazaux could add murder, conspiracy, malicious prosecution, and numerous additional counts of perjury and contempt of court. And Cazaux knew the United States would never be formally charged and tried for any of these crimes, so he would issue the punishment himself. Cazaux's justice was in his heart, his mind, his weapons, and his aircraft.

The Americans had worked to almost put him out of business, permanently. That was going to end. America had yet to feel the fury of a full-scale attack by Henri Cazaux. Now it was time. Cazaux wanted to see America bleed, and attacking its most important and yet most terrifying institution—its air traffic and air travel system—was going to be the way to do it. It was so easy, and yet it was going to be so devastating . . .

It had been a long time since Henri Cazaux had been in an American commercial airport terminal—international terrorists rarely travel by commercial air unless speed is a necessity—and what he saw surprised him. No one, he thought, would consider spending one second longer than necessary in a bus station, or taxi stand, or train station, but modern airports seemed to cater to travelers who obviously spent a great deal of time there. Even relatively small Phoenix–Sky Harbor International Airport had fancy restaurants, video arcades, bookstores, hotels, an art museum, meeting and exercise rooms, even a small amusement park with putt-putt golf and miniature movie theaters right on the airport premises. While Cazaux was busy moving from one restroom to another every fifteen minutes until his flight was called, trying to stay incognito, he noticed people that seemed to hang around, enjoying themselves like tourists. It was crazy . . .

. . . but what an inviting target. This place was packed! There were dozens of planes parked at the gates, with thousands of persons choking the terminal. One bomb in the center of this place could kill hundreds, injure hundreds, destroy perhaps billions of dollars of airplanes and property. But it would take a thousand pounds of explosives, maybe more, to do the kind of damage he needed to do, and he couldn't truck that much nitro all the way into the heart of the terminal . . .

. . . but he could *drop* the explosives on the terminal, just like he did at Mather Jetport and San Francisco International. The Americans had no defense against an aerial assault. Yes, there were air defense fighters, but they were only a few units scattered around the periphery of the country. The FBI, perhaps even the military, would eventually crack down on all unidentified or unauthorized flights, but it would take many days to shut down America's enormous air traffic system, and once shut down it would surely crush the American way of life. Until then, he could take an incredible toll on these mindless Americans. Three attacks, all in less than a week, and he was certain that America would fall to its knees.

It would take lots of planning, and money, and that meant a trip back east, to his American headquarters in New Jersey—the Owl's Nest—to meet with his senior staff to plan the operations. But more importantly, he needed to know if his dreams of destroying America from within was possible. Again, the answer was in the east, in Newburgh, New York. Only one person could advise him on how to proceed, and he needed to see her as soon as possible.

Cazaux remained in his Mexican stronghold in Nogales long enough to disguise himself, effortlessly aging thirty years with simple makeup and posture techniques, then used his forged American passport and boarded a flight from Nogales to Albuquerque. Security was loose and there was no sign of pursuit, and booking a flight to Chicago and beyond was easy. No one gave the bent, alcoholic, emaciated-looking old man more than a passing glance as he boarded the next plane.

PART 2

New York City
August 1995

When his executive assistant found Harold G. Lake, the first thought he had was, *My God, he's going to jump.*

The sealed high-rise windows designed to keep the heat and the odor and the noises of Manhattan out were triple-paned tempered glass, so, of course, it wasn't possible for Lake to jump (from here at least) unless he had a sledgehammer hidden in his closet. But it was the way Lake looked that worried Ted Fell, Harold Lake's attorney, executive assistant, and—if anyone could properly be so categorized—friend and confidant, Harold Lake. He was a brooder even on his best days, and he could be depressing most days. Today, the tall, dark, slim entrepreneur, investor, and Wall Street trader looked like a dog left out in the rain all night.

"Got those letters of intent ready for your signature," Fell reported. "I see no problems at all with the debt restructuring. The next few weeks should be okay. We're in the clear." Fell set a small pile of papers on Lake's desk, the only item on the expansive and empty marble and mahogany desk that looked out of place. Lake continued to stare out the huge picture window of his downtown Park Avenue office into the gray steamy overcast. It was already 80 degrees in the city, and threatening to hit 90-plus with 90-plus-percent humidity—one might actually be cool and comfortable standing out on a forty-first-story ledge right now, Fell thought wryly. "You got my notes there on top, but I got a few minutes to talk about the deal if you—"

"Who did the deal?" Lake asked. When Fell hesitated that extra moment, Lake replied for him: "Universal. Shit. What'd you get?" His voice was uncharacteristically uneven, with a trace of his native New Jersey accent mixed in, even after years of trying to excuse it.

"Universal Equity offered us ten-point-one percent," Fell said quickly.

Lake irritably rubbed his eyes, moved toward the papers as if to confirm what Fell said was true, then sat back in his high-backed black leather chair and continued to stare out the window.

The president and founder of Universal Equity Services, Limited, based in Glasgow, Scotland, was Brennan McSorley, one of the world's richest men, owner of the largest nonpublic investment group in the world. McSorley had his fingers in hundreds of different pies all over the world, everything from oil and gas to banking to shipping to computers. He and Lake, McSorley's one-time disciple, had done business many times in the past, although their version of "business" nowadays was akin to calling the U.S. Civil War a "disagreement." McSorley was like a giant stallion to Lake's horsefly—Lake could irritate the hell out of McSorley and his investors, maybe even cause him to stumble or lose control, but Lake was small potatoes next to Brennan McSorley.

"If I say no to him now, I'm screwed and he knows it." Lake looked at Fell with an accusing glare. "You agreed to his terms?"

"You have final authority, boss, so you can say no to the deal," Fell responded, "but it's what you wanted, right? A done deal, in time to pay the account and retain your shares."

"You fucking agreed to pay Brennan McSorley ten-point-one percent, Ted?"

"No one else gave you the time of day, Harold. You needed eighteen million dollars by close of business *today*. If I had even three days, I could get that for you at eight-point-five. McSorley said yes right away, and I had to move."

"Maybe you moved a bit too fast."

"You may not like McSorley, boss, but he went to the mat for you this time," Fell said. "The money is in escrow, ready to go. McSorley personally guaranteed the loan, boss, he showed up at the bank *himself* to sign the papers."

"He'd like nothing better than to see me default, the prick," Lake said gloomily. "He'd take great pleasure in seeing me file for bankruptcy or selling my assets. He'd be first in line to screw me in bankruptcy court. He probably showed up at the bank to conduct a news conference, to announce to the whole world what a loser I am."

Fell elected to stay silent, but he reminded himself that Harold G. Lake knew a lot about screwing someone, whether it was in court, in the market, or just about any imaginable business or social setting. Along with many other talents, Lake was one of the world's premier options traders. His business was enticing other investors to write option deals to buy or sell their stock. Lake had many ways to sniff out stocks that might come into play—lack of publicity, no returned phone calls, lots of unusual stock trading activity by company officers, even when, where, and how the officers went on vacation. Like a general planning an invasion, Lake was a master at setting an objective and then designing a vast, convoluted, sweeping series of trades to accomplish his ultimate objective—what he called the "perpetual motion machine." Create a series of deals, contracts, and companies whose income and assets always exceeded the expenses and liabilities. Create a network, an empire, that was totally self-sufficient, that made contracts with itself, earned money off itself, paid expenses to itself, owed money to itself. It was a true "money tree," the modern-day answer to Midas's touch of gold.

Lake was a master at this kind of deal-making. After getting an undergraduate degree from Rutgers and an MBA from Harvard, Lake had spent his early career in middle management with a variety of companies and brokerage firms specializing in "creative" financing, long-term corporate debt (junk bonds), and market speculation. In 1980 he joined Universal Equity Services, where he handled all the real estate acquisitions. Then, in 1985, Lake engineered an insider trading scheme in which the price was artificially jacked up in a bidding war between Universal Equity and a company secretly funded by Lake. Lake was fired, but his illegal activities were never confirmed by Universal. Since leaving Universal, Lake worked in a variety of financial and stock trading positions before finally striking out on his own.

"We're still in business, and we've got plenty to keep us afloat for months," Fell said finally, standing up to Lake's glare. "Let's maintain the proper perspective here. Who the hell knew some nutcase in San Francisco was going to wipe out half of an international airport terminal and kill five hundred people? Plenty of investors lost big on this one, boss, including McSorley. It's a glitch in the market, that's all. Everyone in that investment consortium that bailed out on you this morning will be back in a few weeks, looking for fresh meat. They'll know they looked bad when they punched, but they'll come back because you made it happen. We can soak them when they come back, too, because they lost face by bailing out on you."

Ted Fell was one of the few people, in fact the only one, who could really talk to Lake like this. Blunt, no bullshit. But that was because Fell was the best addition to the organization that Lake had made. He complemented Lake's own strengths and made up for Lake's weaknesses in other areas. A graduate of Dartmouth College and Harvard Law School, Fell had held several positions with large law firms in Albany, Wilmington, and New York City, most in the areas of finance, insurance, and corporations. Admitted to the bar in sixteen states, he was considered a leading authority on corporation organization—i.e., dummy corporations and offshore shells. He had worked for Lake since his days at Universal Equity, helping him on his real estate deals and then unwittingly, and then knowingly, participated as an engineer in the stock manipulation scheme that had gotten them both fired.

Lake wasn't totally listening to his attorney, but what little that did register in his head made sense. The terrorist bombing of San Francisco International last night was an aberration, a total fluke—damn it, it *had* to be, or Lake was *really* sunk. Several hundred persons dead, thousands injured, hundreds of millions in damage to aircraft and property, and perhaps billions in lost revenues due to the closing of the airport for perhaps as long as a year.

A one-in-a-million occurrence . . .

But the damage to Lake's portfolio was just as devastating, and simply because it was caused by a random event would not mitigate the damage. Because he rarely used his own money for most deals, Lake liked trading on the edge, leaving himself uncovered for short periods of time. One of Lake's favorite options trading tactics was writing uncovered put and call options, or "naked options," in which he agreed—for a price of course—to buy stocks at a certain price that he didn't have the money to buy, or sell stocks that he did not yet own. In ordinary circumstances, the premiums received for writing such contracts made the risk well worth it. But if the market takes a nosedive and the contract is assigned, as it was during the night by some astute overseas investor, Lake was obligated to sell his stocks at low prices or obligated to buy stocks with cash he did not have. In both cases, he needed cash in a hurry to cover all his contracts.

Normally, in case of impending bad financial news, Harold Lake's overseas brokers usually executed closing purchase transactions that canceled the more risky uncovered options before they were assigned, but the sheer speed of the terrorist attack and the rapid reaction by overseas traders made it impossible. Lake was stuck holding all the IOUs, and they were all due and payable by close of business, or he was out of business. The huge drop in price of Lake's stocks in overseas trading alone was enough to queer several other deals in which he was involved. The New York Stock Exchange was not due to open for another three hours, the Chicago Board of Options Exchange not for four hours, and already Lake had lost 40 percent of his portfolio's value, much of which had to be covered with cash. Dozens of nervous overseas investors bailed out on him through the night, withdrawing money that had been earmarked for scores of other projects—it was a huge maze of dominoes collapsing as quickly as the sunrise moved across the planet. Investors heard of the awful terrorist bombing, took defensive cash-saving positions, and left speculators like Lake sucking wind. Borrowing the money to make up for the losses and to continue his current obligations only prolonged the inevitable. Eighteen million dollars wouldn't last Lake two months, even at zero-percent interest, let alone at an exorbitant 10 percent. Foreclosures and bankruptcy were inevitable.

But even more devastating than just losing your possessions or property was the loss of prestige, the loss of face. Normally talking about losing face was a Japanese notion, but it is very true on Wall Street as well. You are only as good as your last bad trade, the Street version of the old saying goes. No one likes a loser, and the stigma stays with a trader for a long, long time.

Technically, he was out of business right now, because no one would ever do deals with him again, but now it was a matter of survival. Bankruptcy was out of the question—it would save him from a few, but not the ones that mattered. A lot of the people he dealt with did not allow anyone to hide behind lawyers and bankruptcy courts.

Lake took a deep breath, then got to his feet, straightened his shoulders, and tightened his stomach and chest muscles until they tingled. When faced with adversity, he was always taught, get the blood running and the brain working. Start thinking and feeling like a warrior and you'll start acting like a warrior. It was time to get on the offensive: "I'm going to need a face-to-face with George Jacox and get a report," Lake said. Jacox was the outside tax attorney and accountant, leading a staff of two attorneys and six CPAs who managed Lake's affairs. "I need to restructure that debt with McSorley first thing."

"George is in Alaska on that hunting trip," Fell reminded him. "Completely incommunicado until Saturday. I can get in contact with his partner."

"Scherber's an asshole," Lake said. "Besides, George knows where all the bodies are buried. Get the jet and go pick him up. Better yet, pack all his records on a portable computer, grab a satellite transceiver, and take it all to him. Then let's put in a call to—"

"Boss, I think our first move should be to sign those papers and get the loan moving," Fell interjected. He wasn't about to tell Lake, at least not this minute, that they could hardly afford to reserve a court at the YMCA right now, let alone fly the company's private jet from New York to Alaska and back. "We've only got two hours before the last wire transfer from Europe. In an hour and a half the phone's going to be ringing off the hook, and we'd better have a wire receipt to show the institutions that we're covered or we'll *really* be in trouble."

"I am not going to spend all day on the phone with a bunch of nervous bean-counters," Lake said. "They wanted to play, and this is part of the game—let them sweat for a few hours while we get our shit together here. Next time, Jacox doesn't leave the fucking city without a cellular phone or I'm finding a new legal team."

"We don't need Jacox to read a spreadsheet or make a pitch to the venture capital types," Fell said. "I can handle the legal side of the opening negotiations. But let's get solvent first before we start bending anyone's ear."

"You *don't* get it, do you, Ted?" Lake snapped, turning angrily toward his longtime associate. Lake was a bit shorter than Fell and physically smaller, with tight, wiry muscles and a lean physique—physically, he was no match for the huskier, more solidly built attorney. But the air of desperation that hovered around Harold Lake made him seem all the more fearsome. The veneer of cunning control was gone—as much as he tried, Lake was not going to get it back. He ranted, "I am not going to go into eighteen-million-plus dollars in debt, get bombarded by jerkoffs who think they can push me around because the market takes a header suddenly one morning, and then try to pretend everything is going to be okay. This is a *glitch* in the market, nothing more. We're in the middle of a sustained bull market, for God's sake! The market hits new record-high territory every three months! Is it my damned fault that a fucking terrorist drops a bomb on San Francisco International?"

"Take it easy, boss . . ." Fell tried.

The phone on Lake's desk rang—the onslaught of inquiries that Fell was expecting was now beginning. "Tell whoever it is to fuck off," Lake hissed, returning to his desk and resuming staring blankly out the window. Fell answered the phone, leaving instructions that Lake not be disturbed and that he would handle all calls himself. "Get out, Ted," he told his assistant from behind his chair. Fell was going to stay despite his boss's obvious anger, but when Lake appeared to be looking over the loan papers and getting back to work, he relaxed a bit and departed.

The bombing of San Francisco International by some crazed lunatic gunrunner may have been a random, completely unforeseen event, even an accident. But one thing Harold Lake knew for sure was that it could very easily happen again. Yes, a lunatic was behind it . . .

. . . and Lake, like the rest of the world, knew who he was.

Options trading was not the only kind of trading Harold Lake did. Some of the "institutions" he worked with were not listed on Standard and Poor's or Dun & Bradstreet, and some of the CEOs and investors who paid him generous commissions and maintained fat accounts with him were not in any issue of *Who's Who* unless that publication had a version on underworld figures. His biggest secret client was none other than Henri Cazaux, the one responsible for the financial mess Lake was in right now. Lake had never planned on getting involved with men of this caliber. He was far too vain and far too much of a self-preservationist to risk dying at their displeasure. But back in 1987, after being fired from Universal Equity and trying to strike out on his own, Lake kept getting approached by smugglers, hoods, and eventually bigger fish like New York–area mob bosses. They could smell a hungry, smart manipulator of cash, but Lake did all he could to resist their overtures. Until the market crash of 1987. It was then that Harold Lake, fully exposed in all his investments, took a nosedive and lost millions overnight. After that, needing quick cash in a hurry, Lake began to see the appeal of laundering money. He made a few contacts, and before he knew it, drug money was reinforcing his investments. Lake stayed solvent and slowly began to get completely immersed in the science of laundering money. In 1991 Henry Cazaux stepped in and demanded Lake handle all of his accounts. It was an offer, as the saying goes, that Lake couldn't refuse. Unless, of course, he wanted a bullet in the head.

Cazaux was different from your typical sociopath. He was power-hungry, and a megalomaniac, and definitely psychotic, and very smart. Each of his various identities all over the world lived in completely legal surroundings, with proper books, properly filed tax returns, and proper documentation. True, only a small percentage of his total net worth was ever reported, but the funds and the persons that existed aboveground were squeaky clean, thanks to Harold Lake and others like him in other countries. He had to track down the sonofabitch and tell him to crawl back into his Mexico hideout, right fucking *now,* or his source of legitimate, laundered money was going to dry up.

The first thing Harold Lake did was pick up the phone and dial a tollfree number that connected him to a private voice-mail system that was untraceable either to himself or to his calling party. In case someone tried to trace the call, they'd reach a computer with two thousand names and addresses, and if investigators showed up to try to track down the names, they could be erased from computer memory in seconds. In turn, the voice-mail system connected him to a private paging service, again untraceable. Lake entered just three numbers on the pager—911—then hung up.

He then looked over the loan paperwork. Fell had placed Post-It Notes on several important or critical areas of the contract that he had changed or that required special consideration, but his final recommendation was to sign. Reluctantly, Lake did so, adding the words "I hope you choke on it" under the signature line. He then punched his intercom button to Fell's office: "The loan papers are ready, Ted. Come get the fuckers."

Just then he heard a faint beep coming from a desk drawer. He opened the drawer and retrieved his Apple Newton PDA (personal digital assistant), a handheld computer about the size of a paperback book. The PDA had a built-in wireless network system that allowed him to receive packet digital messages anywhere in the world, communicate directly with other computers, or send or receive faxes. He activated the PDA and called up the messaging system, entering a password to access the secret message area. The message read simply, OWL'S NEST. RIGHT NOW.

Stunned, he all but leaped to his feet, then put on a jacket, slipped the PDA computer into his jacket pocket, and left the office via the back door as fast as he could.

Beale Air Force Base, Yuba City, California
That Same Time

Colonel Charles Gaspar, operations group commander of the 144th Fighter Wing (California Air National Guard), asked, "You're standing there telling me that you're *sticking* with this cockamamie story, Vincenti?" The tall, slightly balding officer got to his feet, circled his desk, and stood face to face with Lieutenant Colonel Al Vincenti. The veteran Vincenti defiantly followed Gaspar's movements with his head and eyes while remaining at attention, which angered Gaspar even more. The men were of equal height, but Gaspar was several years younger than Vincenti, and even though he was of higher rank, he couldn't intimidate the older veteran fighter pilot. Gaspar had less than half of Vincenti's flying hours, and the adage that Vincenti had forgotten more than Gaspar had ever known held true—and everyone there knew it.

"Call me on it, Chuck," Vincenti replied hotly. "Try to refute any of it. You'll lose."

"Don't challenge me, Al," Gaspar said angrily. "Don't even bother trying. They don't need *me* to help throw you to the dogs—you've done that all by yourself. The FBI has taken over this case, and the first head they want is *yours*. So you better straighten out your attitude."

Gaspar took a deep breath. It was important for Vincenti to stick to his story—if he couldn't make Gaspar, his longtime friend and wingman, believe his story, no one else was going to believe it either. "You maintain that your last order was to pursue Cazaux, that you believed that the order to land at Beale meant land only when your fuel condition warranted or if you could not reestablish contact with Cazaux. Is that correct, Al?"

"That's what I wrote in my report."

"The controller's tape says otherwise."

"My gun camera tape shows that I acknowledge the order to pursue."

"Played side by side, the tapes don't jive, Al," Gaspar said. Although military aircraft did not have cockpit voice recorders, the F-16's heads-up display system used a color videotape system to record gun camera video. The system, which also recorded radio and intercom conversations and copied flight and aircraft performance data like an airliner's inflight data recorder "black box," was often used by the pilots to record significant events inflight as well. "We hear you acknowledging orders that we never hear on the radio. It looks like the tape's been doctored, or that you simply fake receiving orders to pursue.''

''So now I'm being accused of falsifying orders?'' Vincenti asked. ''Looks like I'm being set up to take the fall for this entire incident. Henri Cazaux blows up two airports and kills hundreds of persons, and I'm to blame. Wonder how the media would react to this?''

''You're prohibited from talking with the media.''

''If the Air Force tries to court-martial me for what happened last night, Chuck, I'm spilling my guts,'' Vincenti said angrily. ''I'm not bullshitting you. I've got a copy of the HUD tape, and I'll give it to every TV and radio station I can think of.''

''What the hell's with you, Al?'' Gaspar exclaimed, his voice serious now, searching his friend's face with a definite edge of concern—Vincenti usually was not evasive or secretive at all. Claiming he had an engine malfunction, Vincenti had landed all the way back at Fresno Air Terminal instead of at Beale Air Force Base, as he had been directed to do. Although Fresno was closer and was his home station, he had plenty of gas to make it to Beale as he was ordered. As the F-16 pilots do every mission, Vincenti pulled his own mission videotapes, and he had it in his possession when he was met by a representative of Fourth Air Force's Judge Advocate General's office about two hours later. The JAG officer confiscated the videotape, supervised a blood-and-urine test, and escorted Vincenti here to Beale Air Force Base, where the accident investigation board was going to be held. Theoretically, Vincenti had time to work on the videotape, doctor it, and duplicate it before someone finally ordered him to surrender it to the judge advocate. Gaspar didn't think he really did all those things—Vincenti had always been a team player—but there was no doubt that Vincenti was pissed enough to do anything right about now.

''I'm sorry about Linda's death,'' Gaspar said softly.

Vincenti swallowed hard, nodded, and let his anger wash away, to be replaced by an empty numbness. Linda McKenzie never got full man-seat separation after ejecting from her Falcon on the runway at McClellan. She was still in the ejection seat, with only a partial parachute, when it hit the ground at over one hundred miles an hour. She mercifully died of her horrible injuries after several hours of emergency surgery.

''That's not your fault, and I understand the pain you're feeling, and the pain you felt last night,'' Gaspar went on. ''But now you're breaking with the program, Rattler. You're abandoning the Force, abandoning your uniform, abandoning your responsibilities.''

''Don't give me that crap, Chuck,'' Vincenti retorted. ''All I see around here is brass rushing to cover their butts. Linda and I did the shitty job we were assigned the best we could. They should have never tried to capture that motherfucking terrorist, especially knowing he had all those explosives on board. And sure as *hell* they should have never herded him over Sacramento or allowed him to get anywhere near San Francisco. We should've either blown his ass away or let him go.''

''I'm not arguing with you, Al, and I'm not going to second-guess the brass,'' Gaspar said. ''All I'm trying to do is get the facts.''

''This is not a debriefing, Chuck. This is not a 'lessons learned' session. This is not even an accident investigation. You don't want my observations or opinions, and you don't care about the facts because everyone's already made up their minds about who's to blame. This is a fucking *inquisition.* Everyone's looking at me and Linda as to why *we* allowed it to happen, why *we* let Cazaux fly over Mather and SFO and drop those explosives, why *we* let Cazaux kill so many persons on the ground. I will tell you right now, bub, I'm not going to allow it. If I'm still getting the third degree, I'll clam up, get an attorney, refuse to talk, take the Fifth, get immunity from prosecution, and screw you and screw the Air Force and the entire federal government. I owe my wingman my full support, even if she's not here, and goddammit, I'm going to give it. Now, how do you want to play it from here on out, Chuck?''

''Okay, Al, I'll add my endorsement over your signature, recommending no disciplinary action and immediate return to flight status—for all the good it'll do,'' Gaspar said. ''I think you're right, chum—the feds want heads to roll because Cazaux got away—and you've been elected. The new director of the FBI herself, Lani 'Trigger' Wilkes, is coming here in a few hours to begin the investigation and to do the press conference at the airport.''

''Great,'' Vincenti muttered. Lani Wilkes, the new director of the FBI, had been given the nickname ''Trigger'' for two reasons—her stand on strict gun control, favoring not just an all-out ban on private purchases of handguns but complete nationwide confiscation of all guns with more than five rounds in them, and because of her hair-trigger temper, first seen during her Senate confirmation hearings and in many courtrooms, press conferences, and congressional hearings since. "Chuck, you might as well just pass my report along to the FBI without your signature. Wilkes is a tough liberal bitch. She'll accuse everyone involved in this thing as being a bunch of screw-ups, tell the press how evil and out of control the military is, then talk about how society, or guns, or the military, has messed up the youth of the country, or some such horseshit. There's no use fighting her."

"Hey, I don't report to Wilkes, Al," said Gaspar.

"I know, but the press and the White House love her, and if she makes you an enemy, she'll bury you alive," Vincenti said. "The further you steer clear of her, the better."

"Well, the wing king wants us to go with him to her press conference at the airport, so I'm going," Gaspar said resignedly. "The press is having a field day with the air traffic controller tapes of you threatening Cazaux and chasing him through the San Francisco Class B airspace. The press thinks you *goaded* Cazaux into blowing up his plane over SFO."

"That's horseshit, Chuck," Vincenti interjected. "Cazaux had no intention of surrendering or safely jettisoning any of those explosives—he jettisoned a palletful of military gear and kept the pallet of explosives on board. His target was either to ram an airliner in midair or bomb SFO, whichever he could do before getting shot down."

"The press and the government don't see it that way, Al," Gaspar said. "Anyway, you're in the hot seat now. If you have any friends in very, very high places, I suggest you call them in."

"Fuck it," Vincenti said bitterly. "If they want my wings, they can have 'em. But I'll tell you something, Chuck—Henri Cazaux is not going to dive underground now. He blew up Mather Jetport on purpose, not by accident, and I think the motherfucker enjoyed watching the fireworks. When he found out I was on his tail, he went right for the next big airfield he could find—San Francisco International. The bastard's going to go after more big airfields, Chuck. I know it. If you have a chance to tell Lani Wilkes that, tell her."

"Forget about Cazaux and Wilkes now, Al," Gaspar said. "Let's deal with *your* problems. My group commander hat is off now, the recorder is off, my fellow fighter pilot hat is on, and it's just you and me. I'm not trying to coach you here—you had better tell the truth during the accident investigation board or your ass is grass—but I want to go over your statement and the sortie chronology minute by minute. Don't leave out a thing."

But as Vincenti started talking, the onus of what he had said started to make an impression on Charles Gaspar—and he realized that Vincenti was right. He too had a feeling that Henri Cazaux would be back, and that no airport in the United States was safe any longer.

The phone in Gaspar's office rang, and he snatched it up irritably: "I thought I told you no calls, Sergeant."

"Sorry, sir, but I just got a call from base operations," the group commander's clerk said. "VIP aircraft inbound, and they just released the plane's passenger list." The clerk told him the plane's lone passenger, and Vincenti saw Gaspar's mouth drop open in surprise. "He wants to meet with you and Colonel Vincenti right away at base ops."

"No shit," Gaspar exclaimed, looking with total amusement at Vincenti's puzzled expression. "We'll be right over." He replaced the phone and smiled broadly at Vincenti. "Well, cowboy, looks like you do have a powerful friend, and he's decided to crash Lani Wilkes' press conference. Let's go."

"The terrorist bombing incidents over Sacramento and San Francisco last night are terrible and tragic ones for all concerned," Lani Helena Wilkes, FBI Director, said to the members of the press from the podium erected on the aircraft parking ramp just outside the base operations building at Beale Air Force Base. This was where the bulk of the FBI's field investigative work for the Cazaux attack was going to be conducted. "Because this is an investigation in progress, I cannot talk about our investigation itself, except to say this: one of the largest manhunts in U.S. history is under way right now in California for Henri Cazaux, who bailed out of the cargo plane seconds before it crashed into San Francisco International. Over three thousand federal agents are on his trail, and I'm confident—no, I'm positive—that he'll be captured soon."

Wilkes was a powerful and dynamic presence, and the press corps treated her with great respect. An accomplished trial lawyer, state and federal district court justice from Alabama, ordained Baptist minister, and political campaign consultant, Lani Wilkes was one of the preeminent personalities in American politics. Rising from a life in the Montgomery slums to leading the number-one criminal investigative force in the world, Wilkes was undoubtedly one of the most notable and most respected figures of either sex in the world. Once mentioned as a vice-presidential candidate, there was no question that the forty-eight-year-old African-American woman, tall and statuesque and beautiful, would be one of the nation's top leaders of the twenty-first century.

"Director Wilkes, do you have any leads yet on the case?" one reporter asked.

"I can't go into details, but we believe we've tracked down the origin of the explosives and other weapons used in the attacks, and the registration of the aircraft used. It was a U.S.-registered aircraft, belonging to a small cargo firm in Redmond, Oregon—obviously a front for Henri Cazaux's operation."

"Henri Cazaux was operating here in California? Why wasn't this discovered earlier?"

"As you all know, Cazaux is extremely intelligent and resourceful," Wilkes responded. "And if I may give the Devil his due, it seems that in this case he played by the rules, which of course in a free society such as ours means that he's relatively free of intrusive government scrutiny. So far we find only legitimate businesses doing legitimate business transactions here in California and much of the western United States and Canada for many years. He pays taxes, sends in his reports, keeps his nose clean. Even a merchant of death can roam free in our society if he doesn't call attention to himself."

"Director Wilkes, can you please go over again the path that Henri Cazaux took after departing Chico Airport last night?" another reported asked. "As I understand it, Marshals Service, ATF agents, and even the U.S. Air Force had a chance to apprehend or shoot him down."

"Unfortunately, I haven't had time to fully study the Bureau of Alcohol, Tobacco, and Firearms' operation, so I can't really comment on it," Wilkes responded, smiling tightly. "I haven't been briefed by the Treasury Department yet, but I understand they were the ones that requested support from the Air Force. As far as the Marshals Service, their role in this incident was to try to apprehend Cazaux as part of his numerous outstanding warrants. Unfortunately, their efforts, as far as I can ascertain, were not coordinated."

"Not coordinated?" A general hubbub followed. Just then an Air Force blue sedan pulled up beside the group of photographers, and several Air Force officers and a civilian got out. Wilkes recognized the civilian who got out of the sedan, one of her assistants, and motioned him to bring the Air Force officers over to the podium.

Being invited to stand on Wilkes' podium didn't mean he had to wait for her expected barrage, so Gaspar took the initiative, stepped right up to the microphone, and without waiting for Wilkes to introduce him, said, "Ladies and gentlemen, my name is Colonel Charles Gaspar, and I'm the operations group commander for the 144th Fighter Wing, California Air National Guard, based at Fresno Air Terminal. With me is Lieutenant Colonel Al Vincenti, the lead pilot involved in last night's incident." Gaspar did not introduce the third officer with them, a young female Air Force captain who stayed away from the podium but within earshot: she was the area defense counsel, the military defense attorney assigned to Al Vincenti, and like any defense attorney her job was to be sure Vincenti was not forced or tricked into answering questions that might harm his defense, should he be brought in front of a court-martial.

"We are here at the request of FBI Director Wilkes to make some general statements about last night's incident," Gaspar continued. "As Colonel Vincenti's superior officer, and as the representative of the 144th Wing, I would like to speak for the Wing and Colonel—"

But the members of the press didn't allow him to finish.

One reporter shouted out, "Colonel Vincenti, why did you chase Henri Cazaux over San Francisco? Tell us why you wanted him dead. Is it because of what he allegedly did to your partner, Linda McKenzie?"

"Why is it," Vincenti blurted out, "that you call what Henri Cazaux did 'alleged,' and what I did you think is a certainty? Cazaux bombed Mather and San Francisco International, for God's sake!" The press corps' photographers snapped away at the pilot's angry face, and within seconds the reporters were inching back in to hear every word. "And I didn't 'chase' him over San Francisco," Vincenti continued. "He flew over the city and into the traffic pattern to try to get away from me."

"But who gave you the order to pursue him into San Francisco? Who gave you the order to attack him?"

This time the area defense counsel pushed her body in front of the microphone. "Ladies and gentlemen, Colonel Vincenti will be appearing in front of an Air Force flight review board and accident investigation board, and he will certainly be part of the FBI's investigation. Please don't try to convict him in the media as well."

"I think the Captain is right," Wilkes said, holding up her hands protectively in front of the area defense counsel. "Colonel Vincenti is not on trial here, and we don't expect him to be responsible for what someone like Henri Cazaux does." Those remarks made Vincenti and his defense counsel relax—and that's when Wilkes continued: "But I think this incident points out the *enormous* hazards involved with asking the military to participate in any way other than in an indirect supporting role in law enforcement operations. The military's primary function is to destroy and kill, and that's what Colonel Vincenti was trying to do last night when he drove Cazaux's plane over San Francisco."

"I did not *drive* Cazaux over San Francisco, he flew there all by himself," Vincenti snapped. He stepped over toward the microphone, and Wilkes had no choice but to give ground. "And the military's primary job is *not* to destroy and kill—our job is to ensure national security by protecting this country from all enemies, domestic as well as foreign. A terrorist in the sky is a threat to our national security, and it calls for a military response. Just because we operate over American soil rather than foreign soil doesn't mean the military can't or shouldn't do the job. The cops and the federal authorities—even the Bureau of Alcohol, Tobacco, and Firearms—are all outgunned. Cazaux realizes this now—"

"Excuse me, Colonel, but this is not the time for a sermon or a call to arms," Wilkes said, smiling benignly as if Vincenti had cracked a joke or was a streetcorner preacher. "The FBI can handle Henri Cazaux—*that* I promise.

"I think that concludes this press conference," Wilkes said into the microphone. "Thank you, ladies and gentlemen, thank you for coming." Wilkes' security team appeared in front of the podium as if by magic, and except for a few questions shouted out by reporters, the briefing was over. But Wilkes was not through. She stepped away from the microphone, turned her back on the cameras and reporters, and seethed at Vincenti, "I strongly advise you, Colonel, to keep your mouth *shut* and to cooperate in every way possible with this investigation. This is not the time to be mouthing off about things you know nothing about. Do you understand me, Colonel?"

Vincenti was going to reply, but a sudden motion got his attention. He saw an Air Force C-20B, a military version of the Gulfstream III business jet, roll up to the parking ramp, aiming directly at the podium—and it kept on coming. Just as it appeared as if it was going to hit the red rope at the edge of the ramp, and just as the FBI security agents started to reach for their concealed weapons, the jet turned away, came to a stop, and shut down engines. As it was obviously intended, the members of the press stopped and turned their full attention to the jet as the airstair opened up and the C-20's passengers emerged.

Vincenti was surprised—no, shocked—not by the look of the man who came down out of the C-20, but by Lani Wilkes' reaction to seeing him. The tall, wiry, gray-haired man that stepped out of the Air Force VIP jet commanded instant attention.

The other men and women that followed the first man were well-known national figures as well—including the former Vice President of the United States, Kevin Martindale; the junior U.S. senator from Texas, Georgette Heyerdahl; the U.S. House of Representatives' Minority Leader from Georgia, Paul Wescott; and a congressman from the San Francisco Bay Area, Samuel Leyland—and it was Martindale who took the lead and headed toward Director Wilkes and the podium, but the press was riveted on the tall, imposing man beside him.

"I sincerely apologize for this late arrival and our intrusion," Kevin Martindale said into the microphone as the members of the press hurriedly assembled back at the podium. "We were watching Judge Wilkes' press conference on the TV, and when we saw it was over I didn't think anyone would mind if we parked here. Sorry for the lousy parking job, but it was my first time at the controls of one of these babies. It's hard to drive and read the instruction booklet at the same time."

He waited for the laughter to die down, then continued: "I'm sure you all know my colleagues here. Mr. Wescott is of course the House Minority Leader, and our gracious host for this fact-finding trip. Senator Heyerdahl is the new cochairman of the Senate Subcommittee on the Future of the Military and National Defense, part of the Senate Military Affairs Committee, the group which is trying to design a framework for the U.S. military in the next fifteen to fifty years. And I believe you all know retired Coast Guard Rear Admiral Ian Hardcastle, former commander of the U.S. Border Security Force, the antismuggling and border security group, also known as the Hammerheads. Paul Wescott was kind enough to notify me that Congressman Leyland from San Jose was heading a congressional investigation on the incident last night, and he invited myself, Senator Heyerdahl, and Admiral Hardcastle to come along as his guests and advisers."

Wilkes tried hard not to show it, but the appearance of these four persons, and especially Ian Hardcastle, was precisely the last thing she needed right now, and her stomach was doing exasperated backflips.

Since the Cabinet-level Department of Border Security was disbanded in 1993 after the new Administration took office, Ian Hardcastle, who founded the paramilitary group called the Border Security Force back around 1990, was regularly on every TV and radio talk show in the country, talking about the decay of the U.S. military in general and of home defense in particular. Every move the Administration made in terms of the military—efforts in Somalia, policies regarding Bosnia, defense cutbacks, gays in the military, base closures, and a hundred other topics—was routinely criticized by Hardcastle, seemingly minutes after a decision was made by the President or his Cabinet, oftentimes even before they made a move. Hardcastle, who was articulate, handsome as hell, well-read, and knowledgeable about every military program, was a formidable opponent.

"I would first like to extend my sincere condolences to the families and colleagues of California Air National Guard Major Linda McKenzie; Bureau of Alcohol, Tobacco, and Firearms Special Agents Russo, Foreman, Wickers, Kritchek, and Bowman, and all those who lost a loved one in San Francisco," former Vice President Martindale continued. "It was a tragedy of simply shocking proportions that has outraged this nation. It is absolutely imperative that Henri Cazaux and all those who were responsible for this insane and ruthless attack be brought to justice immediately.

"But it is also in our best interests to do something to ensure that a tragedy like this never is allowed to happen again in the future," Martindale went on. "As you all know, Admiral Hardcastle has been very actively speaking out against some of the current Administration's policies regarding the military and national security and defense issues. Up until now, his has been largely a lone voice shouting as it were against the winds of change. Since our defeat in the last election, Admiral Hardcastle has been encouraging me to give up my self-imposed exile from the national debates of the issues of the times and get involved in shaping policies for the future. Unwisely, I resisted." He half-turned to Ian Hardcastle, gave him a wry smile, and added, "Frankly, Ian, you old sea dog, you sometimes come on as quietly as a tidal wave.

"But last week, in a speech to the National Press Club, Admiral Hardcastle talked about the threat of terrorism here in the United States. After reading the text of his speech, I made a few inquiries into some of the issues he raised and the accuracy of the facts he presented. In short, Admiral Hardcastle knows what he's talking about. He virtually predicted this very incident. That's when I decided to join forces with him, the American Congressional Citizens Alliance, and the Project 2000 Task Force, and accept an invitation by members of Congress to investigate this tragedy and make some observations about the threat that faces us and what we can do to stop it.''

It was a thinly disguised reason for being here, and Lani Wilkes and most of the members of the national press knew it. The Project 2000 Task Force was a group of right-of-center moderates and conservatives who would in all likelihood form the basis for a major run on the White House in 1996. Formed after the 1992 elections, the American Congressional Citizens Alliance was a mirror image of the Project 2000 Task Force, composed of present and past members of Congress, including one-fourth of the U.S. Senate and about one hundred members of the House of Representatives. After its inception, Project 2000 was most noteworthy for who was *not* in it, namely, the former Vice President, Kevin Martindale, who had always been considered a major front-runner in the next presidential elections. Obviously, with this surprise appearance as a major player in the Task Force, he was now out of seclusion and back in the White House hunt. It was a very unexpected and dramatic coming-out for the former Vice President to take on one of the Administration's toughest and most influential personalities. Worse for her, right in the middle of her own press conference.

But such a move was typical of Martindale. A former U.S. Congressman from Minnesota and former mayor of Minneapolis, Martindale's style of politics was full-speed-ahead, smash-face, down-in-the-dirt nasty. It was those traits that had made him such a prized pit bull in dealing with Congress, the liberal left, and others during his two terms as Vice President during the previous Administration. Tough and conservative, he was one of the country's biggest advocates of tougher laws, tougher sentences, the death penalty, and a strong military. During his term as Vice President, he had been a huge supporter of Admiral Ian Hardcastle's Border Security Force (the Hammerheads) and his disdain for the current Administration had been known practically from the moment the new President was sworn in. Martindale had little use for a man whom he considered a Southern political snake with a duplicitous and questionable private life. He had even less use for the President's wife, a tough-as-nails political infighter he and every other Republican in the capital referred to derisively as the Steel Magnolia.

Representative Wescott, Senator Heyerdahl, and Representative Leyland all made brief comments after Vice President Martindale. The usually outspoken Hardcastle declined to make a comment or take any questions, which probably evoked more questions and surprise than if he had spoken. Afterward, Martindale and his group left the podium and encircled FBI Director Wilkes and her staff. "Judge Wilkes, it's a pleasure to see you again," Martindale said, extending a hand. The press, out of earshot, snapped away as Wilkes took his hand. "I hope you'll apologize for this intrusion, but the Senate subcommittee wanted to be in on this investigation from the very beginning, so we had little choice."

Wilkes tried very hard to continue to maintain her composure. "I would be happy to brief the subcommittee or any other chamber of Congress on the status of this investigation at any time, Mr. Vice President," Wilkes said crisply, not bothering to acknowledge Martindale's apology. It was obvious to all that she was greatly displeased with her press-conference-turned-circus. "It wasn't necessary for the Senate to appoint a commission; I pledge full cooperation. I'm of course happy to see you and pleased to be working with you, but all this congressional attention to an unfortunate but random act of violence seems rather unusual, Mr. Vice President."

"I seem to recall an investigation begun by the Senate Judiciary Committee back a few years ago, around 1991," Martindale said, affixing the beautiful Lani Wilkes with a boyish, mischievous hint of a smile, "that produced a lawsuit against the old Border Security Force in a Mexican drug-smuggling-investigation incident. You might be familiar with that case, Judge Wilkes—that lawsuit was filed in *your* court."

Wilkes did indeed remember the Maria Fuentes incident. A young, pregnant female Mexican drug "mule"—not a drug dealer, not a true smuggler, but someone who, most times knowingly, carries drugs—had swallowed thirty condoms filled with cocaine, almost thirty pounds and two hundred thousand dollars' worth, and had tried to take the drugs into the United States on board a small motorboat, with two young children. She was detected, but could have gone unchallenged had she not panicked and gunned the engine when the Border Security Force's V-22 Sea Lion armed interceptor aircraft flew near her. The chase took two hours, with a small air force of sophisticated aircraft buzzing overhead.

Fuentes ran the boat ran aground near a popular seaside resort at Palmetto Beach, near Mobile, Alabama. The woman grabbed her two kids and tried to flee across the beach on foot. To the astonishment of about a hundred stunned onlookers, she was finally apprehended in a spectacular assault by the V-22 tilt-rotor aircraft. But during the arrest, one of the condoms of cocaine inside the woman broke open, poisoning her and creating an instantaneous stillbirth for everyone to watch, including Fuentes' two terrified children.

The public outcry was deafening—and it was all directed against the Hammerheads; then–Vice President Martindale, who was a strong Department of Border Security ally; and then–co-commander of the Border Security Force Admiral Ian Hardcastle. In response, the Senate Judiciary Committee unexpectedly launched an investigation, "leaking" its supposedly classified information to the press, which led to a lawsuit filed on behalf of the dead woman's family charging the Hammerheads with an unreasonable pursuit, unreasonable "search and seizure"—actually charging the Hammerheads with using the V-22 to force the woman to disgorge the drugs—and unreasonable use of force. Federal Judge Lani Wilkes' court blasted the government, equating the Hammerheads with East German border guards shooting Germans trying to escape over the Berlin Wall.

The government was ordered to pay an incredible ten-million-dollar settlement to the dead woman's family and to some of the onlookers, who claimed they were "traumatized" by watching the incident. Kevin Martindale and Ian Hardcastle were publicly ridiculed. Although the verdict was overturned by the U.S. Supreme Court years later on appeal, the case was regarded as the beginning of the end of the Hammerheads and the Department of Border Security, which was abolished shortly after the new President took the oath of office in 1993.

"I remember the Fuentes case very well, Mr. Vice President," Wilkes said uneasily. "But the Judiciary Committee was completely within its bounds to investigate the incident then. Besides, that was an investigation of a serious incident by the Border Security Force, not of an ongoing FBI criminal investigation. The FBI enjoys a certain immunity from Congressional oversight in the course of an investigation. I'm sure you understand . . ."

"I can't speak for the Senate, Judge Wilkes, but I think the rules have changed—we've been authorized to proceed," Martindale said. He accepted a sealed folder from an aide. It carried the seal of the U.S. Senate on its cover. "And I assure you, we won't interfere with your investigation. We'll just require a briefing—no more than three times per day—with the items stated in this folder included. Also, we have observers that will accompany some of your investigators. If you would, please provide us with a list of your senior investigators, and we'll pair an observer up with him or her right away."

"I'm sorry, Mr. Vice President, but there's been some mistake," Lani Wilkes interrupted. "I can't allow non-Bureau observers on an investigation. And I wish I had the time to give you special briefings on the status of the case, but I don't. The Bureau gives daily press briefings in Washington."

"Our observers are fully trained former FBI, DIA, or CIA investigators, Judge Wilkes," Martindale said. "They know your procedures—our chief Bureau consultant is Jeffrey Peck." Wilkes' eyes grew wide—Peck was the former Bureau deputy director, a longtime FBI veteran, fired from his post as number-two man because of allegations of wrongdoing. No specific charges were ever brought against him. Peck had vehemently argued his innocence and never resigned even though the pressure to do so was enormous, but there had to be a housecleaning when the new Administration came in, so Peck was forced out. The President expended a lot of political capital to fire Peck—now they were going to face him again. Martindale's pleasant smile dimmed a bit as he added, "And I certainly *hope* the three briefings a day won't be too much of a burden for you—because our charter demands nothing less of you. I'm sure you understand."

Wilkes saw the smile diminish and knew that Vice President Martindale wasn't going to spar with her any longer. But she wasn't going to be bullied by any of these outsiders either. "Of course I understand, Mr. Vice President. I'll extend every consideration to you and your people. All I need is confirmation from the president pro tem of the Senate." Wilkes knew the current Vice President would put a halt to all this nonsense right away. "We can start as soon as—"

"I'm sorry, Judge Wilkes, I should have handed this over earlier," Senator Georgette Heyerdahl said. It was a warrant, signed by the Senate Minority Leader. "As you know, the Vice President is overseas, and he turned the gavel over to the Majority Leader. Unfortunately, Senator Collingsworth lost an aunt in the explosion in San Francisco airport last night, and he is on emergency leave. Since the Senate Majority Whip is also out of the country, he allowed the gavel to be transferred to the Senate Minority Leader. Here is his charter for our organization to conduct this investigation."

Wilkes accepted the letter but did not look at it—she was very familiar with this type of provision, called a "roundhouse." Officially, the U.S. Senate is never formally adjourned—the gavel, or presidency of the Senate, is always in someone's hand, day and night, while the Senate is "in recess." The president pro tem of the Senate (the Vice President of the United States) usually leaves it up to the leader of his party in the Senate to choose who would preside in his stead, but there is a definite "pecking order" in case of emergencies or disaster. Usually the day-to-day presidency of the Senate is ceremonial in nature, but it also conveys a lot of power to anyone who knows the law and who has the guts to use it. Establishing a charter to a Senate subcommittee to begin some work is one such power of the president pro tem, and pulling a roundhouse is a quick way to get it enacted. "The charter is only good for five days or until the full Senate can vote to cancel it," Heyerdahl added, as if trying to instruct Wilkes on the law, "but it's in force right now."

"I'm well aware of the law, Senator, thank you," Wilkes interrupted. Of course, the Vice President, who was away in Tokyo, could snatch the gavel back immediately just by stepping aboard Air Force Two or into the American embassy—both were always considered American territory—and he could yank the group's charter away in a New York minute. But at this stage of the game, with a very public press conference just concluded, it was probably not a wise decision. Any hesitancy the Vice President or Wilkes might show toward such a distinguished group as the Project 2000 Task Force might appear like a cover-up.

"As I said, I'll be more than happy to cooperate with your subcommittee, Mr. Vice President." Wilkes sighed. *No use in trying to fight this anymore,* she thought. She had to contact the Justice Department and the President right away and let them handle Martindale and Hardcastle. "An office has been set up in one of the SR-71 hangars for our team, and I'm due to receive a situation briefing as soon as I arrive. You're welcome to sit in."

"Thank you, Judge Wilkes," Martindale said, the famous boyish smile returning. He shook hands again with her, making sure that the press photographers captured the moment.

After the impromptu press conference broke up, Hardcastle noticed several Air Force officers standing by a blue sedan nearby. He walked over to them, extended a hand, and said, "Colonel Vincenti, Colonel Gaspar? I'm Admiral Ian Hardcastle, U.S. Coast Guard, retired." They shook hands, and Hardcastle was introduced to the public affairs officer and Vincenti's area defense counsel. "I'm sorry for what happened to Major McKenzie. I know what it's like to lose a good crewman." The Air Force officers nodded without saying anything—Hardcastle could easily read the distrust in their eyes. "Colonel Vincenti, tell me about Henri Cazaux."

"Colonel Vincenti has been advised not to speak with anyone else, Admiral," the area defense counsel said.

Hardcastle shot her an angry stare, then turned back to Vincenti. "I need to know, Colonel," Hardcastle said. "I'm a part of a Senate investigation into the incident."

"Another government investigation," Vincenti scoffed. "Great. Just what we need."

"We're not trying to pin the blame on you, Colonel—I'm trying to pin the blame on where it belongs: on the White House and the Pentagon," Hardcastle said. "I'm trying to get Congress and the President to act seriously about national defense."

"I appreciate that, Admiral," the area defense counsel said, "but we're still not going to discuss—"

"One question, if that's okay with your ADC," Hardcastle said. Vincenti did not respond, but he did not object, either. "You were the hunter, Colonel. You had your prey in your sights. Now tell me about Henri Cazaux."

At first Vincenti didn't know what to make of this tall, lean, ghostly-looking man. He had seen Hardcastle on all the TV shows, of course, but when Hardcastle said the word "hunter," he heard something else. *Yes . . . yes,* Vincenti thought. *I know what he's talking about.* Al Vincenti knew about the mystique of the hunter.

The hunter, at the moment of unleashing deadly energy against his prey, forms a sort of mind-meld with his quarry. Deer hunters feel it, experience the synergism of minds linked together for a brief instant. Bombardiers sometimes feel as if they are on the ground, watching their bombs fall on their own heads. The inexperienced hunter can't handle it and gets "target fixation" or the "shakes," and the spell is broken and the quarry usually escapes. A young or emotional bombardier that feels it turns to the bottle, gets a Section 8, or gets a .45 and blows himself away. Vincenti remembered that Hardcastle had once lined up lots of targets in the sights of his awesome V-22 Sea Lion tilt-rotor interceptors, so he definitely knew what it felt like to search, track, find, pursue, attack, and destroy a target—Jesus, he had done it for *real.* Hardcastle had fired on many real targets. Vincenti didn't know how many men he had killed, but he knew he had killed before. He knew what it was like. And so did Vincenti . . .

"Defiance," Vincenti said. "No fear. Not at any time did I feel fear from Henri Cazaux. Even in his parachute. He was . . . happy. Satisfied. Ready to begin . . ."

"Begin what, Colonel?"

"I don't know, Admiral." Vincenti shrugged. "I don't even know what I'm talking about. You asked me what I felt when I thought about Cazaux, and that's the first thing that popped into my head. I wish I had taken him out. I won't miss next time."

As the group headed toward their cars to take them to their first meeting, Lani Wilkes turned and noticed Admiral Hardcastle talking with the F-16 pilot involved in the previous night's incident, along with his group commander. She excused herself from the former Vice President and the Senator and walked back to them.

Hardcastle ignored her as she approached. "I hope you get the chance, Colonel," Hardcastle said as Wilkes got closer, a grim, angry expression on her face, "but I rather doubt you will. We'll meet again. No matter what the press says, remember you've got someone on your side—"

"Excuse me, Admiral Hardcastle," Wilkes said testily, standing several paces away from the group. "Can I have a word with you, please?"

Hardcastle closed his notebook, shook hands with both Vincenti and Gaspar, clasped Vincenti reassuringly on the shoulder, and moved aside with Wilkes until the crowd passed her by, with just a few of Wilkes' aides remaining. The press had left, and they were alone. The veteran Coast Guard flier extended a hand to Lani Wilkes and said, "It's very nice to see you again, Judge Wilkes."

Wilkes put her hands on her narrow hips, sliding her jacket open and slightly exposing a shoulder holster with a small automatic pistol as well as a slender waist and a firm bosom. With her sunglasses now in place against the hot summer sun, her lips red with a touch of lipstick, it was hard not to notice that this tough lawmaker and civil rights activist was a very beautiful woman. But, like Sandra Geffar, his partner and co-commander of the old Border Security Force and other good-looking female public figures, Hardcastle knew that a very tough woman still lurked under that beauty.

"Listen, Admiral," Wilkes said testily, "let's get something straight. I'm going along with this charade only because I've got you and Martindale and Wescott in my face in front of the press. Your Senate subcommittee charter is a joke—it'll be nullified by the Vice President before the day's out, and they might even pass a law banning all such charters by the gavel. You may not realize it, even Martindale may not know it, but all this is a sham. I know it and Wescott knows it. After that, you'll be off this base and out of the picture—permanently."

"That remains to be seen, Judge." Hardcastle smiled.

"So what is it you want, Hardcastle?" Wilkes asked. "Is this just another publicity stunt?"

"No more of a stunt than trotting Colonel Vincenti out here in front of the press, accusing him of screwing up the mission, and then letting the press feed on him," Hardcastle snapped. "I heard your press conference, Judge, and I think you're wrong: Henri Cazaux is not just 'a merchant of death,' he is a homicidal maniac. He will kill anyone to escape, *including himself.* He has no conception of the sanctity of life."

"Spare me. We have a full psychological profile on him, Admiral."

"Then *you* haven't read it, Judge—because it would say that trying to apprehend Cazaux would be a waste of lives," Hardcastle continued. "He will slaughter anyone within reach before taking his own life."

"The Bureau has dealt with homicidal personalities before, Admiral, and Cazaux is no different." She sighed, rolling her eyes.

"He's *different,* Judge, because he's got access to aircraft, special weapons, and sophisticated military expertise," Hardcastle said. "He can begin a reign of terror the likes of which this country has never seen before."

"Listen, Admiral, I'm sorry, but I don't have the time for your pro-military speeches—I've got an investigation to run," Wilkes said impatiently. "We will deal with whatever he throws at us—and we'll do it without using the military, without big, expensive tilt-rotor aircraft loaded with machine guns and guided missiles, without one-hundred-million-dollar oil platforms which are now gathering barnacles and rust out in the Gulf of Mexico, without blimps with radars on them, and without weird robot helicopters that crash-land every time you turn around. Unlike *former* so-called law enforcement agencies, the FBI doesn't feel as if we have to harass and scare half the law-abiding population just to find one slimeball.'' Her indirect jab at the Hammerheads, Hardcastle's high-tech drug interdiction and Border Security Force, was fully intentional and heartfelt: Wilkes had always believed the military had no place in law enforcement, and that the rights of all individuals—the accused as well as the innocent—needed to be protected at all times.

''But let me remind you of a few things, Admiral,'' the FBI Director went on. ''This is *my* investigation. I am running the show here. I will not hesitate to throw your tail off this base and into a federal lockup if you try to interfere with my investigation while you're part of this Senate probe. You are not to talk with the crews, you are not to talk with the commanders, you are not to talk with the press about anything you see or hear. Charter or no charter, I'll have you arrested for interfering with an FBI investigation. I may not be able to hold you for long, what with David Brinkley and Larry King, your good TV talk-show buddies, on my ass, but it'll be long enough to disrupt your TV schedule. Is all that clear, Admiral?''

''Yes, it's very clear, Judge,'' Hardcastle replied. ''But I've got one thing to say to you. I've seen this once before. Agusto Salazar, Pablo Escobar, Manuel Noriega—they all thought they could take on the United States and win. Henri Cazaux will hide behind the Bill of Rights and use it to get what he wants. Don't let it happen now. Use all the forces you have available.''

''You're paranoid, Hardcastle. Why don't you run for office? You'd fit right in.'' She spun on a heel and stepped away from Hardcastle as quickly as she could.

The former Vice President's limousine was waiting for Hardcastle, and he joined up with them a few moments later. ''Well, how did it go, Ian?'' Martindale asked Hardcastle as he sat down opposite the Vice President, beside Senator Heyerdahl.

''I don't think she's going to cooperate.'' Hardcastle sighed. ''We're going to have to battle her every step of the way.''

''Too bad,'' Martindale said.

Hardcastle said, ''I think I scared her a bit, and that pissed her off.''

''Well, she's certain to go to the White House and vent now,'' Heyerdahl concluded. ''Our charter will be history by the end of the day, after the press has gone to bed for the night.'' She turned to Hardcastle and said, ''Wilkes is a very powerful and very dangerous opponent.''

Hardcastle said, ''She's tough, and strong, and beautiful. The press loves her. But as tough as she is, Henri Cazaux is tougher. And in a battle of wills, his is superior."

"How do you know this Cazaux so well, Ian?" Wescott, seated next to the former Vice President, asked. "You chase him when you were with the Hammerheads?"

"We'd received a bit of intelligence about him," Hardcastle replied. "We thought he might begin working with Salazar's Cuchillos pilots, using military hardware to protect drug shipments. Cazaux was trained to fly everything from Mirage fighters to Huey helicopters, and he was one of Europe's top commando instructors. Cazaux never moved in, and I lost track of him when the Border Security Force was disbanded. But I know a few Henri Cazauxs, Congressman Wescott, and a few Agusto Salazars."

"I have no doubt that you'd like to see every one of these sleazoids in prison, or better, at the bottom of the deepest ocean you can find," Kevin Martindale said. "But let's keep our ultimate objective in mind—to call attention to the current Administration's piss-poor military utilization and lack of military planning. But we don't want to look like armchair quarterbacks to the press.

"We're here to observe, yes," Martindale went on, affixing a stern glare on all of those around him in the limo, "but our attitude should be that we've got a better way. So the question facing us all during our trip here is simple: if *we* were in the driver's seat, what would we be doing better? Faced with the threat from Henri Cazaux ourselves, what would *we* be doing that the current Administration isn't? We shit in Lani Wilkes' cornflakes by crashing her press conference, but in fact the President is doing pretty much what I'd expect—call for a massive manhunt, order the FBI Director to set up a command center in the area and personally coordinate the investigation. So far, we'd be doing the same thing as the current White House residents.

"We need a specific plan of action, something we can point to and say, 'The President should be doing this,' and the American people lean forward toward their TVs and respond, 'Yeah, the dipshit, he should be doing that, I'm voting for Martindale in ninety-six.' Everyone got the picture?" There were nodding heads and "Yes, sirs" all around. "Okay, good. Comments?"

"Judging by Wilkes' attitude, I'd say the Administration is treating this as a random, isolated, one-in-a-million incident," Hardcastle surmised. "Focus of the FBI's investigation will be the coordination of the federal agencies involved—actually, their *lack* of cooperation. Wilkes has already tipped her hand by trotting Vincenti and Gaspar out in front of the press—no doubt Vincenti's record in Europe will be 'leaked,' and everyone will make the same conclusion—that Vincenti screwed up. The federal government, and the Air Force in particular, will take the heat for a screwed-up pursuit and needless deaths, simply to avoid a general panic."

"You mentioned something about him on the way out here," Martindale said. "What was it again?"

"Vincenti was flying F-4 Phantoms up in Iceland—this was just before Gorbachev came to power," Hardcastle explained. "He scrambled on a Badger bomber that he found flying low-level across the ice pack. The Defense Early Warning radars were out, but he did the pursuit on his own and shoots the damned thing down."

"You're kidding! I never heard about that."

"Hardly anyone did," Hardcastle explained. "Turns out the bomber was a rogue—a crew of fliers sympathetic to Andropov wanted to start World War Three by bombing U.S. bases in Iceland. They had nukes on board, but they say they never would have gone off."

"But Vincenti's not a hero in this story, right?"

"Yes, sir. Problem was, Vincenti never got clearance to shoot—no communications between the controllers and the plane. Vincenti just went ahead and did it, much like the incident last night. He gets a reputation as a hero with the crew dogs, but a wild-dog reputation with the brass. The Badger shoot-down is highly classified—"

"But the Pentagon's recollection of Vincenti isn't," Martindale finished for him. "Vincenti can't follow orders. Vincenti likes to shoot first and ask questions later. Question, Ian: is he a wild dog?"

"No, sir, he's not—but my reputation is not exactly fresh and clean either," Hardcastle said with a wry smile. "In my opinion, putting on my pundit's hat for a moment, I think it would be ill-advised for you to openly support Vincenti. But I want to consult with him on a regular basis. He knows his shit, and he will be very valuable to us and the Air Force when Cazaux tries to take on the authorities again."

"Wait a minute, Ian . . . So you don't think this *is* a random incident?" Martindale asked Hardcastle. He was getting nervous already—his high-profile military guy was thinking in a totally unexpected direction, and with more press conferences scheduled for that day, he had to be brought up to speed immediately. "Just bad luck that Cazaux hit that terminal with a cargo plane and killed several hundred people . . . ?"

"Sir, I can't explain it, but talking with Colonel Vincenti, the F-16 pilot that chased Cazaux's cargo plane, I wonder if this is the last we'll hear from him," Hardcastle said. "Cazaux is not going to dive underground."

As enthusiastic as they were about pointing out the inadequacies of the current White House Administration's military policies, the others in the limo were not at all ready to agree with the former Coast Guard and Border Security Force officer. The former Vice President ran his fingers through his hair in exasperation. "Jesus, Ian," Martindale exclaimed, giving him a tired smile, "I pray you're wrong."

There was no more time for discussion, because just then the limousine pulled up to the aircraft hangar turned investigation center, and the members of the Senate subcommittee task force began to step out. The line of twelve hangars on the parking ramp at Beale Air Force Base once housed the SR-71 Blackbird spy planes, which were the fastest air-breathing aircraft in the world before the advent of the still-classified SR-91 Aurora. "A minute, Mr. Vice President," Hardcastle said. Martindale let everyone else out, and the Secret Service agent closed the door again.

"Spit it out, Admiral."

"Sir, you know that I believe in your campaign," Hardcastle said easily. "No one was happier than I to see you at our board of directors meeting, getting involved, helping to raise money for the Task Force, all that. I know publicly you haven't announced if you're going to run in ninety-six, but I feel you will, and I'm one hundred and ten percent behind you all the way."

"I hear a big 'but' coming . . ."

"Yes, sir. *But,* after speaking with Vincenti, I realized that we are not faced simply with gathering ammunition to use against the current Administration—we need to formulate a policy to make sure that attacks like last night don't happen again."

"Attacks? They weren't *attacks,* Ian, it was the act of a madman trying to escape pursuit," Martindale scoffed. "The odds of Cazaux blowing up another airport in this country are . . . well, hell, they've got to be astronomical."

"I don't think so, sir," Hardcastle said. "I think he'll strike again. I think we need to set up a program to defend this country's major airports from attack. With all due respect, sir, I need to know if you're serious about responding to the threat, or if this is just a way to make some political hay until you're ready to throw your hat in the ring."

"Christ, Hardcastle, ease up a bit with that rhetoric—and the threats," Martindale said, motioning with his body that he was ready to get out of the car. "First of all, whatever use I have for my activities with you and the Project 2000 Task Force *is* part of my campaign. You and the membership agreed to spearhead my campaign. Like it or not, I'm in it, and I'm calling the shots. You know I'm serious about national defense, Ian. When I joined forces with the Task Force, you agreed to my terms. You and the other Task Force members fall in line with me or I walk—it's as simple as that. Understand?"

"Yes, sir."

"I'm Kevin to you, Ian," Martindale said. "Both now and when I'm in the White House. And I *am* going to the White House, my friend, let there be no doubt about *that.*

"As for my thoughts on Cazaux: So far I haven't seen any evidence indicating the beginning of a wave of terrorism. We start creating fear like that, and we'll look bad. Hell, even if we're *right,* we'll look like doomsayers. I don't want to start putting Patriot missiles on the front lawn of the White House, Ian—all I want to do is point out to the people of this country that the current President's got his head up his ass when it comes to the application of military force and his support for the military." Martindale paused for a moment, then seemed to decide to go ahead and say what was on his mind—Kevin Martindale never had any trouble keeping his feelings to himself: "Frankly, Ian, your alarm-ringing reputation is well known in town. I'm not saying you're wrong, but I feel a lot of people might be turning you off. It's been less than twenty-four hours since the attack. Let's not come to any really dire conclusions until we get some more concrete evidence. Okay?"

"That's fine, sir," Hardcastle said. "I'll stand by my reputation and my opinions."

"Don't get me wrong, Ian," Martindale added. "I consider you a valuable asset, and your thoughts mean a lot to me. But let me make the decisions and the public announcements, okay?"

"Yes, sir," Hardcastle said. He exited the limousine, but turned to face Martindale just before the former Vice President stepped out. "But think about this, sir—what if Henri Cazaux strikes again? Then what will *you* be prepared to do to stop him?"

Martindale had already been psyching himself up to get ready to speak with the press that had assembled outside the hangar being used to headquarter the FBI's investigation, so he really wasn't fully listening to Hardcastle—until that very last sentence. If Cazaux *did* return, if this was only the beginning and not the end of a horrible nightmare, then what *could* be done to stop it?

"Damn it, Hardcastle . . ." the former Vice President of the United States muttered. Ignoring Admiral Ian Hardcastle was never an option.

Newburgh, New York
Later That Day

The sleepy little town of Newburgh, about an hour's drive north of New York City, was the perfect place for an American terrorist base of operations. The small city of twenty thousand was easily accessible to New York City by Thruway, train, overland, or even via the nearby Hudson River, but it was much smaller and much more rural than a typical New York City bedroom community, offering lots of seclusion and privacy. Newburgh's first-class airfield, Stewart International, had direct flights to La Guardia; Chicago; Washington, D.C.; Raleigh-Durham International; Hartsfield-Atlanta; and even Toronto and Montreal, but it had fewer than a dozen arrivals and departures a day. The U.S. Military Academy at West Point was just a few miles away, and the resorts and ski areas of the Catskills were just a few hours away.

Passengers liked Stewart International Airport because it was so easygoing and efficient—Henri Cazaux liked Stewart because security there was relatively lax, which made the little airport the perfect place to run a small-scale smuggling operation, or smuggle weapons into the commercial air system. Cazaux had often smuggled a fully loaded Uzi right through security in a briefcase by partially disassembling it and packing it in a candy or gift box with a gold foil wrapper—the wrapper shielded the contents from the X rays, and the guards never bothered to hand-check, especially during the early-morning rush-hour confusion of commuters on their way to New York, Boston, or Washington. The old "gun-in-the-Bible" trick worked every time. If Cazaux ever considered hijacking a plane, it would be from Stewart International.

There were a lot of other factors: the large amount of general aviation activity at the airport, with small planes taxiing and parking very close to commercial traffic, made transporting contraband onto an airliner from the aircraft parking ramp easy; the amount of wooded area and the isolation of many parts of the base from all but roving security; the number of large, isolated vacant buildings and hangars on the airport; and the relative safety and security everyone felt by having a large New York State Police, U.S. Army, and Air Force Reserve contingent stationed there at Stewart. Cazaux used that complacency to his advantage many times. He once dressed like a USAir baggage handler, commandeered a baggage tractor, and personally loaded several hundred pounds of contraband aboard planes parked at the gates, and was never challenged. He had done the same with an Air Force Reserve military cargo plane, posing as a crew chief on a C-5A Galaxy transport. Cazaux stole whole pallets of weapons and equipment right off the back of the giant transports with a forklift, and was never challenged or questioned.

More importantly, the little city was quiet and peaceful—it was a good jumping-off point to just about anyplace in the world, but it was also a good place to lay low and think and plan. That's why when Henri Cazaux safely made it out of Albuquerque, he booked a flight—not a direct flight, but a circuitous route to Chicago to Cleveland to Pittsburgh—and then on to his base of U.S. operations in Newburgh. He needed to get the roar of the destruction he had caused in California, the smell of gunpowder and blood and burning civilization, all out of his head for a while.

There were two other reasons for Henri Cazaux to come to Newburgh, of course. It was a convenient place to meet with his logistics officer, a private Wall Street trader named Harold Lake. When a face-to-face meeting was needed, Lake could be in Newburgh in an hour and a half, and banking transactions begun by Lake in a satellite brokerage house in Newburgh at noon would be on the books and in the system by close of business. Cazaux felt too trapped, too surrounded in New York City itself—Newburgh was more to his liking, large enough to allow him to blend into with the citizens but small and isolated enough to remain anonymous.

The second reason was Madame Rocci, M.M. Her real name, he knew, was Jo Ann Vega. The "M.M." stood for Minister of Metaphysics—it sounded like a phony show title or something out of a 1940s

B-grade movie, but it was not. She was, and had been for several years, the psychic for the world's most dangerous criminal.

For all of Henri Cazaux's intelligence, military training, life experience, toughness, and survival instinct, his one foible, his one departure from clear, perfectly objective analytical thought, was in the realm of astrology—but of course Cazaux would not consider astrology a "weird" science. An astrologer in Denmark whom he visited while in high school told him he would be a great military man—he decided to go into the military based on the woman's advice. During a United Nations deployment to Africa while in the Belgian First Para, another astrologer in Zaire, a shaman, told him he would be a great leader of men, known far and wide for his deeds. Since going into business himself, he had consulted with an astrologer once or twice a year. Their predictions were uncannily accurate, he thought, and he had never made a bad move based on their words.

He had met Madame Vega three years earlier. During a rare time traveling on foot during daylight hours—tactical considerations absolutely forbade travel on roads during daylight except in an emergency—Cazaux had ducked into the back door of her tiny storefront parlor while getting out of sight of a State Police cruiser. He surprised Vega as she came out of the bathroom, but she did not challenge him or try to throw him out. She seemed to know instantly that he was on the run and being pursued. She showed no fear, and offered him instant coffee and two-day-old donuts purchased from the thrift shop down the street, the only things she had to eat in her small kitchen.

Vega was in her early fifties, with long dark kinky hair streaked with gray and with small colored beads braided in her hair near her temples, large round dark eyes, a round, pretty face, large round breasts, strong fingers and hands, a firm waist and buttocks, and slender legs. She looked gypsyish, and said her family were Jewish refugees from Czechoslovakia. Vega did not complain when Cazaux checked the house, the exits, and looked for evidence that she had a boyfriend, roommate, children, or husband living with her. She said she knew that he was afraid, that he was in danger, but that he would eventually prevail, and she would help any way she could.

All he wanted to do was hide and sleep. She showed him a hiding place in the attic, which he accepted—after finding at least three ways to escape—and rested. When he awoke, she was waiting for him. While he slept, she had done a complete astrological analysis on him. He was interested but skeptical—until she started to speak about the life of Henri Cazaux. She predicted his birthdate within a week, his time of birth within two hours, and his country of birth exactly—he was born at a hospital in the Netherlands, although raised in Belgium: she guessed all this.

Being Henri Cazaux, and cautious, he realized Vega could have researched his past—Cazaux was beginning to get a reputation in America equal to the one he had in Europe, although at the time he was not well known outside federal law-enforcement circles. But it would have taken a lot of work and a lot of time, far more than what a near-destitute storefront swami in Newburgh, New York, could ever do. No, she had learned about him simply from looking at the man, then reading her astrological books and putting the terrifying, mystifying pieces together. She talked about his military past, his fearlessness, his lack of regard for others. She talked about his brutal success, his drive for perfection, his intensity. She knew he had once been married, but had no children despite his desire to have them. But that was only the beginning—of what she had to say, and of the astounding accuracy of her predictions:

With the Sun, the blood planet Mars—named after the mythical god of war—the planet Jupiter, and the upper limb of the Moon all in the constellation Scorpio at the time of his birth, Henri Cazaux was a quadruple Scorpio—highly intelligent, secretive, passionate, and powerful. Vega had never seen a chart like his before. If a person could pick all the traits he or she ever desired—the tendency toward great wealth, tremendous sexual energy, animal determination, god-like invincibility, and intelligent introspection—Henri Cazaux had them. Only a few men in history ever had an astrological chart like Cazaux—such multiple-planet generals like Napoleon Bonaparte, Ulysses, and Alexander, politicians like Hitler and Lincoln, military thinkers like Sun-Tzu and Clausewitz. His astrological chart was confirmed by a palm reading and the tarot, but one look at the man would be confirmation enough for anyone. And if his scarred body did not say that his past lay in some expertise in the combat arms, his chart definitely said his future would be in warfare. Mars ruled his chart, and all other "peaceful" signs and planets and influences were nowhere to be seen.

Usually Cazaux liked to "rate" astrologers by how many guesses they got correct—he could not even begin to do this with Jo Ann Vega. It was as if she had written his biography, and then written his eulogy and epitaph. The future she painted was not bright. It was filled with adventure, and excitement, and wealth, and power, but it was a short, violent, lonely life. She said she understood all of those things, and said her life was rich and full despite her loneliness.

She also seemed to understand perfectly when he attacked her. She was so good at her profession that now she knew too much, and when the snarling, cornered beast in Cazaux emerged, she accepted it with professional patience.

Other than killing, raping a woman is tactically the best way to ensure her silence—few women report a rape, especially if they are alone. It is usually the best way to terrorize a woman into silence and cooperation. Cazaux was forceful and violent, but was careful not to cause any visible wounds that might compel others to act. He made her undress for him, made her perform fellatio on him, made her spread her legs and beg him to rape her—not because he enjoyed any of it or thought she might enjoy acting submissive, but because it further implicated her, further shamed her, gave her more events of which most women will not speak, more things for a woman's consciousness to work harder to suppress. As helpless as she was, she was, in a horrible and brutal way, a party to what was happening to her.

The rape was an act of violence—none of it could be considered in the least sexual—but the motivation was not robbery or murder or assault or any other crime. It was an initiation into the life of the world's greatest terrorist, a message that she was now, willingly or not, an acolyte of Henri Cazaux's, a minister to the human incarnation of Satan himself. She could accept the fact, and live, or deny it, and die—but he did not have to tell her these things. Jo Ann Vega—in fact, all of Cazaux's helpless victims—knew this when they looked into the killer's eyes. The rape was an act of violence, yes, but it was more of a promise of the violence to come if the spell was broken.

He made her clean him with her mouth, then departed without saying a word—no threats, no taunting, no innuendos—leaving a small throwing knife stuck into the woodwork around the window behind the back door. It was a tiny warning to her, and a promise that he would return.

He did return, two to three times a year. The violence was gone, and they became lovers. They slept and bathed together, experimented with sex, and talked about each other's worlds in intimate detail. Making love with Henri Cazaux was like trying to wrestle with a bonfire or control a crashing ocean wave—the heat, the power, the sheer energy he released was enormous. Vega was his spiritual adviser, his charge of quarters, his aide-de-camp, but she also got to experience the man when he unleashed his raw, unchained spirit only toward her, and no one else.

Although they shared each other's passion, he was never close—"settling down" was never an option, although he did see to her needs and offered a level of security and protection unlike any other man in the world. He provided her with money—not enough to leave her little storefront or call attention to herself—but enough so she would not have to rely on reading horoscopes to survive. Some of Vega's enemies—a city councilman who tried to have her kicked out of the city for being a drug dealer because she had refused to run a house of prostitution for him, a neighbor kid who liked to get drunk and would occasionally try to break her door down to get at her—both mysteriously disappeared. Jo Ann had never mentioned them to Cazaux.

Jo Ann knew that Henri Cazaux was coming to her, knew this visit would be different. She often read his cards in between visits, and she had just completed a reading on him before she had learned of the attack in San Francisco. She knew he had engineered the attack long before the news told the world so. The cards told of fire, and blood, and darkness. They did not tell of his death, as they usually did. In fact, none of the dark elements of Cazaux's chart—a short lifespan, pain, loneliness—were present. The man coming to visit her soon was a man no longer—he had been transformed. The cards said so.

It was dark outside, and the rain was pounding down so hard it was forcing itself into the house through closed windows. Vega was just finishing a cigarette in her tiny living room/bedroom between the partition to the reading parlor and the kitchen, and was heading back to the kitchen to clean out the ashtray, when she turned and saw him standing in the doorway, watching her. He was already naked from the waist up—he had obviously been there several minutes, judging by the size of the puddle of water under his feet—but he was as silent as a snake. A small automatic pistol was stuck in his jeans waistband.

"Welcome home, Henri," Jo Ann said, a touch of warmth in her eyes and voice. "I'm glad to see you." He did not respond. That was typical—he rarely said ten words to her even on a chatty day. He looked thinner, but his chest was as muscular as ever, his stomach as rippled and hard as an old-fashioned washboard. He had shaved off all his hair. He changed his hair length and style often, although military short-cropped hair was his norm. But Vega's eyes were drawn back to his chest, his rock-hard arms, and his flat stomach. For a brief instant, she felt her nipples erect and felt the slight ache of desire between her legs. She looked into his eyes, and the questions in her head only continued. Cazaux's eyes were on fire—not from anger, or from fear, but from desire. Was it sexual desire? Sometimes she could feel the heat of his need from across a room—Scorpios were all powerful sexual animals, and multiple Scorpios sometimes had an aura of sexual energy that was palpable. Henri was soaking wet, but he was definitely on fire . . .

No, it was not sexual energy this time. He was after something else, something much more significant than Jo Ann. The fire in his eyes seemed to come from visualizing something so vividly that you could see it, touch it.

"Get out of those wet clothes," she suggested. "I'll make us some tea. I have hamburger if you're hungry."

As if he had read her thoughts, he pulled the gun from his waistband, then unbuttoned his jeans and pulled them down to the floor. *My God,* Vega breathed, *he was magnificent!* But her eyes were drawn from the bulge between his legs to the bandages wrapped around his left leg, with quarter-sized spots of blood soaking through. "Henri, you're hurt. Go into the bedroom." The big man silently complied.

After drying the floor carefully with a dishtowel and putting his wet clothes in the washer so no one would notice or question the mess, Jo Ann brought hydrogen peroxide, hydrocortisone cream, and fresh bandages to him. She found him standing naked beside her bed, his injured leg up on the bed, peeling off the old dressing. She sat down on the bed and examined the wound. It was long and deep, like a hot poker or sword had been slashed across his calf. Blood mixed with water and dirt had caked inside the gash itself—this was going to be difficult and painful to clean.

"This was from the chase with the Air Force, wasn't it?"

"Yes," he replied simply. The news of the incredible disaster in San Francisco had of course reached Newburgh. It had been page one in the nation's newspapers, and the lead story on all the networks and CNN. The dragnet was out for Cazaux, but they were concentrating mostly in the west and southwest, thinking that he was on his way to Mexico.

"You came to me for advice," she said, as if reading from Cazaux's unwritten DayTimer itinerary. "You are meeting with your senior staff to plan something . . . but not to hide. You intend on attacking . . . attacking many targets, many persons. I saw much blood in your charts, much destruction. Why, Henri? Is it revenge? I did not see a clear reason . . ."

"You know the reason, Madame Vega," Cazaux hissed in a low voice. "You know damned well."

"Oui, mon cher," Vega responded soothingly, feeling her nipples harden and the lonely region between her legs grow hot and wet. *Oh yes, she knew very well why Henri was on the warpath . . .*

Henri had been a very bad little boy when he was younger. A bastard born in a country foreign to both his parents, now living in a foreign country, Cazaux was a ballistic missile without a guidance system—lots of energy but no sense of direction, no clear path, no destination. He amused himself by stealing and vandalism, and by the age of fifteen had become an accomplished criminal, roaming much of western Europe. He stayed out of the hands of the authorities until 1977. While trying to deal hashish to a U.S. Air Force F-4 Phantom maintenance crew near Antwerp, Belgium, he was caught by Air Force security police and taken to their brig. The Air Force sky cops could not charge him, only release him to the local gendarmes as soon as possible. The Americans had seen many locals get away with vandalism and other crimes because the American military forces had no authority . . . but, either because of manpower shortages, the holidays, or indifference, the local cops had no one to take the boy until Monday, so he stayed in the Air Force brig.

It was the opportunity the Americans had been waiting for to vent their own frustrations at being away in a foreign land among foreign peoples . . .

For the next forty-eight hours, Henri Cazaux had been passed back and forth between the security police teams so they could practice their "interrogation techniques." Cazaux was stuffed into fifty-five-gallon barrels, hosed down naked with icy cold water from fire hoses, questioned by teams of interrogators for hours at a time, made to kneel naked on bricks while chained to concrete pillars, and ordered to dig his own grave and then buried alive in mock firing-squad executions. He was never beaten, never physically harmed . . .

. . . until the nights, the long, awful nights, when Cazaux was alone with just one or two guards in an isolated part of the brig where no one could hear him scream. Then they took turns with him, tying the strong, lean, handsome young man up to a table and performing the ultimate degradation on him again and again, sometimes with a nightstick, sometimes with a broken broom handle and, ultimately, the engorged penises of the men themselves. If they were afraid of the shift commander hearing the prisoner's screams or cries for help, they would order the prisoner to suck on the end of a Colt M1911 pistol while they ravaged him—soon, Cazaux was praying they'd just pull the trigger and put him out of his misery.

Of course, Jo Ann Vega invented most of the more lurid details of the ordeal in her own fertile, twisted mind. Henri Cazaux had been imprisoned and abused for two days in the hands of the American Air Force, that much was known—exactly what had happened to him, Cazaux never said beyond only the vaguest hints. It certainly explained his bloodthirsty attitude toward the Americans, his intense fear and revulsion to the thought of capture, and his intense desire for revenge.

In her own way, Vega relished the idea of some big black soldier treating Henri like a ten-dollar whore . . . It was a fantasy that got her wet just thinking about it.

In any case, the Antwerp incarceration was for Cazaux's third felony crime. He had a choice—ten years in the Auxiliaries (the virtual slave-labor arm of the Belgian Army), or ten years in prison. Cazaux willingly, even happily, joined the Auxiliaries. He reformed himself enough to join the regular army, then the First Para, the special-operations quick-strike brigade known as the Red Berets, flight school, and even received a commission. He stayed on an extra two years after his now long-forgotten sentence, then, as with most soldiers, he was given a Reserve assignment. He left the regular army a finely tuned, well-trained, precision killing machine—and as mentally twisted as a Swiss mountain road.

"I need to know if my plans of destruction will be successful, Madame Vega," Cazaux said. "I need your advice. I cannot issue commands to my staff without some assurances that my plans will be successful."

"I saw much blood, much destruction," Vega said. "I saw death, Henri, lots of death—but I did not see yours, although death is all around you. I saw the wings of the angel of death, the dark master, sweeping across the skies in a fiery chariot, driven by you."

"Your visions are not helping me, Jo Ann," Cazaux said irritably. "All I need to know is, will my campaign be successful?"

She soaked a clean gauze pad with hydrogen peroxide and, without warning or fanfare, scrubbed the exposed wound to loosen the blood and dirt. Fresh water was necessary to clear away the bubbling flesh, but Cazaux did not cry out or even flinch from what had to be incredible pain. "I can see exposed muscle, Henri," Jo Ann said. "You'll need stitches and antibiotics."

"Runyan," Cazaux replied. She nodded. Lewis Runyan was a decertified physician who had tried to set her up as a drug dealer until Cazaux caught up with him. Rather than kill him, he convinced him to become the Cazaux operation's medical officer, and now lived in Newark, New Jersey, under the watchful eyes of Cazaux's lieutenants. "Continue to clean the wound, and pack it tightly. I need to travel within the hour."

"All right." She made no attempt to be gentle, but used her weight to scrub the wound until it bled. She knew she was working harder than necessary—was she trying to cause him pain? Why?

"Tell me what you are thinking, Jo Ann," Cazaux ordered. "You have not answered my question, and you are bound as my spiritual adviser to do so."

She looked up at him, her eyes pausing for a moment on his naked crotch before affixing on his stone-hard face. "I see more blood in your chart, Henri," she said. "I see much more blood, by your hands."

"Yes, yes," he responded impatiently. "My campaign?"

"Have you taken any drugs, any painkillers, any cocaine?" She knew the answer to that even before his flaming eyes rested on hers. Henri Cazaux never did drugs except for antibiotics and aspirin. She touched the leg wound again, with her fingernail. The touch did not register in even one muscle in his angular face. "You have transcended pain, Henri," she said. She wrapped her hand around his calf, stroking his leg. "I see other human traits that are now missing in your soul. You have been touched by Death, Henri, and for some reason, the dark master has released you—for now."

"Yes," he said, his eyes widening as he accepted her words as truth. He couldn't rationalize it before, but her words confirmed what he was thinking: the mission he had just completed, escaping the jaws of death so narrowly as he did, had changed him.

"You have completed a deal with the Devil," she continued as she stroked his right leg, then kissed his left leg, then stroked his rock-hard buttocks. "You have traded what was left of your humanity for a few extra days of life. Show me your right hand." She opened his right hand when he extended it to her. A fresh three-inch-long burn, caused by his grip on the nylon webbing of his parachute risers during his low-altitude bailout over San Francisco International, was etched across his palm, perfectly perpendicular to his already very short lifeline. "Here is the signed contract, Henri. You didn't know this wound was here, did you?" Obviously he did not, because he stared at the cut. "I don't know how long you have—maybe hours, maybe days. Perhaps only . . . minutes."

His eyes flared, knowing she had added that last warning selfishly, that she wanted the next few minutes with him. "No—longer," she admitted. "I see blood, too, a lot of blood. Not all of it is yours."

"It won't be. I can guarantee *that.*"

"This is a serious contract, Henri, a contract with the dark master," Jo Ann said angrily, returning to her nursing. "The contract is irrevocable. The dark master offers you incredible strength, a life without pain, with a tireless body, with sharp eyes. He demands a price for these gifts."

"A price? From *me?*"

"Yes, damn you, the ultimate price—your very life, your *future,*" she said. "Your soul is already his—now he wants control of your mind. He gave you these gifts because he wants to turn you loose on the mortal world, taking your revenge."

"That's exactly what I intend to do."

Her eyes flared, and she took a deep breath as the excitement welled in her chest. *He could do it,* she thought. "Then do it, Henri," Vega said. "I'm telling you, Henri, you've been chosen by the dark master to carry out a baptism of fire on planet Earth. He has given you the gift of freedom from mortal pain. You will not feel hunger, or pain, or weariness. You will defy the laws of nature. You will see with the eyes of a hawk, hear with the ears of a wolf, move with the speed of a cheetah. You will think like no other general has ever done before. It is time to set it all into motion, Henri."

"I have already set it in motion, Jo Ann," Cazaux said, his voice as deep and hollow as if from the bottom of a grave. "Death from the skies, from nowhere, from everywhere. Men think they have conquered the sky; I say they will fear the skies, fear the machines and the physics that carry them aloft. My lack of pain is the sign that I have been given this assignment and that I must carry it out."

"Turn your hatred into blood-lust, Henri," Vega pleaded with him. "You're not just a soldier, not a machine—you're the sword of Satan. Be all that he has commanded you to be. Do it. *Do it!*"

She saw the smile creep to his lips, and it was then that she noticed his erection, and she knew he had indeed changed. Henri Cazaux was not interested in aides, or soulmates, or advisers—he was interested in conquest. The dark master had told him that anything he desired was within his grasp. She had confirmed the voice. Now he was going to act upon that advice.

Her blouse and brassiere ripped off her body in his grasp as easily as if they were of paper. The creature inside Henri Cazaux was free once again, and this time there was no restraining it.

An hour later, Jo Ann Vega wondered with the darkest sense of doom if the country would survive what Henri Cazaux had in mind for it. If the pain and the blood she had just experienced was going to be multiplied by even a fraction of this country's three hundred million inhabitants, she knew that it could very well not survive his onslaught.

Near Bedminster, New Jersey
That Evening

"That is what I desire," Cazaux told the men assembled around him. The staff meeting was in an isolated house in rural New Jersey, owned by Harold Lake through several layers of U.S. and offshore corporations, as safe from government scrutiny as possible. The night was warm and humid, but Cazaux's security forces kept all of the windows and doors tightly closed. Human and canine patrols roamed the thirty-acre walled and gated estate, and electronic trip wires and sensors ringed the compound. Every room of the seven-bedroom home was occupied by an armed guard who constantly checked in with a security monitor.

The men present were members of Cazaux's "senior staff," organized much like an army battalion headquarters with operations and plans, intelligence, logistics, transportation, maintenance, security, and munitions staff officer. Of all of them, Harold Lake—who did not consider himself a staff officer but was generally in charge of procurement, purchasing, and finances for Cazaux's organization—had been with the organization the longest. Surrounded by some of the world's most wanted terrorists, smugglers, murderers, and mercenaries, Lake was definitely the most out-of-place person there.

The "security officer," Tomas Ysidro, was probably the most notorious officer besides Cazaux himself, and Lake had to be careful at all times to not do or say anything to piss the bastard off. Born and raised in Mexico, Ysidro had been one of the Colombian drug cartel's deadliest enforcers before joining Cazaux's small army, and he was quickly elevated to a status very nearly equal to Cazaux himself simply because no one else dared challenge him. Ysidro was in charge of recruitment and training, and his tactics and forms of discipline were a lot harsher than anything the Colombian drug lords used. Only Henri Cazaux's strength and sheer force of superior will could keep Ysidro's psychopathic tendencies in check. They were like two peas in a pod.

"Henri, you're insane," Lake declared. "I don't believe it. You want to blow up *three major airports* in the United States?"

"What I want is revenge on the United States government for chasing me like a scared rabbit," Cazaux said. "What I want is to see the people of this country tremble when they hear my name. What I want is to see this country, this so-called democracy, destroyed by its own military forces. They *shot* at me, Lake, they dared shoot at *me!* I want to destroy the American military by creating fear and distrust in them by their own people. I want to show the world what kind of butchers and wild dogs they really are."

"Hey, Henri, you want it, you got it," Ysidro said, taking his first post-meeting slug of bourbon from a bottle. "Man, this is gonna be awesome. We don't just take out one plane, we take out the whole airport, the whole fucking *airport!*" He laughed.

"Why, Henri?" Lake protested, ignoring Ysidro for the moment. "Why are you doing this? You've already got half the federal government on your tail. You're already the most-wanted man in fifteen countries—"

"Shut up, Drip, you asshole," Ysidro hissed to drown out Lake's voice. Harold Lake shot an angry glance at Ysidro—he hated the nickname "Drip," but everyone there used it in fear and deference of Ysidro. "The man gave us our orders, and now we march. You just need to bring us the money, mule."

"Three airports within thirty days, all attacked by heavy cargo planes or commercial airliners filled with explosives," Gregory Townsend, the British-born chief of plans and operations, mused. Townsend was a former British SAS commando, an expert in planning and setting up all sorts of military operations all around the world. He had lost an eye in a hostage-rescue situation in Belfast several years earlier, and after fifteen illustrious years with the British Army, had been sent packing with only a modest monthly stipend. When Cazaux invited him to join his organization, he readily agreed. "Considering a one- or two-million-dollar deposit per plane, plus a million for fuel, plus a million or two for explosives—we're talking eight to nine million dollars for this operation, Henri, ten million tops. As I recall, we had a balance of eleven million in the war chest. This'll tap us out. What sort of deal did you make with the client? I'd say at least ten million per target struck would be reasonable."

"No client," Cazaux said. "No fee. This I do for myself." Many of the officers around him averted their eyes, disappointed in Cazaux's decision but fearful of showing any hesitation or protest. Lake looked stunned, and showed it; Ysidro looked immensely pleased.

"So, Drip, you might as well close the bank accounts and convert the whole enchilada into greenbacks," Ysidro said. Townsend nodded his agreement. "We expect the cash in three days. Towney, I want to review the aircraft list with you by tomorrow afternoon. We'll have to rig up a trainer system, get charts of the targets, recruit some more flyboys, all that shit. There may be a way to get our hands on some military hardware—imagine using a couple Harpoon missiles or laser-guided bombs on O'Hare or LAX!"

Ysidro took another swig, chuckling at Cazaux's stern expression, noting with relief that Cazaux's anger seemed to be all directed at Lake. Ysidro was a good friend of Henri Cazaux's—at least, if Cazaux had a friend, it was Tomas Ysidro—but he still didn't want to show any weakness to his boss or to the other officers, ever. If Cazaux ever failed to make it back from one of his missions, Ysidro and Townsend would battle for control of the organization and its assets, and he had to appear strong at all times. Townsend was smart and tough, but all those years as a Brit officer gave him an air of superiority that made everyone distrust him.

"Relax, Henri, everything's gonna be fine," Ysidro said to Cazaux. "We got enough in reserve to get started on the explosives payloads for the first couple missions. Butcher and Faker can pick over that Seneschet warehouse in Massachusetts and see what they got, but it'll be no sweat—I think we can pick up about seven or eight thousand kilos of ammonium nitrate from the waste-storage area, and we got about a thousand kilos of TNT in storage for the primer loads. The fuzing will be tougher—we may have to go out on the market for the first few. I got a contact in a National Guard armory in North Carolina where we might get some fuzes."

"I have information on some military ordnance," Townsend said. "Several Air National Guard units recently returned from a European deployment, and much of their ordnance is in warehouses right over at Stewart International awaiting transportation to their home units. Their inventory counts never come out right after a big deployment. We can get gravity bombs, incendiaries, night-vision gear, the works. Drip, I'll need some cash for earnest money."

"The name isn't 'Drip,' you asshole, and there's no fucking cash," Lake finally snapped. All of the other officers turned to him in horror—all but Henri Cazaux, who had been looking in Lake's direction for most of the meeting.

Ysidro cursed. "What the fuck are you talking about? We got eleven million fucking dollars in the bank, Drip. The last meeting before the Chico mission was only eight days ago, and before that we had twenty million."

"That was before Korhonen flew that transport plane into San Francisco International and killed several hundred people," Lake retorted angrily. "That was before three-quarters of the air traffic to the west coast was shut down. That was before every investor in Europe told me to fuck off backwards."

"You telling us you blew eleven million dollars in the stock market just since *yesterday* . . . ?"

"I'm telling you that I lost *one hundred million dollars* yesterday, including this organization's eleven million, because *you*"—Lake jabbed a finger at Cazaux, who was still staring at him—"decided to go on a joyride and blow up SFO. I lost everything I have, damn you, everything! I'm broke! I'm worse than broke. I'm ruined . . ."

Ysidro was on him like a panther, and before Lake could blink, Ysidro had him pressed up against the wall, a knife point pressed into his throat. The other staff officers had surrounded the two to watch the execution. "I think," Ysidro said, his face pressed right up against Lake's so he could feel his last breath as it gushed from his lungs, "we are about to need a new logistics officer."

"No," Cazaux said evenly. "Let him speak."

"This fucker's ripping us off, man."

"Let him *speak,*" Cazaux ordered.

His voice did not change, but the force behind Cazaux's order seemed to everyone several magnitudes higher than the first. Ysidro glared at Lake, then held his head steady, gave him a cut on his neck about two inches long, licked the rivulet of blood, then spit it back in Lake's face. "Fucking bean-counter," he growled. "Unfortunately, you live for now." The air in the room seemed to relax as Ysidro backed away.

Lake was shaking like a man possessed, but more from anger than fear. He wiped blood from his eyes, put a handkerchief to the cut on his neck, and said, "I've been laundering money for this organization for three years, finding legitimate investments and creating legitimate business fronts, and I've done a very good job," Lake said. "I've done a good job because *I* have been steering each mission, preparing the businesses beforehand."

"You haven't done shit, Drip," Ysidro said. "We hardly see you, and all you give us is Jew banker's mumbo-jumbo."

"You think you can just walk into a bank with your terrorist checkbook and write a check for three or four million dollars?" Lake asked angrily. To Townsend he continued, "You think you can take seven million pounds sterling that you just got from an IRA bomber, convert it to dollars, and drop it in the automated teller machine at the corner bank, Townsend? The money has to look clean, and that takes work. The money has to be legitimately traceable down three dozen levels in the United States alone, and a dozen layers down in twenty other countries, all at the same time. Plus, you want me to research the financial on your targets, your clients, their governments, and their relations and principals all the way to the highest levels. I do that, each and every time, so when you make the deal or make the hit, we know exactly what all the players are going to do or say all over the world.

"I can get you what you want and keep the cash in this organization flowing, but only if I call the shots," Lake went on. "I was fully exposed when that LET hit the terminal, Henri, *fully exposed.* I lost everything! Now this damned psycho pulls a knife on me and tries to pin the blame on me. Well, go ahead and fucking kill me, Henri, because if you don't do it, some Japanese or South African investor's hit squad is going to do it."

"He wants to die so bad, Henri, I will be glad to oblige him." Ysidro laughed, brandishing the knife again. "No bean-counter is going to tell me what to do."

"You broke faith with this organization, Harold," Cazaux said in a low voice. "The Army doesn't wait for clearance from a banker before beginning operations. You knew that. Your duty was to keep the funds safe and secure, not engage in wild investment deals."

"Henri, you can't keep eleven million dollars in cash in a shoe box under the bed," Lake said. "You're running an international organization, and you can't efficiently run it with cash. You wanted real estate, business assets, licenses, government contracts, visas, letters of introduction, legitimate tax returns—you can't use bloody cash to pay for legitimate stuff. You can launder a little bit of the stuff offshore in bank accounts, but sure as shit, the FBI or Treasury will eventually track it down, close down your U.S. operations and probably your overseas accounts. If you want legitimacy in the United States you have to dive deeper, get more creative, do more mainstream stuff. And you can't do the same routine two years in a row, or even two months in a row, because the government tracks that stuff quarterly."

"I am tired of this sheep's bleating, Captain," Ysidro said. He reached out with the speed of a cobra and grasped Lake around the neck, digging his fingers deep into the financier's flesh. "Allow me to put an end to it."

"Let him go, Tomas," Cazaux ordered. He pulled out his .45 caliber automatic. "If he is to die, I will do it." The sight of the gun pleased Ysidro, who released Lake and stepped back to watch. "Speak, Harold," Cazaux said. "Say your last words quickly. Tell me why you should not be executed for what you have done."

At first Lake couldn't breathe, which made him panic even more, but the sight of the big pistol squeezed the air out of his lungs. "I got one thing to say, Henri, and if you don't like it, you might as well blow my head off, because my career on the Street is dead anyway. I've got an eighteen-million-dollar loan coming to me later today," Lake said—not pleading, not whimpering, just stating a fact. "I can turn that into fifty million dollars if you follow my—"

"You got our money?" Ysidro asked, grabbing Lake by the lapels instead of the neck this time. "You better hand it over, bean-counter."

"Henri, you want to start a series of operations against U.S. airports, repeating the attack on San Francisco International," Lake said, ignoring Ysidro and looking at Cazaux's fiery eyes. "That's fine with me. All I'm asking is that you let me pick your targets for you."

"You're fuckin' crazy, bean-counter!"

"No, I'm not. Listen to me, Henri. I lost over one hundred million dollars when you attacked SFO last night. But someone *made* money on that attack, Henri, big money. They make money because they predict in what direction a group of stocks will go."

"This is bullshit, Henri," Ysidro said angrily—he had lost track of this conversation long ago. Money, women, and action were the only activities Tomas Ysidro really understood—everything else was bullshit. "He's talkin' buying and selling fucking stocks with our money. Off this sonofabitch, man."

"It's not bullshit," Lake said. "I've got it all set up. Attack U.S.

airports if you want to—just attack the ones that I tell you to do, or give me a few days' notice before you begin an operation against an airport. Give me time to get my contracts lined up. I guarantee you, Henri, we'll make millions every time we do an operation. Best of all, it's one hundred percent legitimate. One hundred percent!"

Cazaux looked as if he wasn't listening, and Lake closed his eyes, not wanting to see the muzzle flash of the big .45—but instead he heard Cazaux say, "Speak, Harold."

Lake opened his eyes. The .45 was lowered. Cazaux was staring at him, but Lake knew he now had his attention. It was now or never, Harold . . .

"Listen, Henri, here's how it works. We do a put-option contract."

"What the hell are you talkin' about, man?"

"Listen, dammit," Lake said. "I'm talking about fast money, one hundred percent legitimate. I'm talking about turning a few thousand dollars into hundreds of thousands or even millions.

"Let's suppose you own one hundred shares of stock that you bought at seven dollars a share, but now it's selling on the market at ten dollars a share," Lake began. "You're not going to sell your stock unless it drops below eight dollars a share because you bought it at seven and you'd start losing money—"

"What is this shit, Henri . . . ?"

"I want your stock, but I don't have the money to pay for it," Lake went on hurriedly. "I think your stock is going to go down to five dollars a share soon, but if I wait until then, you'll sell your shares to someone else at or above seven. And besides, I still don't have the money to buy your shares even at five dollars a share. But I'm still not out of the game, because I'm willing to pay you cash for an *option* to buy your stock. Follow me so far?" Cazaux nodded, but Lake knew he was getting only a few more seconds, and only because he had been a loyal lieutenant of Cazaux's for so long.

"We agree to do the deal. I pay you fifty dollars earnest money, and we write a contract that says that if the stock goes down below eight dollars a share within the next two months, I have the *option* of buying your shares at any time within that two months. If the stock stays at or above eight at the end of sixty days, the contract expires and nothing happens, and you keep the fifty—"

"I thought you said you didn't have the money to buy the stock," Townsend interjected. Of the senior staff, Townsend was by far the most intelligent and worldly of them all—Lake knew he had to not only convince Cazaux that he was honest and sincere, but he had to explain everything carefully to Townsend or it would not work.

"I'm not buying your stock, Towney," Lake replied. "I'm buying an *option* to buy your stock. If the terms of the contract are not met, I don't have the option. If they are, I can choose whether or not to buy. If I buy, I've got to have the cash. But the contract I hold has value—I can sell it to someone who wants the stock, for cash. I'm not trying to own the stock—all I want is cash."

Lake had totally lost Ysidro by this time. Most of the others were watching Cazaux. The arms dealer was carefully paying attention, and Lake believed he understood what was happening and where Lake was leading him. Townsend was starting to get confused. "But how can you get the bloody cash," he asked irritably, "and why do you have to pay someone to buy their stock?"

"I'm paying them to *pledge* their stock, to put it aside until the contract has either been executed or it expires," Lake explained. "Your stock is at ten. I think your stock is going to go to five, and I'm willing to pay you cash to promise to sell it to *me* and no one else if it goes below eight. You basically think I'm nuts, but you want my cash, so you agree to the deal, take the cash, sign the contract, and put your stock in escrow. The cash I pay you is yours no matter what happens." Townsend nodded that he understood. Ysidro took another swig of bourbon, belched, and a few other staff officers fidgeted uneasily, intrigued but bored and anxious to get this over with.

"But how in bloody hell will you know if a stock that you've written this contract for will go down like that—" And then Townsend stopped—and Lake knew then that the English terrorist was on board. "So you're suggesting . . . "

"We *target* our attacks in order to drive the price of the stock in the direction we want," Lake explained, a broad smile on his face now. "We want United Airlines stock to go down, so we hit a United terminal or repair facility. The price of the stock hits rock bottom, and we clean up.

"We can play this game the other way, too," Lake went on. "If airlines go down, other airline-related companies like airplane manufacturers and petroleum companies also go down, and oil prices and other transportation stocks, like auto manufacturers, go way up. We write a contract to buy auto or railroad stocks at a certain price, or write a commodities option contract to do the same with oil, or gold, or aluminum. When the stock or the commodity zooms past the strike price, we execute."

"So what about the federal authorities?" Townsend asked, a trace of old English civility creeping into his voice now that he better understood Lake's plan. "If we start making money like you suggest, won't the federal regulatory agencies become curious?"

"Yes," Lake admitted, after gauging Cazaux's expression. More than information, Lake felt, Cazaux was looking for honesty, and if Lake ever had to be one hundred and ten percent up-front, it was now. "I don't think you can do this for very long—eventually someone will question all these coincidences . . ." His voice regained a lot of the confidence and steel that he had lost since the incident at SFO. "But I think we can plan Henri's three strikes against carefully selected targets, take the proceeds, close up shop, and get away clean before the Securities and Exchange Commission alerts the Treasury Department and the FBI."

"Now you've got three American federal agencies chasing us . . . ?"

"These options trades are done tens of thousands of times a day," Lake explained. "Hundreds of millions of dollars in options are traded every business day. The federal agencies have rules and enforcement officers examining these trades, but it works slowly, and they look for the big fish. Besides, we're not stealing the money—we're just diverting it, spreading it around, with most of it spread in our direction. Lots of other traders will be making money, and the guy who just lost money one day will make it all back, plus a little extra, the next day or the next week. This sounds like big bucks, gents, but it's small potatoes—most big-time traders need to make ten million a day just to keep their spurs.

"We'll be outgunned by the really big traders, the super-big investors and brokers and even some governments. That's the time we take our profits and step back. We'll be lost in the confusion—a perfect opportunity to escape. The feds will go after the elephants, and they'll let the ants scoop up the crumbs and shoo—except our 'crumbs' will be counted in the millions, maybe even the tens of millions of dollars."

"Henri, this bastard is givin' us a snow job," Ysidro said, totally lost and completely exasperated by Lake's attempted explanation. "We gotta get the money this asshole stole from us back, that's the fuckin' bottom line."

Cazaux looked at Ysidro, then Townsend, then at Lake, nodded solemnly, and said in response, "Harold, your plan of action has merit, but it still does not erase what you have done—risk this entire army's very existence by compromising our financial resources. It is nothing short of treason and conspiracy. However, because of your long years of service to us and because I feel your plan should be considered by the general staff, you will not be tried of treason and conspiracy for a period of twelve hours.

"In that twelve hours, while under 'round-the-clock arrest, you are to turn all funds belonging to this organization over to me."

"No problem," Lake said. "I can have the eleven million dollars in your offshore accounts in three—"

"In cash," Ysidro said, "not any of this Jew-banker contract-note shit."

"In cash," Cazaux agreed.

Lake swallowed hard, the back of his mind racing trying to determine the best way to transport a truckful of money to the Owl's Nest from a friendly bank. He quickly determined that it was not possible. "Henri, it can't be done in twelve hours," Lake said. "One or two million, yes, but not eleven. The fastest way to get the money is from the Federal Reserve Bank in New York or Boston, but we don't want to stir up *that* hornet's nest, which means we try going to the commercial and private banks, which will take time. Not many banks carry that kind of cash on hand, which means we'd have to go to several banks, which greatly increases the likelihood of—"

"Then you will die, Harold," Cazaux said, raising the big .45 again.

"Wait!" Lake shouted. "I can get four . . . no, five million with just a phone call. I've dealt with the Win Millions Casino in Atlantic City for emergency cash deals in the past—they can divert five million to me in just a few hours, before the gaming commission inspectors count their receipts tomorrow morning. They'll charge twenty percent—"

"Which you will pay out of your own funds," Cazaux said.

"Of course, of course," Lake agreed. Twenty-percent interest for a one-week loan worked out to an astronomical *one million percent* compounded annual interest rate, but it was his only hope right now. "But Henri, the other six million should stay in the various offshore accounts. We can't write those option contracts with cash." The gun was still trained on him, distrust showing in every man's face around Lake. "Henri, you've *got* to trust me on this one. I've got a loan commitment for eighteen million dollars in my hands. I pay Fraga at the Win Millions Casino six million, I need four million for my other creditors, that leaves you with the rest of the—"

"You will pay us fifteen million dollars," Cazaux said. "Five million now, in cash, and ten million credited to our offshore numbered accounts. You will keep the rest."

"But . . . but I can't do that," Lake protested. "I've got to cover thirty different trust and escrow accounts. The four million is just enough to hold off any legal action for—"

"You will agree to these terms or die," Cazaux said. "That is your only concern right now."

"Henri, I can't step on the floor of any exchange or even talk to a broker unless I—" Cazaux pulled the hammer back on the .45. The sound of the hammer locking into place was as loud as a church bell in Lake's ears. "All right, all right!" Lake shouted. "Fifteen million for you. I agree. Five million now, ten in your accounts." He paused, looking to Cazaux and Townsend, afraid to look at Ysidro, and added, "To be used for Operation Storming Heaven, yes?"

"What the hell is Operation Storming Heaven?" Townsend asked.

"It's an appropriate name for this project," Lake said. "Comes from a quote by the Roman tribune Quintus Horatius Flaccus: 'Nothing is too high for the daring of mortals; they storm heaven in their folly.' Quite good, don't you think?"

Ysidro looked disgusted and angry enough to chew nails, but Cazaux nodded his approval. It was one of those touches that Lake knew that Cazaux appreciated—having a title for any operation he was about to undertake was important to him. Cazaux decocked the pistol and stuck it back in his belt. Lake had to look behind him to see what would have gotten ruined had he pulled the trigger. A nineteenth-century oil painting of Abraham Lincoln, once appraised at over a hundred thousand dollars, would have needed extensive cleaning and repairs to remove Lake's brains and bone fragments if his explanation of Operation Storming Heaven did not convince Henri Cazaux.

Cazaux put the question to a vote of the members of his general staff—merely a formality, because almost no one ever voted against Henri Cazaux. Tomas Ysidro was the only one to vote against the plan, asking again that Lake be executed for what he'd done with the organization's funds. "I'll be on you like stink on shit, Drip," Ysidro told Lake as the staff members were given their instructions to begin planning the three attacks. "You get out of line once, just once, and I'll blow your fuckin' ass off. Cazaux will bitch, and he might even throw me out on the street, but you'll still be dead like you fuckin' deserve."

Ysidro then pulled up a chair and sat right beside Lake, staring at him and taking in every last word as Lake pulled out his cellular telephone and Apple Newton PDA and made the first calls and satellite E-mail messages, first to his office to verify the receipt of the loan money, then to Leonardo Fraga, the vice president and general manager of the Win Millions Hotel and Casino in Atlantic City. Under Ysidro's murderous stare, it was hard to keep his fingers from shaking as he began the first few steps of Operation Storming Heaven.

Beale Air Force Base, Yuba City, California
Two Days Later

"The board has reached an initial evaluation," Colonel Emerson Starr began. He was the operations group commander from McClellan Air Force Base appointed as the chief of the accident investigation board dealing with the crash of the F-16 at McClellan two days earlier. "The scope of the accident investigation has been greatly reduced because of the involvement of the FBI, Marshals Service, and the Bureau of Alcohol, Tobacco, and Firearms—in essence, this board can't come up with a ruling on the cause of the crash because we haven't been granted access to the data now in the hands of the FBI. We know there was an explosion, and we know the F-16 was in close proximity to the explosion, but we don't know anything about the explosion itself. Therefore we can't absolutely conclude that the explosion caused the damage on the F-16. However, based on radio transmissions, ground observers, and a cursory examination of the wreckage, the board determines that the probable cause of the accident was due to the F-16's uncontrolled collision with the ground following sustaining engine and hydraulic damage due to proximity of a large ground explosion at Mather Jetport."

Starr shifted uncomfortably in his seat and continued. "The preliminary report of this accident board in the matter of the death of the pilot Major Linda McKenzie is incomplete; however, we are prepared to issue the following statement to Air Combat Command, the chief of staff of the Air Force, and the adjutant general of the state of California: the death of Major McKenzie was due to violation of Air Combat Command regulation 55-16, 'F-16 Aircrew Procedures,' paragraph 5-53, and Technical Order 1F-16A-1, section three, paragraph—''

''That's bullshit!'' Colonel Al Vincenti snapped, jumping to his feet. ''Don't pull this crap, Colonel. This was not a *pilot error* accident, damn you.''

''Sit *down,* Colonel Vincenti,'' Starr said firmly.

''I want to address the board, sir.''

''The board has already heard your testimony, Colonel,'' Starr replied. ''Sit down or I'll have you removed.''

''You can try, Starr.''

Colonel Gaspar was now on his feet in front of Vincenti. ''Better sit down, Rattler,'' he said. ''You're skating on real thin ice.''

''I assure you, Colonel, I have full authority to hold you in contempt if you don't *shut up,*'' Starr said. ''Now, are you going to be quiet and let me finish, or will I have to ask you to leave?''

Vincenti riveted Starr with his angry stare.

''Colonel Gaspar, can you please escort Colonel Vincenti outside?''

''He'll be fine, Colonel,'' Gaspar said, pulling Vincenti back into his seat.

''Thank you, sir,'' Starr said. ''As I was saying, Major McKenzie violated several aircrew regulations that specifically directed her to eject if she was below two thousand feet above ground level in case of hydraulic failure, catastrophic engine failure, uncontrollability, low airspeed, inability to maintain altitude, unsafe gear indications, flight control transients or failure, inability to fly an approach pattern, electrical failure, center of gravity problems—the list goes on. By every account, and by the testimony of her fellow pilots and technical representatives of the aircraft manufacturer, Major McKenzie should have ejected much sooner and should not have attempted a landing.

''However, the board doubts whether Major McKenzie had full knowledge of exactly what was wrong with her aircraft, since it was dark and she had minimal cockpit indications,'' Starr continued. ''Colonel Vincenti on her wing also could not know the exact condition of her aircraft. The board concludes that it was reasonable for Major McKenzie to attempt a flameout landing with the indications she had. Considering the densely populated areas where the unmanned F-16 would have landed had she ejected, the board also finds that Major McKenzie's and Colonel Vincenti's actions in bringing the damaged aircraft to McClellan Air Force Base saved dozens and perhaps hundreds of lives.

"The board is therefore concluding that the actions of Major McKenzie and Colonel Vincenti were in keeping with the directives and tenets of the United States Air Force regarding safe operation over populated areas, and we conclude that Major Linda McKenzie did indeed risk and eventually sacrifice her own life to save others; although she would have been following prescribed directives by ejecting, and she is indeed guilty of not following those regulations which would have saved her life, failing to do so saved many other lives and much property damage, and Major McKenzie should be commended for her actions."

Colonel Starr then looked over at Vincenti, affixing him with his own angry glare, and added, "The board further finds that damage sustained to Colonel Vincenti's F-16 could have caused the malfunctions in the radios and videotape gun camera being questioned by the Air Combat Command flight evaluation board. Of course, these conclusions are preliminary, since we do not have access to information about the explosion, but it is reasonable for this board to conclude that Colonel Vincenti's aircraft sustained much the same damage as Major McKenzie's plane, and the malfunctions that Colonel Vincenti said were the cause of him disregarding instructions to land could have existed. Given that Colonel Vincenti's last acknowledged instructions were to pursue the suspect aircraft, in our opinion his actions were consistent with his orders as he could have known them at the time. These preliminary findings will be passed along to the flight evaluation board convened to examine Colonel Vincenti's actions subsequent to the crash at McClellan.

"I remind everyone present that the findings of this board are classified confidential, and you are instructed not to reveal any of them or discuss this matter with the press, which I understand is waiting outside. If you are questioned by the press, refer them to Air Force Public Affairs. Until such time as this board is allowed access to data about the explosion at Mather, this board stands in recess."

Everyone in the room rose and departed—everyone except Vincenti and Gaspar, who returned to their seats after the board members had departed. Vincenti, weary and haggard, looked as if he had just been beat up. "Your mouth is going to get you in big trouble one of these days, my friend," Gaspar said to his second-in-command. "You need to make friends with guys like Starr, not shout him down."

"I thought he was going to continue the press's and the government's feeding frenzy and trash Linda, like they've been trashing me and the unit," Vincenti said. "I'm getting tired of this shit, Chuck. I feel so fucking isolated, like it's our fault about San Francisco."

"Since when do you care what anyone else thinks, Rattler?"

"Since I see and hear this stuff ten times a day in the papers, on the radio and TV," Vincenti said. "Everywhere I go, I hear the same thing: I'm the guy that missed Cazaux, I'm the guy who let Cazaux go, I'm the one that screwed up. I'm starting to *believe* all this shit."

"It's all going to continue, Colonel," a voice behind them said. They turned and found Admiral Ian Hardcastle standing in the center aisle listening to them, with his aide guarding the door to the room to keep anyone else out. "The government needs a fall guy, and you're it. McKenzie's name will be cleared—yours won't. In fact, with Major McKenzie's name cleared, you'll appear doubly at fault."

"You know what I think, Hardcastle? I think you're whipping the press up with all this talk of beefing up air defense," Vincenti said angrily, getting to his feet to confront the retired officer. "I've seen disasters like this die away after a day or two, but you're not letting this one die away. Where the hell do you get off?"

"Cazaux will strike again, Colonel," Hardcastle said. "I'm convinced of it."

"So now you're fuckin' Karnac the Magnificent, huh?" Vincenti retorted. "What you're doing here is screwing with people's lives and careers just for your own political bullshit plans."

"That was true two days ago when we showed up here, Colonel," Hardcastle said. "That's why Vice President Martindale and the rest of them are here."

"But you're not?" Gaspar asked.

"Not since I talked to you the first time," Hardcastle replied. "Not after getting the FBI briefing on Cazaux. He's deadly and very dangerous. Yes, I believe he'll strike again. But the government is trying to calm people down by telling them that Cazaux is too crazy to organize another attack, that it was a fluke, that the manhunt will track him down before he can strike again. The FBI's own profile on him says otherwise. The government is also saying that Air National Guard units will be restrained in their overland operations and that no other military precautions are necessary—there's even talk of doing away with all continental air defense units completely. We're giving Cazaux the perfect opportunity to strike."

"With all due respect, Admiral, you don't know shit," Gaspar said. "You're just guessing."

"And all your guesses just happen to follow the party line—*your* party's line," Vincenti added. "You're just as bad as Wilkes and the rest of the Justice Department that are jumping in my shit."

"I'm trying to keep the government from completely dismantling the home-defense infrastructure of this country," Hardcastle said. "That's the truth, and that's from the heart. You're a career air defense pilot—you can tell if I'm bullshitting you or not. Now, you can just sit back and let the Justice Department and the Air Force cut your nuts off and trash your career, or you can cooperate with me and my investigation. If my agenda helps Vice President Martindale and the Project 2000 Task Force, that's fine, I believe in his candidacy and what the Task Force is trying to achieve. You don't have to. But I'm running my show the way *I* want. I'm not a mouthpiece for anyone."

"No, but you want me to be your puppet, right?" Vincenti asked. "You want to use me as the poor downtrodden sob story while you lambaste the White House and anyone else who gets in your way."

"I want you to teach me what you know, Al," Hardcastle said. "You know air defense—I've been out of it for too long. Yeah, I've got a political agenda, but I've also got specific ideas to help the system we have right now, no matter who is in the White House. I need your help to finalize my ideas. In return I can help put you back on flying status, keep your career intact, and help your unit recover from the whitewashing job you're undergoing right now. I'm not saying you and your unit and maybe the entire air defense community will be toast if you don't help me, but you can read the handwriting on the wall just as good as I can."

Vincenti and Gaspar remained silent, defiantly staring at Hardcastle as if trying to recognize any hint of his hidden agenda. Hardcastle let them stare for a moment, then he turned to his aide standing by the door and said, "Marc, show the Colonel here who's waiting to speak to him."

Colonel Marc Sheehan, Hardcastle's aide, unlocked and opened the door behind him, and immediately a throng of reporters tried to muscle their way inside, shouting questions. A few point-and-shoot cameras were poked through the door, rapid-firing at random for pictures.

"I'm not talking to the press," Vincenti said. "No comment."

Hardcastle motioned to Sheehan, who not-too-politely pushed back the reporters and closed and locked the door again. "Sure, you keep on with your no-comment routine, Colonel—without my help this time," Hardcastle said. "You think you look bad on TV now—by tomorrow night's evening news, you'll be called either Cazaux's accomplice or the biggest American military screwup since George Custer."

"I can take care of myself."

"I'm not talking about *you,* Colonel—I'm talking about your career, your future, your retirement, the continued existence of your unit, and everything regarding air defense you've ever believed in. You can't fight the Fourth Estate yourself."

"So now you're blackmailing me, right?" Vincenti asked. "I either help you or swim with the sharks myself."

"I've got work to do, Colonel," Hardcastle said simply. "You're a big boy, an officer and a gentleman. You think you can fight your own battles, go ahead and fight. I'll be fighting too—I just wanted to be fighting together with you, not separately. But I can do it separately. You think you can?"

Vincenti and Gaspar were silent once again. Hardcastle had had enough. He turned and headed for the door. "Have a nice life, Colonel," he said. "I'll lead these bozos away from the front door—slip out in a minute or two. But one last word of advice—try not to make it look like you're running from them. Believe me, you can't."

Hardcastle had just reached the door and was about to open it when he heard, "All right, all *right.* I'll help you."

The retired Coast Guard and Border Security Force officer turned and nodded at Vincenti and Gaspar. "Hangar Bravo, briefing room, six A.M. tomorrow," Hardcastle said. "Bring the original gun camera tapes."

"There are no original tapes. I told you, I told the board—the recorder was damaged."

"Colonel, save that rap for the flight evaluation board," Hardcastle said. "I need your honest inputs. Believe me, no FEB will see or hear those tapes—they belong to the U.S. Senate as of right now, and no one in the military below the Secretary of Defense has the authority to demand them."

"I've got to get permission to be excused from the FEB and released from quarters."

"It's been done. You're a special expert consultant and witness in a Senate investigation—your flight evaluation board and your court-martial have been suspended indefinitely."

"What court-martial? What in hell are you talking about?"

"Oh, that's right, you probably didn't know," Hardcastle said, a wickedly satisfied smile on his face. "Tell him, Marc."

"Air Combat Command was directed by the Secretary of Defense and the President to convene a court-martial," Sheehan said. "Dereliction of duty, actions unbecoming an officer, disobeying a direct and lawful order. Regardless of the outcome of the flight evaluation board, you were going to be summarily court-martialed, sentenced to four years restricted duty—probably as a warehouse officer in Greenland—reduction in grade to captain, then given a less-than-honorable discharge, maybe even a dishonorable discharge. We've seen the paperwork—it's been signed and approved."

"And you were going to just walk out of here and let this happen?" Vincenti moaned, his eyes wide in utter disbelief. "You were going to let me get busted if I didn't cooperate with you?"

"You seem to think this is a game we're playing here, Colonel Vincenti," Hardcastle shot back. "You seem to think you can beat your chest and take everybody on. Let me assure you, it's not a game. I am deadly serious when I say that Henri Cazaux is going to strike again; I'm serious when I say I've got a plan to stop him; and I'm serious when I say I need your help. Now, I didn't sign those court-martial papers—your fellow blue-suiters did, the ones you dedicated your life to almost twenty years ago. I stopped it from happening. Who are you going to help now?"

Vincenti stepped over to Hardcastle—followed closely by Gaspar, ready to intervene if he was needed. But instead of venting his frustration and anger on Hardcastle or Sheehan, Vincenti held out a hand, and Hardcastle took it. "Before I forget what you did for me, before I remember you're a fucking politician now," Vincenti said in a low voice, "thank you."

"Thank you for trusting me—and I hope I can keep your trust," Hardcastle said. "Now, listen up: you and Colonel Gaspar stand beside me—right beside me, not in back of me. Don't try to push your way through the crowd—Marc will do the pushing. Colonel Gaspar, you give them the no-comment routine—after all, you're the military and you're not on trial. Al, you try to answer every question they throw at you—you won't be able to, but you have to look like you've got nothing to hide. Turn toward the reporter asking you questions, make eye contact but ignore the cameras. Don't *react* to a question, don't get pissed off. Think first, then go ahead and answer. Don't listen to what I'm saying. I'm not your lawyer, and we can't look like we're conspiring against telling the truth. Don't worry about what I'll be saying—believe me, we'll be saying the same thing."

"The judge directed us not to talk to the press."

"You work for the U.S. Senate now, Al—and you're fighting for your career, remember that," Hardcastle said. "We control the situation now. Defend your uniform *after* we get Henri Cazaux."

Memphis International Airport
Three Days Later

"Memphis Tower, Express-314 with you, GPS three-six left," the pilot of the Universal Express Boeing 727 reported.

"Express-314, good evening, ident," Bill Gayze, one of the six controllers on duty at Memphis International Airport's control tower, responded. By force of habit, he scanned outside the slanted windows at the direction of the ILS (Instrument Landing System) outer marker, about six miles to the south. He could see a string of lights in the sky, all flying northward—airliners' landing lights. Between eleven P.M. and one A.M., when the big overnight package company Universal Express had its incoming flights (Universal's huge package-sorting "superhub" was located at the north part of Memphis International), it was normal to have one aircraft landing every sixty to ninety seconds.

Gayze checked the tower BRITE (Bright Radar Indicator Tower Equipment) scope, the short-range three-dimensional radar mounted high up on the wall where everyone could see it. An aircraft data block on the top of the BRITE scope in the control tower of Memphis International illuminated briefly—the Delta flight was number seven for landing. "314, radar contact, report five miles out, you're number seven."

"Express-314, wilco." The Universal Express flight was using one of the new GPS instrument approaches, in which aircraft maneuvered from point to point on an instrument approach by means of satellite navigation. The satellite approaches, coupled with differential GPS signals from a nearby radio station, ensured incredible precision for arriving flights—using GPS, an experienced airline captain could make a perfect landing and could even taxi most of the way to his gate, without ever seeing the pavement. Except for an aircraft emergency like an unsafe landing gear, going "missed approach" (where a pilot flies his plane within one or two hundred feet of the ground but has to abort the landing because he or she couldn't see the runway) was almost a thing of the past here in Memphis. The added safety and reliability of the GPS approaches meant that the airport managers and the FAA could safely increase the traffic here at Memphis—every runway at Memphis, and indeed almost every runway in the country, now could have its own precision instrument approach. The concept of "blind flying" and "nonprecision approaches" had almost been eliminated, thanks to GPS.

Gayze's thoughts were interrupted by a call on the interfacility interphone: "Memphis Tower, Romeo-17."

"Memphis Tower."

"Hi, Bill, Doug on seventeen." Doug Latimer, at the sector-seventeen console, was a D-2 controller at Memphis TRACON (Terminal Radar Approach Control), located one hundred and eighty feet below Gayze's feet at the base of the tower at Memphis International. The D-2 controller assisted the sector radar controller by making phone calls to other air traffic control agencies, making radio calls as necessary to back up the radar controller, and maintaining the computerized tracking strips on each flight assigned to the controller. "Arrival report visual three-six left for Universal Express 107, a Shorts 300, one-five miles to the southwest at eight thousand. Can't find his strip. Can you handle him?"

"Sure," Gayze said. Every aircraft on an IFR flight plan has a "strip," or a piece of paper used by air traffic controllers to monitor and log a plane's progress. All Universal Express flights flew on IFR flight plans—company policy—and they were carefully tracked from start to finish by both the company and the FAA. A tracking strip was generated by a Flight Service Station or an Air Route Traffic Control Center and electronically passed from sector to sector as the plane progressed. Although it was not unheard of for a plane to lose its "strip," it was pretty unusual these days.

A plane without a strip was not officially "in the system" and was handled on a workload-permitting basis. This guy was lucky—it wasn't too busy at the moment. Right now there were almost one hundred and fifty planes of all sizes scattered around Universal Express's "super hub," loading up and preparing for departure—it was busy, but not too bad to handle this one straggler.

"Tell him he can have runway two-seven if he wants it," Gayze said.

Runway two-seven lay across the northern part of the airport, right beside Universal Express's freight and package delivery complex. Normally it was a mad race for Universal's pilots to get to their cargo gates ahead of the others—this guy seemed to be taking it easy.

"Stand by," Latimer said. Gayze could hear the controller's conversation with the pilot over the phone line, then: "Okay, Bill, he's taking vectors to two-seven at six thousand feet, two thousand inside ten, D.L."

"Approved, B.G.," Gayze responded, passing the information to the tower controllers handling arrivals to runway two-seven. "How's it looking out there tonight, Doug? Busy?"

"I think every plane in Texas is heading your way tonight, Bill," Latimer said.

"Great," Gayze said wearily. "Ask your boys to vector the southwest arrivals south of Tunica, we're starting to bunch up." The string of lights aiming at runway three-six was starting to get longer and more tightly packed, and the flights were coming in faster. Each airplane under instrument flight rules in the airspace around Memphis International had a protective "cylinder" at least six miles in diameter and two thousand feet thick, with the plane in the center, which could not be violated under any circumstance. If the pilots could see the runway or a preceding aircraft and advised the controller of that, Gayze could tighten the spacing up to about two miles and five hundred feet, but most pilots flying at night were too busy scanning their instruments and running checklists to accept responsibility for separation. Things were going smoothly now, but one plane going too fast or too slow could create a whipsaw effect that could cause problems very quickly. Better to start extending the traffic now, rather than wait.

"You got it, Bill, vector southwest arrivals south of Tunica, D.L.," Latimer replied. "Talk at you later. 'Bye."

"D.G., 'bye." Gayze took a sip of coffee, laced with a little fat-free chocolate milk this time to boost the caffeine level. Things didn't calm down in the tower until after one A.M., nearly four hours away, and it was looking like a busy night. He needed to stay sharp.

* * *

"He wants to take me over to runway two-seven," the young pilot in the right seat of the Shorts 330-200 cargo plane said. "I said okay. He sounded like he was trying to help me out."

Henri Cazaux was in the back of the Shorts, inspecting his deadly cargo, when he heard the call over his wireless intercom. He raised his microphone to his lips: "Follow his vectors, but do not accelerate," Cazaux said. "I'll be up there in a minute." He then continued his inspection.

Although boxy and rather odd-looking, the Northern Ireland–built Shorts 330-200 was a popular short-range turboprop commuter/cargo plane—it had even been purchased by the U.S. Air Force, Army, and National Guard as a short-range utility aircraft. Over two hundred had been built for small airlines or major airline partners, carrying up to thirty passengers or 7,500 pounds of cargo. The twenty-year-old plane no longer flew for the U.S. military, and was now flown only by a handful of commuter and cargo services around the world. The used-airplane market was full of them, and it was easy and relatively inexpensive to build a small fleet of them and to train pilots to fly the small "trash-hauler." Cazaux's bird was a freighter version of the Model 300-200, called a C-23B "Sherpa" in the U.S. Air Force, modified with a rear cargo ramp and integral load rollers in the floor.

Tonight, the Shorts was a bomber.

Cazaux was inspecting three LD3 cargo containers, standard airline-use baggage, cargo, or mail containers, each filled with two thousand pounds of a mixture of waste ammonium nitrate rocket propellant, stolen from an industrial-waste storage facility in western Massachusetts, and TNT. The three containers were chained together, and the forward container was chained to a quick-release lever attached to the forward cargo-bay deck. A fourth pallet in the rear of the plane carried a six-foot-diameter pilot parachute and a forty-foot-diameter main cargo parachute, cabled to the LD3 containers.

This setup comprised a functional and tested parachute-extraction system, similar to the kind used by many tactical transport planes, including the Shorts 300. At the appropriate time, the pilot parachute would be released and inflated in the aircraft's slipstream, applying tension to the three LD3 containers. Once over the target, the pilot parachute would be allowed to release the main parachute, and as soon as the main 'chute fully opened, it would drag the containers out of the Shorts' cargo bay. Deceleration or G-sensors were installed in each container to set off the explosives one second after hitting the target, which would allow the containers to break through the roof of the target before detonating.

Satisfied that all was ready, Cazaux made his way back up to the cockpit and put on a headset. "Say again your last, Roberts?"

"I'm using the Universal call sign you gave me, Captain," the young pilot responded, "and I asked for vectors to runway three-six right, as ordered. Approach Control asked me if I wanted the Universal runway instead, two-seven . . ."

"You should have replied no," Cazaux said. "I ordered you to approach on three-six."

"Sir, in my judgment it would have appeared very suspicious to not accept vectors to two-seven," the pilot said. "Approach Control said I would be number two for landing on two-seven, but number eight on three-six right. The winds are calm, so all runways are in use tonight. I felt I had no choice."

"Get a clearance back to three-six right immediately, Roberts," Cazaux hissed. "You are not paid to exercise *your* judgment, you are paid to fly as you are *directed.* Now get a clearance back on course."

As Roberts got back on the radio, Cazaux checked the portable GPS satellite navigation receiver's moving-map display. They were many miles off course now, almost beyond the extended centerline of three-six right. It might be too late to get two-seven now, and their mission timing was way off. "You had better check your timing, and do whatever it takes to get back on course and back on time," Cazaux warned his young pilot. "I want no more errors in judgment or you'll be a dead man."

A few moments later, the interfacility interphone came alive again: "Bill, Doug, Sierra-12. Universal-107 changed his mind again and now wants three-six right."

"Bless him," Gayze said impatiently, being careful (after listening to his controller tapes many times with a supervisor present) not to swear. This was not the time for new pilots to be messing around with multiple requests and weird clearances. "Send him over to me. I'll give him three-six left and try to fit him in on the right. At least I'll get him out of your hair, B.G."

"Thanks, Bill, I owe you. Here he comes. D.L. 'Bye."

A few moments later, the pilot of the Universal Express Shorts 300 checked in: "Memphis Tower, Universal Express-107, with you descending to two thousand, crossing Arkabutla, requesting vectors ILS three-six right.''

"Express-107, radar contact,'' Bill Gayze responded, double-checking the radarscope. "Turn left heading zero-four-zero, descend and maintain two thousand, slow to one-six-zero, vectors for the GPS three-six left approach course, repeat, left. I'll work on a sidestep to the ILS three-six right.''

"Express-107, roger, zero-four-zero on the heading, leaving six for two.''

The pilot sounded dejected, maybe even pissed off, but he brought it upon himself. Gayze didn't recognize the voice, but the pilot must be a new guy and the old head flying with him must not be paying attention. Most Universal Express flights didn't jam themselves into the normal inbound traffic flow, but overflew or circumnavigated the Memphis Class B airspace direct to Holly Springs VOR or the Loosahatchie NDB, then got their radar vectors to runway two-seven. Even with a stiff crosswind, most Universal pilots took runway two-seven because it cut down on taxi time, and those guys at Universal had to account for every gallon of jet fuel.

Things were going along smoothly for the next few minutes, but a bottleneck was beginning to develop—no surprise who was causing it. The pilot of Universal 107 was still flying over two hundred nautical miles per hour groundspeed and was starting to overtake the slower traffic in front of him. "Express-107, I need you at your final approach speed,'' Gayze radioed. Airspeed glitches like that would create a ripple effect for the next three hours, Gayze thought sourly. Express-107 would slow to one-twenty, which meant that planes behind him would be overtaking him, so Gayze would have to slow everybody down to avoid a "deal,'' or a busted separation. This kid had probably just ruined what could have been a pretty good night, and Gayze punctuated his instructions with a curt *"Acknowledge"* to accent his displeasure.

"107 correcting, slowing to one-two-zero knots,'' the pilot replied.

This guy sure sounded overly green, Gayze thought, and he wasn't getting too much help from his captain. Maybe he better put a bug in Universal's ear about him. Gayze hit a telephone button marked UNIV DISP on his communications console, and a moment later he heard: "Universal Express, dispatcher, Kline.''

"Hey, Rudy—Bill Gayze up in Memphis Tower.''

"Hey, Bill how's it goin' tonight? What's up? Not with any of our birds, I hope."

"Minor problem, thought you might want to mention it to Mike." Mike Chaswick was the chief pilot at Universal Express. He and Gayze were friends and had visited each other's places of business many times on orientation tours. "One of your birds coming up on final approach now. No violations, but he's skating on thin ice."

"Sure, Bill . . . ah, which flight are we talking about?"

"One-oh-seven."

There was a very long pause, then: "107, you said?"

"Yeah," Gayze replied. "A Shorts 330, landing in about two minutes."

"Our flight 107 landed four hours ago," Kline said. "107 is a daily from Shreveport to Memphis, but it usually arrives at eleven P.M., not two A.M. Our last inbound is usually down around one-thirty—we start launching outbounds at three. What kind of plane you say it was? A Shorts?"

"Yep. Tail number November-564W."

"I don't recognize that tail number," Kline said. "We got three Shorts on the flight line, Bill, but we don't use them for the inbound dailies—they're for the short-haul last-minute outbounds. Used very little. I'm flipping through the schedule . . . nope, I don't see any Shorts on the schedule yesterday or today, but that don't mean too much because they come and go on short notice. He might be from the maintenance facility at DFW, but I sure as hell didn't know about him. I'll have to park him on the back forty—all my other gates are full."

This was getting weirder by the second, Gayze thought—and the weird feeling was quickly being replaced by a feeling of fear. "Stand by one." Gayze made a few radio calls for inbound flights, asked one of the other controllers a question, then turned back to the phone line: "We got another inbound Universal flight coming in on two-seven, flight 203 from Cincinnati, a 727."

"We have a daily 203 from Cincinnati, Bill, and it's a 727 usually, but he landed okay at eleven-fifteen. Yep, here's the crew's manifest on 107. Sure he's a Universal flight?"

"Yep, that's what he says," Gayze replied, frowning. "I didn't get a strip on my guy."

"You got a strip on the 727?"

"Stand by one." Sure enough, they did not. Well, he didn't have any more time to work on this screwup, and besides call-sign screwups were common and not that important. Both planes would be on the ground in a few minutes. "Listen, Rudy, I gotta run, but I'll call you back when I get a chance and we'll sort this out after he's on the deck. I'll have Security escort them in. Talk to you later." Well, whatever call sign he had didn't really matter, Gayze thought as he punched off the phone button and returned to the radios.

"Tower, -107, seven miles out, request sidestep for ILS three-six right."

"107, stand by." Gayze canted the strip holder for Universal Express 107, which would remind him that he had something to check on with him, then checked the arrivals counter, which held all the strips for arrivals and departures on the three runways. All counters were absolutely full. The traffic from the east was starting to pile up, so a sidestep maneuver—in which a pilot flies an instrument approach to one runway, then must be prepared to immediately transition to another instrument approach, usually on a parallel runway such as Memphis—was probably not going to be an option. "Unable at this time, -107. Continue on the GPS three-six left, you're number seven, report the outer marker. And give the tower a call on a landline after you land." So it would take the new guy ten extra minutes to taxi to his cargo gate—an extra fifty gallons of jet fuel, about a hundred bucks. Knowing the Scottish tightwad that owned Universal Express, he was probably going to make the poor pilot pay it back. "Break. United Express-231, right on intersection golf-golf without delay, ground point seven when clear." Gayze made a mental note to keep an eye on the Universal Express flight until they made it to their terminal—being new on the job, pissed off at the world, and with a not-so-dynamic captain, on a busy night, this had all the ingredients for trouble.

"You are going to be thirty seconds late, Roberts!" Cazaux shouted. Ken Roberts was one of Cazaux's best pilots, and had been with Cazaux almost as long as Taddele Korhonen had been, but he was much younger and far less experienced. He had been with Cazaux for about a year, and was one of his most capable and experienced pilots, but all he had done prior to this had been cargo missions, hauling drugs or weapons or troops to some dirt strip somewhere and back out. He had never done an aerial assault like this before. Further, Roberts was an American, one of the few Americans on Cazaux's payroll. There had never been any doubt about his loyalty or commitment to following orders—until now. "Push your power up and get back on force timing *now!*"

"But Captain, I was told by the tower to—"

"The tower is not in command of this flight, *I* am!" Cazaux snapped. The kid was a nervous wreck—Cazaux had to take the plane back. He slid back into the pilot's seat, strapped in, took the controls, and slid the throttles up to 85 percent power. "Get back there and stand by on the fucking release mechanism," Cazaux told Roberts. "And be prepared to release the payloads manually if the automatic system fails. Go!" The kid did as he was told, leaping out of his seat.

The terrorist switched radio channels to a discrete, scrambled UHF frequency, and keyed the mike: "Number Two, say status?"

"In the green and ready, lead," Gennady Mikheyev, one of Cazaux's newest and most promising pilots, responded. Mikheyev, a former Russian bomber pilot, was in absolute hog heaven at the controls of a Boeing 727-100, a very old but still reliable airliner, one of several aircraft leased from Valsan Partners, a Norwalk, Connecticut, company that specialized in re-engining and refurbishing Boeing 727s. "I wish I could feel more positive about this release system, Captain. It is giving us a lot of problems."

"I want results, not excuses, Mikheyev!" Cazaux shouted on the scrambled radio channel. "You wanted this mission—you begged me to let you fly the 727 on the primary strike—and your partners were paid to devise a release system."

Mikheyev and several of his fellow Russian aviators devised a complex but clever system to drop their explosives on the primary target—Universal Express's huge package-handling facility at Memphis International. The release system was similar to the one designed by Cazaux for the Shorts 300, but ten tall, skinny CO8 cargo containers, each carrying fifteen hundred pounds of explosives, would be rolled out of the rear airstair door of the 727.

But preceding the main explosives string, six Mk 80 five-hundred-pound bombs would be automatically dropped out of the baggage compartments on the starboard side of the 727—these would hit and explode a few seconds before the main explosive charges, ripping off most of the thirty-acre roof of the Universal Express terminal and creating a nice hole for the main explosives containers to pass through.

Over twelve thousand pounds of explosives would explode inside the building, ensuring maximum destruction.

The system used a handheld computer and GPS navigation unit to roughly compute ballistics for the drop. Mikheyev had guaranteed fifty-foot accuracy on the string of containers from any altitude and at any airspeed, even though the term "ballistics" that he had used with Cazaux for selling his plan was a real stretch because no actual computations had been done on the ballistic flight path of the cargo containers. Mikheyev had been paid handsomely for the ambitious plan, and now, just minutes from his drop, he was trying to back away from his promise. "I will accept *no* excuses for failure," Cazaux warned.

"Captain, the target is too small," Mikheyev complained. The intended target was not the super hub, or aircraft parking and package-handling facility—that was mostly open ramp space, conveyor belts, and packages being sorted for delivery, all easily replaceable in relatively short time. The intended target was the westernmost part of the super hub that housed Universal Express's complex of communications and package-delivery control computers, as well as its main corporate headquarters. The computers cost a whopping three billion dollars to install and modernize over the years—replacing them would cost two to three times that much. Of the entire thirty-acre complex, the target area was about fifteen thousand square feet. With an airliner flying at four hundred feet per second, using a sophisticated but untested release system, there was very little room for error. "I will do my best, but I cannot guarantee—"

"You will ensure that your drop is *precisely* on target," Cazaux shouted on the radio, the anger in his voice barely attenuated by the crackle and warbling of the frequency-hopping system, "or I will personally hunt you and your family down. I know where your family resides in Belize, and I know about your eighteen-year-old mistress. I know the license plate number of the Land-Rover your wife drives. I know which Catholic school your twin daughters go to, and I know that your lovely daughters have just become women . . ." Cazaux let up on the mike button, and sure enough, Mikheyev was letting loose a stream of epithets in Russian.

"If you fail, I will drag your wife, your mistress, and your daughters before you, have my soldiers sodomize them, then strip their skin off, one by one. You will watch them all die, slowly and painfully."

"You bastard!" Mikheyev shouted. He said something unintelligible in Russian, but it was obvious that the force of his anger was subsiding. He knew full well that Cazaux would carry out his threat.

"You are a professional soldier," Cazaux added in a softer tone after Mikheyev had ceased his protests. "You know the price of failure—death, to you and your family. That is the law of the mercenary. My laws were well known to you before you signed up and before you took your very generous payment for this mission. Failure is not allowed.

"On the other hand, if you succeed, I will see to it that your family is paid the full amount of what is owed to you. They will be made comfortable for the rest of their lives. I give you my word as a soldier, and I have never broken faith with a comrade-in-arms. Failure will be severely punished. Success will be rewarded—even if you do not survive."

Cazaux was not going to say anything else to Mikheyev, but the Russian pilot did not reply anyway. He had his choice—perfect accomplishment of his mission, or the undignified, horrible death of every woman close to him, then himself.

Of course, there was only one way Mikheyev could ensure that the target was totally destroyed . . .

At exactly four miles out, the call came in: "Express-107, outer marker."

Aha, Gayze thought, *a new voice!* Definitely older, definitely more professional sounding, with a trace of a foreign accent. The Captain was finally awake . . . "107, roger, traffic ahead is a MetroLiner one mile descending, you're number five."

"107, contact on the Metro, cancel IFR."

This flight was finally starting to sound like they really had a professional pilot at the controls, Gayze thought with relief. Canceling IFR erased the cylinder of protected airspace around his aircraft and really helped to expedite traffic flow, especially since Universal-107 was the one responsible for gumming it up in the first place by keeping his speed up so high. Gayze could now tighten the spacing up on the arrivals and clear out the airspace that much faster. He didn't know for sure if the Universal pilot could really see the much smaller Fairchild Metro commuter airliner, but he was committed to following it now: "Roger, 107, maintain visual contact with the Metro, squawk 1200, you're number four now behind the MetroLiner, cleared to land."

"Universal-107 cleared to land on the left," the Universal pilot responded. *Couple more minutes,* Gayze thought, and this flight would be out of his hair for the night, or at least until it was time for him to turn and depart. Maybe he would be off on break by then.

"Memphis Tower, American-501, with you level seven."

"American-501, good evening, winds three-zero-zero at three, you're number six, report established on GPS inbound course."

"501, wilco."

Things were busy, but not too bad. To an air traffic controller, spacing was the name of the game. After ten years, Gayze could look at the lights in the sky and accurately determine a plane's altitude, speed, and spacing—radar was the best way, but a quick glance at the landing lights usually told him what he needed to know the fastest—

And now there was a glitch developing and, no surprise, it was from the Universal Express newcomer. There was a noticeable gap in the sequence of landing lights—the Universal Express plane had no lights on, which meant its landing gear was probably not down. "Express-107, check wheels down, wind calm." No response. "Universal Express-107, Memphis Tower, check wheels down and verify, over." Gayze didn't wait for an answer this time, but said to the tower supervisor in a loud voice, "John, number four for landing three-six left has no lights—and I get no response."

Simultaneously, someone else shouted out, "John, I got a NORDO and possible no gear down on two-mile final on two-seven. I think he's going missed approach." This was incredible—two radio-out planes landing at once with no radios and no landing lights! The chances of that happening were astronomically high—and so was the potential for disaster.

"Bill, what's your NORDO's altitude?" the supervisor shouted.

Gayze checked the BRITE scope: "Five hundred and level—he might be going missed too."

"Is he turning?"

"No."

"Damn it. Conflict alert procedures!" the supervisor shouted. "Abort all departures! Clear the runways, get on the lights, give those pilots some safe options."

The tower supervisor calmly stepped over to his communications console while watching his radarscope. The phone and radio buttons on his console were arranged precisely in conflict alert procedures order, which connected with Memphis International's two fire departments, the airport security office, the Memphis fire department, and with dispatchers for Universal Express and all of the major airlines on the field. One by one, he hit the buttons without looking at them and calmly started talking: "Victor, Gayze at Memphis Tower, conflict alert procedures, runways three-six left and two-seven, two NORDO aircraft, three inbounds going missed, one takeoff abort . . . Atlanta Center, Memphis Tower, conflict alert procedures, stand by . . . Memphis Crash Network, Memphis Crash Network, this is Memphis International Control Tower, we have an aircraft collision conflict alert, two no-radio airliners, possible landing-gear malfunction on both, on runways three-six left and two-seven, estimated six souls on board, all stations stand by." By the time he finished all those calls, the pilots flying the affected planes should have gotten to the "What was that? What the hell did he say?" stage, and the supervisor went through all the buttons once again and repeated his instructions and notifications.

"Two miles out," someone called out. With a phone in one ear and the radio earpiece in the other, Gayze scanned the BRITE scope. Both no-radio airplanes had accelerated and climbed slightly, both at about five hundred feet above ground. On the radio, Gayze said, "Express-107, are you able to execute the published missed approach? Ident if you are executing the missed approach." No response, either on the radio or on the radarscope.

"Three-six left's clear!" someone in the tower shouted.

Thank God, Gayze thought. On the radio, he called, "Express-107, you are clear to land, runway three-six left, winds calm, eight thousand three hundred feet available, rescue equipment has been alerted. Ident if you can hear me, over." Still no response.

"107's deviating right," the tower supervisor shouted. "The other inbound is deviating right. Neither one of them is executing the proper missed approach, but at least they're not on a collision course. Still at about five hundred feet . . . Jesus, the other Universal flight is accelerating past two-forty." There was a speed limit of 240 miles per hour inside Class B airspace—the aircraft that was trying to land on runway two-seven was about to blow past that. "What in hell is going on? They look like they're doing the exact same thing—they're both accelerating, both flying at five hundred feet, both screaming towards the runway—"

"Like a friggin' air show," someone else remarked.

"Think they got stuck flight controls?" another controller wondered aloud. "Or are they trying to rendezvous? Maybe they're military."

"I hope this isn't some kind of joke," the tower supervisor said. "I'm gonna kick some asses up in Universal if this is some kind of company stunt."

Gayze was still talking on the radios, trying to coach a few of the inbound flights on the proper go-around procedures and coordinating with Memphis Approach for handing off all these airplanes into *their* lap again. Suddenly he paused, and he looked at the spot of dark sky where Universal flight 107 was, as if he could see directly into the cockpit at the pilot. That voice, the pilot's voice—not the young kid, but the newcomer, the older, more experienced voice . . .

It was foreign, slightly French, although the pilot tried hard to conceal it under a phony southern accent. Phony accent, phony call sign, now radio-out and coming in hot . . . "Jesus, I think this is an attack!" Gayze shouted. *"I think we're under attack!"*

"What? What did you say, Bill?"

"Damn it, we gotta warn—" But he stopped, confused. Who could they warn? There was nobody to notify. "I think we should wave off Universal-107 and the other inbound Universal flight until we straighten this out."

"That's not the proper procedure," the tower supervisor said. "The best place for a NORDO plane is on the ground."

"They're not NORDO, they're *attacking,*" Gayze shouted.

"Now hold on, Bill . . ."

The Shorts Sherpa was a military utility and cargo plane, and had been fitted with a simple drop system for paratroop and small-cargo parachute drops. A long boom mounted below the pilot mast on the nose of the aircraft had three arrows on it, calibrated for drops between eight hundred and two thousand feet and two hundred knots airspeed.

One minute before drop time, Cazaux ordered Roberts to open the cargo doors and extend the ramp. When the first arrow passed across the intended drop target, Cazaux issued the get-ready signal, pushed the throttles up to full power, and hit the first green release button.

Ken Roberts watched as a small cannon shot the pilot parachute out the open cargo ramp into the slipstream, and it instantly inflated behind the airplane, putting tension on the release system. When the target—the large main terminal building at the junction of the two angled concourses—passed under the second arrow on the pilot boom, Cazaux hit a red, guarded button. The packing doors on the main parachute case popped open, the pilot parachute pulled the main parachute out of its case, and the latches holding the cargo containers released. As soon as the main parachute was fully inflated, it pulled the cargo containers out of the Shorts' cargo bay with a tremendous thundering sound, like a freight train whizzing by at full speed.

The chains connecting the cargo containers immediately began to break from the immense strain of the slipstream as soon as the wheels of the container ahead of it left the ramp, so the explosives did not drop together. There was nothing clean or aerodynamic about the containers—they cartwheeled, Frisbeed, and spun all across the sky during their fall to earth. The last two containers, with less inertia than the others, almost did not have enough energy to roll out of the cargo bay, but Cazaux lifted the Shorts' nose skyward, providing the last nudge necessary. The last two explosives containers weren't going to hit Cazaux's intended target—but it was still going to do the job.

The eighteen-story control tower at Memphis International was located just north of the main terminal complex, where it had a clear view of most of the gates at the main, cargo, and Universal Express terminals and full view of all runways and taxiways.

Half the tower crew was staring out the windows to the east, waiting to catch a glimpse of the first emergency aircraft; Gayze and the other half were watching out toward the south, staring out into the darkness for the second Universal Express plane and alternately answering questions and vectoring aircraft away from the field. Gayze had a junior controller shining a red signal light at approximately where the northbound Universal flight should be, telling the pilot not to land. Another controller was doing the same toward the east.

Still no radio contact.

The southern part of runway three-six left's hammerhead parking area was brilliantly lit with maintenance floodlights, and as soon as Universal Express-107 crossed just a few hundred yards east of that area, Gayze caught a glimpse of the plane and shouted, "I see 107! Jesus Christ, what is he doing?" The plane was low, but obviously too high to land unless he dumped power and the nose and made a dive for the runway. "I can see him easy—the pilot *must* be able to see the runway, but he's gonna miss three-six left by a hundred yards."

"He could be going for the right," the tower supervisor said. Gayze got on the radio and announced that 107 was not cleared to land on runway three-six right. The eastern parallel runway's approach end was a quarter mile farther north than three-six left, but the Universal pilot was still going to have to do some aerobatics to make it on that runway too. He looked as if he was going to overfly the main commercial terminal building—if he wasn't careful, he could hit some of the tall antennas on top of the building. From the tower, he looked as if he was going nearly three hundred knots—there was no way he'd make it to the runway now. His altitude was not much higher than the control tower.

Suddenly, Gayze saw—well, he wasn't sure what it was . . . "Trouble with Universal-107," he said aloud. "I see debris, something falling out of the plane . . . I think it's his landing gear . . . no, I see . . . a *parachute!* Damn it, someone's parachuting out of the plane!"

"Here he comes," someone in the tower cab shouted, pointing to the east. "Looks like he's going to land on two-seven. I see a landing gear—no, it's not a landing gear. Jesus, he's screaming in! Is he going around? What in *hell* is he doing?"

Gayze turned. The westbound airliner was descending rapidly, aiming for the end of the runway. He was still off a bit to the right of centerline on radar, but his wheels were down and he looked like he was on a fast but good approach. It definitely appeared as if a low-time pilot or perhaps a stricken pilot was flying the westbound flight.

The tower supervisor punched the crash button: "Memphis crash network, this is Memphis Tower, one Universal Express 727 aircraft landing hot on runway two-seven. His gear is down. Be advised, the northbound aircraft is—"

He was going to miss the runway. At less than a half-mile to touchdown, the 727 would not be able to turn fast enough at his present speed to make the runway unless he landed well past midfield. "Crash, be advised, the 727 landing on two-seven is well north of centerline and fast. He may be going into the Air National Guard parking ramp. If he tries to turn back to the runway, he'll mush in with his left wing . . . oh, shit . . . climb, damn you, climb . . . *climb* . . ."

And then the 727 hit the Universal Express package shipping center.

The entire northern part of the airfield illuminated brighter than daylight. The western half of the sprawling cargo complex disappeared in an enormous lake of fire. The fireball that was a 220,000-pound airliner plunged through the western half of the thirty-acre cargo complex, disappeared for a few seconds, bounced on the ground, blew out the northwest side of the building, and cartwheeled several times across the ground, shredding the western half of the building—Universal Express's executive offices, communications center, and computer complex—as it tumbled. The heat of the explosion, nearly a half-mile away, could be felt right through the slanted tower windows, and Gayze was thrown to the floor when the shock wave hit and shattered those windows, the blast-furnace heat rolling across the tower like a fiery tidal wave . . .

But it was not the north windows that blew out—it was the southern windows, behind Gayze. He leaped to his feet as soon as he could shake the shock and noise from his head. A few controllers were rushing for the exit door, but Gayze just stood there, bathing himself in the heat and the noise and the light coming from an explosion—not on the Universal Express cargo facility, but on the main terminal.

Gayze was reaching for the crash phone button again, but the tower supervisor pulled his hand away—the tower was dead. "Get out of here, Bill."

"What the hell happened? Did 107 hit the terminal?"

"The tower's been damaged, Bill. Get going."

But Gayze couldn't make his feet move. As horrible as the spectacular crash on the Universal Express facility was, what had happened behind him on the main terminal was even more shocking. The main terminal building, right at the intersection between the east and west concourses, was on fire, severed and flattened in a fiery crater. Two airliners were on fire, and two more were spun sideways from the force of the blast. Gayze could see inside one L-1011 airliner, and the flickering lights in its windows told him that passengers were rushing toward the exits inside. The fire was still several yards away when Gayze saw doors pop open and emergency escape slides deploy on the side of the plane opposite the fire. A few doors opened on the side of the fire, but no passengers used that exit, thank God. The evacuation seemed rapid and orderly . . .

. . . but it wasn't fast enough, because suddenly the L-1011's left wing caught fire, then exploded, ripping the fuselage of the big airliner in half. Passengers and baggage spilled from the ruptured halves of the airliner onto the fiery tarmac. Gayze ducked when the force of the explosion hit him up in the open tower cab.

"Bill!" someone shouted. "Get out! Let's go!"

But Gayze looked through the clouds of smoke and fire at the terminal. It was not just the main terminal that had been hit—now he could see huge fires breaking out on the north side of the terminal, the northwest corner of the parking garage, and the south side of the Sheraton Hotel, just a few hundred yards west of the control tower. He could hear the roar of the fire, smell the burning kerosene—it was like looking at a firestorm.

"Bill! Damn it, let's go!"

Smoke was rapidly filling the control tower, and Gayze was forced to drop on his knees and crawl to the stairs toward the exit. His eyes were filled with tears, and not all of it was from the smoke.

"Oh . . . my . . . God . . ." Roberts muttered in stunned disbelief as the series of explosions and fires rippled across Memphis International Airport below him. But the sight of the burning terminal and hotel was nothing compared to the horrifying sight of the sea of fire that was once the Universal Express super hub. It looked like a nuclear bomb had simply flattened and vaporized the entire northern half of the airport. The flames still shooting from the impact site seemed to tower far above the Shorts' altitude, and the ripples of fire made it seem like the bottom of a volcano's lava pit.

"I said, close the cargo doors, Roberts," Cazaux ordered over the intercom. Roberts still was too stunned to make his feet or hands move. All that death, all that destruction—and he had witnessed it all, been in on the planning of all of it. It was a terrorist attack on his own people, his own countrymen. It was an attack incomprehensible to the young American, more devastating than anything he had ever heard of since the World Trade Center bombing. They were turning westbound, so he could no longer see the fires at the Sheraton or the main terminal—those attacks *were* by his own hand . . .

"I know it is painful, Kenneth," a voice said. It was Henri Cazaux, standing beside him—obviously the plane was on autopilot. "The destruction, it is horrible, no?"

"God, yes," Roberts said in a low voice. "All those people down there, all that death."

"It is time you joined them," Cazaux said quietly, just before he grasped Roberts by the forehead from behind, drove his infantry knife up through the base of Roberts' skull into his brain, and wiggled the knife point around inside his skull several times to scramble his brain matter. There was virtually no blood—Roberts' heart had stopped beating instantly, as if shut off with a switch. Cazaux merely picked him up by the blade of his knife, still embedded deep in his skull, took him to the edge of the open cargo ramp, and dropped him over the side.

The autopilot was weaving the Shorts around the sky unsteadily, and there was a little turbulence from the heat radiating off the hills of western Tennessee and northern Mississippi, but Cazaux did not seem to notice it. He stood on the edge of the Shorts' cargo ramp, the toes of one foot actually over the edge itself, with no safety line or parachute, looking at the incredibly bright glow of Memphis International Airport on fire.

He dared God, dared the Devil, dared any man or being to take him. It was easy—just a slight buffet, a sudden ripple of air, a short interruption of thousands of circuits running through the Shorts' autopilot system—and he would be thrown into space, just as dead as Ken Roberts.

No, it was not his time to die, not yet. Jo Ann Vega was right: the dark master had given him the gift of invincibility.

He wanted the death to continue . . .

Beale Air Force Base, Yuba City, California
Several Minutes Later

Despite being a retired two-star Coast Guard admiral, Ian Hardcastle preferred the Non-Commissioned Officers lounge on Beale Air Force Base; he and his small staff had virtually taken over the billiard room again with an impromptu drinks-and-dinner meeting.

Colonel Al Vincenti, who, with the help and support of Hardcastle, Martindale, and the Senate subcommittee, had been cleared of all charges (but had not yet been returned to flight status), was haphazardly banging billiard balls around on the well-worn felt with Hardcastle.

Hardcastle's chief of staff, retired Air Force colonel, military analyst, and political consultant Marc Sheehan, his fourth cup of coffee of the night in one hand, was reading from a sheaf of notes: "Admiral, I think we're ready to make this presentation to the Project 2000

Task Force executive committee,'' he said. ''I think this is a masterful piece of work.''

''I'd rather take a bit of time to get more data,'' Hardcastle said, missing a complicated two-rail bank shot. Vincenti cast a questioning eye at Hardcastle's showy but hopeless shot and easily sunk his own. ''There's a lot of stuff this report is missing. And I wish I had more time with Martindale. He's spent more time at fund-raisers and tours than on the business at hand here.''

''Can I speak frankly, sir?'' Sheehan asked.

''That's why I hired you, Marc. Out with it.''

''Sir, in my opinion, you suffer from the H. Ross Perot syndrome,'' Sheehan said. ''Everybody loves Perot. He's a straight shooter, he's knowledgeable—or at least he's got a great staff—he's articulate and polished, and he's not afraid to take on the big boys on their own turf. He also gets no respect, for those very same reasons. He hits people between the eyes with clear-minded logic built on years of experience—''

''And people don't like it.''

''And people don't like it,'' Sheehan echoed. ''And government doesn't like it either. Folks tend to shut you off simply because you come on strong—they think you have a hidden agenda, a secret plan. Right or wrong doesn't matter.''

''Marc, I can't accept that,'' Hardcastle said, lining up another shot after Vincenti intentionally missed an easy shot just so he wouldn't clear the table on Hardcastle again. It seemed Vincenti was scowling at everyone—at Hardcastle, at Sheehan, at the world. He had not said ten words all evening unless asked a specific question, and nothing that anyone had said all evening seemed to please him. ''What I'm writing about here is not fiction—it's real,'' Hardcastle went on. ''My goals and methods are real and workable.''

''Sir, what you're describing is America under siege, America on the defensive,'' Sheehan said. ''Nobody likes to hear that we're so vulnerable. They would rather believe that you're a flake rather than we're facing a major terrorist crisis in this country.''

Hardcastle flubbed another shot by trying a long, difficult shot, scratching in the process. Vincenti put Hardcastle out of his billiards misery by clearing the table again. Hardcastle didn't seem to notice, but asked Vincenti, ''Set 'em up again, Al, double or nothing.''

''I can swim in the beer you owe me already, Admiral,'' Vincenti pointed out.

''You don't drink, remember? You thought betting double-or-nothing beers with you was a sucker bet? I'll never pay off. Set 'em up,'' Hardcastle repeated with a smile. ''Marc, I'm ready to go to the Task Force in the morning.''

''The press conference is set for next week,'' Sheehan reminded him. ''Why not wait a few days, get some more feedback from the congressional leadership? Our little clambake in Virginia Beach is set for this weekend, and so far attendance looks good.''

''Clambake?'' Vincenti asked as he retrieved the billiard balls.

''Good way to feel out the heavy hitters in Congress,'' Hardcastle explained. ''Project 2000 is throwing a party out on Virginia Beach for the leadership and their families—private transportation, plenty of chow and booze, private beach, even parasailing and Jet Skis. We gotta lure the big cheeses to at least listen to what we have to say. Even thirty minutes with them, talking about our programs, would be worth the money.''

''Yeah. Right. Makes sense,'' Vincenti muttered. He finished racking the balls, then put his cue stick on the table. ''Sir, excuse me, but I've got to get going,'' Vincenti said. Hardcastle looked up at him, a hint of a smile on his face. ''If you don't need me anymore, I'll be hitting the road.''

''You got something to say, Al, say it,'' Hardcastle said. ''Spill it.''

''Sir?''

''You've been scowling and shaking your head at me and Marc all night, Vincenti, but you haven't said a word,'' Hardcastle said. ''You got some baggage to unload, so do it.''

''I don't have anything to contribute here.''

''Bullshit. I've got you here for a reason,'' Hardcastle said. ''You read the report.''

''I gave you my comments, sir.''

''Nice, polite, Air Command and Staff College point paper,'' Hardcastle said. ''Standard responses. Pretty disappointing.''

''I guess I'm just not politically savvy, Admiral.''

''I don't need your political savvy, Al,'' Hardcastle said. ''Task Force 2000 and Colonel Sheehan handle that for me.''

''So what do you need, sir?''

''I need you to tell me if I'm right, if I'm close, or if I'm full of shit, Al.''

''I've already commented on your plan.''

''So I'm right, then,'' Hardcastle said. Vincenti was about to speak, but remained silent. ''So I'm not right,'' Hardcastle concluded. ''So which is it, Al? Am I close or full of shit?'' Vincenti stared at Hardcastle, obviously trying to decide what the politically correct answer to *that* question was. "Goddammit, Vincenti, I was told you weren't one for holding back, that you spoke your mind. So let's have it."

"Sir, I'm not really qualified to tell you how to run this."

"It's about Linda, isn't it, Al?"

Vincenti's frown deepened, and darkened. "What are you talking about, Admiral?"

"Linda McKenzie. She's dead, and you think it's your fault."

The rest of Hardcastle's staff had stopped talking and had turned to watch this exchange. *"Sir,"* Vincenti said, looking Hardcastle right in the eyes. "With all due respect, you don't know *shit.*"

"Linda was your wingman."

"Stop calling her by her first name like you knew her, Admiral. She's Major McKenzie to you."

"Whose fault was it that you launched with defective night-vision goggles?" Hardcastle asked. "Whose fault was it that Linda was allowed to close in on Cazaux without her checklist completed? Whose fault was it that she was allowed to approach too close to an armed and dangerous suspect?"

"I don't have to explain anything to you, Hardcastle."

"I don't think she should have even been on alert with you, Al," Hardcastle went on, taking a step towards Vincenti, who was now, Sheehan noticed with some alarm, within arm's reach. "I think you're a piss-poor flight leader, Al. How in hell could you let Linda fly with you after you'd been screwing her?"

A half-dozen bodies moved in unison at that last comment, like runners leaping off the starting block. Vincenti lunged for Hardcastle, Sheehan lunged for Vincenti, and the other staff members dropped notebooks and laptop computers and leaped to their feet in surprise. Vincenti got his hands on Hardcastle's shirt, but Sheehan looped his arms over Vincenti's from behind, and the two Air Force officers were evenly matched. Hardcastle simply smiled, allowing Vincenti to shake him and rage: "You pompous arrogant *asshole.*"

Sheehan dragged Vincenti away from Hardcastle and steered him against the pool table. He was angry at Vincenti for daring to raise a hand toward Hardcastle, but he was even more surprised and angry at Hardcastle for speaking that way to the Air Force pilot. "Knock it off!" Sheehan shouted. His anger turned on Hardcastle, as it should be: "Admiral, you were out of line."

"Yes, I was, and I apologize," Hardcastle said calmly to Vincenti. "But I'm also correct, aren't I, Al?" No response, only a glare. "Talk to me, Al. You're the key to everything I'm trying to do here. Talk to me, damn it."

"Why the hell should I trust you, Hardcastle?" Vincenti shouted. "What are you trying to do here? What's your game? Who gave you the right to poke your nose in any of this?"

"I'm here because I've got a big mouth, Al," Hardcastle said evenly. "I've got a colorful past, and people listen to me because I entertain them with my attitude and my showmanship. But I'm really here because I care."

"Bull*shit,*" Vincenti said. "You're here because you can get some press for yourself and this Project 2000 crap."

"Yeah, I've got some ideas that I want everybody to hear," Hardcastle admitted. "I get shut off and shut down because no one wants to hear my side—they'd rather hear the watered-down, everything-is-beautiful rap coming from the White House. Yeah, I want press for the Project 2000 Task Force because they believe in what I believe in and they have the financial resources I don't. But I've got an agenda, Vincenti, and that is a *strong national defense,* pure and simple. I'm here because this incident is just another example of government *inaction,* another consequence of a weakened military."

"I've heard your big plans already—on TV, in the papers, on the radio, at the speeches," Vincenti said. "But frankly it's all garbage, because you don't know what you're talking about. You made the same damned mistake with the Hammerheads, Hardcastle. But you were too wrapped up in how important you were, with deploying these big-assed air ops platforms, with putting up all these radar balloons, to understand the basic concepts. You had the authority to launch air defense units for your missions, Hardcastle, but did you ever ask an air defense puke how to set up a proper air sovereignty order of battle? You had your Coast Guard guys and your Customs Service guys out there, but did you ever bring an air defense guy on board as part of your staff? Hell no."

"I had Air Force representatives on my staff—"

"Sure—for AWACS and OTH-B, not for the guys who really knew the air sovereignty game, us pilots in the field," Vincenti said. "You sucked up almost the entire E-3 AWACS fleet on drug-interdiction stuff, and you took over all the long-range over-the-horizon backscatter radar ops, but you never employed the F-4s, F-106s, F-15s, and F-16 air defense fighters for your operations except when that crazy bastard Salazar used military hardware on your platforms. Plus you spent billions on all that fancy hardware, when all the time you had the best pilots and the best planes in the business already in place."

Marc Sheehan stepped forward toward Vincenti. "I think you've said enough, Colonel Vincenti."

"No, let him finish, Marc." Hardcastle smiled. "I want to hear this. Go ahead, Al. Continue. You don't like it. Tell me why."

"Because you're doing it half-assed, that's why," Vincenti said. "You did it half-assed wrong with the Hammerheads, and you're doing it half-assed now. You're still thinking two-dimensionally, still thinking in razzle-dazzle terms instead of strategic, layered, logical, multilayered structures. You had fancy, expensive tilt-rotors and drones and a few helicopters and boats, and almost nothing else. When your aviation units got into trouble, when the politicians believed your air units couldn't do the job, your whole infrastructure was weakened and your organization collapsed. Hell, your air units were properly doing their job, and one lousy lawsuit, one lousy smuggler, in which just one of your air units was involved in, brought down your entire Border Security Force in no time flat. Why? Because your basic organization was built on one foundation—your air units.

"The same thing will happen with your current plan," Vincenti went on. "Your current plans are based on air units like the F-16 and F-15 fighters. But an expert can easily blow holes in this plan, and I think Cazaux is smart enough to get by even the toughest air patrols. You wouldn't even survive a comparison between now and your disbanded Hammerheads." Vincenti glared at Sheehan, then at Hardcastle. "I thought you guys were supposed to be smart. You're advising future presidents, formulating policy and laws, spending hundreds of millions of dollars, and you can't even see how fucked up you are."

"Then help me fix it," Hardcastle said. "Help me create a system to stop terrorists like Cazaux."

"You don't have the guts," Vincenti said. "All I see is a bunch of bureaucrats jockeying for position. You throw your beach parties and press conferences and fund-raisers, but when it comes time to actually put the hardware on the line, you back off. I'm not going to waste my breath on a bunch of politicos whose only goal is to rack up percentage points in the polls or electoral votes."

Sheehan, who had stepped away for a few minutes, came back

and said, "Sir, we got a call from Vice President Martindale. He's on his way back from San Francisco now. Cazaux hit another airport. Memphis International. Just a few minutes ago. They're saying the death toll could be in the thousands this time."

"Oh, my God . . ." gasped Hardcastle.

"He got a call from the President, Admiral," Sheehan went on. "He wants you and your staff to report to the White House immediately. They want a complete briefing on your plans to set up an air defense network in the United States."

"Jesus . . . Marc, phone the flight crew, get the Gulfstream ready to go, drop me off at base ops, and get the investigation team together right away," Hardcastle said. He turned to Vincenti: "Al, you're with me."

"I'm not cleared to leave the base, Admiral."

"I just cleared you," Hardcastle said. "You're a member of my staff, effective yesterday, and the President has just ordered you to Washington. We've got about five hours for you to tell me precisely what I need to do to make my air defense plan airtight. Let's go."

PART 3

The White House Cabinet Room
The Next Morning

"I've got only one thing to say to you, Admiral Hardcastle," Deputy Attorney General Elizabeth Lowe said angrily, dramatically waving a bound report in her hand, then tossing it on the Cabinet Room table in disgust just as the door leading to the Oval Office opened and everyone got to their feet. "You must be totally insane, or at the very least so ill-informed as to defy reason and logic." She saw the President of the United States stride in, then said to him, "Mr. President, I can't believe you even allowed that crackpot in this room at a time like this."

"Allow me to respond to the Deputy Attorney General's statement, Mr. President—on the record," Ian Hardcastle said, a slight, challenging smile on his face.

"This meeting *will* come to order," the President's chief of staff said. Lowe quietly took her seat with the others after the President was seated, glaring angrily at Ian Hardcastle. What he did not know was that Elizabeth Lowe, one of the President's most capable political insiders, had met personally with the President just before the meeting and had already been instructed as to how this meeting was going to proceed—her tirade against Hardcastle was part of a hastily but carefully rehearsed trap for Hardcastle and his cohorts.

The members of the Executive Committee on Terrorism, the group responsible to the National Security Council and the President for all antiterrorist matters, had assembled in the White House Cabinet Room to receive the latest briefing on the hunt for Henri

Cazaux. The ECT was composed of senior officials from the Departments of Treasury, Justice, State, Defense, Transportation, and Energy, along with representatives from the Central Intelligence Agency and the National Security Council staff. Because the President had convened this meeting at the White House, most of the Cabinet itself was present along with their ECT representatives, so it was a tight fit in the Cabinet Room.

This was just the latest crisis in what seemed like an Administration plagued by problems from the very beginning, starting with a furor over the President's attempt to drop the ban on gays in the military, to his health care package, to problems within his own White House.

His wife, for instance, known around town as the Steel Magnolia, was conspicuously absent from this and other meetings as of late. A formidable woman who was highly intelligent and, for a while, almost inseparable from her husband, the Steel Magnolia had recently been devoting all her time to extricating herself from a shady real-estate deal that was now threatening to turn into a Watergate-sized problem for the Administration. Things weren't helped when her own counsel killed himself.

But even now, in the midst of a major domestic crisis, the President hardly had time to worry about his wife. There were far bigger problems at hand for this poor boy from what many had laughingly called a hillbilly southern state. This current crisis might be the final straw for his Administration. Depending, of course, on how he handled it.

Joining the President, the ECT members, and Hardcastle were Colonel Al Vincenti; Colonel Marc Sheehan, Hardcastle's aide; and Deborah Harley, who was cleared to come to this meeting as an assistant to Hardcastle but who was in reality an executive assistant to Kevin Martindale—the former Vice President was not invited to attend this meeting, but he made sure he had his spy in place. If the President or his staff knew about Harley, they did not seem to care.

Vincenti's face looked grim as Lani Wilkes, the director of the Federal Bureau of Investigation, began the briefing with a rundown of the attack on Memphis International Airport last evening. He could all-too-easily envision the two airliners barreling in toward the airport, then raining devastation on hundreds of innocent people below. Thankfully, the death toll was not as high as in San Francisco—over two hundred dead and over five hundred injured, mostly at the Universal Express super hub facility—but Vincenti felt responsible for each and every one of their deaths. When he looked up, he saw a few of the ECT members looking back at him, and he felt that they were silently accusing him of not stopping Cazaux when he had the chance.

Hardcastle looked at the oval cherry table, his hands folded in front of him, with a stony, neutral expression; Sheehan was watching the southern President (who was popping M&Ms into his mouth from a jar on the table) and Hardcastle, waiting for the sparks to fly.

"We're assisting the local authorities in hunting down the aircraft," Judge Lani Wilkes was saying, "but the attack on the airport knocked out all the radar control centers in the entire region—both Approach and Center radar control centers are located at Memphis International—and we couldn't track any of the aircraft.

"Our best lead right now circles on aircraft dealers in the south and southeast, particularly ones handling civil and military-surplus cargo aircraft. But there are two hundred and thirty such dealers and brokers in the region; plus, getting a plane from Central or South America flown into the southern U.S. is too easy. Getting warrants to search each establishment will take time. We—"

Hardcastle let out an exasperated sigh at the mention of warrants. A few eyes darted in his direction, but Hardcastle did not speak and no one else said a word. Wilkes, pretending she did not notice, continued, "Sir, I've said this before: we can't let our concern over Cazaux's attacks force us to degenerate into simply lashing out at every hint of criminal or suspected terrorist activities—it's stretching my manpower too thin, and it's creating more panic. We've got every available federal agent involved in this manhunt. I've got agents in Mexico and Canada. I've diverted extra agents to four different locations following up investigations on suspicious explosions, and each one has come up with nothing. The Bureau has investigated over one hundred bombings in the United States just last month, and none of them were tied in to Cazaux."

"But now Cazaux's finally gone over the edge, and I believe we've got to investigate each incident," said Transportation Secretary Ralph Mersky. He turned to the President and said, "Mr. President, under the Federal Aviation Regulations, I've had the FAA close Tucson International Airport because a suspected terrorist incident is under investigation—we think Cazaux was flying on a commercial airliner, and he was afraid of getting caught and killed some airline service workers to make his escape. By the law, I should close every other major airport near any of these other suspected terrorist incidents as well—whether or not Judge Wilkes believes they have anything to do with Cazaux. But I've had meetings with every major air carrier in the country, and to a man they've pleaded with me not to shut down the airports."

"What in hell would you expect them to say?" Deputy Attorney General Lowe interjected. Under the National Security Act of 1949, the Deputy Attorney General of the United States was the most senior manager of any domestic terrorism crisis. Elizabeth Lowe was a hard-nosed Army veteran, attorney, and Washington lobbyist—perfectly suited for the job of dealing with the exclusive men's domains of defense and antiterrorist strategy and response. "They need to keep making money, and they're willing to bet other people's lives on the long odds that Cazaux will strike anywhere else but *their* location or *their* planes."

"I know that, Liz," Mersky shot back, "but I need the White House's direction on this one." To the President, he continued: "We've already enacted Level Three security, which deals primarily with terrorist threats such as bombs in baggage, sabotaging planes at the gate, car bombs near terminals, that sort of thing. The law says I must enact Level Two security measures at all airports that carry more than eighteen passengers per plane if terrorist activity is suspected in the vicinity or on a national level, Mr. President."

The President of the United States, sitting half-slouched at his big desk in the Cabinet Room, looked as if sleep and he were complete strangers. He was tall, young compared to recent Chief Executives, well-built and handsome, with prematurely gray hair that was thick and bushy. But the dark bags under his eyes from lack of sleep, and the wrinkles around the eyes caused by stress and squinting at reports and televisions without using his glasses, made him look considerably older. He wrapped his big hands around a coffee cup and took a sip—cold again. He let the cup rattle back onto its saucer, popped some more M&Ms into his mouth (his affection for junk food was legendary), then drawled, "Ralph, it doesn't sound like this Level Three protects anyone if Cazaux drops a damned bomb on their heads. Why hasn't stricter security been set up already?"

"Sir, the reason is that we have *no* procedures for dealing with air raids against major airports inside the United States except for closing them down," Mersky said. "We have Civil Defense procedures drawn up thirty years ago for use in case of Soviet air raids, and even then they mostly deal with evacuation, medical care, restricting access to navigation facilities—"

"So the only option we have right now is to close the airports until we track this Cazaux down?" the President asked incredulously. God, how he hated these meetings without his wife present. That fucking real-estate deal was consuming all of her time, time that she could have been spending helping him. Damn her. They should have never invested in that fucking land in the first place. Oh, well. They'd just have to live with it. And he, unfortunately, was having to live without her at a time when he needed her most—like now. "Hey, you don't need to be a rocket scientist to understand what a disaster that would be. Remember how disrupted everything was when American Airlines' flight attendants went on strike. Remember the panic? Jesus. I want to hear more options." He turned to Hardcastle, Vincenti, and his Secretary of Defense, Dr. Donald Scheer, and said, "Admiral Hardcastle, I asked you to come down here because I've heard of your"—he took a moment to consider his next words, then decided to just say it—"genius, concerning this disaster.

"I don't agree with it, and I frankly suspect that much of it stems from your political agenda with the Project 2000 Task Force and Vice President Martindale's campaign," he continued. "We don't need partisan politics interfering with this investigation. I think the little stunt you orchestrated in the Senate to step into the middle of the FBI's investigation of the San Francisco attack was a cheap, dirty trick to take advantage of the situation to promote your own agenda."

"Except Cazaux *did* strike again," Hardcastle pointed out bluntly.

The President spread his hands and nodded. "Yes, he did," he drawled. "I thought he'd be long gone, but he's not, and he's got to be dealt with. And you offered your technical assistance, which I deeply appreciate." He picked up Hardcastle's point paper on the air defense emergency and added angrily, "But showing this report to the press at the same time as handing it to me stinks. The American people see you on TV promoting this plan, and they cling to it because it's a 'do-something, do-anything' move. It makes me question your motivation here, Admiral: do you really want to help me solve this crisis or are you just pushing a political agenda?"

"I'm trying to stop Cazaux, Mr. President," Hardcastle said evenly. "It's that simple. With all due respect, sir, how *you* respond to this crisis affects your own political agenda more than how *I* respond."

"When I need your advice on politics, Admiral, I'll ask," the President snapped. "With all due respect, Admiral, dealing with you is worse than Cazaux—at least that maniac is not on TV every two hours. But let's get back to what we should do about Cazaux. Dr. Scheer's staff has outlined your suggestions for me, and although I consider your response dangerous, it could be the only one available to us."

"I believe it *is* your only response, Mr. President," Hardcastle said, "and I've encouraged your advisers to just come out and say so. FAA Level One security is the only set of procedures on the civilian side for dealing with this emergency, and it won't help stop or find Cazaux. Civil and strategic defense is virtually nonexistent in this country. The FAA's SCATANA procedures basically entail shutting down all but a few major airports and most navigation radio facilities, and we're still faced with finding and stopping Cazaux."

"So your solution is to turn security for this crisis over to the *military?*" Lani Wilkes asked incredulously. She motioned to Hardcastle's report. "You want to use the military *inside the United States* for law enforcement?"

"This is no longer a law enforcement question, Judge Wilkes, this is a *national defense* crisis."

"You're wrong, Hardcastle. This is a criminal investigation, and it should be handled like one. Mr. President, there is no doubt whatsoever that this is a serious crisis, but imposing martial law is not the answer."

"I *do not* want to impose martial law," the President said immediately, running his hand through his hair. "Let's make that real clear right from the get-go."

"Mr. President, I've read Admiral Hardcastle's proposed plan," Wilkes said, "and it's nothing but a reactionary, grandstanding power grab."

"I couldn't agree more," Deputy Attorney General Lowe said. "We don't need the military to secure the skies and hunt down Henri Cazaux. Mr. President, the Executive Committee on Terrorism is in charge and in control of this situation."

"Judge Wilkes, Liz, hold on a minute," the President said evenly. "I brought Hardcastle and the Colonel in here to get their thoughts." He turned to Hardcastle again. "I was briefed on your proposal, Admiral. It's pretty severe. Tell me why this isn't martial law."

"Mr. President, *critics* can label this plan whatever they like," Hardcastle responded. "My objective is simply to defend our major international airports from aerial attack."

"Mr. President, I think the FBI can handle this crisis without having to resort to this extreme military option," Lowe said, holding up her copy of the plan Hardcastle had proposed to the Secretary of Defense. "You're talking about surface-to-air missiles, fighters escorting commercial airliners, *free-fire zones* around major *cities* and *airports* . . . ?" She shook her head in disbelief. "Ludicrous. This is not some damned Dale Brown novel, this is real-life."

"It has to be set up and executed as if this was an overseas American military installation under attack by a foreign hostile military force," Hardcastle explained. "Sir, the plan presupposes that we want air traffic in this country to continue at the highest possible level of efficiency."

"That goes without saying, Admiral."

"Then, sir, it will be easier than taking candy from a baby for Henri Cazaux to attack any airport at will, unless we have a layered, iron-clad defense network around every major U.S. airport. It is absolutely essential that we act to screen air traffic moving in and out of our major airports in case Cazaux slips past our dragnets and tries to attack."

"I don't like the sound of this one bit," the President remarked, wishing like hell that it wasn't *his* Administration that had to deal with this shit. Why couldn't they have just elected his wife? Let her handle it, that's what he wanted. "But I invited you here because enough people think your plan might have merit during this emergency. What is it you propose, Admiral?"

"Sir, my plan has two major elements," Hardcastle explained. "First, we control and monitor the movement of every aircraft in the United States, using civilian and military radar systems. Second, we use airborne and ground-based air defense systems to track, identify, and, if necessary, engage any aircraft that is not properly identified or deviates from its proper course."

"This is the Hammerheads all over again," Lani Wilkes said with an expression of disgust, as if someone had passed gas. "Another assault on the Bill of Rights, eh, Admiral?"

"Until you catch Cazaux, there is no other way to keep air traffic in this country moving safely, Judge Wilkes."

"You make it sound so sterile, Admiral," Transportation Secretary Mersky interjected. "Putting every aircraft in the United States on an instrument flight plan? That'll overload our air traffic controllers. All others can't fly? That'll ground hundreds of thousands of planes. And your term 'engage' is a polite term for 'shoot down,' as in 'shoot down a commercial airliner' if it strays too far off course or turns the wrong way on a missed approach in bad weather."

"Admiral Hardcastle, I simply don't think this plan will work—or if it is implemented, it won't do any good and will cause more panic and confusion than it will help," the Vice President added stiffly. "Every plane flying into a major airport in the country has to be escorted by an *armed* fighter? This has got to be a violation of Constitutional rights."

"The only way to positively identify a suspect aircraft is to intercept it and check it visually, sir," Vincenti interjected. "And in many cases, the only way to divert a suspect away from a restricted area is by a fighter intercept. The ground-based air defense systems are a last resort only. Obviously, shooting at a terrorist plane only a few miles from a major airport will still cause massive destruction on the airport, although if it doesn't hit its intended target then the engagement was a success.

"The intercept must be as far from the intended target and as far from major population centers as possible. A Stinger missile has a range of perhaps one to two miles, and the cannon on an Avenger mobile air defense unit has an effective range of half that. But a terrorist hit by an Avenger cannon or a Stinger missile will more than likely still crash on the airport, although the damage and death it causes should be greatly reduced. Patriot has a maximum range of about sixty miles, the Hawk missile perhaps twenty—this is the minimum range a suspected terrorist should be allowed to approach."

"This is nuts . . ." someone muttered.

There were murmurs of concurrence around the room.

"The main means of identification, control, and engagement must be by armed fighter interceptors, which are vectored into the intercept by AWACS radar planes. Then, intercept the suspect as far from the target as possible—preferably hundreds of miles away," Vincenti went on. "All suspected terrorist aircraft must be kept away from major airports, and the best way to divert an airliner to another airport where it can be inspected is with an interceptor."

"This is insane!" Deputy Attorney General Lowe said. "Can you imagine an American Airlines flight with two hundred people on board looking out and seeing a fighter on its wing? Jesus, what if there's an *accident?* An accidental shoot-down will cause mass hysteria."

"General Lowe, I think we've already got mass confusion bordering on hysteria right now," Hardcastle said. "My flight from California to Washington was delayed for hours because someone's flight plan was lost and they wouldn't allow the aircraft into their airspace. I heard air traffic controllers panicking on the radio every time a plane strayed a couple miles off course—it didn't matter that the plane was a little corporate job hundred miles away from any major airport. Sir, we've got to take control of this situation or the public *will* panic."

"Mr. President, with all due respect to Colonel Vincenti, we should ask Admiral Hardcastle and his staff to pack up their Patriot missiles and F-16 fighter planes and go back to the TV talk shows," Lowe said bitterly. "We don't need his brand of frontier justice to keep control of this situation."

"I agree, Mr. President," FBI Director Lani Wilkes chimed in. "Sir, Cazaux is going to make a mistake. If that was his handiwork in Memphis, the net will only pull tighter."

"Okay, Liz," the President said, holding up his hands. "Tell me what you've got in mind for restoring confidence in air travelers?"

While Lowe spoke, Deborah Harley, Martindale's special assistant assigned to Hardcastle for this meeting, leaned forward in her seat behind Hardcastle and slipped him a note. He turned to her. Harley was in her late forties, a pretty blonde with bright green eyes and a thin but persistent smile. "What's this, Miss Harley?" he asked.

"An observation, Admiral," she whispered. Her smile seemed pleasant enough, but her eyes were hard and insistent.

Hardcastle frowned. He did not know Harley, but had seen her on numerous occasions with Martindale in a variety of functions—sometimes she acted as a secretary, a chauffeur, a bodyguard, or even as a wife. Martindale, divorced after being voted out of office in the last election, had a variety of beautiful women drifting in and out of his life—the tabloids kept constant tabs on Martindale's frequent flings—but only Deborah Harley returned. She was beautiful and mysterious and could even be considered alluring—perfect "tabloid bait"—but the tabloids never pursued her. Hardcastle had never spoken more than a few pleasantries to her. She was all business.

He had trouble reading her unfamiliar handwriting—the message looked like, "It's a SITREP." He was about to ask her what she meant when the President addressed him: "How does that sound to you, Admiral?"

"I'm sorry, sir," Hardcastle responded, folding the note and shoving it into a pocket, unread. "Say again?"

"Jesus, Admiral, we're having a meeting over *here,*" Lowe muttered irritably. "I suggested to the President that one way to monitor air traffic is to restrict all flights from and to towered fields on IFR flight plans only, where tower personnel can visually identify all departing aircraft and we can use the ATC computers to help monitor all traffic. In that way, we can keep a good portion of general aviation traffic moving, eliminate the pop-up radar targets, and we don't endanger civil air traffic with missiles and guns."

"If you'll notice, that's all part of my plan, General Lowe," Hardcastle said. "I think it's essential for authorities to know precisely what the origin of each and every flight is. As the system works now, a flight under visual flight rules can enter the air traffic control system anywhere. This is called a 'pop-up' flight plan, and we need to eliminate them. Cazaux can load up a cargo plane with explosives from some isolated desert base, take off, then simply call up ATC and get a flight plan to a major airport. He'll get first-class ATC service—right to his bomb-release point. By restricting flights from only towered airports, federal authorities can directly determine who's in the system. If a personal inspection is warranted, we have a chance to do it—"

"A visual inspection?" Lowe interjected. "You mean visually inspect *every* plane that looks suspicious? Hardcastle, do you have any idea how many planes that is?"

"On average, one plane over seventy-five thousand pounds gross weight takes off every five seconds from the thirty largest American airports," Hardcastle replied. "That's over seventeen thousand flights per day. But three-quarters of those are scheduled passenger flights, which leaves about four thousand flights per day that are cargo flights or flights of unknown purpose or cargo—business, private, small commercial, expedited freight, all that. That's about one hundred and thirty flights per day from each of the nation's thirty largest airports, or about five per hour. I believe those flights can be inspected. If we organize local, state, and federal authorities, including reserve law enforcement personnel and the military, we can inspect each and every flight.

"But I don't have any illusions that this system will be airtight," Hardcastle went on. "The Border Security Force had a tight, overlapping, redundant air surveillance network, and smugglers still found ways around it. Cazaux is clever as well as dangerous—I work under the assumption that he'll figure out a way to beat the system. But we must have a way to stop Cazaux before he gets over the airport terminal, and that means an integrated air defense network. We must have the ability to monitor, precisely track, and, if necessary, attack *any* hostile aircraft *anywhere* in the airspace system, primarily around the thirty-three major airports under Class B airspace in the United States."

"I'm strongly opposed to this idea, Mr. President," Lowe insisted. "I think it'll result in accidents and needless civilian deaths. It's like letting Dirty Harry loose on the airports."

"I'm afraid I'm opposed to the idea as well, Mr. President," Transportation Secretary Mersky interjected. "There will be problems integrating civil air traffic control functions with military requirements."

"But it *can* be done, Secretary Mersky," Hardcastle said. "I proved that with the Hammerheads. I've had plenty of success with this type of emergency, Mr. President. We can implement this program in just a few days. I think it's vital, sir."

The President fell silent, apparently thinking it over; then he turned to Hardcastle and said, "All right, Ian. I don't like the idea, but we gotta move on this thing." The President withdrew a card from his jacket pocket, glanced at it, then said, "Ladies and gentlemen, Deputy Attorney General Lowe, I'm going to announce to Congress that under 10 U.S.C. 332 and 333, I'm directing a military response to this crisis situation. Deputy Lowe, under the law I'm appointing a military representative as your deputy director of the Executive Committee on Terrorism. He'll interface with Justice and various branches of the military and coordinate an effective response. I want to emphasize that the military's involvement is limited to protection of major airports around the country, not in law enforcement matters."

The President then turned toward Hardcastle and continued, "It's time to put your money where your mouth is, Admiral, so I'll just come right out and say it: I want *you* to head the program, Admiral. You are going to be the military liaison to the Executive Committee on Terrorism."

Hardcastle could have fallen out of his chair in surprise. He gasped, "Excuse me, sir . . . ?"

"I've got no other choice," the President drawled simply, sounding a bit defeated. "Cazaux's out there. Judge Wilkes is closing in on him, but until she nails him, we've got to act decisively. My own Cabinet is divided on the subject. I need the best in the business to head this thing, and as much as I hate to admit it, you're the best candidate. What'd you say, Admiral? You want in?" Hardcastle glanced quickly at Scheer, Mersky, Lowe, and Wilkes: all but Wilkes stared straight ahead, emotionless. Only Wilkes seemed angry enough to spit bullets. "I need your answer, Ian. This can't wait any longer. I need you to get together with Dr. Scheer and get the hardware moving into place."

"Then I'm your man, Mr. President," Hardcastle said. "I'll start immediately."

"Good answer," the President said, relieved, hoping he could get the hell out of there. "I'll announce it at this afternoon's press conference. You'll be under Mike Lifter, title of Special Assistant to the President for National Security. However, I'd still like all of you to report to Deputy Attorney General Lowe on all antiterrorist stuff—let her talk to me about our responses. You'll get commensurate three-star pay, standard nondisclosure agreement, you know the drill. Happy to have you aboard, Admiral. I'll let you, Mike, and Don Scheer get at it. Good luck."

With that, Hardcastle had been dismissed. He rose, led his staff out with him, and was joined outside the Oval Office by National Security Advisor Michael Lifter and a military aide.

"We've set up a staff meeting at the Pentagon," Lifter said. He was a tall, thin, severe-looking man with small, dark, nervous eyes and a high forehead that made him look sinister and secretive. "Secretary Scheer will meet us there along with the Chairman. I'm sure they'll have a videoconference set up with General Lawson of A-COM." The Chairman, Hardcastle knew, was the popular (at least with the media, the military, and the public—less so with the President and the Cabinet) and powerful Chairman of the Joint Chiefs of Staff, Army General Philip T. Freeman. Army General Thomas Lawson was CINCACOM, Commander in Chief, U.S. Atlantic Command, the major military command charged with the defense of the "lower forty-eight" states. Hardcastle did not know Lawson; he would have chosen Air Force General Charles Skye instead—perfect name for an Air Force four-star general and former Thunderbirds demonstration-team solo pilot—who was commander of U.S. Space Command and automatically "triple-hatted" as commander of the U.S. Aerospace Defense Command and the joint U.S.-Canadian North American Air Defense Command. But it was the President's call. "We can take my car . . ."

"Sir, if you don't mind, we'll follow you over," Deborah Harley suddenly interjected.

Lifter looked a bit puzzled. He glanced at Harley, dismissed her with an impassive blink of his snakelike eyes, then back at Hardcastle: "I have some important matters to go over with *you,* Admiral."

"*We'll* meet *you* over there in the Chairman's office, Mr. Lifter," Harley said.

There was no ignoring her this time. Lifter nodded, swallowed, muttered a curt "Very well. One hour. The secretary has your toll passes and plates."

As they collected their government plates and toll plaza passes from the White House Operations secretary and exited the White House, Hardcastle said, "Miss Harley, what in the hell was that about? And what in blazes did that note say?"

"It said, Admiral, that you were being *set up,* and they executed it perfectly," Harley said. "You didn't see it coming?"

"See what coming?" Sheehan asked.

"How about you, Colonel Vincenti?" Harley asked. "What did you see?"

"I saw 'good cop, bad cop,' " Vincenti said. "Hate to say it, Admiral, but they played you like a fiddle."

"Did you really think it was a good idea to *head* this air defense task force, Admiral?" Harley asked. "May I ask why you agreed to do it?"

"Because I can help with this situation," Hardcastle replied. His mind's eye was furiously replaying the sequence of events in his head, and the more he recalled, the worse he realized he looked. "Damn it, I *can* help with this situation. I can directly implement my plan."

"Admiral, your plan has merit," Harley said, "but you're not part of this Administration. You won't be allowed to implement your program the way you want—you're an assistant to the National Security Advisor, and Lifter's only an adviser, not in the military chain of command. Furthermore, you won't be permitted to speak to the press or the public, including the Project 2000 Task Force. Under the terms of the White House Non-Disclosure Agreement, the Chief of Staff, through the director of White House communications, tells you to whom you can and cannot give statements. If you bust their guidelines—and I guarantee, if they want you to bust the rules, you *will*—they can throw you in prison. They've done it many times in the past. While you're stuffing some congressman's newsletters in minimum security, they'll roast your reputation so badly you'll be lucky to be allowed to lead a Cub Scout pack anywhere near Washington. Minority Leader Wescott, Senator Heyerdahl, even former

Vice President Martindale can't help you then. You've been very effectively squelched, Admiral Hardcastle, and you did it to yourself. Looks like you just canceled all your TV appearances for a while." Harley shrugged, giving him a cheerful but tired smile. "Don't feel bad, Admiral. The President is very good at flimflamming someone—so good, he does it to himself and his wife all the time."

Hardcastle was tight-lipped and scowling as he emerged from the White House, but just as their car was driven over to them at the entrance to the West Wing, he turned to Harley and said, "I may have been porked by the President, Miss Harley, but they still appointed me Special Assistant to the National Security Advisor. I want to test the boundaries of that office, and you're going to help me do it."

Deborah Harley's shoulders quivered and her eyes brightened in anticipation for a moment, but then her expression turned downcast. "I'm sorry, Admiral, but I've got a job—"

"I don't know exactly in what capacity you serve Kevin Martindale, Miss Harley, but one thing's for sure—I've got a toe in the White House right now. I think you would serve the Vice President and the Project 2000 Task Force better if you were with me instead of spying on Martindale's political enemies—isn't that what you do, Miss Harley?"

Harley blushed—something Hardcastle never thought he'd see her do. "I don't think it's relevant to discuss—"

"What's wrong, Miss Harley? Don't you think you can pass the White House security check?"

"Admiral, I don't think that'll be a problem," Harley said. "I know precisely what my White House security file says—I designed it. In fact, I've seen the White House's security report on *you*. I'll even *show* it to you later on."

Hardcastle nodded—he could tell by her confident half-smile and steady gaze that she was telling the truth. This woman was much more than a simple executive assistant—she was obviously Martindale's chief troubleshooter, an invisible insider able to pass through the inner sanctums of the current Administration with apparent ease—definitely not someone to piss off. "Find anything interesting to you, Miss Harley?"

She laughed, pointed a finger accusingly at Hardcastle, and replied, "All I can say is, Admiral, that if you plan on doing only half the things to Henri Cazaux that you did to the Haitian, Bahamian, and Colombian governments while you were with the Hammerheads, Cazaux is in big, big trouble."

Fallon Naval Air Station, Nevada
Three Days Later

Before any aircraft carrier air wing begins a cruise, its crews must certify to the carrier air group commander that they are fully qualified and ready to perform their assigned duties. For Navy and Marine Corps strike units in the western half of the United States, that means a trip to Navy Fallon in northern Nevada for a very intensive two-month training and evaluation course on aerial gunnery, bombardment, and missile tactics. With thousands of square miles of ranges spread out over three counties, mostly desolate hills and dry lake beds, hundreds of men (and now women) per year streak over the high desert and mountains, line up on plywood tanks or airfields scratched into the hard-baked earth by bulldozers, and drop thousands of tons of live bombs, rockets, missiles, and cannon rounds. The ranges are also used for operational evaluations of new weapons about to be deployed for the first time. Because of its very isolated location, Navy Fallon is also one of the country's largest ordnance depots, from which thousands of tons of weapons and explosives are stored, distributed, repaired, refurbished, dismantled, and disposed.

For aircrew members, the eight-week TDY to Navy Fallon is a mixed blessing. Although the base facilities are first-rate, the surrounding town is so isolated and small that, apart from the temptation to visit one of the many legal brothels nearby, there was little to do in Fallon for relaxation or enjoyment. But it was a good opportunity to prepare oneself for a long deployment at sea, where the facilities and chances for rest and relaxation were even less available, and it was definitely some of the best flying around. Crew members actually looked forward to Fallon's open skies, big ranges, plenty of live ordnance, and the chance to show the brass what you can do with the Navy's most modern warplanes.

It was also a weapons smorgasbord for arms dealers and smugglers, if you had the money and the right connections.

After a flight into Fallon Municipal Airport, five miles northwest of the Naval Air Station, Gregory Townsend, Henri Cazaux's third-in-command and chief of plans and operations, signed a lease for a large hangar, the flight crew fueled and prepared their aged de Havilland C-8 Buffalo cargo plane for departure, and Ysidro and his crew made preparations for their meeting.

Just after midnight, they heard the sounds of heavy truck engines approaching outside the hangar. After an hour-long wait, undoubtedly so their counterparts could move toward them and surround the hangar, Ysidro and Townsend were met by several men in a Navy Humvee. Six men emerged from the big vehicle, all armed to the teeth with M-16 rifles and military-issue Beretta automatic pistols. Two men wore Navy utility uniforms; three others were in civilian clothes but had military haircuts; and one, who stepped out of the front passenger side of the Humvee and looked like the leader, looked like a civilian all the way. While two men stood before Ysidro and Townsend, armed with M-16 rifles, two of the gunsels herded the smuggler's crewmen inside the de Havilland to watch them, and two others stationed themselves at the front and rear hangar doors.

Both Townsend and Ysidro were frisked, and their weapons taken from them. Ysidro was heavily armed with an automatic submachine gun, two pistols, and two knives—those were taken from him—but he was allowed to keep the aluminum briefcase he carried, after a careful inspection. Inside the suitcase was U.S. cash in twenties, fifties, and one hundreds, along with Swiss and German bearer bonds. "They brought the cash," the soldier reported to the civilian after checking the case for hidden weapons.

"We've been doing business a long time," Townsend said to the leader. "We want it to stay that way. We'll play fair with you in return for good service. Cash for quality goods."

But even then, reassuring words did not tone down the rough search he had to undergo. Townsend carried only one gun, a Colt .45 auto pistol, along with a Tekna three-cell flashlight—which was carefully inspected, even to the point of unscrewing the butt cap and sliding out the batteries—and, to the gunsel's surprise, a sixteen-inch Bowie knife in a sheath strapped to his back, handle down so he could draw it easily. After showing the huge knife to the others, the gunsel rasped, "Like fucking' *Crocodile Dundee.* What's this for, bobbie?"

"Skinning snakes," Townsend spat back. "Be careful with it. It has special sentimental value."

"From your mother, I suppose."

"My father beat up and killed my mother when I was a child," Townsend said in a conversational, matter-of-fact tone. "I took that knife from Mohammar Kaddafi's bedroom during a botched SAS assassination mission. Three of my best soldiers were killed on that raid, and the bastard wasn't even home.'' He leaned forward, and in a low, ghostly tone of voice, said, ''I was so upset I resigned from the SAS, returned home, got drunk, and sliced off my father's head with that knife.''

The soldier didn't know if Townsend was telling the truth, but one look at his crocodile's smile and he decided not to make any more smart comments. He placed all the weapons and gear inside the front seat of the Humvee and backed away without further comment.

Relieved of his weapons and gear, Townsend took a moment to carefully study the men around him. They all looked like professional soldiers, although he noticed how quickly and easily they relaxed when Ysidro's and his own weapons were confiscated. If the gunsels knew anything about unarmed combat, they would know that a professional soldier never relaxed, even with ten-versus-two odds. Two of the Navy men in uniform were known to Ysidro and Townsend, but the rest were strangers, which Townsend didn't like. ''Who the hell are these blokes? We agreed only us four at the setup.''

''That was before you asked for the *heavy* stuff, Townsend.'' Crenshaw laughed. ''Our first deal was easy—six thousand pounds of waste ammonium nitrate and perchlorate. Hell, the Navy dumps at least six thousand pounds a day of waste chemicals and explosives into open pits out here—drink the well water around here for a couple years and if you fart you blow your ass off.''

''All right, let's get on with it,'' Townsend said impatiently. ''Perchlorate and hydrazine we can get anywhere—the state of Nevada practically gives the shit away. You got the rest of it?''

''What I'm telling you, bobbie, is that the prize is gonna be worth the price.'' Crenshaw turned to the guard at the front hangar door, who made a signal with a flashlight. Soon two five-ton utility trucks, painted Navy gray with desert-camouflaged canvas tops over the cargo beds, rumbled toward them. When the trucks pulled up to the group and the hangar doors were closed, Crenshaw stepped behind the first truck and flipped open the canvas cover on the back, and Townsend jumped up on the back of the truck to examine the contents. There were eight 55-gallon drums marked HIGH EXPLOSIVE, and four drums marked FLAMMABLE. He found an opener tool in the bed of the truck and opened each screw opening of the first eight drums, and the unmistakable acidic-aluminum-blood smell of aluminum perchlorate filtered out. He inspected the last four drums, this time mixing two ounces of the liquid in the second barrel with a pinch of the powder in the first set of barrels in a small plastic tube. After swirling the mixture in the tube, he carefully held a lighter to the opening of the tube, and a long cylinder of blue fire shot out with a loud *pop.*

He repeated the test with all four barrels, satisfied that he had the good stuff. Hydrazine and aluminum perchlorate were two highly explosive compounds all by themselves, but mixed together they formed a thick, unstable vapor that, mixed with oxygen and ignited with a spark, created a huge, violent explosion hundreds of times more powerful than gasoline or TNT. "Drove all this way across the desert at night with simple nylon ropes securing these barrels, did you?" Townsend asked as he stepped out of the truck. He knew that there was enough aluminum perchlorate and hydrazine in that truck to once and for all bring down one of the World Trade Center towers. "You're either braver or stupider than I suspected."

"Not as stupid as you two are, Townsend," Crenshaw said, motioning with glee at the twin-engined de Havilland cargo plane. "We got here in one piece. Let's see how brave you two are when you gotta fly outta here in that piece-of-shit cargo plane. You opened the drums. One wisp of hydrazine lingering in the air or near those engines when you start them up—*poof.* You blow the hydrazine, scatter the perchlorate, make an even bigger boom." Townsend had to nod at that last remark—yes, it was going to be tricky going.

"These are the real prizes, gents." Crenshaw stepped over to the second truck and opened a canvas flap, revealing several different oddly shaped weapons. There were eight devices in all, all about four to five feet long. "Took some time collecting these bad boys," he said proudly. "All Gulf War veterans, all fully operational. Three Mark-77 napalm canisters, three CBU-55 fuel-air explosives units, and six CBU-59 cluster bombs units. Best stuff in the arsenal."

"Very good," Townsend said. It was indeed an impressive haul—perhaps too impressive. The Navy didn't let ordnance like this just lie around. Crenshaw was a top munitions maintenance man, but even he had to carefully account for stuff like this. "My flashlight, if you please?"

"Suit yourself," Crenshaw said, motioning to one of his men, who handed Townsend his flashlight. Townsend jumped up onto the truck, placed the flashlight in his teeth, and carefully examined each weapon.

The Mark-77 was little more than a large blunt-ended gas tank filled with chemical beads, which Townsend checked. Once filled with gasoline, the beads dissolved to form napalm, which could blanket nearly an entire city block with a sheet of fire. The CBU-59, with the words CONTENTS: LIVE LOADED BLU-77/B stenciled on the sides, were metal containers that, when released and opened by a barometric nose fuze, scattered seven hundred APAM (anti-personnel, antimaterial) bomblets across a four-hundred-foot oval swath. The one-pound baseball-sized bomblets were filled with steel dartlike projectiles that could mutilate anything—or anyone—in their path. Some of the bomblets exploded on contact, while others had timer fuzes which would detonate them minutes or even hours later.

The real prize was the fuel-air explosives bombs. The CBU-55 canisters were simply very large fuel tanks that would be filled with the hydrazine and aluminum perchlorate, the stuff in the other truck. Behind the endplate of each canister was a dispenser holding three BLU-73 bomblets. When released, the two compounds would mix, the canister would automatically spray the target area with a large cloud of explosive gas, and then the parachute-retarded bomblets would ignite the gas—the resulting explosion would be equivalent to ten 2,000-pound bombs going off at once. Pound for pound, the CBU-55 was the most powerful non-nuclear bomb in the American military arsenal. In limited service in the Vietnam War because the dense foliage dissipated its explosive effects, it was the weapon of choice in the wide-open deserts of Iraq. Officially it was used only to "clear minefields," but it was used with terrible effect on large masses of Iraqi troops, squashing and incinerating anything within five hundred yards of ground zero. Its devastating killing power was considered unethical, almost on a par with chemical, biological, or nuclear weapons.

"Very impressive, Crenshaw," Townsend said, swinging the flashlight beam into Crenshaw's face, then snapping it off. Acquiring the fuel-air explosive weapons would make Cazaux very happy indeed. "I hope bearer bonds are acceptable. They have been in the past."

"As long as you got my share in U.S. greenbacks in there, I don't care about that shit," Crenshaw said. "The officers want the fuckin' Kraut bonds, not me. Now get the fuck down and—"

Distracted by the flashlight beam, Crenshaw didn't see what Townsend was doing until he had nearly finished doing it—he had unscrewed the butt cap off the three-cell flashlight, removed the two rear D-cell batteries, screwed them together, and aimed it at him. Before Crenshaw could raise his submachine gun, Townsend pressed a button, and with a barely audible *pufff,* a two-inch razor-edged arrow pierced his chest, sliced through his heart, deflected off a rib, and ricocheted around inside his body like a pinball, slicing up blood vessels and lungs in the blink of an eye. He turned and shot darts into the first truck driver and two more gunsels standing nearby, then leaped off the truck. Everything had happened so fast that the driver of the first truck was still idly sitting behind his wheel when Townsend ran over to his door, put the weapon to his left temple, and fired a bolt into his brain.

Ysidro disdained the use of any sort of fancy James Bond–type weapons. As soon as he saw Crenshaw go down, Ysidro was on the move. He bashed the heavy metal briefcase into the soldier nearest him, grabbed his gun as he went down, and started pumping bullets at anything that moved, remembering not to shoot toward the explosives-laden trucks and counting on Townsend to kill anyone near him. The massacre of the three soldiers near him was complete in a matter of seconds. The guard at the rear of the hangar took off running as soon as he saw Ysidro sprinting after him, but luckily the back door to the hangar was locked. Ysidro dropped him with a bullet in his chest from fifty feet, then stepped up to him and put a second bullet in his brain.

"Jesus Christ, Ysidro, one bullet ricocheting in the wrong direction could've cooked us all," Townsend said.

"Hey, we're already fuckin' stupid for accepting this assignment in the first place—this is a job for the grunts," Ysidro said. "I'm a guerrilla, not a trash-hauler, and if we blow, we blow. Let's just get the hell out of here. Linnares, get your ass out here and load these explosives *now!*" Johann Linnares, the leader of the flight crew, stepped out of the de Havilland along with his crew—they had killed the two guards who tried to lock them up in the plane as soon as they were alone.

"I still don't fucking understand why we had to kill these guys this time around," Ysidro said as the crews began to load the explosives and weapons aboard the cargo plane. "These guys were swaggering assholes, but they were generally straight with us, and we been trading with them for a long time. What gives?"

"Things are going to get too hot around the clubhouse once we begin the next series of attacks," Townsend said. "We paid these blokes pretty well, but when the feds see what we're about to do, the heat gets turned up and the reward money for our heads will undoubtedly be more than assholes like Crenshaw could resist. I think Henri was correct—once these attacks are completed, it'll be time to open up some new sources of hardware. By then, we'll be the top dogs in the terror-for-hire game. We'll have the world's pick of the litter."

"*If* we survive," Ysidro said. "Henri really *is* fuckin' possessed, and I think we're gonna need the Devil's help to get out of this alive."

Dallas–Fort Worth International Airport, Sunrise
Two Days Later

If you had to go to war, had to deploy at a moment's notice, had to hump all night to get your unit set up and operational as fast as humanly possible, there were worse places to do it than Dallas, Texas.

Lieutenant Colonel Valerie Witt, U.S. Army, emerged onto the catwalk with a cup of coffee just as the first rays of sunlight peeked over the horizon, putting the skyline of the city of Dallas in stark profile. The dawn was hazy and cool, but she had ditched her field jacket back in her new office downstairs hours ago. She allowed herself the luxury of drinking in the sunrise, letting the brilliant yellow sun charge her batteries. For a moment, she was back in her hometown of Ogunquit, Maine, watching the sunrise from her parents' home on the coast, or on the beach at Treasure Cay in the Bahamas on her honeymoon. Beautiful. Just beautiful . . .

But as she scanned the horizon an unusual sight brought her back to reality very quickly—and Avenger FAADS (Forward Area Air Defense System) unit parked a few hundred yards beyond the approach end of runway 35 Right. It was hardly more than a speck out there, but its two box launchers aimed skyward, each containing four Stinger heat-seeking antiaircraft missiles, could be seen. This was not her honeymoon. This was not home. Yes, it was Fort Worth, Texas, but it was also war.

Valerie Witt was the commander of Third Battalion, 43rd Regiment, and was the senior air defense artillery battalion commander deployed to the defense of Dallas–Fort Worth Airport. Her communications headquarters were on the second level of Dallas–Fort Worth's multistory control tower, where she had a clear view of all her air defense units at DFW; but her weapon command center, the AN/MSQ-16 MICC (Master Information and Coordination Central), a large steel green-painted box crammed full of radar sets, radios, and air conditioners (for the electronics, not the humans who work inside), had been hoisted up onto the roof of terminal 2W of Dallas–Fort Worth. Beside the MICC was the AMG, or Antenna Mast Group, a truck carrying two UHF antennas that linked Witt's MICC with all the air defense units surrounding Dallas–Fort Worth. Because DFW was one of the busiest and most important airports in the United States, there were a lot of air defense units deployed here to try to stop Henri Cazaux if he tried to attack here.

Eleventh Brigade, from Fort Bliss, El Paso, Texas, had deployed six of Witt's Third Battalion Patriot missile batteries in the area—two at Carswell Air Force Base, west of Dallas–Fort Worth, two at Naval Air Station Dallas to the south, and two batteries at Fort Worth–Alliance Airport, north of the city of Fort Worth. Each battery had four Patriot missile launchers—half the normal number, because so many airports in the nation had to be covered—and each launcher contained four missiles.

In addition, there were four platoons of Hawk medium-range surface-to-air missiles spread out on the outskirts of Dallas–Fort Worth, twelve launcher units for a total of thirty-six Hawk missiles; and eight Avenger units, stationed at each end of the four runways kept active at DFW, for a total of sixty-four short-range Stinger missiles. Patriot Communications Relay Groups scattered all across Tarrant and Dallas counties ensured tight coordination between the Patriot batteries and Witt's battalion MICC, which controlled all the Patriot, Hawk, Avenger, and Stinger surface-to-air missile sites surrounding Dallas–Fort Worth Airport. In turn, Witt's command center was tied directly into the overall Air Defense Force Commander, an Air Force officer she did not know, orbiting over El Dorado, Texas, in an E-3C Sentry AWACS (Airborne Warning and Control System) radar plane. Although Witt could launch any of the missiles defending Dallas–Fort Worth, primary responsibility of launching missiles at any one of the major airports in the south-central United States—Dallas–Fort Worth, Houston-Intercontinental, Houston-Hobby, Memphis, Tulsa, Nashville, and New Orleans—or directing any fighters on intercepts, was in the Air Force officer's hands.

Witt finished a walkaround of the catwalk around the control tower, checking the weather, checking the airport, and catching a glimpse of all the HAWK and Avenger units deployed around the huge airport. Far to the south, she could see two F-16 Fighting Falcon fighters leaping into the sky from Naval Air Station Dallas, then peeling away to the east with afterburners roaring. Air defense units, fighters—this was something you'd expect to see in Beirut, or Baghdad, or Tel Aviv—not Texas. What was going on in this world when a single terrorist could hold a nation hostage like this, force it to restrict the rights of its own citizens in order to defend itself?

Witt returned to her little headquarters—consisting of several banks of radios, computers, and radar repeater—just as the secure radio crackled to life: "All Tiger units, all Tiger units, stand by for a poll of the air defense force."

Witt reached over and picked up a telephone, which was wired directly into her MICC van down below: "Tiger 100, report."

It looked huge from the outside, but the Master Information and Coordination Central van was barely big enough for three persons inside. The Battalion Engagement Officer, Captain Jim Connor, sat on the left in front of a large twelve-inch digital radarscope, surrounded by switchlights, indicators, and a keyboard; he was responsible for making the decision on whether or not any missile unit in the battalion would fire on a hostile target, and for taking over as Battalion Force Commander if communications between the Air Defense Force Mission Commander on board the AWACS radar plane were lost. The Battalion Fire Unit Technician, Master Sergeant Mike Pierini, sat on the right, with a virtually identical radar setup as the Engagement Officer. Pierini was responsible for identifying all targets on radar and classifying them as friendly, hostile, or unknown (if the crews aboard the AWACS plane had not already done so), assisting the Engagement Officer, and maintaining communications with the battalion's missile units.

Between them was a dot-matrix printer, and above that the LED readouts and status displays of all the rounds remaining of all the missile units under Witt's command. Reading off the status display, Connor responded: "Ma'am, Tiger 100 shows all units in the green: Ninety-six Patriot, thirty-six HAWK, and sixty-four Avenger Stingers ready. All units acknowledging HOLD FIRE command."

"Very well, Tiger 100, out."

Aboard the E-3C Sentry AWACS Radar Plane Orbiting Over El Dorado, Texas

Army Lieutenant Colonel Valerie Witt might have been incensed to learn that the overall Air Defense Force Mission Commander for the south-central United States was about ten years younger than she, had five years less time in the military, and was only an Air Force major, but that described William "Kid" Kestrel, the Mission Crew Commander (MCC) aboard Tiger Nine-Zero, the E-3C Sentry Airborne Warning and Control System radar plane. Kestrel was short, blue-eyed, fair-haired, and slight, and he looked even younger than age thirty-eight—he looked far younger than anybody else on the twenty-two-person AWACS crew, although he was probably the oldest.

Kestrel was one of eleven Air Defense Force Mission Commanders airborne at that moment aboard E-3C Sentry radar planes, covering the entire continental United States—the others were stationed over Elizabeth City, North Carolina, Allentown, Pennsylvania, and Indianapolis, Indiana, covering the northeast; Gainesville, Florida, covering the southeast; Des Moines, Iowa, covering the Midwest; Cimmaron, New Mexico, and Billings, Montana, covering the Rocky Mountain region; Mormon Mesa, Nevada, and Porterville, California, covering the southwest; and Lakeview, Oregon, covering the northwest. Flying one-hundred-mile racetrack patterns at twenty-nine thousand feet, the E-3C Sentry, with its powerful AN/APY-2 Overland Downlook Radar mounted on a thirty-foot saucer rotodome atop the converted Boeing 707 aircraft, could detect and track any aircraft in flight for three hundred miles in all directions.

After one aerial refueling three hours ago, Kestrel's crew had been on station now for eight hours, with four more hours to go before another plane would launch from Tinker Air Force Base in Oklahoma City to take their place. Under normal circumstances, this might be boring work. Air traffic had subsided to a fraction of its normal levels after the government ordered that all aircraft flying within the United States had to take off and land at airports with control towers, had to file an IFR (Instrument Flight Rules) flight plan, and had to be under positive radar control at all times—and of course, the prospect of having several tons of high explosives dropped on your head inside an airport terminal kept a lot of people from flying as well.

But a lot of civilian and commercial aircraft that stayed on the ground were replaced by other aircraft: military fighters, escorting airliners all over the United States. The best estimate said that over two hundred F-16 ADF and F-15 fighters of the Air National Guard's total inventory of three hundred air defense fighters were airborne at any one time, shadowing any aircraft, big or small, that violated any of the new flight rules or did or said something suspicious. Every airport in the United States with a five-thousand-foot concrete runway and jet fuel available probably had a fighter land there at one time or another in the past twelve hours.

On Major Kestrel's radarscope, it appeared that he had every one of the military planes in his airspace—and he needed them all, because it also seemed that all the flakeoid pilots, bad radios, garbled transmissions, incorrect assumptions, and lost flight plans were rattling around in his assigned sector. Last night, the first full night of the new emergency flight rules, was the worst—but now it was dawn and the wrong decisions, rule violations, confusion, and just plain dumb-shit moves still showed no signs of letting up.

"All Tiger units, all Tiger units, this is Tiger Control with a poll of the air defense units," Kestrel began. Satellite communications downlinks allowed him to speak with units many miles away as if he were orbiting right over them. "Tiger 100."

"Tiger 100, all units in the green, all units acknowledge HOLD FIRE command," Colonel Witt at Dallas–Fort Worth Airport responded.

"Tiger 200."

"Tiger 200, all units in the green, all units acknowledge HOLD FIRE," the battalion commander at Houston-Hobby International reported, which also secured Houston-Intercontinental Airport. The poll continued with all of Kestrel's assigned units at New Orleans, Memphis, Little Rock, Oklahoma City, Tulsa, Jackson, and Springfield. Not all of these locations had Patriot missiles stationed there, but all had at least two Avenger-Stinger units and one HAWK missile unit, all controlled by Kestrel in the E-3C AWACS.

"Well, everybody's in place, and it looks like we survived the night all in one piece," Major Bill Kestrel told Admiral Ian Hardcastle and Lieutenant Colonel Al Vincenti, as they observed the progress of the emergency operation. Since Dallas–Fort Worth was one of the busiest in the nation, and since Cazaux's last attack in Memphis was not far away, it was a logical target, and a lot of planning, personnel, and hardware had gone into defending it. It was the perfect place to watch how the system was running—and the perfect place to watch potential problems occur. "But I'm seeing signs of pilots testing the system already."

"What do you mean, Kid?" Hardcastle asked.

"It's a pilot thing, I believe," Kestrel replied, giving veteran F-16 pilot Vincenti a mischievous smile. "Airline pilots need to be on time—their jobs depend on it—so they stretch the rules, probe the boundaries of the new authority. See, here's a good example." Kestrel reduced the range on his scope to show better detail. "This USAir flight from Little Rock is a 757 and he thinks he owns the sky. He's an hour late, but so what?—everybody in the system is at least an hour late. But he's real cranky. First, he won't stay on the Blue Ridge Four Arrival—he wants vectors to runway 35 Left final. We closed 36 Right and 35 Left, the runways closest to the terminal, so naturally that's what this bozo asks for. ATC says no, we want him out to GACHO intersection, fifteen miles out, and we want him on the ILS glideslope.

"Now he's really pissed, and he's making mistakes. He's screaming onto the localizer, going like a bat out of hell. He's cutting the corner, see?—he's never going to reach GACHO intersection. He's still going 250 knots, which is legal but not very smart since he's got about a ninety-degree turn coming up in a few seconds. Ninety-nine-percent chance he's a good guy, but he's doing bad-guy stuff. I got no choice." He hit the intercom button to his Senior Director—although the Senior Director was sitting right beside him, the intercom call alerted the entire crew to what he was doing—and said, "Active scramble on target ID uniform-seven-one-one-three, two F-16s. Continue the hold-fire on all batteries but tell Tiger 124, 125, 146, and 148 that ID number U7113 is a possible hostile. Tell Tiger 112 that a 757 will be flying real close from the east. I want all units to hold fire—don't get excited to see that idiot barreling in."

Kestrel pointed to his scope. "See that? He's blown through the localizer inbound course, still going like a bat out of hell—good thing he's not running up someone's ass. Now watch." Kestrel pointed to a spot at the top of his scope, and sure enough, a white rectangle with the words EMER appeared and began blinking. "They all do that—they argue, get excited, make a mistake, then realize what they've done and squawk emergency. Look, he's practically into Naval Air Station Dallas' airspace, overflying the Patriot missile site. Jesus . . ."

"So what can you do?" Hardcastle asked.

"I've got no choice, Admiral," Kestrel said. "But it ain't gonna fly. Listen . . ." He pressed another button on his communications panel: "Dallas East Approach, this is Tiger Control, that USAir Flight, ID U7113, is in violation. I need him kicked out to Scurry VOR until we can get a fighter visual ID . . . affirmative, U7113 . . . deviated more than two miles off assigned course within twenty miles of Dallas–Fort Worth Airport." Hardcastle and Vincenti could hear the approach controller, and he did not sound happy at all. "I've got two F-16s airborne from NAS Dallas now, and I'll declare him MARSA with the USAir flight at this time . . . I know he's declared an emergency, Approach, but he's in violation, he *still* hasn't gotten back on the localizer . . . what's your controller number, ma'am? . . . fine, my commander will call your supervisor. Request you advise that flight that he is an air defense item of interest and that if he violates the flight parameters again, he will be fired upon without further warning . . . yes, damn it, I'm serious. Tiger out."

He clicked over to another channel with an angry stab on the button: "All Tiger units, this is Tiger control, ID U7113 has declared an emergency and is being cleared to land on runway 31 Right at Dallas–Fort Worth. Interceptor units are airborne from NAS Dallas. At DIVVR intersection, repeat, at DIVVR intersection, all Hawk and Avenger batteries are released tight, repeat, at five miles out, all Hawk and Avenger batteries are released tight." He switched channels again, this time to the VHF GUARD emergency frequency, which was linked to a repeater station near Dallas–Fort Worth Airport: "Attention all aircraft, attention all aircraft, this is the United States Air Force airborne defense controller Tiger, we have an air defense item of interest landing on runway 31 Right, Dallas–Fort Worth Airport, warning, do not violate your flight clearances or you may be fired upon in the interest of national security. Repeat, all aircraft, do not violate your flight clearances or you may be fired upon without warning. Tiger out."

Kestrel turned to Hardcastle and Vincenti and said, "Okay, gents, I've just given the order for the short-range air defense systems to open fire on the inbound 757 if he strays more than a mile off course within five miles from the runway, more than a half-mile within two miles of the extended runway centerline, or more than one thousand feet toward the terminals within one mile. Meanwhile, the F-16s will try to join on him or orbit nearby until he's turned off the runway. This jet jockey is screwing up by the numbers, and now he—and his passengers, don't forget—are looking down the barrel of about twenty-four missiles and two F-16 fighters with missiles and guns of their own. Just plain stupid. He can die at any time between now and about two minutes from now, and you'll have a major disaster on your hands."

It was a very tense wait as they watched the final two minutes of the approach. The F-16 fighter joined on the 757 when the airliner was about two miles from touchdown: "Tiger Control, Tango X-Ray-311 flight, target looks clean, no open panels or devices, wheels are down. I see passengers in the windows. Looking good . . ." There was a short pause as the F-16 pilot configured his own plane for landing. He would fly to the right and above the airliner as long as he could, away from the Hawk and Avenger missile units arrayed between the runway and the east terminals of Dallas–Fort Worth Airport. "Control, -311 going around."

"Control, this is Tiger-148, I've got a visual on the target," reported one of the Avenger ground units, stationed at the approach end of the runway and tracking the airliner all the way on a telescopic infrared camera. "He's looking good, wheels and flaps down . . . Control, the target has touched down . . . Control, I see thrust reversers and spoilers, looks like a normal rollout . . . Control, he's turned off onto the high-speed taxiway one-north, moving onto taxiway 21 . . . Control, security units are on the scene. Request permission to disengage. Over."

"Attention all Tiger units, this is Tiger Control, all batteries hold fire, repeat, all batteries hold fire. Target ID U7113 is down. Tiger Control clear." Kestrel slid off his headset after telling his Senior Director he was going off the air for a few minutes, then motioned to Hardcastle and Vincenti toward the back of the AWACS plane: "I gotta take a break."

Hardcastle and Vincenti followed Kestrel to the galley, where Kestrel hit the lavatory and stayed in there for what seemed like a long time. When he finally emerged, his face still damp from the water he had splashed on it, he slugged down a couple of antacid tablets with a grimace. "It's gonna be a long day, I can see that now," he muttered.

"Very good work over there, Major," Hardcastle offered.

"That routine happens about twice, maybe three times an hour, gents," Kestrel said to Hardcastle and Vincenti, as if he hadn't heard Hardcastle's compliment. The strain really showed. "The pilots declare an emergency, and all our rules go out the window. All the air traffic controllers want to do is get these guys on the ground, so they clear them for landing before we can check them out. It's wearing my crews down real fast, and this is only the second day."

"But aren't your crews accustomed to this?" Hardcastle asked. "You've got some Desert Storm veterans on your crew. In the Middle East you were flying thousands of sorties a day, controlling hundreds of aircraft."

"In Desert Storm, and in most controller situations, most of the targets on the scope are good guys, and we're on the lookout for the bad guys," Kestrel explained. "Here, *every target* is a potential bad guy, right up until he turns off the runway after landing. Furthermore, *all* of our 'bad guys' are flying right toward the spot that we're assigned to defend—and we have to *let them!* That's pretty unheard-of in the AWACS game. We're used to playing on a much bigger scale—here, most of the real tense action occurs close to the ground and close to the defended spot, where if something goes wrong we don't have a lot of time to react—"

"Nothing personal, Major, but I'd rather burn out a few AWACS crews rather than see Cazaux bomb another terminal," Vincenti said. "Air defense is a shitty game, but we gotta play it."

"I hear you, Al, and I can't argue with that—it's our job and we're going to do it," Kestrel said. "I'm getting an ulcer because some flyboy wants to land five minutes earlier than his buddies—fine. But I wonder if that pilot realizes that if he does so much as wag his wings toward the terminal when he's on final approach, sirs, one of those kids riding in the Avengers is going to pull the trigger and send two Stinger missiles into an airliner full of civilians. It's something you guys from Washington are going to have to deal with if this thing drags on and a mistake happens. Either we turn up the heat and catch this Cazaux bastard right away, or you'll have to tighten up the rules a bit more, before we start flaming a lot of innocent Americans."

"We can't do much about the tactical situation," Hardcastle said. "We can nail the pilots busting the rules or declaring an emergency in order to circumvent the rules and get on the ground faster, but for the time being I don't think Washington is going to want to hear any more plans to restrict air traffic any more than what we're doing right now. I'd like to see the FBI take off the kid gloves and beat the bushes a little harder for Cazaux, but I believe they're working as hard as they—"

"Major Kestrel, another target just busted the arrival routing," one of the surveillance technicians said as he approached the group. "SD wants you back up on headsets."

"On my way," Kestrel said, popping one more antacid before leading Hardcastle and Vincenti back to the Weapons Controller section of the AWACS radar plane. He reached his seat, slapped on his headset, and turned to his Senior Director: "What do we have, Todd?"

"A private 727 on the Acton Two Arrival with a lost flight plan," the Senior Director reported. "Departed San Antonio International about a hour ago—that's been confirmed by the tower crew."

"Can't let him into DFW without a flight plan," Kestrel said emphatically. "Why the hell didn't ATC kick him out and tell him to return to San Antonio?" He knew that was a rhetorical question that his Senior Director couldn't answer, so he flipped his communications panel to his discrete Dallas Approach channel: "Dallas West Approach, Tiger Airborne Control."

"This is Dallas West Regional, go ahead."

"Yes, sir, that private 727, radar ID 35T90, doesn't have a flight plan for Dallas–Fort Worth International. Landing is prohibited without an IFR flight plan coordinated through me. Landing at DFW, Love, or Alliance is not authorized."

"Stand by one, I'll give you to my military operations desk." Kestrel was put on hold for about a minute, and then he had to explain the situation all over again to the Dallas TRACON military operations officer again, who responded, "We've been losing lots of flight plans, Tiger. The system is jammed. We'd lose five percent of the flight plans on a normal full-up day—now, with every plane in the sky filing a flight plan, we can't keep up."

"I understand your problem, Approach, but let's deal with this guy first," Kestrel interjected. "Reroute the guy either to one of the satellite airports or back to San Antonio—he can't land at DFW, Alliance, or Love."

"I thought the procedure stated that you military types would visually identify any aircraft that was not on a flight plan or that was not following his clearance."

"That's correct," Kestrel said. "If he tries to fly toward the primary airport in Class B airspace without a flight plan, without a clearance, or if he's not following his clearance, he will be intercepted."

"So why not just intercept this guy, visually check him out, then make the decision to let him land?"

"Sir, that's not the purpose of the procedure," Kestrel said patiently. "The purpose of an intercept is not to visually identify him, but to *shoot him down* as far away from the primary airport and from populated areas, if that becomes necessary."

"Why do you want to shoot him down, for God's sake?"

"I don't *want* to shoot him down," Kestrel said. He looked at Hardcastle, who was listening in on the conversation with an expression of absolute disbelief on his face. "Sir, the aircraft does *not* have a proper flight plan in the system—that's a violation, and it makes him a suspected terrorist. He's approaching a high-volume primary airport in Class B airspace, one of the airports designated as a high-value asset by the federal government. He's supposed to be on the Acton Two arrival, but I have him three miles east of HULEN intersection and one thousand feet low."

"Is he on a vector?"

"I don't know, sir," Kestrel said, ready to tear his hair out in utter frustration. He turned to his Senior Director, who nodded his head "yes" at the question. "My senior director says he is on a vector, Approach, but that doesn't matter. All I know is that he doesn't have a flight plan, he's not on a published standard arrival routing, and he's not on a published approach procedure. I'm asking you to divert him to a satellite airport or back to his departure airport."

There was a slight but maddening pause, then: "Okay, Tiger Control, I . . . sir, it's really busy here, and I'm not quite sure what the problem is . . ."

"I'm trying to explain it to you, if you'd just listen to me."

"I didn't catch that last, Tiger," the supervisor said in a detached, bureaucratic way that told everyone listening in that he heard what Kestrel said but was ignoring him. "If you think you've got a terrorist situation, perhaps I'd better turn you over to the chief of security operations or the deputy director. Stand by one."

Hardcastle keyed his headset mike button: "Dallas Approach, this is Admiral Ian Hardcastle speaking. I'm the Special Assistant to the President for Air Defense Operations." Kestrel was shaking his head at Hardcastle, silently asking him not to get into it, but it was too late now. "I'm in charge of this antiterrorist operation. I'm ordering you to divert this suspect aircraft away from Dallas–Fort Worth Airport until his identity can be verified. Do you understand me?"

"Who is this again?"

"This is Admiral Hardcastle, Special Assistant to the President."

"President of . . . the United States? Is that what you're saying?"

Hardcastle's back stiffened angrily, his cheek muscles quivering. He grasped his headset mike, pulled it closer to his lips, and shouted, "The name's *Hardcastle,* sir. I am the man who is going to make your life *miserable* if you don't comply with my instructions."

"Ah . . . right—*Mister* Hardcastle." It was obvious by the controller's voice that he wasn't accustomed to being threatened and he was done talking. "I'm turning you over to the deputy facility director—you can make your requests and your threats to him. Stand by, please." And the line went dead, replaced by soothing mood music.

"Damn it, he cut us off," Kestrel said. On intercom, he said to his senior director, "Todd, divert Tango X-Ray-311 for an ID intercept on target ID 35T90. Classify that target ID as 'unknown.' Transmit an alert to Tiger units 112, 113, 131, and 132, but send a HOLD FIRE and have all units acknowledge." Kestrel turned to Hardcastle and said bitterly, "I've got a bad feeling about this one, Admiral. The shit's starting to pile up real fast."

Air Defense Battalion Master Information and Coordination Central, DFW Airport

Lieutenant Colonel Valerie Witt was breathing heavily from the run from the control tower to the access elevator that took her up to the roof of terminal 2W. This was where her Master Information and Coordination Central van was set up, as she hurried into the van and stood between the battalion engagement officer, Captain Jim Connor, and the battalion fire unit technician, Master Sergeant Mike Pierini, in the front of the cab. "What do we got, Jim?"

"Tiger Control just made this guy an UNKNOWN," Connor replied, tapping the eraser point of his pencil on his radarscreen. "No flight plan on him. Tiger is scrambling two fighters, and they've alerted NAS Dallas and Carswell Patriot batteries and HAWK units 131 and 132. We've acknowledged the HOLD FIRE order."

Witt relaxed and got her breathing under control. It was just another alert, probably the fifteenth one since she set up operations here less than two days ago. As it was during the Persian Gulf War of 1991, the brass aboard the AWACS radar planes flag everybody even marginally suspect as UNKNOWN during the first few days of a conflict. When the friendly forces became more organized, everyone got more comfortable, and procedures became better understood and more routine, the numbers of alerts decreased, even to the point where engaging a SCUD missile was considered routine. This was shaping up to be the same. Witt checked the status readouts—yes, every Patriot, HAWK, and Avenger fire unit was reporting "HOLD FIRE." The unknown was still over thirty miles out, well within range of Patriot and coming within range of HAWK batteries in a few minutes. The Air Force fighters were airborne, and MICC had a solid track on them. No crisis yet.

Witt studied the battalion engagement officer's radarscreen as the fighters converged on the suspect airliner. The airspace for fifty miles around Dallas–Fort Worth had been divided up into safe-fly corridors, which corresponded to the FAA's published STAR, or Standard Terminal Arrival, procedures. The corridors were like gradually narrowing chutes beginning at four radio navigation beacons surrounding DFW, angling down from the higher en route altitudes to lower terminal and approach altitudes. If they were heading toward DFW in a threatening way—a combination of high airspeed, low altitude, not following airways, and no identification beacon meant "threatening" to the Patriot fire control computers—any aircraft straying outside the safe-fly corridors could legally be shot at by Patriot surface-to-air missiles. Inside twenty miles to the airport, the corridors became narrow funnels, and within two miles of the runway, the safe-fly zone was a thin tube only a few hundred feet wide. Although Patriot missiles could hit a hostile plane anywhere along its route of flight, even at very low altitude and close to the terminal buildings, their assigned fire area was from twenty to fifty miles from DFW. The HAWK missiles would engage between twenty and two miles from the terminal buildings, and the Avenger Stinger missiles and .50-caliber cannons would engage inside two miles.

"I don't get it—what's going on here?" Witt murmured. Until a few seconds ago, this new unknown had been a regular inbound, a private Boeing 727 executive corporate or charter job, squawking all its normal beacon codes and doing generally normal things in a very confusing airspace system. Now, the Air Force AWACS radar crew had made it an "unknown."

"We got a kill code of 0.75 from Patriot," Sergeant Pierini called out. The Patriot fire control computer was programmed with a set of hostile-aircraft flight parameters—distance, speed, heading, altitude, flight path, location in or away from the safe-fly zones, general tactical situation—and every target was assigned a hostile track code, or "kill code." A score of 1.0 meant that Patriot believed the hostile was going to strike either the Patriot site or Patriot's assigned protection zone. Next to the target's kill code was Patriot's estimate of a successful kill if it launched on the hostile track—right now, patriot's confidence of a kill was 0.95. It was probably an underestimate.

"Hold fire, Sergeant," Witt said. "The fighters are on him. Let them deal with this sucker."

"All units acknowledging HOLD FIRE," Pierini replied.

Aboard the F-16 ADF Fighter Tango X-Ray-311

The vertical and horizontal antenna sweep indexers on the F-16 ADF's AN/APG-66 radarscope continued to move, but a small white box had appeared at the upper-left portion of his F-16 Fighter Falcon ADF's radarscreen. Captain Ron Himes, 111th Fighter Squadron "Texans," Ellington Field, Houston, Texas, clicked a button on his throttle, moving two white lines called the target acquisition symbol onto the white box, then pressing and releasing the button to lock the cursor onto the target. He switched to medium PRF, or pulse-repetition frequency, to get a clearer look at the target. The fire control computer displayed the unknown target's flight parameters—range thirty miles, speed three hundred knots, altitude five thousand feet and descending. Himes clicked open his radio and reported, "Tango X-Ray-311, judy," indicating he had the target on radar and needed no further intercept information.

"Roger, 311," the weapons controller aboard the E-3C AWACS radar plane responded. "Check nose cold, ID only. You're cleared in the block angels six to eight."

"311 copies, ID pass only, nose is cold," Himes responded, letting the controller know—for the third time since takeoff—that all his weapons were safe. He transitioned from the radarscope on his instrument panel to his heads-up display, which also showed the radar target lock, and prepared for the intercept. Unlike the past few years, when all the F-16 Air Defense Fighter birds carried was ammunition for the cannon, Himes' and his wingman's birds were fully armed in air defense/intercept configuration. Himes carried six AIM-120A Ram radar-guided missiles on this mission, plus one fuel tank on each inboard wing pylon and two hundred rounds of ammunition for his 20-millimeter cannon; his wingman carried four AIM-9P Sidewinder heat-seeking missiles instead of the newer Ram missiles. The AIM-120A Ram missile was a medium-range "robot" missile, capable of guiding itself to a target at over twice the speed of sound from twenty-five miles away with its own on-board radar, rather than having the launch aircraft illuminate the target for it.

A lot of low-level humidity haze and a few summertime thundercloud buildups in the vicinity of Dallas–Fort Worth Airport were the only obstructions in the sky. Himes encountered a little thermal turbulence at all altitudes, and the cockpit glass acted like a greenhouse, trapping the hot Texas sun inside the cockpit and baking his slate-gray helmet. Himes usually enjoyed flying, even in these conditions, but this assignment was demanding and very frustrating. Only two F-16 fighters from his unit had deployed to DFW Airport, since Texas Air National Guard fighters were being sent as far away as Ohio to fly air defense missions over major airports, and resources were very scarce. That meant Himes and his wingman, Captain Jhani McCallum, one of the first black female combat pilots in the world, took all the scramble calls for this very busy airport.

It was never anticipated that the interceptors would be used so much, and the strain was starting to wear on Himes. On average, an Air National Guard fighter on alert would launch once in a three-day alert shift and spend about two hours in the air. Here at DFW, they were launching every few hours, day or night, good weather or bad. No sooner would they land from one scramble and refuel, and they'd be off on another chase. A sortie lasted only twenty to thirty minutes, but the tension was ten times greater than anything most of them had ever experienced. They were chasing down a deadly terrorist who could kill hundreds of people in one pass if the interceptor pilots didn't do their job. But so far all they had accomplished was to train live missiles and guns on airliners filled with travelers, not explosives. It was a deadly game.

Himes saw the airliner's smoke trail first. He wagged his vertical stabilizer, a visual signal to McCallum to extend into combat spread formation left, then gently eased into a left rolling climb. As the airliner slid underneath him, Himes continued his roll until he was above and to the 727's right side, beside the tail. He made a fast check—good, McCallum was in position above and behind the airliner's left wingtip. She would stay in that support position until this 727 was either on the ground, no longer classified an unknown—or they destroyed it.

"Tiger Control, 311 in position, nose cold, radar down, wingman on guard," Himes reported to the AWACS Weapons Controller assigned to him. "Stand by for visual ID."

"Tiger Control, ready."

"Tango X-Ray-311 lead has intercepted a Boeing 727 airliner, registration number November 357 Whiskey. Beige in color with royal blue stripe across the windows, no lettering. Large heraldic crest in gold on the blue vertical stabilizer." Himes slid a few more yards to the left, close enough to see a shadow of his number-one AIM-120 Ram missile on the airliner's tail. "Reads 'U-N-I-V-E-R-S-A-L' on the scroll. I observe several sealed windows on the right side over the wing. The aircraft appears to be in Westfall Air livery, repeat, Westfall Air charter livery. Moving underneath." Westfall Air, based at Dallas–Fort Worth and owned by the same company in Scotland that owned Universal Express overnight package service in Memphis and Sky Partner International Airlines in New York City, was one of the largest air charter operations in the south, and its planes were well known to most Texas fliers.

Himes gently eased below the fuselage until he could see the entire underside of the jet. It was filthy dirty from years of accumulated tire smoke and perhaps some rough handling, but otherwise normal. "311 is underneath the target aircraft. No open panels, no underslung devices. No unusual antennas. Moving forward in visual range of the target's crew."

"Clear," the weapons controller acknowledged.

Himes carefully slid out, then above the airliner, then eased forward until he was abeam the cockpit windows. Then he slid forward and gently in toward the airliner until he could see the pilots turn their heads toward him—he knew he had their attention now. "Tiger Control, I have positive visual contact on two male individuals in the target's cockpit, and they do see me as well, repeat, they do see me." He hit a button on his multifunction display, which activated a video camera that had been mounted on the right wingtip. The video was displayed on the multifunction display. Himes adjusted the steerable camera with a toggle switch on the instrument panel until he could see the cockpit, then zoomed in until he could clearly see the faces of the men in the airliner cockpit looking back at him. "Smile for the camera, boys," he said half-aloud as he zoomed in for a nice tight shot.

"Tango X-Ray-311, this is Tiger Control, you are clear to divert the flight, preferred destination airport from your present position is Fort Worth–Meacham, heading three-five-one at two thousand feet, do not overfly Carswell Air Force Base or Naval Air Station Dallas.

Landing at Alliance Airport or Dallas Love Field not authorized. Weapon status is HOLD FIRE, repeat, HOLD FIRE, acknowledge."

"Tango X-Ray-311 acknowledges weapon status HOLD FIRE, my nose is cold. Switching." He punched up FTW on his navigation computer, got a heading to Fort Worth–Meacham Airport, just fifteen miles west of DFW, switched his radio frequency to simultaneous VHF and UHF GUARD, the international aviation emergency channels, and clicked open his mike. "Attention, 727 airliner November 357-Whiskey, this is the United States Air Force fighter Tango X-Ray-311 abeam your right cockpit. You are in violation of emergency federal air regulations. All previous ATC clearances are hereby canceled and continued flight toward Dallas–Fort Worth Airport is denied. You are hereby ordered to turn left and fly heading three-five-zero, descend and maintain two thousand feet, and lower your landing gear immediately. Prepare for a VFR approach and landing at Fort Worth–Meacham Airport. Acknowledge these instructions on VHF frequency 121.5 or UHF 243.0 now. Over."

On the GUARD frequency, Himes heard, "Tango X-Ray-311, this is Westfall Air 357-Whiskey, I acknowledge your transmission." The accent was typical Texas, smooth but firm, maybe a Houstonian. "Our destination is Dallas–Fort Worth Airport, we've got the field in sight, and Approach has cleared us to the field. Is there a problem?"

"Westfall 357-W, this is Tango X-Ray-311, all previous clearances are canceled. You are ordered to land at Meacham Airport. Do not overfly Carswell Air Force Base. We will be escorting you for landing. Lower your landing gear and turn left heading three-four-five. Over."

"Roger . . ." Himes was afraid he might argue some more, but just then the airliner banked left and settled on a three-four-zero heading, lining up almost perfectly with Meacham Airport. The landing gear then came down, and Himes had to lower flaps to stay in formation as the airliner decelerated. "Tiger, Westfall-357-W is slant-Romeo direct Meacham at this time, over."

"Tango X-Ray-311 copies, descend and maintain two thousand, airport is twelve o'clock, twenty-one miles, contact Meacham Tower on 118.3. Acknowledge."

"Switching to Meacham tower, Westfall . . . stand by one, Tango . . ." *Oh shit,* Himes thought. *Here it comes.* Obviously, when the landing gear came down, the charter client woke up—those VIP 727s had a bedroom that rivaled anything on the ground—and now he was undoubtedly being heard from. "Ah, Tango X-Ray-311, my client wants to know why we can't land at DFW. We had a valid clearance from San Antonio. Over."

"Westfall 357-W, I don't have that information, sir, but you must comply with my instructions. All previous clearances have been canceled. You cannot land at Dallas–Fort Worth. Over."

"Okay, Tango X-Ray, but I really need to know . . ." There was a momentary rustle on the frequency, like paper being crumpled. Himes looked over to the airliner's cockpit and saw the copilot rising out of his seat and another man, in a white shirt, tie, and dark beard, drop into his vacated seat. Then, a definitely Middle Eastern voice came on the frequency: "Listen to me, Air Force fighter plane, we land at big Dallas airport. *Right* now. *Right* now. You understand . . . ?" And at that, Himes saw the bastard grab the 727's control wheel and turn it hard to the right—directly in the F-16's flight path.

"Holy mother of God!" Himes pulled on his control stick and shoved in full military power. He caught a glimpse of the airliner's nose rolling toward him, and then a hard *slap!* under his seat as the airflow buffet from the big airliner hit the F-16. They had missed by just a few feet. Himes continued his climb, raised his flaps, and fought to roll wings-level. When he finally got himself stabilized, he had climbed over five thousand feet above the airliner—it was no longer in sight. "Tiger flight, this is lead, check."

"Two's in," McCallum reported. "I've got you in sight, Ron. I'm at your seven o'clock low."

"Stay on the airliner, Jhani."

"Thought you needed help, came to see if you needed help."

"No, damn it, stay on the target." *Too late now,* Himes thought angrily. He switched back to Tiger Control: "Tiger Control, Tango X-Ray-311 flight, we had to break away from the target, he made a sudden turn across our flight path. Over."

Aboard the E-3C AWACS Radar Plane Tiger Control

Without the fighters tailing the airliner, Kestrel and his weapons controllers had lost their "eyes" on the scene, and without visual contact they had only a two-dimensional radar image to use. "Lost visual contact on the 'unknown,' " the weapons controller shouted to everyone in the weapons section of the radar plane.

Kestrel leaned closer to his screen. The airliner was fifteen miles out, over Lake Arlington, well outside the safe-fly corridor, five hundred feet below the programmed approach altitude, a little faster than normal, and still heading for Dallas–Fort Worth Airport. According to the rules of engagement, that bastard was dead right now. "Comm, broadcast warning message on GUARD, on all DFW tower freqs, and all DFW regional approach control freqs, try to get that unknown turned westbound."

The assigned weapons controller was already back on his radio. "Tango X-Ray-311, this is Tiger Control, your bogey is at two o'clock, three miles, fly heading zero-six-five, descend and maintain angels two."

"Tallyho, Tiger," the lead F-16 pilot reported. "Descending."

But it wasn't going to happen fast enough, and Kestrel knew it. The sonofabitch was heading right for the west terminals of Dallas–Fort Worth. He looked up and saw Hardcastle and Vincenti carefully studying him. "All right, Admiral, Colonel," he said. "I could use a little advice here."

"You still got time to reacquire the intercept," Vincenti said immediately. "He's still five minutes from landing. Get on his ass and try to turn him away. If he doesn't turn by five miles—"

"—nail him."

"Admiral?"

Hardcastle hesitated. It was he who headed the Pentagon staff that designed the air defense parameters, not more than three days ago. A staff of over one hundred had pored over charts and diagrams of the thirty-three largest airports in the United States, deciding the safest and simplest way an airliner could approach the airport in a hostile situation. In the short space of time they had to work the problem, the staff had designed a plan that, even if a pilot screwed up every possible rule in the book and did everything wrong, there was still a margin of safety that would save a nonterrorist but still destroy a terrorist before he got close enough to bomb a terminal.

Well, that was theory, done on charts and diagrams and computers. This guy had busted every rule, exceeded every parameter. He could not look more hostile unless he was launching cruise missiles. He should have been dead sixty seconds ago, the minute he turned into the F-16 . . .

But Hardcastle heard himself say, "Continue the intercept," and all the planning and all the theory went right out the window—as it usually does in situations like this. "Get Approach Control and

DFW Tower to divert all other flights. No one approaches DFW until this is sorted out.'' Kestrel breathed a sigh of relief that could be heard over the roar of the engines in the AWACS' cabin, and he had every free technician on board AWACS calling the airliner.

Aboard an Airtech CN-235 Twin-Turboprop Transport Northwest of DFW Airport

''Attention all aircraft, air defense emergency in progress over Dallas–Fort Worth Airport, stand by for divert instructions. Hazardous flight precaution, all aircraft, do not approach closer than ten miles of the Dallas–Fort Worth VOR or you may be fired upon without warning.'' The message, broadcast on the tower frequency, was repeated several times; then: ''Airtech-75-Delta, turn right heading two-four-zero, vectors clear of emergency airspace, sorry for the delay.''

''Right to two-four-zero, Airtech-75-Delta,'' the copilot of the Canadian-built Airtech CN-235 turboprop transport plane replied. He switched frequencies and shook his head, then laughed out loud. ''Jesus, what a stupid motherfucker,'' he said to his pilot. ''That guy's going to get his ass shot off if he's not careful.''

The pilot finished a long drag on his marijuana joint, keeping the pungent smoke in his lungs for a full fifteen seconds before letting it slowly trickle out. ''Sounded like a raghead to me,'' the pilot said. ''Serves him right.''

''So what are we gonna do?'' the copilot asked.

''What the hell can we do? We bust that ten-mile ring, they're liable to put a Hawk missile in our face. Better make the turn.'' The big transport plane turned right and headed southwest.

''The boss will be pissed if we don't make this delivery,'' the copilot fretted. ''We're already late as it is.''

The answer to that one came a few moments later: ''Airtech-75-Delta, Dallas Airport has just closed temporarily due to the air defense emergency,'' the approach controller told him. ''I can give you vectors to Redbird or Meacham. Say intentions.''

''Stand by one,'' the copilot radioed. Cross-cockpit, he said, ''Oh shit, the boss is going to skewer us. Now what?''

The pilot was too stoned to care what happened to him. He lazily shrugged his shoulders, enjoying the view. ''Hell, we got the gas—let's head over to Meacham.''

But as he glanced out the windows to his left, he saw an airport—and, to the west of the airport, something that he had never seen before but had no trouble at all recognizing. "I got an idea," the pilot said, banking hard left toward the airport and beginning a steep descent. "If we can't make the delivery, we might as well make a splash."

Air Defense Battalion MICC
Dallas–Fort Worth Airport

"Range eight miles and closing," Sergeant Pierini said aloud. "Tiger 111 Patriot battery reports confidence down to 0.89. Tiger 112 Patriot battery confidence at 0.92, and Tiger 113 is 0.93. Recommend degrading Patriot and committing HAWK batteries 131 and 132 to engage."

"Agree," Captain Connor said. "Uplink the engagement change to Tiger Control. Engagement status remains HOLD FIRE." The Patriot missiles at Carswell Air Force Base, Alliance Airport, and Naval Air Station Dallas were still capable of destroying the airliner, but the farther away and lower it flew, the less capable Patriot would be. Patriot would still track the airliner, but now only the HAWK and Avenger missiles would open fire if the order came.

That order could come any second, Colonel Witt thought as the airliner continued to drive toward DFW. "Even if the pilot of that thing isn't a terrorist," she said half-aloud, "he *should* die in a huge fireball, because he's so stupid he shouldn't be allowed to breed."

"Six miles . . . still have a HOLD FIRE command," Connor reported. "Five-point-five miles . . ."

"Stand by batteries 131 and 132," Witt said. She had reached up over Connor's head and was repeatedly mashing the battalion klaxon button, warning anyone within earshot to get away from the launchers before a missile motor ignited in their face. "Sarge, notify DFW security, tell them we may be launching."

"Target turning!" Connor suddenly shouted. "Unknown eighteen-track heading now two-niner-zero, continuing turn to heading two-seven-zero, climbing through three thousand feet."

"Jesus, that sonofabitch was lucky," Witt exclaimed, feeling her heart pounding in her chest. She took a deep breath, the first in what seemed like several minutes. "I hope the feds bust that asshole just for taking five years off my life. Get a poll of the battalion, Jim, and check—''

Suddenly, one of the aircraft data blocks on Connor's radarscope began to blink. ''Mike—what is that . . . ?''

Pierini caught it at the same moment: ''Track ID 4Q121 made a sudden turn toward Alliance Airport,'' he reported. ''He was on a vector heading from Dallas Tower during the emergency . . . Tiger Control still showing him as a valid track . . . now Tiger is making him an 'UNKNOWN,' sir, we've got an unknown, number 19, three miles east of Alliance Airport, altitude rapidly decreasing, now less than two thousand feet, airspeed two hundred knots . . . range two miles, still closing, altitude one point five, still decreasing . . .''

''Jesus . . .'' Witt hurriedly changed to Tiger Control's frequency and pulled her headset microphone closer to her lips as she watched the radarscope: ''Tiger Control, this is 100, I need an engagement command on unknown 19 blowing into Alliance,'' Witt radioed immediately to the AWACS radar plane. ''He's diving on Alliance Airport, range less than two miles.''

''Lost contact with Tiger-113,'' Pierini shouted. ''Datalink is down, switching to landlines . . . hard lines down. No connectivity with Tiger-113.''

''What the hell happened?'' Witt cried. She turned to the VHF radio and tried that—no response. ''Shit, we lost everything. Check your systems and do a BIT test.'' She clicked on the UHF radio to the Air Force AWACS plane: ''Tiger Control, this is 100, check connectivity with Tiger 113, datalink and connectivity lost at Battalion MICC. Over.''

Aboard the E-3C AWACS Radar Plane Tiger-90

''I see it, I see it,'' Kestrel said, studying his radar display. The surveillance technicians had assigned an unknown code 19 to the newcomer that had just blown past his approach clearance into Dallas–Fort Worth, and now they had put a giant flashing arrow on the radarscreen, pointing at UNK 19, to get his attention. He was silently kicking himself for not seeing the guy turn toward Alliance Airport earlier, but he was trying to watch a half-dozen major airports at once, and he had turned his attention away from DFW once the Westfall plane had turned away. The tiny blue square that marked the locations of the two Patriot missile batteries at Alliance

Airport was gone—not flashing, which would have indicated that the datalink was down but the site was operational, but completely gone, as if it never had been set up. "The Patriot site at Alliance went down. Todd, get one of the fighters over there and have him take a look."

As if the fighter pilot had heard him, Kestrel heard, "Tiger Control, Tango X-Ray-311, I'm about fifteen miles southeast of Alliance Airport, following the 727 airliner. I can see a lot of smoke and fire coming from Alliance Airport. I see . . . Tiger, I think I see secondary explosions—yes, definitely secondary explosions. I think one of the Patriot batteries went up."

Kestrel swore under his breath, then said, "Where are our unknowns, Senior Director?"

"One unknown, target ID 18, ten miles east of Meacham Airport," the Senior Director responded. "One unknown, target ID 19, now two miles northwest of Alliance Airport."

"MC, call from Meacham Tower, unknown 18 has requested clearance through the class D airspace westbound, destination Will Rogers Airport."

"Denied," Kestrel said. "I want Tango X-Ray-311's wingman to intercept unknown 18, and Tango X-Ray-311 leader to intercept unknown 19. Comm, this is MC, I want—"

"MC, target 19 turning right and descending . . . now heading zero-niner-zero, altitude one thousand . . ."

There was no time to warn this guy, no time for an intercept or visual identification. Kestrel wet his lips, prayed for a cigarette—but there was no time for praying for anything. "MC, unknown 19 passing through heading one-two-zero . . ."

Kestrel reached up and hit a button on his upper-left communications panel, marked simply "B," and said, "Tiger 100, Tiger, unknown target ID 19, batteries released tight, I repeat, batteries released tight."

Air Defense Battalion MICC, Dallas–Fort Worth Airport

The Patriot fire control computer had already placed a blinking diamond symbol around the red caret on the radarscreen marked UNK 19, signifying that it was ready to attack the aircraft. Captain Connor reached up to his upper instrument panel and hit a button, activating a loud klaxon in the area of the Patriot missile launchers stationed at Carswell Air Force Base and NAS Dallas. He checked and there was only one blinking diamond on the screen—the Westfall airliner still had a diamond around it, meaning the computer was tracking it as a hostile but was not yet prepared to launch on it. He then pressed a switch on the lower-right corner of his instrument panel marked LAUNCH.

The MICC computer had a choice—the target was within range of Tiger 111, the Patriot site at Carswell AFB, and Tiger 136, a HAWK site at Dallas–Fort Worth Airport—and it selected the northernmost Patriot battery at Carswell, launcher number one. It took only five seconds for the order to be relayed via microwave to the Engagement Control Center van at Carswell, which selected the proper launcher, activated the first two missiles, dumped the initial targeting information to the missiles' guidance units, released the safeties, and fired the solid rocket motor on missile number one. The first missile's motor blew out a protective fiberglass rear cover and shot a column of fire and smoke out the back end of the boxlike launcher, and the missile's quartz dielectric nose cap pierced another fiberglass cover on the front of the missile canister as the missile shot out of the launcher. The launch computer waited three seconds for the first missile to clear the launcher and for the launcher to stop shaking from the exhaust blast of the first missile before commanding the second missile launch.

Patriot engagements were always done in pairs for maximum effectiveness . . .

Aboard Airtech 75-D

"Man oh man, did you *see* that?" the copilot of Cazaux's plane shouted gleefully. The pallet of four cluster bomb units they had just dropped on the Patriot missile site at Alliance Airport was doing an unbelievable job. The exploding cluster bombs made the sun-dried brown earth west of the runway look as if it were boiling, with tiny flashes of yellow fire erupting in a large area the size of two full city blocks. Then, one of those tiny explosions would hit next to one of the upraised Patriot launchers, and the whole unit would disappear in a huge explosion that would rock their little transport plane. After one such explosion, one Patriot missile cooked off, and the two terrorists could see it spinning along the ground in wide arcs until it skipped across the runway and plowed into a group of buildings in the northern part of the airport, causing another huge explosion and fire. "Hey, go around once more. I gotta see this again."

"No sweat, man," the totally relaxed pilot murmured, starting a right turn back toward the airport so he could give the copilot a better look out the right cockpit windows. "Hey, that was fun." He rolled out momentarily, checking outside, then looked over to his copilot and said lazily, "It was nice flyin' with ya, bud."

"Say what?" The pilot pointed out the left cockpit window with his thumb. On the horizon, they could see a white line suddenly appear from the ground, speeding skyward out of sight. He squinted, trying to look up at its origin, but it was too high up and moving too fast to see. "What in the hell's th—"

Launcher number one was set at a fixed 60-degree up angle, and it was pointed far to the northwest, well away from the eastbound aircraft, but Patriot didn't need to be pointed directly at its quarry at launch. The missile quickly adjusted course, sending a white streak of smoke across the early-morning Texas sky. It climbed to fifteen thousand feet in less than three seconds before starting its terminal dive. Traveling at over twice the speed of sound, it took only six seconds for the first missile to find its target. After the hit, the Patriot engagement radar locked on to the biggest piece of the stricken aircraft, the aft half of the fuselage, and that's what it steered the second missile into—but one missile was all that was needed.

"Splash unknown 19," Connor reported in a monotone, detached voice. The plane—he wasn't even sure what kind of plane it was or how many persons were aboard—was destroyed, clean, simple, and quick. Radar return one moment, the next moment nothing. Connor felt horribly tense, almost nauseated. All their actions were precisely like the simulator sessions they constantly ran—the little Patriot missile "football" symbols racing across the screen, the dotted lines showing the missile's track intersecting with the target's track, the "coffin" symbol around the target as the computed time of intercept ran out and as the radar tried to determine if the target was still flying. But, of course, this was no simulation. "Set HOLD FIRE all units," he murmured, his voice barely audible over the whir of the van's air conditioning units, "and let's get a status report."

Aboard Tiger 90

It was an eerie feeling on the AWACS radar plane at that moment. In the Weapons and Surveillance sections, most of the controllers were busy with their own sectors and were not aware that a Patriot missile had just destroyed an aircraft near Fort Worth, Texas. But the Senior Director and Major Kestrel, the Mission Crew Commander, simply wore blank expressions as they stared straight ahead at their scopes. The other controllers and technicians that had participated in the shootdown were on their feet, silently looking over toward Kestrel. Most of them had helped kill things before for real—but they had been SCUD missiles over Saudi Arabia or Israel, or drones over the Gulf of Mexico or Pacific Ocean during live-fire exercises, never a manned aircraft flying over America.

"Get me a status on all Tiger units," Kestrel said, forcing as much steel into his voice as he could. "Verify all units acknowledging HOLD FIRE." He could see the status of all his assigned air and ground air defense systems himself, but he wanted to hear it for himself, direct from the unit operators and commanders, to reassure him that he was back in control and that no one else would die unless he gave the command.

"MCC, unknown 18 is still looking for clearance to Oklahoma City . . ."

"I want that bastard on the ground at Meacham," Kestrel ordered. "I want both Tango X-Ray-311 units to intercept unknown 18, and if they have to blow out his windscreen or shoot off an engine, I want that sonofabitch on the ground immediately. I want federal agents to arrest the crew."

"It's being done, Will," Ian Hardcastle replied. "Marshals Service agents and the FBI are on the way." He had been speaking on a headset to Marshals Service agents on the ground at Dallas–Fort Worth as the incident was occurring.

"Major . . . there was nothing you could do," Hardcastle said. Hardcastle could see the pain and the anger in Kestrel's face. These men were professional soldiers, trained to defend their country, yet killing was not part of their nature. It was even more difficult because it was so easy, so detached, so remote—say a word, and seconds later, men die and a very large air machine is destroyed. "You did everything right, and you exercised proper judgment."

"Then why in hell did we lose a Patriot site, Admiral?" Kestrel said. "There were a hundred soldiers at that site out there at Alliance."

"You got the guy who attacked them, Will. There was no way we could know unknown 19 was a terrorist. He had a proper flight plan, followed the proper procedures."

"Then what are we doing here, Admiral?" Kestrel shouted, whipping off his headset and shooting to his feet before Hardcastle. "We can't stop anyone who wants to come in. That Westfall flight is doing everything completely wrong!" He pointed to his radarscreen, his eyes bulging in anger. "He's *still* doing everything wrong, and he's getting away scot-free."

"We gotta deal with that, Will."

"Are you saying I should blow away that Westfall flight?"

"I'm not saying that, either," Hardcastle replied. "Your job is to protect your assigned airports from aerial assault."

"Well, I obviously failed at that."

"If one plane screws up and gets away, and a terrorist is allowed to attack, then it's the system that's failed, not you," Al Vincenti interjected. "You're doing everything you can."

"Sir, I need you on headsets," the senior director interjected. Hardcastle could see real, serious stress etched on that man's face—the pressure was on early in the game, and it showed no signs of letting up at all. "We've got another unknown, over Houston-Hobby, declaring an emergency."

"Shit!" Kestrel exclaimed, slipping wearily into his seat and donning his headset once again. "Admiral, I don't know what the answer is. But this is not going to work. It is just not going to fucking work."

Near Bedminster, New Jersey
That Evening

The television was on, and CNN was giving its hourly wrap-up of the hunt for Henri Cazaux. Jo Ann Vega shivered with excitement as she saw pictures of the aftermath of the latest attack, a cargo plane shot down north of Fort Worth, Texas, after it had dropped several cluster bombs on an Army Patriot missile site. Military commentators were now talking about the capabilities of the Patriot missile, assuring everyone that the advanced surface-to-air missile could easily defend its assigned airports.

She rose from her leather sofa and walked toward the windows, which looked out through the front of the house past the four-acre, tree-lined front lawn, and shook her head while she thought of the commentator's words. No one, she thought, was safe from Henri Cazaux. Even a Patriot missile could not stop him. Only Henri Cazaux himself could stop the killing.

Looking out the third-story window through the driving rain, Jo Ann Vega could see the guards in the front of the mansion, who had been sullenly pacing back and forth around the grounds through the warm summer rain, suddenly snap to attention. Cigarette butts went flying and submachine guns appeared from under long coats back up to carry-arms position. A few minutes later, a big one-ton dually six-passenger extended cab pickup truck zoomed around through the trees at the edge of the grassy front lawn and down the gravel driveway toward the mansion, stopping about fifty yards from the front door. While one guard covered the driver and another covered the passenger cab, a third guard shined a flashlight inside the front passenger side, checking IDs.

The truck was allowed to pass, parking just underneath the breezeway that covered the front entryway. A man she had never seen before emerged from the back of the truck, stood out on the lawn as he finished his cigarette. As he tossed it away, he looked up and saw Vega standing in the window, watching him. Their eyes locked for several moments before he pulled up his raincoat collar and headed inside.

Vega began to quiver, and she reached for a pack of cigarettes. Empty. She shivered again, and she felt as cold and as sweaty as if she was out there in the humidity and rain with the guards.

Henri was home. Good . . .

She had evacuated her home in Newburgh, New York, several days ago, right after the attack on Memphis. As they had expected, Newburgh and Stewart International had become a major supply depot for the effort to stop Henri Cazaux, with dozens of flights of C-5 Galaxy, C-141 Starlifter, and C-17 Globemaster transports bringing soldiers and air defense missile batteries into Stewart and trucking them to New York City and airports in Connecticut. Stewart International was also the southeastern New York headquarters of the New York State Police, with the FBI and Bureau of Alcohol, Tobacco, and Firearms setting up shop at the Army barracks at Stewart as well, so clearly it was no longer practical for Cazaux to visit her there.

Vega now occupied the entire third floor of the spacious mansion, with luxurious furniture, a little galley, a fully equipped entertainment center, and plenty of windows to watch the deer and other animals scamper across the property. Her new bedroom was almost as large as her entire storefront apartment in Newburgh had been. It was a lovely, peaceful, tranquil . . . prison. She had no company and was not allowed any guests. Her meals were brought to her by guards, who patrolled the hallways and who would periodically enter her room, even her bathroom, unannounced, to check on her. The guards never spoke to her, hardly ever looked at her, even when they would burst in on her in the shower or dressing in front of the mirror. Of course, she had no phone. She had no one she desired to call, but it effectively sealed her isolation.

She was allowed to have all her astrological books, charts, cards, runes, and even had a new computer with her charting software installed on it, so she spent a lot of time doing Henri's charts and readings, mapping out the progress of his campaign of terror, and writing what amounted to a script, a Book of Revelations, about how his private war would turn out. There was no doubt that his strength was growing each and every day. Every life, every existence could of course take a number of different paths, and Jo Ann tried to search each of the strongest and best-defined paths that her Henri would most likely take each day. They all went in the same direction—horrible death. Henri's death was clear, but his was not the only soul that she saw feel the pain of vengeful, wicked, bloodthirsty death. She saw thousands of tortured souls crying into the mists of the future, thousands of souls painfully ripped from this life and thrust into the next like hair being pulled from the skin by the roots.

But even more horrible than that was of a nation torn apart by a desperate, cold-blooded act of hatred by Henri Cazaux, an incredible act of destruction that would change millions of lives . . .

"Hello, Jo Ann."

Vega whirled around and saw him. Jesus, he was as silent as a snake. His hair, brown and curly with a hint of gray around the temples, was growing back with astounding speed, so fast that he appeared a completely different person. He seemed thinner, but that only helped to accentuate his wiry, muscular frame and lean, cheetah-like profile. He wore a sports coat over a black T-shirt, which he removed as soon as he entered her room.

"Henri," she greeted him, suddenly short of breath both by

being startled by him and by the excitement of seeing him again. "It's good to see you."

"You look good, Jo Ann," Cazaux said casually. His words made her heart flutter. They were the most caring words he had ever said to her. He stepped toward her, his eyes roaming her body momentarily, and then he said in French, *"Ça va,* Jo Ann. How have you been?"

"*Ça va bien, merci,* Henri," she replied. "I'm lonely without you, Henri. I wish you would stay with me, but—"

"You have already seen otherwise," Cazaux finished for her. "You know the forces that drive me, Jo Ann. You know that the power that is the instrument of my revenge is stronger than both of us. I have come so that you can tell me more about my future."

"I don't know that the forces that propel you are too strong to be overcome, Henri," Vega interrupted. "I've seen many of your futures. You are vulnerable now."

"Vulnerable? How?"

"The forces of good are organizing against you," Vega said. "There is weakness among your troops. Their resolve is not as strong as yours. You must use your power to keep all those around you in line."

"I have seen to that," Cazaux said with a smile. "You shall see."

"Good," Vega said. She averted her eyes slightly, as if embarrassed to tell all. Cazaux reached out and grasped her arm, wordlessly ordering her to continue: "The master, he is concerned about your targets," the woman said. "These small airports, this emphasis on these little companies."

"I don't understand, Jo Ann."

"The dark master has given you an enormous gift, Henri," Vega said. "Eternal life, power beyond any mortal, the vision, the strength—and you waste it on whatever this stockbroker tells you to attack."

"He has chosen his targets carefully," Cazaux said. "I don't understand all that he does, but the money he earns for us is far beyond anything I've ever seen before in my life."

"Do you think the dark master cares about how much money you make, Henri?" Vega asked. "He has given you a gift much more precious than money. Are you going to waste it on earning a few more dollars?"

"Then what?" Cazaux asked. "You're my adviser! Tell me!"

She stared at him, said nothing, then they both diverted their attention to the television. A group of men and women were standing in front of the White House for an impromptu press conference: "Henri Cazaux is a menace to American society, and I think it's time the White House and the Pentagon take off the kid gloves and get serious about stopping this bastard," the man in the lead said. He was identified by a caption as former Vice President Kevin Martindale. He continued, "So far the White House has put a gag order on their plans on how to deal with this crisis, which claimed thirty-one more victims this morning near Dallas. The American people deserve to be told how the Administration is responding to the crisis."

"There," Vega said. "That is your target."

"What? Those men? I agree they should be executed, but I don't—"

"I and my colleagues on both sides of the aisle are calling for a bipartisan Senate hearing on the terrorist crisis that is paralyzing our country," another person, identified as Senator Georgette Heyerdahl, said. "What we are demanding is a full-scale military-led manhunt for Henri Cazaux."

"A manhunt!" Cazaux laughed. "Those idiots are incapable of mounting a manhunt for a child, let alone a group of trained soldiers."

"Congress will enact legislation authorizing full military participation in the hunt for Cazaux," Heyerdahl continued. "We are asking that the President federalize the National Guard to assist law enforcement agencies to patrol the airports, protect the air defense units, fly along on scheduled commercial flights, and assist in the FBI investigation." The image shifted to shots of soldiers with Stinger shoulder-fired antiaircraft missiles, and then to an aerial shot of the White House.

"There," Vega said, a smile coming to her full red lips. "That is your target." Cazaux was staring with complete surprise at the aerial view of the White House and of the Capitol Mall.

The *White House?* The *Capitol?* But . . . But, of course . . .

"Yes," he breathed, his chest tightening in anticipation. "Yes, that's it. No more airports, no more little business run by nobodies."

Oh yes, he was going to be unstoppable.

"The attack on Dallas–Fort Worth Airport was a complete failure," Cazaux said later to his assembled staff officers. Almost everyone except Tomas Ysidro remained perfectly still in case any movement might be noticed by their angry commander. He tossed a plastic bag onto the circular glass coffee table before them. "I will not tolerate any more failures from this staff. Is that clear?"

The plastic bag landed on the table with a gut-wrenching *splut!* and flopped open, but no one dared to touch it—no one except Ysidro, who was sick enough to do just about anything anyone could possibly imagine. Under Cazaux's stern gaze, Ysidro held the bag up, examined its contents, smiled at Cazaux and nodded approvingly, then reached in and pulled a black, sticky blob out of the bag by a long rubbery tube.

"This belonged to Georges Lechamps, the butthead who hired those two dope-smoking pilots for the Dallas mission, eh, Henri?" Ysidro said, holding the thing up and twirling the tube as if he were carefully studying the thing, although he was really looking to see everyone else's reaction. Cazaux said nothing, but watched as everyone stared in horror at the squishy black blob that Ysidro was handling and examining. "Well, I guess ol' Georges' heart *really* wasn't in his work!" Ysidro laughed, letting the now-recognizable mass drop back into the bag.

That was enough for Harold Lake's assistant, Ted Fell—he barely made it out of the dining room before vomiting in a bathroom off the billiard room down the hall. Harold Lake felt equally as nauseated, but he was glad he could control his stomach, because Cazaux and Ysidro watched Fell run out of the room with utter disgust and disdain.

"I'll agree, Lechamps paid too much and got two worthless pilots to fly that mission," Gregory Townsend said, quickly ignoring the blood-filled bag of gore on the table in front of him. "But the mission was important because it pointed out the military's defense setup. Our field people report that our Airtech was destroyed by a Patriot missile fired from Carswell Air Force Base while the Airtech was less than a thousand feet aboveground. That was a shot from about fifteen miles away; a double missile launch, as I believe all Patriot attacks are done. That tells us that the Patriot missiles alone have extraordinary capability.

"What we learned about the other near-engagement was important as well. The Army let that first unidentified 727 fly right to five miles outside Dallas–Fort Worth Airport and still did not engage—at cruise speeds, that's less than forty-five seconds to a bomb-release point. Our people saw two F-16 fighters scramble from the Dallas

Naval Air Station, and those fighters did not engage either. At least one and possibly several Hawk antiair batteries were within range, and possibly even an Avenger Stinger mobile unit, and yet *no one* fired on the unidentified 727."

"You can believe that will not be the case the next time," one of the other staff officers said.

"The next target will have to be saturated for any attack to be successful," Townsend summarized. "Multiple aircraft, multiple axes of attack. Follow the flight plan as best as possible, then strike as close as possible to the aerodrome. As we saw with the very first unidentified-aircraft alert in Dallas, the mobile air defense units and the fighters escorting the suspect are not in a favorable position to attack the suspect once he's on the ground—they still track him, to some extent, but they assume he is not a hostile target when his wheels actually touch ground. We can use that fact to our advantage. Of course, timing and speed are essential."

"The problem is getting pilots to fly these missions," Ysidro said. "The money ain't attracting 'em anymore, Henri—everyone knows it's a one-way trip."

"That's not a problem," Townsend said confidently. "We have a system that can fly any of our planes by remote control now."

"It ain't gonna fucking work, Townie," Ysidro said. "Just find some cocky slug pilot who wants the money. Stupid pilots will do anything."

"My GPS system has tested very well on a small single-engine plane," Townsend said emphatically. "It's simple and basic, like a large radio-controlled model plane except much more sophisticated. It uses a simple digital autopilot system with altitude and vertical speed presets, hooked into a Global Positioning System navigation set. I can launch the plane by remote control, tie in the autopilot and the satellite navigator, and it'll fly right to the coordinates I punch in. With the GPS controlling the plane's altitude, I can have it dive-bomb right on top of whatever coordinates you like."

"The GPS satellite system's accuracy can be degraded by the Department of Defense," Cazaux said. "Our attacks call for precise guidance and accurate delivery."

"With those fuel-air explosives, Henri, you can miss the target by almost a half-mile and still blow the shit out of it," Townsend added.

Cazaux thought about that idea for a moment, then nodded his agreement. "Very well, we will use the GPS-controlled planes as well, but only with the smaller planes—I want human pilots controlling the larger aircraft. Where are your GPS-controlled planes, Gregory?"

"I just flew the first one into Boone County Airport for testing," Townsend replied. "I can pick up the fuel-air explosives canisters and fly it anywhere you want."

"Very well." Cazaux gave him a destination airport, then said, "Tomas is correct—there seems to be no shortage of pilots who will fly these missions for the proper sum of money. You are authorized to offer any amount necessary to get a crew to fly our planes. But understand this: any crew we contract with will either deliver the weapons on target as specified, or they will die the same fate as Monsieur Lechamps. Is that clear?" There was an immediate chorus of "Yes, sir" all round the table and its grisly centerpiece.

"The key to a successful strike now is to destroy the ground-based air defense sites nearest the designated target," Cazaux said. "We shall stage commando raids on the nearest Patriot, Hawk, and Avenger batteries to the designated target, and on the master command and control van on the ground. Our scouts can locate each of these assets and plan coordinated attacks at every point."

"That leaves the fighters and the radar systems that control them," Townsend said. "We can attack the terminal radar antennas to knock out the ground-based radars; we know their locations precisely. But the airborne radar planes and the fighters will still be in operation. If they're on the ground, we can hit them. We know the radar planes' main operating base is in Oklahoma City, Oklahoma, and our scouts can locate any other aerodromes they may deploy their radar planes. The fighters are widely deployed—we've seen them at the most unlikely aerodromes, parked beside fabric-winged planes and tiny line service plywood shacks trying to top up on jet fuel—and they fly more aerial patrols instead of returning to ground alert after a run. That means they'll be harder to target. But we've got the manpower and the hardware to raid a dozen locations simultaneously, Henri. Just give us a target and a time. A few days after we get the planes, we can—"

"I've got a better suggestion," Harold Lake interjected. "Why don't we quit while we're ahead here?"

The entire room turned as quiet as a tomb. The other staff officers looked at Lake in astonishment, wondering how he or any man who knew Henri Cazaux could dare to suggest such a thing as stopping an operation that Cazaux was actively directing. Lake noticed the sudden, deathly silence, took another deep swig of Scotch, and went on. "Look at you bums, looking at me like I just developed four fucking heads. Henri, I'm serious about this." Lake turned to Cazaux. He knew the terrorist respected strength and military protocol, and so he straightened his shoulders and said in a clear, steady voice, "Permission to speak, Henri."

"Of course, Harold," Cazaux said, nodding his approval. "You have earned the right. I have been remiss in not acknowledging your contribution to this campaign. I was distrustful and wary of your idea concerning using the stock and options markets to raise money for our operations, but you have far exceeded all expectations. I congratulate you, and I admit that my hesitation about your plan was because of my ignorance. Speak."

"Thank you, Henri. I'll preface my suggestion with the quartermaster's report, gentlemen: we have almost ninety million dollars in cash or liquid securities in our hands right now. The options that will expire in the next three to five days will net us another ten to twelve million—"

"You're shitting me!" Ysidro cried enthusiastically. "I don't believe it, Drip—you really made that stock option shit work!"

"This is by far the largest war chest we've ever had," Lake went on. "The only payables we have right now is the refurbishment and reregistration of the Shorts Sherpa following Henri's Memphis mission. We're not just repainting it, of course, but we've got to create new airworthiness certificates and registration documents, and all that takes time and money—and of course the prepurchase of the new aircraft, weapons, and hardware for the next mission.

"But each securities transaction I accomplish now is getting more and more attention, and it's only a matter of time before someone starts a Securities and Exchange Commission investigation. I'm not worried about that—the source of the money is very well covered, and besides, everything I'm doing is completely legal—but it will create a little attention, and we can always do without that. But when we purchased the Airtech transport we used on the Dallas raid, I'm sure our paperwork was scrutinized by the FBI or the Marshals Service. Any plane that even slightly appears as if it might be used in a Henri Cazaux–style raid will be subject to a more intensive search. In short, Henri, the heat's being turned up everywhere—not just over the target, but in the brokerage houses, banks, and the airplane dealers."

"So what's the point, Drip?"

"The point is, this might be a good time to take the cash, fold up our tents, and get out of the country," Lake went on. "Our operating expenses from our normal smuggling and tactical operations were about six million dollars a year. That's *half* of what we'll make on *interest* on our war chest alone, without ever touching the principal. In addition, I've established several iron-clad legitimate business entities in seven countries just in the past two weeks, all completely untraceable to any of us. I've got entrées into the defense and aviation ministries from countries like the Czech Republic, Indonesia, and mainland China, which means they will sell us weapons and aircraft with a phone call and a wire from a bank *that we own.*

"Henri, this is no shit, I swear it—I've got us tapped into resources, government officials, bank accounts, letters of credit, and industry pipelines to over ten *billion* dollars' worth of airplanes, weapons, real estate, anything you want," Lake went on excitedly. "We're players now, Henri—global, international, zero-frontier players. With all due respect, Henri, we're almost as big now as we were as just Henri Cazaux's smuggling gang, and far more legitimate-looking. We can pull the strings from anywhere on the planet that has a phone—not even a phone, man, as long as we could see the sky to aim at a satellite—and we could get away from the FBI and the regulators forever. And if we turned our backs on it all, flew the Shorts down to South America, bought a plantation outside Caracas or Rio or Cartagena, we could live like kings and have enough dough to set our *grandchildren* up in business fifty years from now."

Harold Lake had mesmerized this audience—he even seemed to have Cazaux's full attention. Tomas Ysidro said, "Hey, Henri, the Drip is paintin' a pretty smooth picture right now. I see stuff on the news about the feds closing in on us—I don't see it happening, but, you know, it kinda gets stuck in your brain, you know . . . ?"

"Ysidro is babbling as usual," Townsend said, "but I share his thoughts. In any previous operation, Henri, we have never stayed in a country as long as we have for this one. Staying on the move, and especially outside the States, has helped us keep out of the reach of the authorities. I feel we've overstayed our welcome here, as well. Perhaps it is time to consider taking the cash and laying low for a few weeks."

To everyone's surprise, Cazaux nodded—the sense of relief was obvious. "Very well," he said, crossing his arms on his chest. "My adviser has indicated to me that the authorities are indeed closing in on us, and so we shall close our operation, disperse, and meet again in a new location—after one more mission.'' He turned to Lake and said, ''Harold, you indicated that Universal Equity still has two major companies in America untouched—Westfall Air at Dallas–Fort Worth Airport, and Sky Partners Airlines in New York City.''

''Sure,'' Lake replied, ''and they're trying to make a comeback of sorts, using the public's fear as a marketing tool. Universal Express has moved most of the package stuff to other airports, and the blowhard president, McSorley, is promising to fly even if all the other carriers close up shop during the air emergency. We missed Westfall Charter when those dopers failed to attack Dallas–Fort Worth, Henri, but Westfall is small potatoes—Sky Partners is the real prize. The stock is on the upswing—ripe for another fall.''

''Then that will be our objective . . . our *secondary* objective,'' Cazaux said. ''And now I will brief you on our primary objective—and what I demand of all of you.''

After completely destroying a corner of a very expensive Persian carpet in the billiards room, Ted Fell leaned on the pool table, his eyes filled with tears, trying to block out the grisly image of a murdered man's heart being dangled in front of his face. Cazaux had butchered a man and brought his heart back, obviously as a warning to everyone else. What was really sick was that Mexican bastard Ysidro. Cutting out a man's heart and stuffing it into a Ziploc bag was one thing—pulling it out and gleefully examining it as if it were a pet mouse or a newly discovered seashell was another thing. Fell thought he had never seen anything as disgusting in his life.

A few guards checked Fell, but they ignored him as the attorney continued to dry-heave in the corner, chuckling at the bean-counter's cowardice as they walked away. The image would simply not go away—Fell saw that gruesome piece of flesh everywhere in his mind's eye. He finally stood upright and tried to force fresh air into his lungs, noticing that the front of his suit was stained with vomit. He left the billiards room to find a bathroom and clean his suit, and perhaps get some help in cleaning the room. It was obvious that Henri Cazaux and most of the others were out of place in that big New Jersey mansion—Cazaux looked as if he belonged in a southeast Asia jungle or an African swamp—but he still feared meeting the wrath of Cazaux or Ysidro if they found the mess he had made, so he thought he better clean it up.

Fell heard voices coming from the kitchen, but he decided to avoid that place—the guards, most likely on break or getting dry. He noticed what looked like a broom closet at the top of the stairs, so he quietly stepped upstairs. No guards were nearby to stop him. He reached the top of the stairs and found some towels and cleaning supplies, then went down the hallway to the bathroom to wet the towels. He was about to enter the bathroom when he passed a set of stairs leading up to the third floor—and he heard a woman's faint sobs coming from upstairs.

At first Fell told himself to forget what he just heard, forget all about whoever was up there. He thought that Cazaux probably didn't have a wife or girlfriend—who in hell would want a psychopath like Cazaux? Was she a captive? Some kind of sex slave? Was she a hostage? In any case, he didn't think Cazaux would take too kindly to someone sneaking around his house. Fell heard a groan and a labored cough—she obviously sounded hurt, perhaps recovering from being strangled or hit. Beating up on women was the mark of a coward—and so was terrorism. Henri Cazaux fit both descriptions perfectly. And what was Ted Fell made of? He was either very brave or very stupid, because he found himself quietly tiptoeing up the stairs and pushing open the one door.

The attic had been turned into a very nice little studio apartment—but what else he found was not so pretty. Fell saw a woman lying on her back on the bed in the center of the apartment, her clothing ripped away from her body, her breasts exposed, her dress piled up around her waist, exposing her crotch, her legs dangling off the side of the bed. She was facing away from him, so she could not see him. Her dark hair was a tangled mess, her hands and fingers were stained with . . .

"It is not safe for you to be here," she said suddenly. There was a slight pause while she sniffed and let out a painful breath; then she added, "Mr. Fell."

Fell resisted the urge to run down the stairs and back to the billiards room as fast as he could—obviously he had made a lot more noise than he thought he did, even though he had tried to be quiet. But her shaking voice and trembling hands and shoulders told him that she was in real trouble. "Who are you?" he asked in a loud whisper. "How do you know my name? What happened to you? Was it Cazaux?"

"My name is not important," she replied weakly. "I know all

who come to this place, except you, so you must be Mr. Lake's assistant, whom I have not met. I . . ."

She had tried to rise onto her elbows, but a shot of pain had cut her off. Fell darted into the room, closed the door, and sat on the bed beside her. Her face had been savagely beaten, covered with red and black bruises. Her nose was broken, and it did not look like the first time it had been done. He pushed her skirt back down over her knees, but couldn't help noticing the blood that stained the bedspread under her anus. "My God . . . the sonofabitch . . ."

"He is no longer in control of himself," the woman mumbled. "The dark master controls him."

"Cazaux? Who controls Cazaux . . . ?"

"I tried to stop him," she said. "I tried to tell him that he still had a choice, that he can still control his destiny. But his soul has been taken. He no longer listens to human reason."

"Forget Cazaux," Fell said. "Is there a way out of here? I think you need medical attention."

"I cannot leave here," the woman said. "There is no way out for me while Henri lives—but you can leave." Her eyes no longer reflected the extreme pain she was suffering, but locked firmly on his, riveting him. A plan came instantly to mind—she just hoped she'd be there to watch it. "You are my only hope. You must stop Cazaux before he flies this last mission."

"What last mission? What do you mean?" The thought of he, Ted Fell, trying to stop Cazaux from doing anything was both laughable and terrifying. "Hey, I'm trying to help you, miss, but I'm not going to try to get in Cazaux's way. The last guy who crossed Cazaux—well, there's a human heart on the coffee table downstairs. I'd like to keep mine for a while longer."

Vega didn't know about the heart, and she had to force herself to suppress a smile. *My God, Henri really* has *gone over the edge!* She hoped she could see the heart, see the knife that he did it with, maybe listen to him describe how he did it. But she forced a horrified expression on her face. "Ted Fell, listen to me," the woman said. "You must kill Henri Cazaux."

"What . . . ?"

"You must do it, Ted Fell," she said. She reached under her mattress and came up with a tiny .22 caliber automatic pistol. "I'm too weak to do it. If he comes back for me, he'll kill me, I know he will." Vega let the remains of her blouse fall away, revealing her breasts to him, and she noticed with a tiny smile that, despite her face and the beating she took, he was admiring her chest. *A typical male,* she thought, *wanting to suck tits and screw pussy without one single thought regarding the woman.* He was going to do just fine, she thought—this little tit-sucking weasel was going to pull a gun on Henri Cazaux, and when he did she was going to watch Henri, Townsend, and Ysidro chop him up into fish food. She pressed the gun into his hands. "You must do it, Ted . . . for me. You want to help me, don't you?"

She brushed her breasts against him, averting her eyes and letting a few wisps of hair fall innocently across her face—and he was hooked. He took the pistol, hefted it, then set his jaw and stuck the pistol in his pants pocket. Even if he never pulled it out, Vega thought, someone would notice it. She would be listening, and the first sense of commotion she heard, she'd rush downstairs and hopefully be just in time to watch. "Go, Ted. Save me—please!" She pushed him off the bed with surprising strength, but Fell didn't need too much prompting—he was already racing for the door. "Do not stop!" Her voice was cut off by another fit of coughing, but by then Fell was taking the steps three at a time, landing on each step on tiptoes.

He reached the first floor without anyone seeing him. He glanced back upstairs, wondering if any guards were chasing him or had heard him stomping down the stairs, and had just walked past the double doors to the billiards room when he ran headlong into Thomas Ysidro. The Mexican executioner pushed him away, but held him tightly by his jacket. "Where the fuck did you go, asshole?" Ysidro growled.

Fell's mouth flapped open and closed like a dying fish—he was so scared he couldn't answer. Ysidro's expression went from suspicious to angry to murderous, and he grabbed Fell by the lapel and pulled him closer, shaking him like a dirty throw-rug. "I said, where the fuck did you . . . ?" Then he noticed the green and yellow stain on Fell's shirt, then sniffed at the same smell coming from the billiards room. With Fell still in his grasp, he peeked around the corner and saw the mess on the carpet. "Shit, bean-counter, you barfed on my fuckin' rug!"

"I . . . I couldn't help it . . ."

"Well, clean it the fuck up!" Ysidro said, pushing Fell onto the floor in front of the vomit. Fell waited for the follow-up kick, but all he heard was another "Shee-it" as Ysidro left. Fell found some rags in the cue rack on the wall, and used his hankerchief to mop up the rest and take out as much of the stain as he could. He stayed on his hands and knees after cleaning up the mess, thinking hard.

Could he do it? Could he kill Henri Cazaux? No doubt the world would be better without that psychopathic woman-beating bastard, but certainly Ysidro and the others would execute him right away . . . or would they? It did not take a genius to see the power struggle going on in Cazaux's organization. Maybe he'd be doing them a big favor . . . yes, maybe . . .

"Hey, asshole, on your feet," Fell heard a voice say behind him. He struggled to his feet, feeling his knees wobble and his fingers shake. The guard had a small, mean-looking submachine gun in his hands, held at port-arms in front of him. He noticed the vomit on Fell's jacket and sneered. "Back in the other room, the others are leaving."

Fell was prodded back into the foyer outside the den where the meeting was held, only to find the meeting breaking up and Cazaux's officers putting on coats, preparing to depart. Fell caught Cazaux's gaze on him, a mixture of hatred and suspicion. *Jesus, does he know I made contact with his captive upstairs?* But Cazaux's eyes only glanced down at the vomit stain, and his eyes told Fell that he was being dismissed as too weak to be a threat to him. He was so smug, so confident, ignoring the little weak guys simply because they were smaller and less imposing. Cazaux was an animal, a human animal. He deserved to die, the bastard, he *deserved* to die, long and hard and painfully. Ysidro might even reward him for daring to do something that he obviously wanted very badly to do himself.

But even more fearful than Cazaux's questioning stare was Harold Lake's face—he looked horrified, shocked, as white and colorless as if he had been dead for several hours. He nearly stumbled into Fell as Fell tried to help him on with his coat.

"Harold, what is it?" he whispered as they headed outside. "What's going on?"

"Just go," Lake said. "Out."

"My briefcase," Fell said, hesitating as long as he could. "I'll get it."

Fell went back into the conference room for the briefcase and picked it up. He was alone. The nearest guard was back in the hallway, almost completely out of sight, and Henri Cazaux was standing on the opposite side of the room, his back turned to him, looking out the window. The perfect opportunity. There was an inside slit in his raincoat that allowed Fell to access his pants pocket. Fell reached into the slit, then into his pants pocket . . .

"Look out, Henri!" he heard a voice—a female voice—shout behind him. "Look out, he's got a gun!"

Cazaux spun, crouched, a knife appearing in his hands as if by magic. Fell turned. It was the woman, dressed in a red silk robe, the blood cleaned off her face, even wearing makeup. She was pointing toward him. Cazaux hesitated, seeing who it was threatening him, then he chuckled softly and lowered the knife from its throwing position. Fell was confused—why was she doing this?

Three guards pounced on Fell, wrestling him to the ground, pinning his arms behind his back so hard and so high that Fell thought they'd snap off. Hands were all over him, searching him, then dragging him up to his feet before Cazaux. The big Belgian mercenary looked at Fell with an amused expression.

"Nothing, Captain," the guards said. Ted Fell had lost his nerve after rushing downstairs and had placed the gun underneath a large tree planter in the second-floor hallway. The guards released Fell, then turned toward the dark-haired woman. She looked momentarily confused.

"He is not armed, Madame Vega," Cazaux said. "Why did you think he had a gun?"

"I . . . I'm sorry, I guess I'm just too keyed up," she said. "I've never seen this man before. He scared me."

"He was just leaving," Cazaux said. He gave Fell one last menacing look, and Fell felt sweat pop out on his forehead and felt urine uncontrollably rush out of his bladder. He barely caught it in time before he wet himself. Fell was escorted out of the house by the two guards and virtually dumped into the duallie with Lake.

Lake refused—or was unable—to say anything until they were outside and back into the six-passenger pickup with the security glass between the front and rear seat closed. Fell waited several minutes for his heart to start hammering in his chest. *The damn bitch tried to get me killed,* Fell thought. *Who in hell is she?* But soon the curiosity of what was happening with his boss, Lake, finally took over. "Harold, what happened? What's going on?"

"We're folding up shop," Lake said finally. "First thing tomorrow morning, we put stop orders on all outstanding contracts, negotiate for cash closings. We need to arrange for a cash-asset transfer—probably use Win Millions Casino again."

"Sure, sure, Harold, they'll give us whatever we want," Fell said.

"So we're bugging out? Time to see what Brazil is like in the wintertime?"

"We'll be out of the country by tomorrow night . . . two nights, tops. While Henri is counting the cash, we'll be on the *Challenger* to Belo Horizonte."

"Great, great," Fell said. That was a relief—the farther he was away from that dark-haired bitch, the better. "I've been checking on the plane and the crew every day for a week, making sure they're ready to blast off. Flight plans are no problem if you're *leaving* the country. One stop in Belize for gas and maybe a few señoritas, and we're out of here with twenty million dollars in cash at our disposal, all nice and safe in numbered bank accounts. We'll live like kings in that little town, what's its name, Abaete or something . . . ?" Lake wasn't sharing in the image one bit—in fact, he looked as if he were turning to stone, or wax. "What the hell's the problem, Harold? Cazaux will never find the cash we've been siphoning off from the Asian contracts. Did he accuse you of something? What—"

"There's going to be one more operation," Lake said. "One more big strike . . ."

"As long as we're out of it, I don't really care," Fell said. "We close up shop and we're done . . . right?"

Lake said nothing else during the rest of the ride to the garage, where their limo was waiting for them. The image of them relaxing on the red-tiled veranda of their two-thousand-acre ranch in central Brazil was gone . . . replaced by the woman's struggled plea to stop Cazaux. Obviously he was planning something so deadly, so monstrous, so devastating, that not even Lake could talk about it.

It didn't matter, Fell decided. In two days they were going to be out of the country. Twenty million dollars and a Gulfstream bizjet bought a lot of comfort, especially in Brazil—it bought a lot of forgetfulness, too. He was going to have to forget the woman's piercing eyes, her plea that reached down to the core of his soul . . .

. . . and remember, if he could ever forget, what happened to experienced mercenary soldiers who crossed Henri Cazaux. Remember that bloody bag, the black mass dangling from an artery, remember Ysidro's sick grin. What chance did an attorney from Springfield, Massachusetts, have? Silence and a life of luxury in equatorial Brazil, or go to the authorities and face Henri Cazaux, Tomas Ysidro, Gregory Townsend, and almost certain death.

Ted Fell didn't need to be a Harvard Law School grad to figure that one out.

Mojave, California
Two Days Later

"They're coming in here faster than we can handle them," the man said. "I'll be of any help I can. You have your pick of the litter, I can assure you."

Harold Lake did not say anything—he was too surprised to speak. He was looking not at a puppy kennel or thoroughbred racehorse stable, but at two mile-and-a-half-long lines of airliners—all shapes and sizes, in various states of repair but all generally in very good condition. It seemed every airline in the world had an airplane here, and the paint jobs looked brand new. Even Ted Fell, Lake's assistant, who hated airplanes and anything having to do with flying, was suitably impressed. "My God, I never dreamed anything like this existed," he said, gaping at what he saw.

"I imagine most folks don't," the facility manager responded, smiling at Lake's amazed expression as they drove down a taxiway in a thankfully well-air-conditioned Range-Rover. "Mojave Commercial Air Services used to be a boneyard for airliners—much like Davis-Monthan Air Force Base in Tucson stores and parts-out old military aircraft. We've cut up and recycled over ten thousand aircraft since we opened back after World War Two.

"But airliners last longer and are much more expensive, so when times get tough and nobody's flying, companies send their planes out here for storage—low humidity, not much rain, pretty good conditions for outdoor storage. Some companies buy them and immediately fly them directly out here for storage. When they signed the contract to buy them three years ago, the industry wasn't in quite bad shape. Now they own it, and it's a big investment, but it wouldn't pay to fly it half-filled with passengers, so they bring it out here for storage. The industry will bounce back, and when it does these babies will be put on the line." He motioned to one airplane, obviously the size of a DC-10 or L-1011, completely cocooned in shiny aluminized plastic. "We used to just fly them in, weatherize them, and let 'em sit, but more companies want a bit more protection from blowing sand and moisture, so we shrink-wrap some planes."

"That's shrink-wrapped?" Fell asked. "You're kidding!"

"Nope. Shrink-wrapped just like a copy of *Playboy* on the magazine racks," the manager said. "Actually, it's much better than that. It takes only a couple hours to apply it, and it protects the planes against most every hazard. It's completely sealed—all the air is pumped out, so it's impervious to the elements. A plane in shrinkwrap like that will be as good as new ten years from now—we guarantee it, in fact. No mildew, no critters, no corrosion."

"Incredible," Lake exclaimed. The array of planes out here was amazing—he saw quite a few MD-11 and Boeing 757 and 767 airliners, the cream of the airline crop, sitting here idle. "There has to be four or five billion dollars' worth of machines sitting out here."

"Pretty good guess, Mr. Lake," the manager said. "The actual figure is three-point-seven-two-billion dollars—we keep a weekly tally." He pulled up to a plane and put the Range-Rover in park. "Here's 331. We started the prepurchase inspection as soon as your people showed up. Isn't she a sweetheart?"

Lake distrusted and usually discounted anyone who talked about inanimate objects in human terms, and he was proved correct on this one. They were looking at an Aeritalia G222 twin turboprop heavy transport plane, and it was a short, squat-looking airplane with a tall tail and high-mounted wings—not exactly a "sweetheart" unless you were into ugly-looking planes. This one was painted up with high-visibility white-and-orange stripes, with the words SISTEMA AERONAUTICO ANTI-INCENDIO painted on both sides. Lake opened a thick information folder on the plane: "This is a 1988-model waterbomber? It looks in great condition."

"The G222 is the finest pure water-bombing aircraft on the market today," the facility manager said. "These actually have the newer uprated Rolls-Royce Tyne turboprops, so they each put out closer to four thousand shaft horsepower instead of the normal three thousand four hundred. She's also been strengthened to pull over four Gs instead of the normal two-point-eight—pretty important when your clients are diving into the bottom of a deep canyon chasing that last stubborn torcher. I've got to hand it to you water-bomber guys—you got balls the size of coconuts. Which group did you say you were representing?"

"I'm acting as the finance manager for a broker representing Walter Willis and Company," Lake said. "The G222 and any other aircraft I can find within the next thirty days will be going to his ranch in Colorado for modification and training—and possibly go operational if this summer stays hot and dry like this." It was all a lie, of course, but he had laid enough groundwork over the past few days, with this deal and with a half-dozen others, to make the fiction work unless a real in-depth investigation was begun. Years ago, Lake, working with the skinflint president of Universal Express, Brennan McSorley himself, had helped finance the lease of several aerial firefighting aircraft to Walter Willis, the biggest private aerial firefighting company in the world. Lake had been involved in several other financing deals since, so he had the credentials to visit this place in Mojave and talk turkey.

"I've never worked with Mr. Willis himself," the facility manager said. "How is the old buzzard doing?"

Fell looked at the guy, then at Lake, and he could immediately sense that his boss's mood had suddenly turned as dark as the inside of a thunderstorm. He stepped back a pace to watch the fireworks . . .

"He's doing fine," Lake said tightly. He glanced at the manager, who was suddenly eyeing him with a great deal of suspicion, then added, "Walter is doing fine—for a guy who's been dead for eleven *fucking* months, you cold-hearted son of a bitch!" The manager's jaw dropped open in surprise, and Lake used his dumbfounded expression as a target for his anger: "His son Brad Willis and the Universal investor group own the company; I was an usher at Brad's wedding last January in Aspen. Do you know the Willises?"

"Ah, no, but you see . . ."

"Then why did you ask about Walter? My friend Brad almost had a nervous breakdown at the death of his father." Lake did not know Brad Willis except by his ultra-irresponsible playboy reputation—Brennan McSorley and Universal got a good deal when they bought the company from Brad. "And Walter was certainly not an 'old buzzard' when he died—he was only in his early sixties, in the best physical condition of his life." Lake turned toward the manager, enjoying watching the bastard wilt under his glare. "Is this some kind of test, Mr. Adams?" Lake asked. "Are you actually *testing* me?"

"I would never even *consider* . . ."

"Sir, I do not have to submit to this," Lake said, truly indignant that this old bastard would dare to try to clumsily trap him like that. "I can drop names all day to you, and you might be impressed or you might not. But I let my credentials, my reputation, and my money speak for me, sir."

"I assure you, Mr. Lake, I did not mean to . . ."

"As I recall, I deposited a certified check in the amount of nine million dollars in your bank account in Los Angeles two days ago, along with enough credit references that my submission can be measured by the pound. It took a staff of four two days to complete it, working night and day.'' He reached into his jacket breast pocket and withdrew an envelope, opened it, and showed the contents to the manager. ''This is another certified check for sixteen million four hundred thousand dollars, made out to your company, with today's date, as the second deposit for the two aircraft.''

Lake waited until he could see the facility manager's eyes grow wide with surprise and want—then crumpled the check up in his right hand, right in front of the man's face. Lake held his clenched fist with the check inside it up in the man's face until he saw sweat pop out of his forehead. ''I am not accustomed to being treated like a teenager trying to buy a bottle of cheap wine at the Safeway, sir. Ted?''

Fell turned to the Aeritalia G222, put his fingers to his lips, and whistled. The three men he had hired to do the prepurchase inspection on the freighter looked up and turned toward him. ''Pack it up,'' he shouted. ''The deal has been canceled.''

''Wait a minute, Mr. Lake,'' the manager pleaded. ''Hold on. It wasn't a test, I swear it wasn't. I wouldn't do such a thing.''

''No, and after your company finds out what happened, I would think you won't be selling too many aircraft, either.''

''C'mon, Mr. Lake, I didn't mean anything by it,'' the manager said. ''It's all these federal boys out here—I guess I started thinking like some bozo gumshoe detective.''

Both Lake and Fell twisted their necks around to stare at the manager when he mentioned ''federal boys.'' Fell shot a subdued, panicked look at his boss, but Lake quickly regained his composure and shot a warning glance at Fell, who turned away and walked toward the G222 so he could effectively hide his shocked expression. ''Federal boys? What are you talking about?''

''This place gets a visit by someone or other from Los Angeles or Washington or Las Vegas or Sacramento damned near every day,'' the facility manager said. ''I guess it has to do with that terrorist that's dropping bombs on American airports. The feds ask tricky questions all the time, trying to trip you up, like I can hand Henri Cazaux to them on some shiny silver platter.''

''I think that's the last straw,'' Lake said quickly. ''Federal agents, indeed! You're just trying to pin your clumsy attempt at making me feel uncomfortable on someone that doesn't exist.''

''No, Mr. Lake, they're here—look, there's one now,'' the man said. He pointed at a dark gray Chevrolet Caprice sedan cruising up and down the flight line. ''That's . . . damn, I can't remember his name . . ." He fished around in a pocket and came up with a business card. "Yeah, here he is—Timothy Lassen, Deputy U.S. Marshal. Here's his card."

Lake snatched the card away—he didn't want to be so obviously upset, but a thrill of panic had just settled into Lake's brain, and he was no longer totally in control of himself. Yes, the card said he was a U.S. Marshal, from Sacramento . . . and now the man in the Caprice had spotted him talking with the facility manager and had turned in their direction.

"Well . . . perhaps I've been a bit hasty," Lake said as the sedan approached. "I should've realized you're under considerable scrutiny these days."

"That is the truth, Mr. Lake, it certainly is," the manager said, relieved that the sale would actually go through. Lake motioned to Fell, who told the inspectors to go back to work.

"I will direct my bank to cut another check for you—it'll take an extra day, I'm sure you understand."

"I certainly do, Mr. Lake," the manager said, practically kissing Lake's hand in gratitude. "And I sincerely apologize for my behavior. I'm very, *very* sorry . . ."

"I'd like *nothing* more to be said about it," Lake said, adding a touch of his command voice into his request. "My clients appreciate discretion as well as efficiency. There will be questions about why the transaction is to be delayed an extra day, and that'll have to be handled."

"You can count on me, Mr. Lake," the manager said. "Don't worry about a thing." Just then the sedan pulled up to them, and a tall, good-looking man a bit older than Lake emerged. His plain dark-gray suit coat was unbuttoned, revealing a plain white shirt and plain dark-blue tie with diagonal red stripes. The sun was hot and merciless already that morning, but the man kept the jacket on. "Excuse me, Mr. Fennelli, but how do I get out of here? I'm lost already."

"Easy enough, Agent Lassen," the facility manager said, pointing southwest. "Just head for the gap between the big hangars out there, you'll see the front gate. Be sure to watch out for planes taxiing around."

"Got it," Lassen said. It was obvious that Lassen didn't need any assistance getting off the airport. He looked at Lake, and the investor could practically see the marshal going through the mental exercise taught to all law enforcement officers that would imprint a man's face on their memories for years. He held out a hand toward Lake: "Hi. Tim Lassen—how're you doing?"

"Harold Lake, Marshal Lassen," Lake responded, shaking Lassen's hand. "My associate, Ted Fell." They shook hands. "Mr. Fennelli tells me you're a federal marshal," Lake said. He motioned to the expanse of high desert and rocky mountains surrounding Mojave Airport. "Seems like the perfect setting for a marshal, like the Old West. All you need is a horse and a big six-gun."

Lassen chuckled easily and genuinely enough, but his eyes never left Lake's. He said, "Actually, you're pretty close, Mr. Lake," Lassen said. "This area used to be one of the roughest and toughest in the country. Claim jumpers, fugitives on the run from justice, hijackers, bank robbers . . . terrorists . . . the scum of the earth always seemed to congregate around this area, as if the desert would protect them from the law . . . This your plane, Mr. Lake? It's Italian, isn't it?"

The federal agent eased into the questioning even more smoothly and naturally than Lake had expected. Lake responded, "No, it's not my plane. I know very little about planes, actually."

"Your plane, Mr. Fell?" Lassen asked, turning toward Lake's assistant, who thought himself completely out of the conversation.

"No," Fell replied much too hastily, too nervously. "Actually, I hate airplanes. I have to practically be sedated into unconsciousness before takeoff."

"It's a beauty," Lassen said. "I don't know too much about them, either, but of course the job lately has introduced me to lots of different kinds."

"You're investigating the terrorist Cazaux," Lake said knowingly. "The lunatic who isn't satisfied with blowing up one plane—he's got to blow up the entire terminal."

"Exactly," Lassen said. "This kind of plane, as you might know, is just like the one Cazaux might use—big, relatively inexpensive, heavy payload, designed to drop things out the back. This is a firebomber, right?"

"A water-bomber, to be exact," Lake corrected him. "And yes, it is Italian. It is used all over the world for firefighting, military transport, even civilian and commercial passengers. So how's the investigation going? You going to catch that bastard yet?"

"Oh, I think Cazaux will either slip away out of the country, do something really stupid and get himself caught, or one of his soldiers will rat him out for money or to make a deal with prosecutors," Lassen said matter-of-factly.

"You sound pretty sure of this," Lake observed, trying to act disinterested.

"I wish I could say that most crimes are solved by expert, meticulous investigation by wise, insightful, observant agents, but in fact most crimes get solved because the bad guy screws up . . . or someone very close to him turns him in." He paused, his eyes affixing on Lake, and the New York investor felt the first prickle of perspiration on the back of his neck.

"Most criminals, Mr. Lake, are dishonest, egotistical, greedy slimeballs," Lassen explained. "Many of the people that psychopaths like Henri Cazaux surround themselves with are also slimeballs, but they're usually smarter. These guys are not quite as violent or psychopathic as their boss—they're usually motivated by greed, not by the thrill of killing or some voice inside their head telling them to kill. They are cowed by the psychopathic leader into following him, even when the killing grows beyond anything anyone could imagine.

"But sooner or later it appears that the leader is getting too far out of control, and the smart underling realizes that he'd better cut and run and make a deal with the authorities before everyone lands in prison for life plus two hundred years—or dead. The smart underling turns in the psychopath, gets a reduced sentence or maybe even put in a Witness Protection Program, and thanks his lucky stars he saw the light before it was too late . . . I'm sorry, I've been chatting on here. What is it you do, Mr. Lake?"

At first Lake acted as if he didn't hear the federal agent's question—and in fact he hadn't, because he was too stunned by what Lassen had said. He had precisely described the dilemma Lake was in.

Cazaux was getting more and more violent every day, urging his troops to take more chances, go to any lengths to carry out his orders. Lake had been looking for his chance to scrape together enough cash to disappear to a ranch in Brazil or Thailand, but it seemed Cazaux was always around, watching him, ordering him around. This trip was exactly a case in point: Lake knew nothing about doing prepurchase inspections on cargo planes, but Cazaux had him come out here anyway instead of just staying in his office and monitoring their ever-growing portfolio of options contracts.

They were making ten, sometimes fifteen million dollars a *day* from their series of investments, and it required careful study and analysis to keep it all going. But Cazaux ordered him out here, and now he was being confronted by a fed from Sacramento, a damned *fed* who seemed to see right through him.

"I'm a smart underling," Lake finally responded with an easy smile, "and I work for a broker who can really terrorize a tiramisù or an apricot flambé if he sets his mind to it. I'm going to turn him over to Jenny Craig any day now."

The ploy thankfully worked—everyone laughed, and Lassen finally disengaged his piercing gaze, laughed loudly, and shook a finger at Lake as if to say, *Okay, okay, okay, you got me.* "Hey, have a great day, everyone, I've got a long drive back to Sacramento ahead of me. Nice to meet all of you. Thanks again, Mr. Fennelli." He shook hands with Lake and Fell and headed back to his car, casually studying the G222 as he did. He finally took off his jacket just before getting into the sedan, and Lake noticed he seemed to wear no gun.

A pencil-pusher, Lake guessed, pressed into field service in Hell's half-acre in Mojave because the feds were stretched so thin. "Seems like a nice guy," Lake said to Fennelli as the fed departed.

"That's the most I've heard him say the whole time he's been here, about four days now," Fennelli replied. "Pokes around here and there, flies off, shows up again a couple days later, never asks for anything, pokes around some more, flies off again. That's his Cheyenne over there."

That made Lake relax a bit—the guy really did seem like nothing but a pencil-pusher, not a real investigator. But as soon as Lake took some comfort in that thought, his mind went on the alert again. Lassen was a deputy U.S. Marshal—that was not a ceremonial or political post. Lake wished he had taken more time to study the fed better. He was going to have Fell check him out.

"I'll be returning to Los Angeles this afternoon," Lake told Fennelli. "My staff will conclude the transaction."

"Yes, Mr. Lake," Fennelli said. He extended a hand to Lake; he did not accept it. "Everything will be ready for your ferry crews. If there's anything else you require, please let me—"

"All I require, Mr. Fennelli, is for you to do your job," Lake said, "and to leave the sleuthing to Deputy Marshal Lassen there."

"Of course, Mr. Lake," Fennelli said contritely. He led Lake and Fell back to the Range-Rover. He started heading back toward the flight-line offices where his customer's Learjet was parked, then did a sudden one-eighty turn and headed back down the flight line. "I'm sorry, Mr. Lake, I almost forgot," Fennelli said. "You'll be wanting to see your other plane, I'm sure." Lake really didn't care to see it, but he said nothing as Fennelli sped down the row of airliners. It did not take long to reach it. "Here we are. It looks like they're further along the prepurchase inspection on this one."

Lake found his legs and hands shaky as he stepped out of the Land-Rover and looked up at the huge aircraft before them. He glanced at Ted Fell, and he was just as white-faced and nervous as his boss.

This had to be some kind of joke, Lake thought bitterly. Henri Cazaux had issued his order that he wanted this plane, and Lake had found him one right away without really asking why he wanted it. Now, seeing it like this, Lake understood exactly why Cazaux wanted it.

It was a Boeing 747-200F freighter, still in Nippon Cargo Airlines livery, although the markings on the vertical stabilizer from its former owner had already been painted over in bright white. The aircraft was a cargo-carrying version of the 747 airliner, with a huge nose loading door hinged at the top just below the flight deck, which opens out and up, like a huge sun visor. Almost two hundred thousand pounds of cargo could be rolled into the cavernous cargo bay through the front or through large side doors. "It's a beauty, all right," Fennelli was saying. "JA8167 is one of the earlier models, built in 1980. Relatively low-cycle airframe, treated fairly well in over ten years of service although it's had its share of short fields and tropical weather. It's still got its RB211 engines, so its max payload is about ten percent less than if it had JT9Ds or CF6s, but it's got its quiet kits installed and it's fully certified for Stage Three noise level operations, so you can fly it anywhere. You got yourself one fine bargain. Who's going to do the paint job on it?"

"Excuse me?"

"The paint work," Fennelli said. "Your ferry crew indicated that its first stop is the paint and mod shop. Where are you taking it? You know, we do a really fine job of configuring your bird to your exact specifications. Since you're a customer, of course, we can offer you a substantial discount. Nobody does a better paint job on large aircraft like Mojave. Please consider it, Mr. Lake."

Damn flyboys, Lake cursed silently. The stupid bastards that Cazaux and Townsend were digging out of the woodwork to fly these missions had real big mouths. The modifications and paint job were going to be done at one of four facilities already hired to do the job—Little Rock, Arkansas; Salina, Kansas; Portsmouth, New Hampshire; or Newark, New Jersey, depending on which had all the necessary personnel, equipment, and cargo ready to go, and which was under the least surveillance by the authorities. Fennelli would obviously want the job badly, so he might try to contact some of the names in the application to ask them directly. Lake had sewn up most of those traps so Fennelli might not get anywhere—but then again, he might if he tried hard enough.

"I'm afraid that's up to the buyer, Mr. Fennelli, and he hasn't confided in me about his plans for the airplanes," Lake said. "But I will certainly pass along your offer."

Lake couldn't have been more relieved to get on the Learjet and head back toward Los Angeles.

"Ted, get on the damned phone and contact the ferry crews," Lake ordered. "Tell them that if they don't keep their mouths shut from now on, I will personally see to it that Cazaux deals with them. Then I want—"

"Harold, it's not a good idea to use the Flitephone for something like that," Fell interrupted. "The phone on the airplane has to go through a UHF radio station before it hooks into the landline phone system. It's worse than a cellular phone system—everybody with a thirty-dollar scanner can listen in."

"We're still using the secure phone system and the dead-drop line, aren't we?"

"Yes, but I'm not so sure how well it works over an ARINC network." The scrambled phone system was a simple but usually very effective analog voice-scrambling system that would protect against unauthorized recording and casual surveillance; the dead-drop line was an 800 number that tied into the local and long-distance phone lines so all calls made would appear to go only to the 800 number, not to any particular phone or person. Fell knew that sometimes calls from the plane were not scrambled, or could not be descrambled on the other end, because of the properties of the additional Aeronautical Radio, Inc., radio link.

"The damned system cost well over a thousand dollars a month to operate—it better work," Lake said. "I need the bank to cut a replacement check for Fennelli, and I want to make sure the taps on Universal's branch offices and to Worthington Enterprises brokerage are in place—if Fennelli tries to contact them directly, I need to know about it. Get on it, Ted, right *now.*"

Lassen, in a Piper Cheyenne II turboprop plane shuttling northward to visit another airport, was undoing another button of his shirt to try to get a bit cooler when his transportable phone insistently beeped at him. He plugged his headset into the unit, pressed the green SYNC button, and waited until the scramble-synchronization circuits between the caller and his unit agreed and allowed the call to connect. When it did a few seconds later, he heard a tone and responded, "Sweeper."

"Sweeper, this is Peepshow," came the reply. "Peepshow" was the tactical mission commander aboard an RC-12K Guardrail communications and intelligence aircraft. Because cellular and radio communications were difficult to maintain so far out away from large cities, federal agents involved in special investigations in remote areas often set up communications relays, which allowed them to maintain constant contact. One such communications relay system was the U.S. Army's Guardrail system, which was a modified Beech Super King Air turboprop plane loaded with communications and signals intelligence equipment. Along with providing a secure, efficient communications link, Guardrail could also eavesdrop on radio, TV, cellular, telephone, and data communications for a hundred miles in any direction, and could break in on conversations or broadcast on civil channels or frequencies. "We got some information on your subject."

"Stand by one." Lassen pulled out a personal digital assistant computer, created a new note file, and readied his electronic stencil. "Go ahead."

"Your target filed an IFR flight plan direct Santa Monica Airport," the tactical mission commander reported. "Normal air traffic control communications. We monitored three separate radiotelephone calls via ARINC Mojave to a WATS number. Do you need the number? Over."

"Let me guess," Lassen said, retrieving another note file from the PDA and reading off an 800 number.

"The same," Peepshow responded. "The conversation was scrambled, but the ARINC transmission was garbled and they had to repeat the password sequence several times. Finally, your target ordered the WATS operator to turn off the scrambler so he could log on to the service. We copied the ID number and password.'' Peepshow passed Harold Lake's service ID number and password to Lassen. It would probably not do too much good—Lake would undoubtedly change the password at his first opportunity. ''We copied several phone numbers, account numbers, and what appear to be code names before they scrambled the transmission again.'' The tactical mission commander passed that information to Lassen. ''In addition, we got a good analysis of the scrambler algorithm routine as they shut it off and then turned it back on again, so we can probably give you their scrambler's algorithm to plug into your descrambler once we get back on the ground. That's about all. Over.''

''Great work, Peepshow,'' Lassen said. ''Sweeper out.'' Well, it didn't prove too much, but it was a start. Using blind phone drops was not illegal—blind or dead drops prevented someone from knowing what number was called—although it looked very suspicious. It was going to take time to check out all these names, and he had six other airports between Mojave and Reno to check out. He decided to transmit his notes from the PDA via his radiotelephone back to his office in Sacramento so his staff could get to work on it; using Guardrail, the task took only a few moments.

Harold Lake and Ted Fell were two new names in this investigation, so this trip may not have been a total bust. Two guys from New York who admitted not knowing that much about planes, traveling all the way out to Mojave, California, to buy two very large transport planes. It might take a warrant for Fennelli to give him any information on Lake, his company, his financial institutions, and the persons he worked for. With a little push and some carefully veiled threats, Lassen was sure that Fennelli would easily roll on Lake or anybody else and hand over the files on Lake. But if Fennelli was smart and called in his attorney, Lassen would get into hot water with the U.S. Attorney, that avenue of information would snap shut, and, if he was dirty, Lake would disappear.

More pieces to the puzzle, Lassen thought—a little patience and determination, and eventually the pieces of this puzzle would start fitting together. Harold Lake was being evasive, and Lassen's instincts told him Lake was dirty. Meanwhile, there were still a thousand more pieces of the puzzle to examine.

PART 4

Atlantic City International Airport
That Night

"November-Juliet-641 flight, report altitude passing, radar contact, climb and maintain one-zero thousand." A few seconds later, on the same frequency, he heard, "Lead, give me a few knots, okay?" followed by a loud feminine voice in his headset that seductively said, *"Caution! Caution!"*

Major Greg Mundy shook himself alert—as intended, Bitching Betty had that effect on guys. The feminine audio "caution" warning in his F-16 ADF Fighting Falcon air defense fighter was better known as Bitching Betty, a computerized female voice that calls the pilot's attention to a problem in the aircraft; the warning was repeated visually in his heads-up display with a large flashing CAUTION message in the center. The male voice just before Bitching Betty's was from Mundy's wingman, Captain Tom Humphrey, who was apparently having trouble closing in on his leader and was asking Mundy to pull off a little power.

Mundy pinched his nose through his oxygen mask and blew against his nostrils to help clear his head—knowing full well that he was just blowing the shit in his head further in, which wasn't going to help later on—and checked around the cockpit. He finally realized he was passing three hundred knots indicated airspeed in his F-16, still in zone-five afterburner—and he still had his landing gear down. He immediately flipped the gear handle up, pulled the throttle back to military power, and then flipped his oxygen panel supply lever to OXYGEN 100% to get a shot of pure oxygen into his lungs.

"November-Juliet-641 flight of two departing A-City, passing five for ten thousand, check," he radioed, realizing he had not checked in with Atlantic City Approach Control either.

"Two," Captain Tom Humphrey responded. "Tied on radar, three miles." Good wingmen rarely said more than their formation position on the radios; Humphrey was fairly new in the unit, having come directly from undergraduate pilot training, Fighter Lead-In, and F-16 Air Defense Fighter training directly to the New Jersey Air National Guard. Being a new guy, he was still a bit wordy on the radios—that would pass soon, Mundy thought.

It was a big, big mistake to do this flight, Mundy told himself. Members of the 119th Fighter Squadron "Red Devils" of the New Jersey Air National Guard, Mundy and five other F-16 ADF fighter crews had been flying six straight days of air defense alert since the terrorist emergency, pulling 'round-the-clock four-on, eight-off shifts out of Atlantic City International. But a flu bug was starting to make its way through the fighter group, and two pilots assigned to air defense duties in the Philadelphia Class B airspace had gone DNIF—Duties Not Involving Flying, which with this flu meant little more than stay in bed—so the other crews were on four-on, four-off shifts. In addition to feeling the first few chills and achiness of an oncoming bout of the flu, Mundy and his fellow Falcon pilots were just plain exhausted, and it was starting to show in his flying.

"November-Juliet-641," Atlantic City Approach Control radioed, "have your wingman squawk standby when he gets within two miles of you. Passing ten thousand feet, contact Washington Center, button eight."

"641 copies all, check."

"Two."

With the gear properly up and locked, it didn't take long to climb through ten thousand feet on their way to fifteen thousand feet, and Mundy took his wingman over to Washington Air Route Traffic Control Center's VHF frequency and checked in. They were almost immediately shuttled off to their UHF tactical frequency, and shortly made contact with Liberty-90, their AWACS controller for the next four hours. The E-3C AWACS radar plane was orbiting over Allentown, Pennsylvania, about one hundred miles to the north, providing enhanced low-altitude radar coverage for all airspace as far south as Richmond, Virginia, as far north as Boston. Having an AWACS radar plane in the northeast United States was not as critical as in the midwest or western United States. Because of the sheer density of airports, ground-based radar coverage was so extensive in the northeast that any aircraft flying higher than two or three hundred feet aboveground was in radar contact with some FAA agency.

First order of business was an air refueling, out over the ocean about fifty miles east of Long Branch, New Jersey—the two F-16 Fighting Falcons would top off from the aerial refueling tankers at least three times during their four-hour patrol. The night was clear and beautiful, visibility about a hundred miles; the lights of New York City, Newark, Long Island, Trenton, Wilmington, Camden, Philadelphia, and even Allentown were all clearly visible. Mundy's wingman picked out the tanker's powerful recognition lights a few moments before the radar locked on, and they set up for the air refueling. They were going to refuel in an "anchor," a small, tight oval pattern in which the aircraft would be in a turn for half of the contact time.

The flight of two F-16s approached the KC-135 Stratotanker from one thousand feet below the tanker's altitude, and as Mundy closed within five miles he made sure his precontact checklists were completed and turned all his attention to the rendezvous. He checked his blue RDY light to the right of the heads-up display, meaning that the slipway door was open, the fuel system was depressurized, the slipway lights were on, and the system ready for refueling. "November-Juliet flight, five miles," he called. He had the tanker's lights clearly in view, and there was no chance of flying through any clouds and losing sight of him, so he turned his attack radar to STANDBY to keep from spraying the tanker with electromagnetic energy.

"November-Juliet flight cleared to precontact position, One-Five ready," the tanker's boom operator radioed. Mundy, with Humphrey on his left wing, started a slow climb, following the tanker's rotating beacon. "One-Five coming left." The tanker's wingtip lights rolled gently left. Mundy used the left turn to "cut the corner" and speed up the closure, and he carefully guided himself onto the white light at the tip of the air refueling boom trailing down below the tanker's tail.

The left turn pointed them north toward Long Island. The lights of New York that were so beautiful just a few minutes ago were serious distractions now, and Mundy had to concentrate hard on the tanker's wingtip lights to tell how much the tanker was turning—his visual horizon was gone. "Halfway through the turn," the tanker pilot radioed.

Soon, Mundy and Humphrey had moved to within fifty feet of

the aerial refueling boom, slightly low, and they rolled out of the turn heading south. "641 stabilized precontact, ready," Mundy radioed.

"642's cleared to the wing," the boom operator radioed, and Humphrey moved away from Mundy and took a position just off to the left and behind the tanker's left wing. "641, cleared to the contact position, One-Five ready."

"641, contact," Mundy responded as the nozzle clunked into the F-16's air refueling receptacle. The director lights, which were two rows of colored lights along the tanker's belly that graphically depicted the limits of the air refueling boom, came alive, showing him slightly low and slightly behind the center of the boom's envelope. He began maneuvering to correct, not really moving the stick but "willing" the fighter to the correct position—the F-16 was far too nimble for a pilot to make any huge corrections, especially flying five miles per minute just a few feet from another aircraft. He stole a quick peek at the fuel quantity gauge to the right of his right knee and watched the forward and aft fuel quantity pointers creep clockwise and the fuel totalizer rolling upwards.

"One-Five coming left," the tanker pilot again reported. Mundy turned his attention back to the tanker—and the world started to spin on him.

"641, down two . . . 641, down four . . . come left, 641 . . ."

Mundy thought that he was in a tight left diving spiral, and he instinctively tried to compensate by rolling right and climbing. The combination of the left turn, no visual horizon, and his head movement to the right to check the fuel gauge caused the "spins." He recognized it, hit the NWS A/R DISC MSL STEP button on the outside of his control stick, pushed the stick forward, and transitioned to his heads-up display to get his bearings back. "One-Five, disconnect," the boom operator reported.

"641, disconnect," Mundy confirmed. His first priority was separation. He descended a few hundred feet and pulled a little power back. His head was still telling him he was in a hard left diving death-spiral, but for now his hands were believing his eyes, and his eyes were watching the flight instruments, which were telling the truth. "Ah . . . roger, I got about three thousand pounds, fuel transfer looks good, let's get 642 on the boom to make sure he can get his gas, then I'll cycle back on to top off."

It was a pretty weak excuse—boom operators could recognize the onset of spatial disorientation and were usually quick to either call a disconnect or guide the receiver pilot back—but everyone allowed Mundy to keep his pride. "Rrrr . . . roger, 641," the boom operator responded, his voice telling everyone that he knew what was *really* happening. "You're cleared to the right wing." When Mundy was out of view of the boom operator, he called, "642, cleared to the contact position, One-Five ready."

It was a tremendous relief to climb safely away from the tanker. Once safely on the tanker's wingtip, flying very loose relaxed formation, Mundy dropped his oxygen mask, found a handkerchief in his left flight suit leg pocket, blew his nose, then massaged his sinuses to try to clear his head. No damn good. He had no choice—he retrieved a tiny bottle of nasal spray from his left leg pocket. Flight surgeons would argue, but the fighter pilot's unwritten but widely followed credo was, "Don't Hesitate: Self-Medicate."

The secure-voice UHF radio crackled to life: "November-Juliet-641 flight, Control, say status."

"641 in the green, eight-point-one," Mundy replied. He was about three thousand pounds shy of a full fuel load. "642's on the boom." Actually, Humphrey was having just as much trouble as Mundy did staying on the boom, but that was part of the new-guy jitters as well. Humphrey was a good stick, a good wingman.

"We're tracking a pop-up target about one hundred and twenty miles bull's-eye," the controller said. "Bull's-eye," the navigation reference point for the air intercepts, was Atlantic City International. "Too far out for a good track. We're doing a manual groundspeed, and he's gone from two-forty to about three hundred in the past few minutes. Better top off and stand by to go take a look."

"641 copies." Mundy knew that the AWACS controllers had three minutes from first detection to decide if an unknown aircraft was a hostile or not—that's how much time Mundy had to get his gas. He rocked his mike button forward to the VHF channel: "642, I need to cycle back on. What's your status?"

At that moment the boom operator reported, "Forward limit disconnect, 642." The boom nozzle popped free of the receptacle on the F-16's spine behind the cockpit, the lights illuminating a brief spray of fuel vapor. Humphrey had slid in so far that his F-16's vertical stabilizer was dangerously close to the Stratotanker's tail. He descended slightly and quickly backed away.

"I'm showing ten-point-one," Humphrey radioed. "One more plug and I should be full."

"Better let me get in there, -42," Mundy said. "We might have visitors."

"Roger," Humphrey acknowledged. "Clearing to the left wing."

"Copy, 642, clear to the tanker's left wing." As Humphrey moved away from the boom, the boom operator said, "641, cleared to the contact position, One-Five ready."

"641, moving in . . ."

"Taking fuel, 641, no leaks"

Mundy was doing pretty well this time—in fact, he was so steady, and concentrating so hard on staying that way, that a new problem cropped up: autokinesis. The green "forward/aft" director light suddenly seemed to move, but not up and down along the row of director lights, but in a slow clockwise spiral. Mundy knew what it was—a form of spatial disorientation when a stationary point of light would appear to move by itself, following tiny movements of the eyeballs. He tried hard not to follow the light, but there was no way of stopping the slight, almost subconscious commands to go to the flight controls.

"641, stabilize . . . down four . . ."

It was no use—the spinning was getting worse by the second. Mundy hit the disconnect button just as the director light hit the aft limit: "641, disconnect . . ."

"641, *breakaway, breakaway, breakaway!*" the boom operator shouted on the radio. Mundy's reaction was automatic: throttle to idle, nose down, positive rate of descent. He glanced up and saw the boom operator's observation window just a few scant feet away—he had come just a few milliseconds from hitting the tanker. The tanker pilot had cobbed his four throttles to military power and hauled back on the stick at the "breakaway" call, and they had still avoided hitting each other by less than a yard.

Get on the instruments, Mundy commanded himself. The sudden deceleration was causing his head to spin downwards, making him pull the F-16's nose up, but he knew it would cause a collision if he let that happen. He choked back the overwhelming sensation of tumbling and spinning and focused on the attitude indicator, forcing it to stay at wings level and 5 degrees nose down. He saw the altimeter spinning downwards and applied a little power to level off. "641 is clear, One-Five," he radioed. Mundy took his hands off the control stick momentarily, felt around his right instrument panel, and flipped on all the exterior lights.

"I've got a visual on you, 641," the boom operator said. "Our next turn is coming up. Do you have a visual on us?"

"I've got a pretty good case of the leans," Mundy said, still staring at the attitude indicator but finally getting enough stability back to glance at the heads-up display and other indicators. "I'll stay straight and level at the bottom of the block. Make your turn in the anchor. 642, come join on me after you've made the turn. I'll let Liberty know what's going on." He pressed the mike button aft to the SECURE UHF position: "Control, 641 flight is rejoining, two in the green, about eleven apiece."

"Copy, 641," the weapons controller aboard the AWACS radar plane responded. "641 flight, vector heading one-six-zero, your bogey is at one hundred bull's-eye low, speed three-twenty, ID only, report tied on."

"641 flight copies, check."

"Two," Humphrey replied.

"641 turning right," Mundy radioed. His case of the leans was just about cleared up, but his congestion was as bad as ever and probably getting worse. The shit was starting to pile up, he warned himself . . . "642, I'm at zero-two-zero for seventy-five bull's-eye at angels seventeen."

"Tallyho." Humphrey had visual contact on him, so Mundy pushed the throttle up to military power, got on his vector heading, and started his pursuit. Humphrey would catch up as he could, and report when he was back in formation with his leader.

With a closure rate of almost a thousand miles per hour, the intercept did not take long. Mundy's radar found a lone blip on the screen about seventy miles from the New Jersey coast. Mundy used the radar cursor control on the throttle quadrant to move the cursor on the radar return, then hit his DESIGNATE TARGET button on his control stick and received an audio LOCK in his headphones and a LOCK indication on his heads-up display. He then hit the IFF INTERROGATE button on his control stick, and a row of code letters appeared on his radarscope, 1X 2X 3X 4X CX, which meant that the target he had locked on to was transmitting no air traffic control signals. With wackos like Cazaux flying around, this was definitely a hostile act, not to mention a really stupid thing to do—if I had an IFF or radio malfunction at night, Mundy thought, I wouldn't fly anywhere near U.S. airspace these days.

"Control, 641, radar contact, twelve o'clock, thirty miles low, no paint."

"That's your bogey," the weapons controller confirmed, "641 flight, check noses cold, ID only."

Mundy checked the weapons status readouts on his left multifunction display. He carried two AIM-120 Ram radar-guided missiles and four AIM-9P Sidewinder heat-seeking missiles, plus two hundred rounds of ammunition for the gun and two external fuel tanks. Right now he had no weapons selected, none armed. "641 confirms nose cold for the ID pass, check."

"Two," Humphrey responded. He was supposed to do a complete weapons status check and report, but, Mundy thought as he tried to clear his head and ears, for now the less said on the radios, the better.

The last ten miles to the intercept turn passed very quickly. The bogey was screaming now, almost four hundred miles an hour, and he had descended to barely three thousand feet above the ocean. This was not a smuggler or a terrorist—this guy appeared on a military attack profile! Mundy remembered that the Cuban drug smugglers stopped by the Hammerheads a few years earlier had used military aircraft to deliver drugs—maybe Cazaux had turned to military aircraft as well. That thought didn't cheer Mundy up one bit.

Well, it was time to see what the story was. At fifteen miles distance, high and slightly to the left of the unknown aircraft's nose, Mundy started a tight left turn and a rapid descent. He was passing twelve thousand feet on his way to four thousand . . .

. . . when suddenly a red-hot jab of pain spiked through his sinuses like a knife driven into his head, threatening to blow out his eyeballs. Mundy's vision and hearing both disappeared in the incredible pain, and his entire face seemed to creak and pop like a slowly collapsing building. Mundy knew what it was, and he was fully expecting it—what he had not been expecting was the enormous amount of pain it caused. With a head cold and sinus infection, the rapid climb during takeoff forced mucus tightly into the Eustachian tubes of Mundy's inner ear, reducing the air pressure inside the sinuses and inner ear and jamming the sinuses and inner ear closed. As the ambient air pressure increased during the rapid descent, the outside air rushed in and tried to fill the partial vacuum in the inner ear and sinuses. The few extra pounds of air pressure on the delicate sinus membrane and eardrums caused intense pain. Mundy tried rolling his head, tried a Valsalva maneuver, tried swallowing, but the pain only continued. He dropped his mask and tried to squirt more nasal spray into his impacted sinuses.

Suddenly, the pressure in his left ear went away, followed shortly by relief in his right ear, and he could see his instruments again as most of the pain washed away. But as he felt a warm trickle of fluid running down his neck, he knew the relief wasn't because of the nasal spray—it was because he had just ruptured both eardrums. He had to turn the radio volume up all the way to hear it. Mundy ran his finger up into his helmet's earcups to scoop out sticky blobs of blood, but it didn't help much.

Somehow, through all that, he managed to stay on the bogey, and now Mundy and Humphrey were closing in within three miles of the unknown aircraft. It had no exterior lights on—another sign of a hostile. As he moved closer, Mundy could start to make out its shape and size—commercial, not military, at least no military aircraft Mundy was familiar with. "Control, 641 flight, I have visual contact on a commercial aircraft, two engines, possibly three engines, aft-mounted. No exterior lights, no interior lights visible from the windows. It appears to be a Hawker or Gulfstream-class bizjet. Activating ID light." Mundy could barely hear himself talking through the radio, like listening to a conversation going on in another room. The pain in his head was tolerable, but now his loss of hearing and an occasional bout of the spins and the leans made it difficult to concentrate.

"Copy, 641."

If the AWACS weapon controller responded, Mundy didn't hear him, but he went ahead anyway. By the time he had moved within one mile of the bandit—he had stopped considering him just an "unknown" and now thought of the aircraft as a "hostile"—they were over the coast of New Jersey just north of Sea Isle City, heading northwest. They had climbed slightly, to about four thousand feet, but were still traveling about six miles per minute. The bright lights of the Philadelphia metropolitan area were dazzling on the horizon, only fifty miles away.

"Control, 641 has a visual ID on a Falcon- or Learjet-series twin-engine turbojet aircraft, tail number November-114 Charlie Mike. Color appears silver or gray over dark blue. Still no exterior lights. No visible external weapons, no open doors. Moving forward. Acknowledge." Mundy heard a faint "Clear, 641," from the AWACS controller, so he activated his ID searchlight on the left side of his F-16 ADF fighter and started forward, maneuvering the agile fighter so the searchlight trained along the right side of the bandit's fuselage and across the row of windows.

Mundy reached a point where the searchlight was shining inside the right side of the bandit's cockpit, then switched his VHF radio to 121.5, the international GUARD frequency, and said, "Unidentified bizjet-N114CM, this is the United States Air Force fighter off your right side. You are in violation of emergency federal air regulations. You are hereby ordered to decrease speed, turn left immediately to a heading of one-seven-zero direct to the Sea Isle City VOR, and lower your landing gear. Respond on 121.5 immediately. Over."

"Welcome, Air Force F-16," came the response. "This is Barry Kendall of the TV news program 'Whispers.' I'm speaking to you on the international aviation emergency frequency. Can you hear me? How are you tonight?" The Gulfstream's exterior lights popped on, and its airspeed began to decrease. "Can you tell us your name, please, and where you're from?"

"November-114CM, you are in deep shit." Mundy had to restrain himself from coming completely unglued at this point. He recognized the TV show, of course, one of a series of trashy "tabloid TV" shows that liked to bring cameras into the most unlikely places to videotape people in compromising positions. Why the hell they'd risk their lives to pull this stunt, Mundy couldn't figure. "I mean, 114CM, you are in serious violation. If you proceed any farther you may be fired upon without warning. Turn left immediately towards Sea Isle City VOR and prepare for an approach and landing at Atlantic City International. Over."

"Air Force pilot, this is Barry, we're live right now on national TV, and about twenty million viewers are watching this intercept. I must say, it took you boys longer than I expected to find us. Did you have us on radar the whole time, watching us, or did it take some time to track us down?" Mundy was going to repeat his warning, but the bastard continued, "Now that you have us identified, my cockpit crew is going to reactivate our flight plan and we'll proceed up the coast to our destination at Newark Airport. We're going to switch off the low-light camera and take some footage with the regular camera. Thanks for your cooperation, guys." At that, a blinding beam of light stabbed out from the bizjet's cockpit, aimed right at Mundy.

The beam momentarily blinded him—not painfully, but irritating enough—but when Mundy swung his head down and away to shield his eyes, he got an instantaneous case of the leans. The F-16 seemed to do a tailflip right over onto its back. In a reflex action, Mundy screamed on the radio and pulled the control stick back hard before realizing that it was the leans, not an uncommanded flight control pitch-down. He climbed nearly a thousand feet before he finally regained control and started believing the attitude indicator again . . .

But at the instant Mundy screamed on the radio, Tom Humphrey had reacted reflexively as well. He hit the DOGFIGHT button on his throttle, which changed the F-16's weapons and fire control computer mode instantly from VID (visual identification) mode to "Air-to-Air" mode, arming his AIM-9 Sidewinder heat-seeking missiles and his 20-millimeter cannon, then flipped the MASTER ARM/SIMULATE switch on his stores control panel to MASTER ARM. He immediately got an RDY 4A-9LM indication on his stores control panel, meaning that the four missiles were armed. He then hit the large UNCAGE button on his throttle, which unlocked the seeker heads of his missiles. Seconds later Humphrey got a blinking diamond in the middle right side of his heads-up display, indicating that the first-up Sidewinder had locked on to the bizjet and was in the launch zone. He pressed the weapon-release button on his control stick. The whole procedure took about three seconds.

An AIM-9L missile slid off the number-two-weapon-station rail in a brief burst of light and hit the bizjet's left engine a split second later.

Mundy didn't—couldn't—see any of this. He saw a brief flash of light out of the corner of an eye, then heard someone shouting "Mayday! Mayday! Mayday!" on the radios. He heard a brace of loud static, then a brief "Oh, shit . . ." then nothing.

"641 flight, Liberty Control."

"641, go."

"641, was that your mayday? Say status."

"641 is in the green," Mundy said. "I got blinded by a spotlight from the Lear, and I had to split from the intercept. I heard the mayday call. 641 has lost visual contact with the target. 641 flight, check." No response. "November-Juliet-642, check in on Liberty Control button nine." Still no response. Mundy searched out his cockpit canopy—pretty useless gesture at night—then said urgently on the radio, "Tom, damn it, are you up?"

"Two's up," Humphrey finally responded. "Shit, I thought you were under attack, lead."

Mundy heard the sheer panic in his wingman's voice, and his throat turned as dry as sand. *"Say again,* 642?"

"I thought he was shooting at you," Humphrey said. Mundy could hear sobs coming from his wingman—Jesus, he was *crying* . . .

"I thought he was shooting at you, Greg, I thought you were hit . . ."

Mundy finally realized what his wingman had done. "Tom, this is Greg, do you have a visual on me? Do you see my lights? What's your position?" There was no response. "Tom, say your position." He thought he'd try a more rigid, formal approach: "641 flight, *check!*"

"Two's . . . up . . . oh God oh God . . . I shot the fucking plane *down* . . ." Humphrey responded.

"Tom, you were doing your job. Rejoin now, get back on my wing," Mundy shouted. "Where are you? Say your position? Do you have me in sight? Control, give me a vector to 642. Tom, damn it, *answer.*"

A sudden bright tongue of fire caught Mundy's attention. He saw an F-16 in full afterburner streak across the sky from his nine o'clock position, heading northward, then turn suddenly in front of him and head eastbound, back out over the Atlantic. "Tom, I see your burner, I'll be tied on radar in a second, stand by . . . you can cut your burner now, Tom." The afterburner plume remained. At nearly one hundred thousand pounds of fuel burned per hour at zone 5 afterburner, he would exhaust his fuel in less than three minutes.

Mundy turned eastward to follow his wingman. "642, I've got you tied on radar, cut your burner and I'll join on your right side . . . cut your burner, I said!" Mundy had to kick in afterburner himself to keep Humphrey on radar. "Tom . . . Cut your burner! I've got you in a descent, climb and maintain eight thousand, I'll be at your five o'clock position."

Ninety seconds later, November-Juliet-642 plunged into the Atlantic twelve miles east of Longport, New Jersey, still in full afterburner, hitting the ocean at well over the speed of sound. Vacationers on the Boardwalk at Atlantic City reported a streak of light across the sky out over the ocean and wondered if it was a shooting star.

In case it was, some made a wish.

New Executive Office Building, Washington, D.C.
Less Than an Hour Later

Lieutenant Colonel Al Vincenti trotted into Hardcastle's makeshift office in the New Executive Office Building, across the street from the White House. He had finally been convinced to keep his flight suit in the closet and put on a class A uniform while working in the general proximity of the White House, but it was obvious he was uncomfortable with it; it was also obvious that he had shaved in the car on the way over, because he missed a few spots. Deborah Harley, on the other hand, looked as scrubbed and as ready to go as she always did, even though she arrived several minutes before Vincenti. "What's happened, Admiral?" Vincenti asked. "The operator said something about an accident."

Hardcastle handed him an electric razor and a desk mirror—obviously Hardcastle was an expert at shaving on the run. "Clean up while I run it down for you," he told Vincenti. "About an hour ago, the Atlantic City fighter group intercepted a bizjet running with its lights and transponder off, trying to race in off the Atlantic toward Philadelphia. Turns out it was a camera crew from that trash TV show 'Whispers.' "

"Don't tell me," Vincenti said. "A midair?"

"Worse—a Sidewinder up the tailpipe, *after* the intercept and the ID," Hardcastle said. Vincenti swore under his breath—it was an interceptor pilot's nightmare in the best of conditions, but under the present emergency it was only a matter of time before it actually happened. "Worse yet—the shooter decides he's done a really bad thing and crashes his F-16 into the ocean."

"Oh, God, no," Vincenti exclaimed. "The President's going to have a shit-fit."

"We'll find out," Hardcastle said as his office phone rang. "Lifter's calling in the staff for a meeting in two hours; the President will be awakened at four A.M., and the first meeting in the Oval Office will probably be at five. We got a long day ahead of us." Hardcastle's secretary was out—it was after midnight—so Hardcastle picked the phone up himself. "Hardcastle . . ."

"Is this Admiral Ian Hardcastle, the one hunting down Henri Cazaux?"

Hardcastle pointed to an extension line in the secretary's alcove; Harley immediately ran for it, checked to see if it had a dead switch—it did—and picked it up. The dead switch would kill the mouthpiece unless the button was pushed. She also started recording the conversation and starting a caller ID trace with the push of one button on the secretary's phone console. When she was on, Hardcastle asked, "Who is this?"

"No names," the caller said. "Just listen. Henri Cazaux's base of operations is a three-story mansion on Cottage Road, Bedminster, New Jersey. It's protected by heavily armed gunmen. He was there a few hours ago; I don't know if he's there now. Cazaux is planning something big.'' The line went dead.

''Damn it! He hung up,'' Hardcastle said. To Vincenti he said, ''Someone calling telling us Cazaux's whereabouts.''

''Another one? This makes . . . what, the one-thousandth . . . ?''

''This sounded more genuine to me.''

''Just let the FBI have it, Ian, and let's get back to—''

Hardcastle ignored him. ''Deborah . . . ?''

''Got the phone number from caller ID,'' Harley said. All phone calls going to any federal government office are automatically traced, using caller ID, which instantly reports the caller's phone number, and by instantaneous computer phone-record checks. ''Manhattan exchange. I can run the address through the FBI . . . but let me take this one, okay?'' Harley smiled. ''It might tie into some stuff I've heard. The Marshals Service interviewed a Wall Street investor at an aircraft reclamation firm in Mojave who was acting as a third-party broker buying several large aircraft for an aerial firefighting firm in Montana. He mentioned a part of their investigation on this sent them to a secretarial service in north-central New Jersey. Their investigation dead-ended there—''

''But maybe it's just come alive again,'' Hardcastle said. ''Wonder why we never heard anything about this investigation?''

''Because the Marshals said they turned everything over to the FBI,'' Harley said. ''Briefed Director Wilkes personally.'' Hardcastle nodded. ''Ian, if we dump this on Wilkes, it'll get pushed into the wacko pile. Let me have it. I'll give it to the Marshals Service. They deserve a try at Cazaux for what happened to them in California.''

Hardcastle looked decidedly uncomfortable. He said, ''I'm not sure, Deborah. I'm not averse to letting the Marshals redeem their reputation after the Chico raid, but I'm not winning any points butting heads with Lani Wilkes and the President.''

''You handed the wacko call to me and told me to notify the authorities,'' Harley suggested. ''You meant the FBI; I took it to the Marshals Service. I can handle the heat from the Justice Department, believe me.''

''I believe you,'' Hardcastle said. ''Okay, you got it. Notify the proper authorities about this call immediately, Miss Harley.''

''Yes, sir,'' she responded with a smile.

''As long as I'm sticking my neck out, Deborah, I might as well stick it out all the way," Hardcastle said. He made two phone calls from his desk, quickly typed out a letter on Office of the National Security Advisor letterhead, and handed it to Harley. She read it quickly, her smile becoming brighter and wider by the moment. "You've received blanket authorization from me to requisition some hardware the 'authorities' will need for their operation. Take the Executive shuttle to the Pentagon heliport—an NSC helicopter will take you. The crews at Patuxent River Naval Weapons Center are waiting."

"Yes, *sir,*" Harley said. "I'm on my way. Thanks, Ian."

New York City
That Same Time

"Who the hell are you calling this time of night?"

Ted Fell nearly fell over backwards in his seat in surprise. Harold Lake never prowled the hallways and never stopped in Fell's tiny office—until tonight. Fell could feel his heart hammering away in his chest, and he had to fight to control his tone of voice: "Jesus, Harold, what are you skulking around for?"

"I needed the option contract summary on the Isakawa house holdings—the Japanese markets open in thirty minutes. Who were you on the phone with?"

"Kim," Fell said. Lake briefly recalled that Fell had a somewhat steady girlfriend whom he brought on occasion to a cocktail party—that must be her. "Told her I wouldn't be home tonight."

"Thought you called her after we got back from Jersey."

Fell shrugged. "Doesn't hurt to make her feel included, I guess." It was ambiguous enough, and Fell hoped that would disinterest Lake enough to drop this line of questioning. Harold Lake never showed an ounce of interest in anyone else's personal life—it was strange he was asking questions about it now. "I put the summary in your E-mail folder. We're looking good, as long as Isakawa doesn't think we're on the ropes because we're selling our portfolio. If he does, we'll be down around the fifteen-percent range again." Fell remembered when making 15 percent a day was considered incredibly good. Now it was one-half to one-third of what they were making, and would be considered a very bad day.

"We're liquidating, but it doesn't mean we gotta take any bullshit from the Japanese or from that asshole Quek Poh Liao in Singapore," Lake said. He studied Fell for a moment, his eyes narrowing suspiciously. "That crazy fucker Ysidro really rattled you, didn't he?"

"I don't see how you could just sit there and watch him play with that . . . that human heart," Fell said, his eyes growing distant. "It was horrible, disgusting."

"You gotta detach yourself from their world, Ted," Lake said, but even as he said that, his mind's eye was obviously replaying that gruesome sight. "Forget about it."

That was the understatement of the year, Fell thought, remembering his bizarre encounter with the woman in Cazaux's place. She obviously got her kicks out of setting men up to die. "How did you ever get involved with those animals, Harold?"

Lake shrugged, then leaned against the door as if the very thought had taken all his strength away. "The money, at first," he replied. "Cazaux had a guy on his payroll whose job it was to launder money, except he was a jerk. He was openly skimming at least ten percent from Cazaux's funds, I mean, he didn't even *try* to account for the loss. Cazaux eventually caught him—you saw a heart, Ted, but my first meeting with Henri Cazaux, he was carrying this banker's severed fucking *head* in a bag. I got the old *'ploma o plata'* offer then—lead or silver, a bullet in the head or wealth beyond reason, if I joined him. It's a hard offer to refuse.

"Hey, I *know* who I work for. A bigger assassin than the Jackal, bigger terrorist than Abu Nidal, a bigger arms dealer than Adnan Khashoggi. It's like being the chief designer for Lee Iacocca or Ralph Lauren. You're working for the *best*—"

"Harold, think about what you're saying," Fell interrupted. "You're working for a killer, a murderer, a terrorist. He kills without thinking, without caring. He kills for money."

"So what? We all do something for money, one way or another. If I think about it, I'll go fucking nuts." Fell noticed that Lake had all but lost his sophisticated accent and speech pattern, and had digressed almost all the way back to his New Jersey accent. It was a fitting signal of how he had slid into the depths of the criminal world. "Check on the plane and the security setup again, Ted."

"It's too early, Harold."

"I want them ready in twenty-four hours," Lake said. "They're ready when I say they're ready. And no more calling your bimbos. We'll be out of the damned country and out of her and everyone else's life in just a few days. Ted . . . get used to the idea." He stepped away from Fell's door and back down the hallway, but glanced back at his attorney. Fell was staring blankly at the telephone again, as if trying to check on something—or someone—far away.

Lake couldn't stand it any longer. He charged back into Fell's office, reached Fell's desk before the attorney's eyes even registered that he was back in the room, and hit the REDIAL button on Fell's phone. On the small LCD screen at the top of the phone, a number with a 202 area code popped up. "All right, Ted, what in hell's going on? That's Washington, D.C. Your girlfriend lives here in Manhattan. We don't have any brokers in D.C. Whose fucking number is that?"

"It's the forwarding number for the new deputy of the security team we hired, Ha—"

"Don't fucking lie to me!" Lake shouted. "What in hell did you do? Who did you call, Ted?" Fell appeared as if he were going to try his story one more time, but Lake grabbed his shirt collar in both hands and shouted, *"Answer me!"*

"Hardcastle," Fell said in a weak voice. "National Security Council . . . the guy on TV, in charge of the air defense stuff . . ."

"Oh, shit, tell me you're fucking kidding . . . oh, shit, oh shit," Lake said. He unplugged the PBX cable from the phone, dumping the phone log memory from the unit, then left it unplugged. "You asshole—you didn't use the secure exchange. Cazaux is bound to find out."

"I am out of this, Harold," Fell said. "I am out of this entire operation. I'm getting the hell away from butchers like Cazaux and psychos like Ysidro, and if you had any brains you'd get out too."

"But what did you say? What did you do?"

"I was going to leave a message on the NSC's voice mail," Fell said. "Hardcastle himself answered it. I told him the location of Cazaux's mansion in Bedminster, and I told him about the hostage he's got in there."

"What hostage? What in hell are you talking about?"

"He's holding a woman in a third-floor apartment, Harold. He's beating the hell out of her."

"Dark hair, exotic-looking, kind of spacey?" Fell's expression told Lake that he had guessed correctly. "That's Cazaux's astrologer, you *idiot.* Varga, or Vega—I don't know the bitch's fucking name. She's no hostage, Ted—she *likes* getting beat up. She gets off on it. You called the authorities to try to rescue *her?* She's the one who's probably been telling Cazaux to do all this in the first place! She's as weird as he is. They're like both out of a fuckin' horror movie."

"Oh, God . . ." It made sense now—he thought he was helping her, while all along the woman was going to get her kicks watching Cazaux slice him up into little pieces. *Shit,* Fell thought, *what in the hell am I doing here?* "Well, that doesn't matter," Fell said, thinking hard and fast. "I'm not doing this for her—I'm doing it for me. I'm tired of standing by and watching Cazaux rip this country apart."

"So you ratted him out," Lake said. "Jesus, Fell, our lives aren't worth *spit* anymore."

"We've got an escape plan worked out, Harold. Let's do it. Let's get the hell out of here."

"I've got forty million dollars in options contracts being executed in the next six to ten hours, Ted. I can't leave. I'll have to sign a proxy, pay someone to execute the contracts, sign for the cash. I can't risk this operation with any of that."

"Harold, I'm out of here," Fell said. He told him about the woman, about how she had tried to get him to pull a gun on Henri Cazaux and then watch Cazaux kill him. "I told the authorities about Cazaux and how they can find him. If anyone escapes the raid, they'll try to hunt us down. I want to be safely hidden long before that. I'll help you get out, too, but if you want to stay I can't help you."

Lake thought about it, but only for a moment—he knew that Fell was right. Cazaux and his cronies were completely out of control, and the slightest screwup would mean instant, deadly retaliation. Even if Fell hadn't already made the decision for them, Lake knew it was time to get out. "All right, Ted, you're right," Lake decided. "Notify the flight crew and the security detail—we leave immediately. I'll execute the contracts and the cancel orders and have the funds sent by the bank to Townsend at the mansion—he'll know what to do with the cashier's check. Jesus, I hope the FBI nails Cazaux, because he will hunt us down for sure."

Bedminster, New Jersey
Three Hours Later

The first guard heard it while it was still a long way off, a heavy, slow rhythmic beating against the sky. He raised his left hand to his ear until the cuff of his left sleeve was even with his lips and said, "Station three, chopper, south, big one."

"Copy," the security shift officer responded. Everyone knew that Tomas Ysidro, the chief of security, would be listening in to the guard's channel, so responses were quick.

The first guard withdrew a Russian-made monocular night-vision scope from a case at his side and scanned the sky. His line-of-sight visibility was extremely limited, but his job wasn't to scan the sky, but the treeline, about seventy yards away, and the long gravel driveway leading to the main dirt road. The rain had stopped, but the clouds were thick, scuttling across the sky on strong low-level winds as the summer night storm passed. He could see the glowing yellow eyes of a small animal, a raccoon or possum, scurrying from tree to tree, doing some nocturnal hunting. The night-vision scope always revealed all sorts of animals—deer, foxes, rabbits by the barn-ful . . .

. . . and men. The guard chuckled as he watched one of the other guards emerge from the trees, about a hundred and fifty yards away, zipping up his fly after taking a piss in the trees. He saw a puff of smoke trickle from his mouth—the asshole was smoking on duty with the brass in the house. He was using a light shield around his cigarette so Ysidro or Cazaux wouldn't see his glowing cig, but the night-vision equipment clearly showed the smoke. If Ysidro saw that, he'd kick his ass. It was a hell of a chance to take just for a lousy cigarette.

He lowered his night-vision binoculars and listened for the helicopter—nothing. "Station three, clear," he reported.

"Copy."

The guard relaxed a bit, letting the scope dangle on its neck strap and crossing the Colt AR-15 assault rifle, the semiautomatic version of the standard Army M-16, in his arms. Bedminster had very little air traffic at night, but the estate was just a few miles from Interstate 78 and State Route 206, so they got visitors once in a while. Interstate 78 was the main drag between Newark and Allentown, and choppers and light planes often followed the interstate at night when—

A sudden sound made the guard alert. He put the AR-15 in his hands and dropped to one knee, scanning the treeline for any hint of motion. He knew from Army training that at night the edges of the eye picked up motion better, so he carefully scanned the treeline. He was fully exposed where he was standing—too far away from the house, but close enough to be illuminated by the light from a few windows and too far from the trees to take cover. He reached for the scope . . .

"What the hell are you doing out in the open like this, asshole?" The guard was so startled he nearly fell over into the wet grass. Tomas Ysidro had succeeded in stepping out of the front door of the house right up beside him, and he didn't hear a thing. The guard shot to his feet, swinging the AR-15's muzzle around at Ysidro, who caught the barrel of the rifle and yanked it out of his hands. "Jesus, Vaccarro, what's with you?" Ysidro asked, giving the rifle back.

"Thought I heard a noise, sir."

"Yeah, it was me, burping and farting all the way from the house," Ysidro said. Cazaux's third-in-command was carrying a side-arm holstered in a quick-draw shoulder rig, but his hands were full with a burger and a mug of coffee. "Now get the hell out of the light."

"Yes, sir."

"What about that chopper?"

"Heard it for about thirty seconds, well to the south," the guard said. "Didn't hear it approach. Big one."

"Good call—it helps to keep the whole detail on their toes," Ysidro said. "I'll send one of the new guys out to spell you in about—"

This time they both heard it—a loud *snap!* of a twig, on the tree-line. Ysidro pushed the guard hard to the right to get him out of the light, the coffee and burger went flying, and a SIG Sauer P226 9-millimeter automatic was in his hands in the blink of an eye. "Call it in, damn it!" Ysidro said in a loud whisper.

"Station three, intruder east on the treeline," the guard radioed. He took cover behind a tall bush and retrieved the night-vision scope, quickly scanning the—

He saw a lone figure, running toward the house beside the gravel driveway. The guard raised his AR-15, sighted with the scope—then recognized the runner. "Mick, damn it, what the hell are you doing?" the guard whispered into his radio. The running man dropped to the ground, waving his rifle at the treeline. "Mick, answer up!"

"What?" the second guard radioed back—the first guard could see him talk into his left sleeve while holding his earpiece in his left ear. "Was that you talking, Tommy, you asshole?"

"Was that you on the treeline?" the first guard radioed back. He saw the guard named Mick lower his head in nervous exasperation.

He lifted his sleeve mike to his lips. "Station three, secure. Stand by and I'll clear the treeline." He saw the second guard start to get to his feet, angrily brushing himself off and shouldering his rifle on its strap. "Mick, stay put until I clear the—"

Tommy saw the second guard named Mick suddenly turn toward the treeline, and seconds later he heard another sound—but this one wasn't a twig.

An unknown voice shouted, "Freeze! Federal agents!"

Mick fumbled with his rifle, but he didn't get it up to his waist to try a shot from the hip before he heard three quick *pop-pop-pop*'s from a suppressed automatic three-burst submachine gun, and Mick went down.

"Intruders, treeline east—federal agents!" Tommy radioed. He scanned the treeline and saw only one figure, dressed completely in black, with a military-style helmet, ballistic face mask under a pair of night-vision goggles, black fatigues, and black body armor with the words U.S. MARSHAL on the front under a combat harness. "I only see one, treeline east! I—"

The greenish image of the marshal suddenly disappeared in a puff of fire, and the guard dropped the night-vision scope and rubbed the pain from his eyes. The security supervisor inside the mansion had activated the motion-sensing land mines that ringed the compound, and the first marshal was history.

"Lost contact with Davis on the ground team at target thirteen," the airborne assault leader reported. "I heard a challenge, then shots, then nothing."

"I'd call that an 'officer needs assistance,' " Deputy Chief Marshal William Landers said. "Should've known it would be target thirteen—my unlucky number." Dressed in full body armor and protective headgear, Landers was aboard one of the three CV-22 PAVE HAMMER tilt-rotor aircraft just outside Cazaux's Bedminster home. Landers was the number-two man in the U.S. Marshals Service, a twenty-one-year veteran, an experienced field agent, and former commander of the Marshals' Special Operations Group, also known as SOG. "Let's go in using assault plan Alpha." The PAVE HAMMER, formerly one of the Hammerheads' antismuggling aircraft and still sporting its distinctive Department of Border Security high-visibility orange markings, lifted off from the interstate rest-stop parking lot and leaped into the sky, rotating its wingtip engine nacelles so the two large rotors were pointing at a 45-degree angle for more forward speed.

From other staging areas nearby, two more CV-22 tilt-rotor aircraft lifted off at the same time and raced for the estate. There were several large homes in the Bedminster area described by the unknown informant during his brief phone call, so the Marshals Service had immediately dispatched several agents from the New York City, Philadelphia, and Newark offices into the area to start surveillance on each suspected residence. Unfortunately, it had taken the apparent death of a marshal to find the right one. Now, the three CV-22 aircraft, each carrying ten fully armed SOG agents, were encircling Henri Cazaux's mansion in the hopes of capturing the world's most wanted criminal.

Landers' CV-22 took only two minutes to approach the estate. Flying low and slow, the hybrid airplane-helicopter slowed by swiveling the rotors to full helicopter position. When it was about five hundred yards from the mansion, it activated its bank of four 3,000-candlepower NightSun searchlights and turned them onto the front door of the mansion. Landers, standing between the pilot's and copilot's seats, watched their approach through the CV-22's telescopic TV camera. At two hundred yards, Landers clicked on the public address speaker: "Attention. This is the U.S. Marshals Service. We have a federal search warrant and demand entry. Come out of the house immediately with your hands up."

"U.S. Marshals, my ass," Tomas Ysidro said to Henri Cazaux. "Let's take care of those motherfuckers ourselves, Henri."

The two terrorists finished donning their own assault uniforms—skin-tight protective black body suit, Reactor combat gloves, balaclava hood, black Hi-Tec trail sneakers, and a combat ALICE harness laden with pistols, knives, grenades, and other tools and devices. "Can't risk it, especially not with assault aircraft out there," Cazaux said.

"We play it right, one of those choppers could be ours."

"I said, we cannot risk it," Cazaux snapped. "The time to play action hero will come, Tomas, and I want you with me when it comes. But for now, we need to survive to execute the rest of our plan. Execute the escape plan and we will meet in the Catskill ranch in six hours. We're going after a prize much greater than a few tilt-rotor aircraft,'' Cazaux said, extending a hand. Ysidro took it, then they embraced. *"Bonne chance, mon ami."*

''Fuck you too, my friend,'' Ysidro said in return. He pulled up his balaclava, then turned to his security supervisor. ''Deactivate the land mines for ten seconds after you see the DOOR OPEN light, then turn 'em back on.'' His eyes flared for an instant, punctuating his last order: ''And I want to hear plenty of fireworks out here or I'll come back and stuff your nuts down your throat. Hear me?''

''I heard an explosion, then lost contact with Davis,'' one of the other ground agents reported. ''I'm thinking the place is mined.''

''Shit,'' Landers said. ''That entire front lawn might be mined—that takes care of our landing zone.'' He turned to another person watching the scene below next to him. ''Thoughts, Agent Harley?''

U.S. Secret Service Agent Deborah Harley, wearing the same body armor and assault gear as the U.S. Marshals—except her body armor said TREASURY AGENT on the front—studied the TV image carefully. ''I don't see those guards on the rooftop anymore—we're going to have to assume the roof and that balcony over the front entrance are booby-trapped too. Let's—''

''Unit One, this is Three, four motorcycles leaving the house at high speed,'' one of the other CV-22 pilots radioed. ''One each cardinal direction.'' Harley and Landers picked up one of the motorcycles barreling northbound, going at least sixty miles an hour straight for the woods.

''Try to stop them without killing them!'' Harley shouted.

''All units, clear to engage riders, try to interdict only, do not shoot to kill.'' Landers knew it was a useless command—anytime a weapon was used during a mission like this, death was always a possibility, especially with the weapons the CV-22s had. Trying to wound someone with a weapon designed to destroy an armored vehicle or a building was sometimes just not possible.

The pilot of Landers' CV-22 pulled the trigger on his control stick to the first detent, which activated the gun camera and slaved both the tilt-rotor aircraft's Hughes Chain Gun and the thermal sight in the CV-22's nose to the pilot's line-of-sight—the forward-looking infrared sight followed the pilot's head movements, and the Chain Gun slaved itself to the aiming crosshairs superimposed on a clear glass reticle in front of the pilot's right eye. When the crosshairs settled on a spot just a few feet in front of the motorcycle's tires, the pilot pulled the trigger to the second detent. A fifty-round burst of cannon fire that sounded like a chain-saw blade cutting through the aircraft's aluminum skin rattled through the PAVE HAMMER aircraft.

The motorcycle rider obviously saw the Chain Gun's muzzle flash, because he veered hard left as soon as the cannon fired. The motorcycle skidded on the slippery grass, and the rider threw himself clear as he went down. The motorcycle skidded straight ahead and was instantly turned into scrap metal by cannon fire.

The CV-22 pilot swooped lower. The rider rolled along the ground for several feet before coming to rest in a half-sitting, half-prone position, shaking cobwebs out of his head. He was wearing a dark skin-tight suit with a mask—Harley or Landers couldn't recognize him. "Turn facedown and spread your arms and legs," Landers shouted over the PA speaker when they hit the rider with the spotlight. To the pilots, Landers said, "Hover right over him, guys. We'll fastrope right over him and haul him up with the rescue winch. We'd just better hope he's not laying right on top of a mine or we'll—"

"He's moving . . . damn it!" the pilot swore. He was distracted enough to lose sight of him as the rider got up and ran underneath the PAVE HAMMER. "Aft gunners, keep an eye out for—"

There was a loud *bang!* and the CV-22 heeled sharply over to the left. The pilot corrected for the shove, gained a little altitude, and experimentally swung the tilt-rotor aircraft's tail around so they were facing the forest. No caution lights illuminated, and the aircraft responded normally. "What happened?" he called on interphone. "Someone sing out."

"Land mine," one of the aft gunners called out. "The suspect had just reached the edge of the trees when he tripped it. He exploded like a rotten tomato."

"Well, we know the land mines have been activated again," Landers said. "Pretty sophisticated—a fucking remote-controlled perimeter defense system. Any doubt we got the right house?"

The guard named Tommy watched the whole thing—watched the motorcycle rider zoom away from the house toward the forest, watched the huge helicopter open up on him, watched the rider do a triple-flip through the air, then watched as he was blown into a hundred pieces by one of the land mines. The big boxy-looking twin-rotor helicopter with airplane wings was now hovering at the edge of the clearing, pointing not quite at the front door but a little off to the right, as if deciding what to do. Tommy had traded his semiautomatic AR-15 for a full-automatic M-16 with a fifty-round magazine and an M206 40-millimeter grenade launcher, and had taken his position at one of the bulletproof polycarbonate front windows inside the mansion.

Suddenly the big chopper's blinding searchlights swung around and hit the house full force. Tommy lowered his night-vision goggles—they were useless with so much light. A voice came over the chopper's PA. "Come out of the house with your hands in the air! This is your last warning!"

"Two more of those things, surrounding the house," someone radioed.

"Did the boss make it?"

"I don't think so."

"What do we do?" Tommy shouted back over his shoulder. "They got a damned big gun on that thing!"

"Sit tight," the security supervisor said. "Everyone hold your fire. They won't use the heavy stuff unless we—"

"What are you doing?" a female voice behind Tommy shouted. Tommy whirled around, pointing the M-16. It was "the witch," as everyone called her—Cazaux's squeeze, the crazy woman who lived upstairs. She was wearing a silky red robe. Her long dark hair like a lion's mane was around her shoulders. The robe was not tied, and her breasts and crotch were exposed. "Why aren't you attacking?"

"Shut up and get out of here," Tommy said, pausing to get a good look at the witch's body. Pretty nice rack, he thought, but she had to be as crazy as they come to be walking around half-naked like that in the middle of a firefight. "Go downstairs in the wine cellar until this is over."

Jo Ann Vega saw the gunsel's eyes roving over her body before turning back toward the window. Another typical male, she thought angrily. "Listen, you little son of a bitch, *get out there* and kill them. Avenge Henri."

"Those are U.S. Marshals out there, and they got heavy stuff. We'll wait them out until we know the boss is safe."

"Henri is already dead," the witch said. "I saw him get hit out there." Tommy swallowed, finding it hard to believe that Henri Cazaux was dead, but he stayed at his position. "You've got to avenge him," the witch shrieked. "Get out there and kill those federals, *now!*"

"I said, shut up, take your big tits downstairs and take cover, lady."

That did it—the male pig deserved it now. Jo Ann Vega raised her Lorcin .380 automatic and fired three shots into the back of the man's head from two feet away. There were a few other shots as other gunners nervously fired a few rounds. Vega reached down, pulled the M-16 out of the dead man's arms, walked quickly to the front door, and swung it open.

"I'll take care of them for you, Henri, my love," Vega said aloud. "God how I loathe weak men." She stepped outside, her robe flying open in the wind. As she emerged out from under the breezeway in front of the house, she leveled the M-16 at the searchlights on the big aircraft on the other side of the expansive lawn and pulled the trigger. Her first shot came the closest, missing the searchlights by only a few feet, but the other shots went high and to the right.

She had fired almost the entire magazine, most of it almost straight up in the air, and was trying to figure out how to launch one of the inch-and-a-half-diameter grenades from the launcher slung under the rifle when the marshals' aircraft's cannon opened fire. Three 12.7-millimeter shells hit, one in the head and two in the torso, and Jo Ann Vega was split apart as easily as a hammer hitting a banana. The cannon then sprayed the rest of the front of the house, hitting each and every window with a gunner in it. Then, a long cylindrical pod on the left side of the PAVE HAMMER aircraft popped out of the left sponson, and three rockets ripple-fired into the front of the house, blowing out the front door and creating two more man-sized flaming holes.

Skidding to the left to shield the right side of the aircraft from the gunners in the front of the house, the CV-22 flew toward it. A few shots of automatic gunfire from the upper floors were immediately answered by Chain Gun fire. The Chain Gun then fired a path into the front lawn toward the house, creating a terrific explosion as one of the shells found a land mine close to the house. Two more rockets blasted into the house near the front door, the CV-22 stopped about twenty yards from the front of the house with its nose high in the air, hovered for a few seconds, then veered sharply to the left and climbed over the house.

Leading six U.S. Marshals, Deborah Harley and William Landers jumped off the back cargo ramp of the PAVE HAMMER. Following the chewed-up path created by the Chain Gun, they were safe from land mines. Firing into the windows, most of which were ablaze, Harley and the seven Marshals burst into the house.

The ground floor was decimated. The walls were blackened by smoke and fire, furniture was upended and smashed, and smoking, crumpled bodies lay everywhere. Harley, wearing a gas mask, shot one armed guard running toward the stairs from the kitchen, then ran upstairs. She tossed two tear gas grenades upstairs, then, with more agents behind her, started clearing rooms. She shot two more gunsels stupid enough to have guns in their hand and turned over six more blinded and choking guards to the Marshals.

Clearing the entire mansion took only five minutes of careful searching by twelve U.S. Marshals, and the assault was over. A New Jersey National Guard ordnance-disposal team from nearby Picatinny Arsenal had to come out to create a safe ingress path toward the mansion, but within minutes the cleanup was under way.

Hardcastle arrived about an hour after the raid was over. He admired the large, lumbering PAVE HAMMER hovering nearby. "Good to see you boys back on the job," he said half-aloud to the ungainly hybrid aircraft—they belonged to the U.S. Navy now, but he'd always think of them as his. Hardcastle then turned to Deborah Harley, checked her TREASURY AGENT body armor, and said with a smile, "It's good to see you too, Agent Harley. I should have known you were Secret Service. It would explain why you seemed to have the run of the White House, and how you seemed to have access to a lot more intelligence information than the average executive assistant."

"Vice President Martindale hates Secret Service around him, so I'm less of a bodyguard and more assistant," Harley said. They were given the all-clear by the Army ordnance-disposal units to reenter the mansion, and Harley began shrugging out of her body armor.

"Have you ID'd the bodies yet?" Hardcastle asked. "Was Cazaux here? Did you get him?"

"Yes, yes, and I think so," Harley said. She led Hardcastle to a line of corpses outside the mansion, where U.S. Marshals were taking fingerprints and photos of the bodies for identification. "Hired gunners, ex- and retired GIs, a few known felons and mercenaries—Cazaux recruited only the best." She kicked aside a sheet high enough for Hardcastle to see a mass of blood-caked hair and bloodied but recognizable womanly features. "One woman, might be a local—we're putting a rush on her ID."

Harley unzipped a black body bag with three strips of tape on it. The badly bullet-mutilated body of a tall, well-built man was inside—he had been hit several times by cannon fire from one of the CV-22s. "This looks like him, Admiral. One of the Navy flyboys got a little antsy and hit him with his Chain Gun. Based on my best description, I think that's Henri Cazaux."

"Fingerprints? Dental records?"

"We've already called the FBI," Harley said. She noticed Hardcastle's disappointed expression at having the FBI called in, and Harley added, "The Marshals have printed and photoed the bodies, but the FBI Pictures and Prints lab has the best gear to do a positive ID, Ian, and they can do it fast. The only other place to get Cazaux's ID records is from the Belgian Army or from Interpol, since Cazaux's never been a guest in an American prison. I know you and Judge Wilkes are having this thing with each other, but you want an iron-clad positive ID, and so you're talking FBI. The Marshals are working on it, top priority. But I might be able to give you something for the Executive Committee or the White House."

Harley checked a notebook retrieved from a camouflage field briefcase, then knelt next to the corpse: "Cazaux was supposed to have had paratrooper tattoos on both his left and right hand between the thumb and forefinger." She picked up the grisly bullet-shattered hands and removed the thin Reactor gloves. One of the nearby Marshals had to turn away at the sight of the mutilated body, but Harley handled it as casually as if she were giving a baby a bath. "Here's one tattoo on his left hand . . . and here's a scar on his right hand from laser surgery. It looked like he was having the tattoos removed. They were apparently executing a well-rehearsed escape plan—we've found vehicles, disguises, even a little two-man helicopter stashed nearby."

"Damn," Colonel Marc Sheehan said in admiration. "You got him. You actually got Henri Cazaux!"

"I'm not celebrating until those fingerprints and dental records match," Hardcastle said. "In the meantime I've got some information on the guy who called with information on Cazaux."

"Compare notes with this gent," Harley suggested. She stepped over to one of the Marshals taking notes over the bodies. "Admiral Hardcastle, meet Timothy Lassen, chief deputy U.S. Marshal from Sacramento. He's been tracking the money from an aircraft transaction a few days ago. I radioed him about the raid. Tim, the Admiral's got a name for you."

The Marshal checked a notebook, and before Hardcastle had a chance to speak, said, "Ted Fell. Works for a Wall Street greaser named Harold Lake."

"Jesus," Hardcastle exclaimed. As fast as things were happening, Hardcastle thought, the Marshals and people like Deborah Harley were moving even faster. "How in the hell did you know, Deputy Lassen?"

"Good ol'-fashioned pure dumb luck," Lassen admitted. "Lake brokered several large aircraft deals for buyers all over the country. At first blush they all checked out—aerial fire-fighters, corporate planes, parts, that kind of thing. But one buyer didn't know it was Lake who was brokering the deal, and he told me some stories about Lake—about how he was in debt up to his chin, about how he was sure to get caught in some money-laundering scheme someday. I checked further. Turns out Lake's financial fortunes changed right after Cazaux's attack on Memphis."

"Changed? I thought you said he was already in debt."

"I did," Lassen explained. "He was bankrupt, worse than bankrupt. But two days before the attack on Universal Express, Lake writes this complicated and outrageous stock option deal, in effect betting that Universal Express stock is going to drop in value, and I mean *really* drop—he wants to trade hundreds of thousands of shares of stock."

"Lake had that kind of money just lying around?"

"You don't need a lot of cash to do one of these options deals," Lassen said. "Four or five million was enough to get the ball rolling."

"Where could he get that kind of cash?"

"You won't believe it," Lassen said. "He borrows the money from McSorley, Brennan McSorley—the president of Universal Equity Services, with whom he used to do business—they had a falling-out some time back. Talk about balls—Lake makes a bet that Universal Equity stock is going to take a hit, using Universal's money! It's like betting the 'Don't Come' line with your mother rolling the dice.

"Anyway, two days after Lake makes this option deal, Cazaux blows up Universal Express. Universal stock falls through the floor. Lake now owns all this stock for pennies on the dollar, and he turns right around and sells it when the stock recovers. Lake is now rolling in money—something like seventy million dollars' worth."

"Maybe I'd better open an account with this guy," Harley said.

"Maybe not, Debbie," Lassen said. "Lake is flush now, but instead of going back to stocks and bonds, he goes into aircraft leasing—big aircraft, cargo aircraft. One of the planes he buys is from this place in Atlanta, where those two FBI guys were killed in that hangar. Another one of his planes is shot down over Fort Worth. And guess what—one of the unexploded bombs recovered from the Fort Worth bombing matches a military lot-number of several cluster bomb units stolen from a Nevada Navy arsenal several days prior."

"Christ—Harold Lake and this Ted Fell are the bankers for Henri Cazaux?"

"It's looking that way," Lassen agreed. "But apparently Fell had a change of heart—I guess working with a psychopath like Cazaux will do that to a man, no matter how good the money is. So Harold Lake dropped a dime on Henri Cazaux, eh, Admiral?"

"The phone call was made from Lake's private office in Manhattan," Hardcastle said. "I turned the information over to Judge Wilkes and the FBI before I came out here. As usual, I haven't heard a thing. What about other aircraft that Lake and Fell purchased, Agent Lassen? Have you kept track of them?"

"Unfortunately, I dropped the aircraft line when they checked out in my initial investigation," Lassen replied. "When I matched Lake with the Fort Worth plane, I tried going back to pick up their trails. One I found—it's one of the smaller bizjets, going through an avionics refit up in Newburgh. So far I haven't found the rest yet. They still might be legitimate."

"And they might not," Hardcastle said. "We've got to find those planes."

"Newburgh might be the place to start," Lassen said eagerly. "Maybe we can take one of your awesome birds up there. They're surely a couple of mean-looking choppers."

"Sounds good," Hardcastle said. He had his aide Marc Sheehan radio for a CV-22 PAVE HAMMER to pick them up on the hastily prepared helipad on the front lawn. While Sheehan was on the radio, he received another message and gave it to Hardcastle, who turned to Lassen and Harley and said, "Guess what, guys? Judge Wilkes herself is on the way. She wants everyone to stop what they're doing and wait until her and her team check in on the scene."

"Well, I think things have just ground to a halt here," Lassen said. "FBI's in charge of a terrorist incident, not the Marshals or Secret Service."

"Do you have enough to arrest Lake or Fell, Agent Lassen?"

"Definitely," Lassen replied. "You gave me the caller ID with

Lake's number, telling us about Cazaux in this place—that makes him a witness. I've circumstantially linked Lake with the aircraft used in two of the bombings."

"Then I'd suggest you go pick him up," Hardcastle said. "We can explain things to the FBI later. Besides, you have to make room for Judge Wilkes' chopper."

"Gotcha," Lassen said. He waited until the big white-and-orange PAVE HAMMER touched down, then plugged his ears against the noise and trotted off. No sooner had the aircraft roared off out of sight than a small blue-and-white Bell JetRanger zoomed into view, circled the landing zone until a small smoke marker was set out for them, then rapidly touched down.

Judge Lani Wilkes, Director of the FBI, was the first off the JetRanger, and she was ready to explode with anger. Two agents followed her off, both armed with Uzi submachine guns. She didn't wait for the screech of her helicopter's turbine engine to subside before laying into Hardcastle: "You're coming with me, Admiral. You and Agent Harley and Agent Landers there and anyone else who was responsible for this raid."

William Landers, still wearing his body armor and still carrying his H & K MP5 submachine gun, asked, "Would you like a briefing on the operation before we depart, Judge?"

"Shut up, Bill," Wilkes interjected. "You know damned well that SOG was involving itself in an FBI-directed investigation, yet you proceeded without my authorization. I'm responsible for all the casualties here, and I can assure you, I'm going to rake you over the coals for each and every one of them. Hardcastle, where was that . . . that *thing,* that tilt-rotor thing of yours going?"

"It doesn't belong to me, Judge Wilkes," Hardcastle replied, yawning. "It belongs to the Navy. We borrowed it for this operation."

"This *operation?* . . . This *massacre,* you mean!" Wilkes shouted. "Where the fuck was that aircraft going?"

"Following up on the tip we got this morning."

"We checked those offices in Manhattan. They look like they've been evacuated."

"We think we know where Harold Lake and Ted Fell might've gone," Deborah Harley said. "Agents of the Marshals Service are going to check it out."

"I told everyone to stay put," Wilkes seethed. "The *FBI* is in charge of this investigation, Hardcastle. You're interfering. You're not authorized to conduct any arrests or investigations without my office's authorization. I'm going to bust all—"

"We think we got Henri Cazaux, Judge," Hardcastle announced.

Wilkes stopped in midsentence, staring in complete shock first at Hardcastle, then at Landers and Harley, and finally at the line of body bags in front of the mansion. "Where is he?" she asked skeptically, her voice a weak gasp. "Show me." She turned to one of her aides and said, "Get a P and P satellite ID unit in here and secure this area. Get everyone out of that house. *Now! Move it, move it!*"

Wilkes followed Harley and Landers over to the body bag with the bullet-shattered body of Henri Cazaux inside, and Landers explained how they made their identification. "It's not confirmed," Landers reminded her, "but from my operational notes, one of the bodies we recovered could be him. He was trying to escape in a motorcycle along with three others; we got one of the other riders. Two escaped. State Police and the sheriffs are out looking for them." He then explained what happened to the fourth rider, and gave a thumbnail sketch of the raid itself.

When he was finished, one of his agents handed Landers a note. "We ID'd the woman killed in the raid," he said. "Jo Ann Rocci, a.k.a. Jo Ann Vega, address, Newburgh, New York."

"That's where the Marshals are headed to see if they can find Lake and Fell," Hardcastle said. "This place and Newburgh look like Cazaux's entire U.S. base of operations."

"I hope congratulations are in order," Wilkes said as she examined the body, then ordered it to be zipped up and guarded, "but you still violated my procedures. I expected no less from you, Admiral Hardcastle, and I'm very disappointed with the Secret Service and the Marshals for letting themselves be led around by the nose by you, Admiral. Well, this will be your last cowboy stunt, Hardcastle, I promise you. We have a debriefing at the Justice Department, all of you. The Bureau takes charge of these bodies and this crime scene as of right now. Let's go."

Stewart International Airport, Newburgh, New York
That Same Time

The roadblocks were still in place, but all cars were no longer being stopped and searched. The limousine driver simply showed the bored rent-a-cop an airport pass, and they were waved in. Things had definitely calmed down here at Stewart International Airport, and the commuter flights were flying again.

To Harold Lake, it made perfect sense—Henri Cazaux abandoned Newburgh, so why not use it? So what if it had State Police, Army, Air Force, and FBI swarming all around it? Evading the authorities was Cazaux's headache, not his. The presence of all these uniformed men gave Lake great peace of mind.

Of course, being surrounded by his own personal security detail helped. Using a portion of the money he was skimming from the option contract deals he was doing for Cazaux, Lake had hired his own small, well-equipped army and air force. Starting with a new personal secretary—a beautiful statuesque redhead who could take Gregg dictation, type sixty words a minute, and had a Browning 9-millimeter automatic hidden in a holster beside her ample left breast—Lake had a new chauffeur and bodyguard, a new armored Lincoln sedan, inside and outside guards at his East Side apartment, a Gulfstream III jet with a six-thousand-mile range, and a ranch in central Brazil with yet another contingent of guards stationed there.

All this security had cost him one-third of all the money he had skimmed from Cazaux over the past few weeks, but it was well worth it. Henri Cazaux was relentless. Many of these guards were nothing more than trip wires—their quick, silent deaths would hopefully alert the inner guards that Cazaux was on the hunt and closing in. Lake had no illusions about evading Cazaux—he just hoped that the world's law enforcement authorities and his own security force would get Cazaux before he got too close.

The first thing Lake had done when he bought the Gulfstream was get the registration number changed and get it repainted, which guaranteed both that it would look different and would be out of sight until he needed it. He didn't recognize the plane himself when they drove up to it, and he was about to question the driver when the chief of his security detail, a big, football-player tight-end-looking guy named Mantooth, emerged from it when the sedan pulled up.

The sedan stopped several yards away from the plane until it was quickly searched, then it pulled up right to the foot of the open airstair door. Mantooth stood in front of the sedan's door, blocking the view of anyone from the main commercial air terminal, but he did not open it himself—Lake and Fell had to open their own doors. According to Mantooth, the bodyguards' job was to stay on the lookout with *their* hands free to reach for *their* guns or subdue an attacker, not open doors or carry luggage. "Everything's ready, Mr. Lake," Mantooth said. "We're ready to go."

"Then let's go," Lake said and quickly stepped aboard the aircraft. The doors were closed as soon as Fell stepped aboard. The big, roomy VIP interior of the Gulfstream already made him feel safe, and the increasing snarl of the bizjet's two big turbofans and the sweet, husky smell of jet fuel helped to soothe his jangled nerves. Lake met the ship's stewardess, a brunette named Diane, who led him to the big, light-gray-leather, fully reclining master's chair on the right center side, buckled him in, and fixed him a Bloody Mary as the jet began to move. Ted Fell busied himself at the desk behind Lake, checking that the phone and fax machine were working. "Forget all that, Ted," Lake said. "No one is going to call or fax us—that stuff's not even hooked up."

Fell looked at Lake as if he were surprised at his boss's words; then, realizing he was right and that these phones had never been activated, fearing that Cazaux could easily find out about their escape plans that way, he averted his eyes to the richly carpeted floor and put his hands on his lap. "It . . . it doesn't seem real," Fell said. "We're on the run. We're never coming back."

"At least not as long as Cazaux, Townsend, or Ysidro are walking the earth—which hopefully won't be for too long," Lake said. "Just think of it as an extended and very, very secluded vacation, Ted. We'll start developing our offshore banking and brokerage ties in a year or so, making sure that everything is numbered and convoluted enough so no one can trace the trading activity to us. We'll be back in the trading pits before you know it. Meanwhile we work on our tans while—" Just then the big Gulfstream came to a stop, the engines wound down to low idle power, and the intercom phone beeped. Fell reached for it, but Lake picked it up. "What's going on . . . ?"

"Orders from the tower, sir," the pilot said. "Takeoff clearances have been canceled for all flights. They're ordering everyone back to the ramp."

"Why the hell are they doing that?"

"Don't know, sir," the pilot responded. "I don't see any police activity."

Lake knew why. He shot a murderous glare at Fell and said, "Damn it, Ted, the fucking FBI tracked us down."

"But how? I made the call from New York. No one knows about

this plane or its location, Harold. Maybe we were followed from the city. What are we going to do?"

"How the hell should I know? Let me think," Lake said angrily. He searched out the large oval window near him, looking to see if any police were converging on them, but he was facing away from the main terminal. The Gulfstream was on the parallel taxiway approaching the end of the runway, with a United Airlines MD-80 the only plane ahead of them. On the intercom phone, Lake asked, "What are your instructions, pilot?"

"All aircraft were told to back-taxi on the runway back to their original locations, sir," the pilot responded. "We'll be back-taxiing shortly and be back on the ramp in about five minutes."

"Are they blocking the runway?" Lake asked. There was a rather long, uncomfortable pause as the flight crew was obviously considering the possible ramifications of this question. Lake shouted, *"Well . . . ?"*

"No, sir, nothing is blocking this runway," the pilot finally replied.

"Good. When that United Airlines plane gets out of the way, you will ignore all instructions from the tower and make the takeoff," Lake said. "That's an order."

"Sir, I can't follow an order like that."

"If you don't, I'll come up there and shoot you in the back of the head," Lake said as calmly and as truthfully as he could. He carried a gun, but he had fired it only once, several months ago, and wasn't even sure if it was loaded. Mantooth, who was sitting in a seat near the airstair, heard Lake's words but did not register any surprise at all—it looked as if it was okay with him if his employer shot the pilots.

"Then I hope you can fly this plane, sir," the pilot said, "without a windshield. If you shoot or try to open the cockpit door, we'll stomp on the brakes, bust open the windscreens, jump out, and run like hell."

Lake obviously wasn't very good at threatening anyone with bodily harm. "Okay, let's try it this way," Lake said. "Make the takeoff and I'll give you twenty thousand dollars."

"Fifty thousand," the pilot immediately responded.

"Each," the copilot chimed in.

"Carter, Luce, you boneheads are getting paid plenty to fly this machine—do as Mr. Lake instructs you, or I'll shoot you myself," a deep, menacing voice said behind them. It was the chief of the security company, the bodyguard named Mantooth. "Take your seat, Mr. Lake."

"Are we taking off or not?"

"My job is to protect you, Mr. Lake," Mantooth said. "You're assuming it's the FBI or some other law enforcement agency out there, but I've seen no evidence of that. This airfield has obviously been compromised—whatever's going on, I think you'll be safer in the air than on the ground. We'll deal with the FAA later. Now sit down and strap in. And if there's a problem, let me know—there's no reason for you to talk to the pilots. Is that clear, Mr. Lake?" Lake was very unaccustomed to taking orders from anyone, but he could do nothing else but nod silently at the big bodyguard—he obviously knew what he was doing.

The Gulfstream moved up into the hammerhead, poised for takeoff as soon as the airliner ahead pulled off. Lake could just barely see the MD-80 leave the runway when the pilot lined the Gulfstream up on the centerline, spooled up the engines to takeoff power, and released the . . .

. . . but suddenly Lake could see a bright light shining on the wing's leading edges and on the pavement beside his jet, and even before the pilot again chopped the power to idle, he knew they weren't going to make it. On the intercom, he heard, "Emergency vehicles on the runway, sir. We're blocked."

Mantooth had drawn the biggest, meanest-looking automatic pistol Lake had ever seen from a shoulder rig, but Lake said, "Put it away, Mantooth, it's the FBI out there. You have a permit for that, I assume?"

"Of course, Mr. Lake, but you'd better let me—"

"Put the gun in your holster and take off your jacket so they see your gun first thing," Lake said. "Everyone stays calm, everyone does as they're told, no one resists, and no one, I repeat, *no one* says *anything*. Not a word. If they tell you you're under arrest, you immediately say, 'I want to speak with my attorney right now.' Got it?" To the pilots behind the closed cockpit doors, Lake shouted, "Shut 'em down right here," then he undogged the entry hatch.

"No! Shut only the left engine down!" Mantooth shouted to the cockpit. He turned to Lake angrily: "Sir, you stay put. I'll see what they want."

"This is my problem, Mantooth."

"No, it's *my* problem," Mantooth said. "You hired me to protect you, sir. I'm a practicing attorney here in New York State as well as former military. We cooperate, but you don't have to expose yourself to danger or get your rights violated. Now, stay out—"

"You're a good man, Mantooth," Lake said, "and your people are first-rate, but this shit started long before you came on board."

"Sir, you may have gotten yourself in deep shit, but now your problems are my problems," Mantooth said. "If you have to surrender to the police, we'll do it in a controlled, orderly manner."

"I need the government's cooperation . . . their protection . . . to stay alive," Lake said. "I have to give them whatever they want."

"Why do you need government protection, sir?"

"It's too complicated," Lake said. "I . . . I've got to go out there."

"I said, stay put, and that's an order," Mantooth said. He nodded to Diane, the stewardess, who had produced a 10-millimeter automatic pistol from nowhere and was guarding the emergency exits, making sure no one came in from behind them. "I'm your attorney in New York State, representing you. You don't have to say a word. Understand me?" Lake nodded—for the first time in a long time, he felt as if things were truly under control. Mantooth deployed the airstairs and stepped outside.

A huge, boxy-looking aircraft with two huge helicopter rotors mounted on the tips of short fat wings—certainly not a standard little helicopter—hovered just a few hundred yards in front of the Gulfstream, shining a large searchlight right at them. It slowly began to descend onto the runway as a yellow-and-blue New York State Police cruiser with lights flashing sped onto the runway, turning around in front of the Gulfstream and parking about twenty yards in front of the jet's nose. A lone trooper got out of the car, right hand on the butt of his service weapon, partially shielding himself with his car door. On the car's PA speaker, he asked, "How many others in the aircraft?"

"Five," Mantooth shouted back.

"Any armed?"

"One, a private security employee."

"Have him, Harold Lake, and Ted Fell step out, hands in sight." Mantooth turned and motioned toward the entry door—but instead of anyone stepping outside, the airstairs retracted and the hatch closed tight. "I said I want Lake and Fell out here—right now!" the trooper shouted.

But Mantooth wasn't watching the trooper—he was watching

the approaching aircraft. He recognized it as a V-22 Osprey, used by the Border Security Force for stopping drug smugglers a few years earlier. A door opened on the right side and several armed men got out . . . and at that same moment, both rear passenger doors on the State Police car burst open, two men rolled out carrying submachine guns, aimed their guns at the V-22, and opened fire.

Mantooth pounded on the side of the Gulfstream and shouted, "Get out of here, *now!*" He drew his sidearm, but it was too late—he saw the red glint of a laser aiming beam flash across his eyes, and then the whole world turned black.

The Gulfstream's right engine roared almost to full power, and the nose did a tight pirouette to the right, the left wingtip barely edging over the roof of the sedan. Gregory Townsend, dressed as a New York State trooper, calmly reached into the front seat of the car, withdrew a LAWS (Light Antitank Weapon System) rocket, raised its sights, waited until the Gulfstream was about seventy yards away, aimed, and fired. The Gulfstream III bizjet exploded in a huge fireball, singeing the man's hair and eyebrows with the heat. Townsend dropped the spent fiberglass launcher tube, ignored the heat, the destruction, and his two dead comrades behind him, calmly stepped into the sedan, and raced away. He was picked up by a waiting helicopter on the other side of the airport and was gone minutes later with no possible pursuit.

The White House
That Same Time

The bedside phone was programmed with a gentle wakeup cycle: the ring started out soft and barely audible, and gradually rose in intensity, depending on the urgency of the call as determined by the White House operator. On all but a national defense–level emergency call, the President usually needed three or four good rings to wake up—but not the First Lady. At the first gentle buzz of the phone she was quickly and silently out of bed, her lean, agile body barely flexing the super-king-size mattress. By the second ring, without turning on a light, she had her Armani robe and slippers on and was all the way around to the President's side of the bed. By the third ring she had touched the ACKNOWLEDGE button on the phone and lightly touched her husband's shoulder: "I'll be outside," she said simply, giving him a peck on the cheek as he struggled to shake out the cobwebs.

The First Lady walked briskly across the bedroom, opened one of the double doors, and stepped out into the outer apartment, leaving the door partially open. Theodore, the President's valet, was just showing a steward inside, carrying a tray with a pot of strong black Kona and walnut-covered pastries for the President, a pot of Earl Grey tea and cold cucumber slices for the First Lady, and a small stack of messages for the President's immediate attention. A Secret Service agent stood by the door, hands folded in front of his body, casually scanning the outer apartment and occasionally talking into the microphone mounted inside his left sleeve, reporting to Inside Security that everything was secure. "Good morning, ma'am," Theodore greeted her pleasantly.

"Good morning," the First Lady said distractedly. She immediately snatched the messages off the tray, sat down on the sofa, and began to read as the tray was placed on the table before her and her tea was poured. Theodore had been the White House valet for two Administrations now, and it was damned unusual to be greeted by the First Lady when these early-morning crisis calls came in. Most First Ladies stayed in the inner apartment and waited for the hubbub to die down in the outer apartment and their own personal staff to arrive and brief them—not this First Lady. She always got up ahead of her husband, never bothered to dress before coming out, always helped herself to the messages from the Communication Center, and rarely waited for her husband to come out before making notes or phone calls or even going out to the Yellow Oval Room, the main living room in the center of the second floor, to talk to the Chief of Staff or whoever else might out there waiting for a reply.

"Anyone outside yet, Theodore?" the First Lady asked.

"No, ma'am," the valet replied.

The First Lady picked up the phone beside the sofa. She heard the standard "Yes, Mr. President" from the operator, silently suffered the gender gaffe, and said, "Location of the Chief of Staff and the Deputy Attorney General."

"One moment, ma'am . . . the Chief of Staff is en route, ETA five minutes. The Deputy Attorney General is also en route, ETA fifteen minutes."

"Ask the FBI Director, the Attorney General, and the Communications Director to report to the White House immediately," the

First Lady said and hung up. The word "ask" was, of course, superfluous—it was an order, not a request. Besides, the First Lady thought angrily, if the President had to be awakened, the damned staff had better be wide awake and in their seats by the time he was up. "You can go in and see to the President, Theodore," the First Lady said without looking up from her reading.

"Yes, ma'am." The Secret Service agent reported that he was leaving the door, then walked briskly over to the door of the inner apartment, and went inside, followed by the valet. Another Secret Service agent, a woman this time, took his place at the outer apartment door and reported the room secure.

A few moments later, wearing a short-sleeved college sweatshirt, jogging pants, and running shoes without socks, his hair slicked back with cold water, the President emerged from the inner apartment. "I really could've used another four hours' sleep today," he said, yawning. "Is this a coffee call or not?"

"It's a coffee call," the First Lady said.

"Great," the President muttered. "Coffee calls" meant he should have coffee because he probably wasn't going to get any sleep the rest of the morning. "What's the beef now? Not another Cazaux attack, I hope."

"Bad news and not-so-bad news," the First Lady said, handing her husband the messages. "A plane carrying a TV crew was accidentally shot down by the Air Force."

The President shook his head in exasperation, reaching for his coffee and stuffing a pastry in his mouth. "Ah, jeez . . ."

"It happened earlier this morning, but the staff decided not to wake you about it until later—I think that was an error in judgment. You should have been called."

"I agree," the President muttered, not really agreeing with her—he was thankful for every bit of sleep he was allowed to get these days. "What's the not-so-bad news?"

"The FBI thinks they got Henri Cazaux."

"Hot *damn!*" the President crowed. "That ain't not-so-bad news, honey, that's *great* news! Dead, I hope?"

"Dead," the First Lady said. "Killed in a shoot-out at an estate in northern New Jersey, in a raid organized by the U.S. Marshals Service and Admiral Hardcastle."

"That Hardcastle is an arrogant sonofabitch," the President said happily, "but I could kiss him on the damned lips if he engineered that raid."

"The problem is, *we* didn't engineer it," the First Lady said coldly. "We weren't briefed by Judge Wilkes or Deputy AG Lowe about the operation, so we can only assume that Hardcastle exceeded his authority and free-lanced this raid."

"Baby doll, I don't really care," the President said, "as long as that Belgian bastard is dead. We need to get confirmation on this, and they better do it quick—maybe we can get the morning news shows."

"You are *not* going to show this kind . . . of *glee* on international TV," the First Lady decided. "You are going to praise the FBI, the Justice Department, Governor Seale of New Jersey—I'm sure there were some New Jersey cops in on the raid too—and the Marshals Service for their efforts. No mention whatsoever of Hardcastle." The First Lady paused momentarily, then added, *"Except* when it comes to an explanation of this accidental shooting of that civilian plane. The message stated the civilian plane was at fault and that the pilot who fired the missile killed himself by flying his plane into the ocean . . ."

"Oh, my . . ." the President exclaimed, reaching for a muffin now.

". . . and we'll put Hardcastle's fingerprints all over that screwup," the First Lady said, her mind turning to high gear. "This will prove that Judge Wilkes was right all along: the FBI was better suited to solve this Cazaux problem after all, and that Hardcastle's plan to use military forces was a failure right from the start. You see, we've got to wipe *your* fingerprints off this military idea."

"It ain't gonna matter, sweetie," the President drawled casually, sipping coffee. "It's over. We can go back to normal now."

"What matters, *dear,* is the political fallout. You approved using Hardcastle, so it's your fault if innocent people got killed. We've got to portray that fucker Hardcastle as a loose cannon, a maverick . . . I know, we'll put him up in front of a Congressional panel." The First Lady's legal mind was turning; she was in full damage-control mode: "If Hardcastle's a witness, he can't talk to the press. You may have to strip him of his authority, maybe even fire him."

"That's easy," the President said, swallowing the last of the muffin. "No one likes him anyway. What I need to do is get back on the *road,* honey. I've got an election to win yet. Kemp and Bennett have been on the move in the east all during this Cazaux thing, Wilson and Brown have been slam-dunking me on the west coast, and Dole's been in Kansas whipping up the midwest against me—I've been stuck here in Washington too long."

"I told you before, hiding behind the trappings of power doesn't look good," the First lady said. "If you simply declare the emergency over, some might say it's political. Let Lowe and Wilkes and the terrorism committee make a statement to the press declaring the air defense emergency over, and have Hardcastle's office release a statement taking the fighters and the surface-to-air missiles off alert status pending the investigation of the accident. The press will listen to Lowe and Wilkes. When the press starts wondering why you haven't gone on the road yet, suddenly they'll find you on a six-state 'fact-finding mission,' beginning in California. But let the staff take the heat. I told you before."

"I know, I know . . . let public opinion make the tough decisions," the President said. "Don't make headlines—embrace them."

"Right," the First Lady said. "And we need to make our peace with the producers of the TV show that had their crew shot down by Hardcastle's goons—we might have to feed them an exclusive interview from the White House or from Air Force One while we're on the road."

"Let's do it on Air Force One—that always impresses the hell out of the media."

"We'll decide that later," the First Lady said dismissively. "Again, it's important to emphasize that Hardcastle's mismanagement caused the accident—the Air Force crews were following orders. The pressure Hardcastle was creating with these 'round-the-clock patrols and missiles everywhere caused this terrible accident. Remember that."

"Gotcha," the President said. "I'm gonna go take a nap for an hour while the staff gets their act together."

"Let's get the photos done first," the First Lady reminded him.

"Photos?"

"Of you and me, up in the middle of the night, working after being notified of this terrible tragedy," the First Lady said, reaching for the phone. "We've got to show the people we're on the job, and need to show them ratty sweatshirts and unshaven faces. Remember: You're concerned over the accident. Look concerned. You share their pain."

The President sighed but nodded okay. Sometimes even he had to admit his wife was a bit much.

U.S. Department of Justice
Office of the Deputy Attorney General
Washington, D.C.
Four Hours Later

"I'm glad this is over," Deputy Attorney General Elizabeth Lowe said during the day's first meeting of the President's Executive Committee on Terrorism. "If this got any bloodier . . . well, I'm just glad it's over." Left unsaid were the words "It might *really* hurt the President's reelection chances," but everyone present in the Oval Office knew what Lowe meant to say. To Ian Hardcastle, Lowe said, "Admiral, the President is meeting with the producers of that trash TV show 'Whispers.' What's the final opinion as to the cause of the accident—and what happened to the pilot who fired the missile?"

"Captain Humphrey killed himself, plain and simple," Lieutenant Colonel Al Vincenti said to the Deputy Attorney General. "He was overcome with grief because of the accidental shoot-down, and he flew out over the ocean and crashed his plane where he wouldn't hurt anyone else."

The room got very quiet at that point—but not for very long. "Jesus, what a damned mess," someone muttered. Vincenti angrily searched for whoever it was that spoke, but all he saw were averted eyes. Finally one of the Assistant Secretaries of Defense that Vincenti did not recognize said, "Did he have a family? A wife and kids?"

"Tom Humphrey was a newlywed," Vincenti replied. "They're—she's—expecting her first."

"How the hell could this happen, Admiral Hardcastle?" Ralph Mersky, the Secretary of Transportation, asked. "This was a tragic but avoidable accident, in my opinion. The Air Force has very specific procedures to follow during an intercept—and they weren't followed."

"It was an accidental missile launch, Secretary Mersky," Admiral Ian Hardcastle responded. "He made a mistake, that's all. They were chasing a hostile aircraft."

"It was a TV *news* plane, for God's sake! They *identified* themselves."

"It was violating the law and flying like a hostile aircraft, with its transponder and lights off," Hardcastle said. "The fighter leader got disorientated."

"Screwed the pooch, you mean."

"I mean, got *disorientated,*" Hardcastle snapped. "You should know about spatial disorientation, Mr. Mersky—you're a licensed pilot. Mundy lost control of his plane due to the sudden flash of light from the TV crew on board the Learjet and because of spatial disorientation, and Humphrey reacted as if his leader had just gotten hit by hostile fire. It was a mistake."

"A damned costly mistake," Lowe interjected. "Admiral, we've received word that Congress is going to begin an investigation of the shoot-down incident, and you've been subpoenaed to appear." She nodded to one of her aides, who handed a document to Hardcastle. He did not open it, but handed it to Sheehan—he was so furious, he thought he would tear it up into tiny pieces if he even touched it. "Until the matter has been resolved, your duties and responsibilities with the Executive Committee on Terrorism have been suspended, effective immediately."

"*What?*" Hardcastle retorted. "You've suspended me? Why?"

"We've been heavily criticized for your approach to solving this problem, Admiral," Lowe said. "Your tactics regarding the air defense setup simply havn't worked—the accident tonight near Atlantic City was a good example. In addition, your actions concerning the raid on that mansion in New Jersey, although probably successful, were beyond your authority."

"Secretary Lowe, I did what I had to do."

"As we all knew you would, Admiral," Lowe said, averting her eyes so Hardcastle could not see the contempt in them. *Yes, we all knew you'd come in with guns blazing and the Bill of Rights be damned,* the Deputy Attorney General thought. *I just wished we made a stronger connection between you and Martindale.* There was still time to build that, Lowe reminded herself. "I'm sorry, Admiral. The Congressional investigation will commence shortly; we can assist you in obtaining legal counsel." Lowe turned to Vincenti and said, "Colonel Vincenti, you're under similar subpoena, as an expert witness, so like Admiral Hardcastle, you're prevented from talking with the media about the incident.

"The President has directed that the Air Force will make a statement about the accidental shoot-down," Lowe told the rest of her advisers seated around her, "expressing our condolences to all the families of that TV crew who suffered a loss." It was obvious that the President wanted to distance himself from that situation as well, Lowe thought—yes, the crew on that Lear screwed up, but if there was some political hay to be made out of his sorrow for the deaths suffered, the President wanted to do it. "General Skye . . . ?"

"First of all, ma'am, if I may, we should offer condolences to the family of Captain Humphrey, the F-16 pilot lost after the accident," General Charles Skye replied. Skye was the fifty-eight-year-old "triple-hat" commander of U.S. Space Command, U.S. Aerospace Defense Command, and the North American Air Defense Command, charged with the air defense of the continental United States, North America, and all U.S. assets in space. Tall, distinguished, and completely no-nonsense, Skye showed his exasperation at these endless meetings for the entire world to see. "It was obvious that the remorse and guilt he felt caused him to crash his aircraft into the sea."

"General . . ."

"If you only offer condolences to the TV crew that violated the law and caused the accident to occur in the first place, ma'am, you and the President will lose a lot of faith from your military supporters," Skye said. "Captain Humphrey, his wife and kid, and his unit deserve better."

"I didn't forget, General," Lowe shot back angrily. "We weren't *only* going to offer our condolences just to the TV crew. *Thank you* for reminding me."

But there was not much chance of General Skye's taking the hint. "I'll go to Atlantic City and meet with the unit commander myself."

"I'd like to accompany you, General," Hardcastle said immediately.

"Same here, General," Vincenti echoed.

"Permission granted, gents," Skye said, "if the Justice Department or the Senate or whoever wants a piece of your ass lets you come out and pay your respects. Thank you. We'll arrange to talk with the TV people later."

"I'm so glad we got that settled," Lowe said, rolling her eyes. "Now, about dismantling the air defense stuff . . ."

"What?" Hardcastle retorted. "I think that's a bit premature, Miss Lowe."

"That's a real stupid idea," Skye said, not bothering to use polite words in this meeting. "Real big mistake. The fighters are the first line of defense—you've gotta have eyes up there to see who's coming down on you."

"General, perhaps you didn't understand—we *got* Henri Cazaux," FBI Director Lani Wilkes said. "The emergency is over."

"Tell that to Lake, Fell, and that Gulfstream crew up in Newburgh," Hardcastle said. "It was a summary execution all the way—maybe it wasn't Cazaux, but it was probably one of his men."

"Cazaux's operation has been blown away, Admiral," Wilkes said. "We got his mansion, several of his soldiers, his bimbo, and his banker. We've got a line on several million dollars belonging to Cazaux's organization—he's frozen, bankrupt."

"We can't account for several aircraft that Lake purchased," Hardcastle said, "and several of the weapons stolen from Naval Air Station Fallon that have been linked to Cazaux. He's still got to be considered dangerous."

"Cazaux or not, Judge Wilkes, if the Commander in Chief orders me to take the air defense stuff down, I'll do it," Skye said. "I haven't received such an order, so they stay. It's that simple."

"I'm concerned that there will be more accidents if we have all these missiles and fighters in the air, especially with air traffic controls lifted," Transportation Secretary Mersky said. "Besides, the fighters didn't help over Atlantic City or over Fort Worth, did they?"

"You don't turn these boys loose to do their jobs, Mr. Mersky, and the job won't get done," Skye said. "You set up an air cordon and tell civilians they can operate inside the cordon, they better understand that if they play games and dick around, they'll get their asses shot off, pure and simple."

"General, the President is afraid to publicly announce that the emergency is over, because he feels, and I concur, that such an announcement will only attract the copycat bombers or Cazaux's lieutenants out there to blow up a terminal or airliner," Deputy Attorney General Lowe said. "Instead, we want to recommend to the President to quickly but quietly take down the air defense network and return the air traffic system in this country back to normal. Airport security will still be at maximum levels, and we want to implement an air marshal program again, but we want to do away with the special air cordons, the military weapons in place around the airports under Class B airspace, and all military control of access to the air traffic control system."

"The President wants a gradual *increase* in the number of flights," Mersky added. "I'll concede that giving access to uncontrolled or VFR air traffic should be phased in over a much longer time frame, but the President's top priority is to do everything he can to encourage the airlines to start flying again."

"General Lowe, Secretary Mersky, if all you propose is allowed to happen, the military won't be able to stop a Cazaux type again," Hardcastle said. "There are just too many aircraft out there doing suspicious or even downright illegal things."

"The only way to make sure we can pick a terrorist flight out from all the rest of the inbound flights is to increase the number of interceptors and decrease the number of flights until the two balance out," Colonel Vincenti added.

"And we're telling you, Colonel, that's not what the President wants, and that's not what the American people want," Elizabeth Lowe said finally. "Besides, it's not the military's job to find and stop these terrorists—it's my job, and the FBI's job.

"I'll pass along your reservations, General Skye, Admiral Hardcastle, but I'm recommending to the President that we immediately ground all fighter patrols over the United States."

"Maybe we should go tell the President our opinions together, General Lowe," Skye suggested.

"General, the purpose of having this committee is so a horde of people with a horde of different opinions aren't marching in and out of the Oval Office all day," Lowe said, refusing to let the four-star Air Force general bully her around. "My job as chairman of the Executive Committee on Terrorism is not only to coordinate day-to-day antiterrorist operations, but to analyze the threshold of danger existing in the country, determine what are the best possible options to deal with the danger, and present my opinions to the President.

"In my opinion and in the opinion of the majority of members of this committee, the danger has subsided to a sufficient level, and the hazards of continued military interceptor and military air traffic control have increased to such a dangerous level, that we feel we can recommend that the military's involvement in this emergency can be substantially decreased."

"General Lowe, I caution you about using the President's wishes to form the basis of this committee's policy decisions," Hardcastle interjected. "The President wants everything back to normal—we all do. But we feel the time's not right. At least let's wait a few more weeks until the FBI analyzes Cazaux's financial records from Lake's computers, sifts through the debris at the mansion in

New Jersey, tracks down whoever killed Lake and Fell in Newburgh, and bags more members of Cazaux's organization."

"This committee is not a Presidential rubber stamp, Admiral," Lowe snapped. "Our respective staffs have been working overtime on this problem, and we've all come up with the same conclusion: we don't need the military anymore."

"In my opinion we never did," FBI Director Wilkes said. "All we needed was a little more *cooperation,* and this situation probably could've been solved earlier."

"We don't want to totally dismantle the emergency system or cut out the military," Mersky said. He opened his staff's summary sheet and went on: "I propose the following: we keep all military surveillance in place except for the fighter interceptors. We keep the short-range ground-based air defense systems in place, namely the mobile Avenger Stinger systems, but deactivate all Patriot and HAWK systems. Airport and aircraft security will stay at maximum levels, with security situations reevaluated daily on a case-by-case basis. We deactivate all emergency air cordons in Class B airspace, but we mandate that all aircraft in Class B airspace must be on a flight plan—no aircraft allowed in Class B airspace with pop-up clearances."

"Any other discussion?" Lowe asked.

"Discussion seems to be pointless," Skye said.

"Very well," Lowe said. "I move that Secretary Mersky's and the Department of Transportation's recommendations be adopted by the committee and presented to the President immediately." The motion was seconded and approved. The Secretary of Defense's representative voted in the affirmative for General Skye, and, because he had been suspended from the Executive Committee on Terrorism, Hardcastle's negative vote was counted as an abstention. "Thank you all. Our next meeting will be tomorrow morning, unless the situation changes. General Skye, I don't think we'll require your presence unless a member of the committee requests it."

"Fine with me, *General* Lowe," Skye said. "This little game of power politics is a total waste of my friggin' time anyway. But I'll tell you this, Miss Lowe: I'm sending my strongest reservations about this committee's actions up my chain of command. I'm advising the Chief of Staff of the Air Force that your recommendations do not reflect my opinion, and I'll ask that he present my opinions to the Secretary of the Air Force and on to the White House—frankly, I don't trust you to give the President the word for me. It's nothing personal, General Lowe . . ." Skye paused, looked at Lowe, then shrugged and said, "Okay, it *is* personal. In my humble and insignificant opinion, any person who lets her people, even guys like Hardcastle, hang out to dry like you did and ignores all the danger signs around her is an asshole—ma'am. And any committee who allows all of the above to happen on their watch should be publicly kicked in the ass."

"I encourage free expression in my meetings, General Skye," Lowe said tightly, "but now I'm giving you fair warning—get control of your tongue and your attitude before they get you into serious trouble."

"My comments are totally on the record, ma'am—I trust they'll stay there."

"Count on it, General," Lowe responded bitterly.

"Then my apologies if I've offended anyone—you know who you are," Skye said, collecting his papers and rising to depart. "I hope the President knows what he's doing, that's all." He got to his feet and dismissed himself from the meeting; Hardcastle, Vincenti, and Sheehan followed.

"I hope you get around to busting Skye's nuts when you get a chance," Wilkes said after the rest of the committee had departed.

"Skye's already dug himself a hole he can't crawl out of," Lowe said. "We've got a bigger concern to talk about—namely, the President's fund-raiser in California."

"Security will be airtight," Lani Wilkes said. "The President will be perfectly safe, especially once we get those missiles and fighters put away."

"I agree," Lowe said. "But I need all your best efforts on making sure that the body you got in the morgue is Cazaux, and that his organization is shut down. I'm putting the President's security in your hands because you said you could handle it."

"It'll be taken care of, General Lowe," Wilkes assured her.

"It'd better be," Lowe said. "The President's advance team deploys in less than two days from now, and once they're on the road, every crazy and nut case will be out there hunting the President down." She silently looked at the FBI Director for a moment, then added, "Frankly, Judge, you've been one step behind the Marshals and Hardcastle this entire crisis. In case you've forgotten, there's an election coming up next year, and how the President reacts to this crisis is important. He wants to be seen in the sky and on the road again, and he doesn't want to be seen hiding behind F-16 fighters or Patriot missiles—or too many government agents.''

Pease International Tradeport
Portsmouth, New Hampshire
Two Nights Later

Pease International Tradeport was once Pease Air Force Base, a small but vital Strategic Air Command bomber base, closed in 1990 and converted to civilian use. The eight large hangars that once housed B-52 Stratofortress bombers and KC-135 Stratotanker aerial refueling tankers now housed a collection of small fixed-base operators servicing light civilian planes—one hangar now held two dozen light planes in the same space that once could house only one B-52. The base operations building had been converted into a Bar Harbor Airlines commuter terminal, flying passengers throughout New England.

The original company which gave Pease Tradeport its ''international'' designation was Lufthansa Airlines, who in 1992 built a modern office complex in nearby Kittery, Maine, and converted three of the large maintenance hangars at Pease to a jumbo aircraft refurbishment and inspection facility, one of the most modern facilities of its kind in the world. The location was perfect—within an hour's flying time of six of the top ten busiest airports in North America, close to many European and Asian transpolar flight routes, good schools, generous tax incentives, no income tax, a rural atmosphere but close to Boston and the high-tech Route 128 Corridor of northeastern Massachusetts. Pease International Tradeport was on the verge of becoming a major American airport, a vital reliever to already crowded and expensive Boston-Logan International.

Its popularity and success soon became its number-one problem. There had been two major crashes per year since the facility was opened.

Seacoast-area residents, backwoods environmentalists, and perturbed rich Massachusetts vacationers with beach homes in the Vineyard and Narragansett kicked the golden goose and told Lufthansa to scale back; indignant Lufthansa did them one better and left for the open arms, tax breaks, and relative peace of Raleigh, North Carolina. Pease International Tradeport became a virtual ghost town practically overnight.

But there were still high-tech heavy jet maintenance facilities at Pease, so occasionally the three-thousand-pound Cessnas would get a visit from one of their three-hundred-thousand-pound cousins. The busiest destination was Portsmouth Air, which leased about a third of Lufthansa's aircraft refurbishment facility at Pease but still struggled to stay in business.

The Boeing 747-200 jetliner with Nippon Air livery had been flown into Pease the day after its prepurchase inspection at Mojave, and since then was locked away inside one of the remodeled hangars, one big enough to house the entire plane instead of leaving a tail section sticking out through a hole in the hangar doors. The hangars were designed to allow environmentally safe aircraft painting, completely sealing toxic fumes in and allowing multiple painting crews to work at the same time. Tanker trucks filled with paint were brought in to repaint the airliner, and work continued on for several days.

Pease's air traffic control tower closed at nine P.M., and by nightfall the airport was silent, but it was not unusual to get after-hours traffic. At several minutes past one A.M., a Piper Aerostar twin-engine plane self-announced on Pease's tower frequency, entered right traffic for runway 30, and lined up to land. Since Pease was one of the pilot's favorite and frequent destinations, he knew it was best to stay high and delay landing until after midfield, still with six thousand feet of runway remaining, in order to shorten the taxi time to the general aviation ramp on the northern half of the field. No problems with the landing, no problems taxiing clear of the runway and heading toward the dead-quiet transient parking ramp. The pilot noticed activity at the Portsmouth Air maintenance facility, but that was normal—those guys worked day and night on the few jumbo jets that came in these days.

Everything was going fine until the pilot, by himself in the Aerostar, decided to shut off the electric fuel-boost pumps after turning onto the parallel taxiway. Seconds later, both engines sputtered and quit, vapor-locked. He nearly drained his battery trying to restart an engine. Disgusted, he braked to a halt, shut his plane down except for the strobes to keep another plane from ramming his Aerostar, grabbed his briefcase, locked up, and headed toward the terminal to find someone to help him tow his six-thousand-pound plane to the ramp.

The general aviation FBO and the Bar Harbor Airlines terminals were long closed. The only other sign of life at the airport was

Portsmouth Air, so he walked over to the huge hangar complex. The complex was surrounded by a twelve-foot fence topped with barbed wire, but a CypherLock gate near the parking lot was not fully closed, so the pilot walked in. The front door to the main office was locked. He walked around the offices to the west side of the hangar itself and tried another door—locked too. But just as he walked past it to find another door, the steel-sheathed door banged open, someone loudly hawked and spit outside, then let the door go—whoever it was never saw the pilot behind it. The Aerostar pilot caught the door before it closed and stepped inside the hangar . . .

. . . and what he saw inside made his jaw drop in surprise—it was Air Force One, the President of the United States' plane!

The huge Boeing 747 airliner completely filled the hangar. White on the top, light blue and black on the bottom, with a dark-blue accent running from the upper half of the nose section and sweeping along the mid-fuselage windows to the tail, it was an awesome sight to behold. The pilot, a professor at Dartmouth, knew that Air Force One used to come to Pease quite often when President Bush would fly here on his way to his family retreat in Kennebunkport years ago, but he never had the chance to see him or his entourage arrive—now he was getting a good firsthand look at one of the most distinctive planes in the world!

He could plainly see the words UNITED STATES OF AMERICA on the side of the fuselage, although the lettering looked . . . well, a bit sloppy, not even or symmetrical at all. He was near the tail section, and he could see the Air Force chevron at the base of the vertical stabilizer, and the serial number 28000 and the American flag midway up the vertical stabilizer, painted as if the staff side were forward and the flag were stretched taut and blowing aft. The smell of paint fumes was very strong—it looked as if Air Force One was getting a touchup or a good cleaning. Funny—the pilot never would've guessed they'd do maintenance on Air Force Ones up here in little Portsmouth, New Hampshire, although they'd obviously keep that kind of information secret.

The pilot began walking toward the front of the plane, under the right wingtip. He passed a few workers, but they didn't pay too much attention to him. He stood along the wall of the hangar, watching a guy painting the Seal of the President of the United States near the nose, and, like the lettering on top, the paint job on the seal was passable but not very professional. It looked okay from a distance, but up close it—

"Excuse me, sir," he heard. The pilot turned and was confronted by a tall, very mean-looking guy with short-cropped hair, wearing a dark-green flight suit. He looked like a Marine Corps aviator. He looked mean and nasty enough to kill with his bare hands, but fortunately he seemed in a good—or at least a forgiving—mood. "This is a restricted area."

"I'm sorry," the Aerostar pilot said. "I'm Doctor Clemenz, professor of history at Dartmouth. "Clemens with a *z,*" he added, as if often asked how to spell his last name to make it jive with the unusual pronunciation. "My Aerostar is stuck out there on the taxiway. I was looking for someone who might give me a tow."

"No problem, sir," the Marine said with a thick Brooklyn accent. "But I better get you out of this area before we all get our dicks in a wringer." He escorted the pilot along the wall toward the front of the hangar. Workers saw the big Marine, wore shocked expressions on their faces, and stepped toward him but retreated after a few steps.

"You guys actually service Air Force One here?"

"Not much use in denying it, is there, sir?" the Marine said jovially. "But please keep it under your hat, all right, sir? I've already got a lot to explain—like how you got inside here."

"Front gate was ajar, side door was opened by someone wanting to get a breath of fresh air . . . listen, am I under arrest? I probably shouldn't say anything else if I am."

"I'm not placing you under arrest, sir—unless you try to run."

"I assure you, I won't . . . uh, I'm sorry, your name . . . ?"

"Captain Cook, Dave Cook," the big guy said, extending a hand.

Clemenz accepted it. "Marines?" Cook nodded. "I always thought the Air Force took care of Air Force One."

"The Air Force flies it—the Marines are supposed to guard it," Cook said after a short, uncomfortable pause. Clemenz nodded, accepting that explanation—the Marines guarded the White House, why not Air Force One? "The operative words here are 'supposed to.' "

"Shit happens," Clemenz said, trying to console the soldier and sorry that his trespassing was probably going to get the friendly Marine into big trouble, maybe even ruin his career.

"Yes, sir, it surely does," the big Marine said. He led the doctor through a doorway into an office, past more startled men. Most of them wore civilian clothes but were very heavily armed. Cook waved them away before they could grab Clemenz, dismissing them with a sharp shake of his head—Clemenz could easily feel the daggers darting from Cook's blazing eyes to the guards, silently admonishing them for their miss. He grabbed one man tightly by his upper arm and whispered something in his ear, then let him go. "Have a seat, Doctor Clemenz. Coffee? Tea?"

"Not unless I'm going to be here awhile, Captain," Clemenz said with a wry smile, afraid that's exactly what was going to happen.

"I don't think so, Doctor Clemenz," the soldier said, picking up a clipboard and finding a pencil in a desk drawer. He copied Clemenz's Hanover, New Hampshire, address, employment information, and names and addresses of any relatives and friends nearby—no relatives in Portsmouth, only a few acquaintances. Clemenz enjoyed fishing and lobstering and came to Portsmouth often, but he was fairly new to the area and usually came only in the summer, so he knew few people in town. He said he shared a house with another professor up in York Harbor. "How were you going to get to the house, sir?"

"Airport car," Clemenz said. "Airport lets us park a car here for fifty dollars a month. It's just an old beat-up Datsun. It's parked right over by the DOT building . . . is this going to take much longer, Captain? I left my strobes on so nobody would run over my Aerostar. Can you help me tow it to the main parking ramp? I don't mean to rush you, since I was doing the trespassing, but it's getting late and I—"

"Of course, sir," Cook replied. "If you don't mind, sir, we'll follow you to your house in York Harbor, just to verify your destination. Will that be a problem, sir?"

"No . . . no, I suppose not . . ."

"Was there someone you needed to call? Leave a message at the FBO about your plane?"

"When they see the plane parked out front, they'll know it's me."

"Very well. I think we're done here," Cook said. "I would like to take some pictures for our files. Do you have any objections to that?"

"No, I guess not."

"Good. And sir, I'll probably say this two or three times before you leave, but you must be absolutely clear on this: what you've seen tonight must be kept secret. I'm sure you can easily imagine the danger if any terrorists, saboteurs, or kooks knew that Air Force One is serviced here. Our security is usually very good, but if an amateur can stumble into this place, imagine what a trained terrorist squad can do."

"I understand perfectly," Clemenz said earnestly.

"Good," Cook said. "Let's get some pictures and we'll wrap this up. This way, sir." Cook led the way through the door back out to the main hangar, allowing Clemenz to pass in front of him . . .

. . . and when the professor exited the office, he saw about three dozen men, the workers that had been working on Air Force One, standing a few paces outside the door, backdropped by Air Force One itself towering over them. They were looking at Clemenz with a collective expression mix of surprise and . . . What? Pity? until Captain Cook emerged from the office. Then their expressions changed to one of downright, undisguised, genuine fear.

Clemenz somehow knew he was a dead man even before he felt the hand grasp his hair, yank his head up and forward, and felt the sharp prick against the back of his neck at the base of his skull as the knife was driven up along the top of his vertebrae and into the base of his brain. He gave a short cry, not necessarily from the pain as much as from the surprise and the resignation. He did not feel anything else after that.

Henri Cazaux let the corpse dangle at the end of his knife for several seconds, letting all the workers and security men get a good look. No one dared avert his eyes, although one man mercifully fainted when he saw the body quiver in its last throes of death. "This man just walked in here!" Cazaux shouted. "He just *walked in!* No one bothered to stop him, challenge him, even look at him, although he is obviously not wearing an identification badge or the clothing code of the day. He is going to hang here in front of the hangar as a reminder to every one of you to keep vigilant. Now get back to work—the timetable is going to be moved up. *Move!*"

Armed guards were taking three men away in handcuffs as Tomas Ysidro and Gregory Townsend came up to Cazaux. Cazaux tossed the dead professor off his knife against the wall—the man had died so quickly that almost no blood seeped from the knife wound. "Sorry about that, Henri," Ysidro said casually, kicking the corpse so the small trickle of blood from the wound dripped on the man's clothes and not onto the hangar floor. "If I would've gotten here earlier I could have supervised these bozos better, but I can't be at two places at once."

"Can you be in position by tomorrow night?" Cazaux asked.

Townsend thought for a moment; then: "I think so, Henri. We'll need the Shorts to move the guys and their equipment, but I think we—"

"Don't think, Townsend," Cazaux said menacingly. *"Can you be in position by tomorrow night or not?"*

"I'd prefer two nights to get everyone into proper position, Henri," Townsend said, "but the answer is yes. I can be ready to go tomorrow night."

"This man will be missed in two nights' time, perhaps sooner—we must go tomorrow night," Cazaux said, wiping his blade clean and putting it back into its hidden sheath. "You will leave as soon as you can get the Shorts loaded. I'll see to the loading and preflight here."

"You'll take care of the flight plan, Henri?" Townsend asked. "Remember the FAA order 7210.3—we need sixteen hours."

"I remember, Townie, I remember," Cazaux said, his mind racing several hours ahead.

Since Air Force One was a SAM, or Special Air Mission, military aircraft, a flight plan for their flight to Washington could be filed only through a special teletype system. Fortunately, they had access to such a terminal at Pease International Tradeport. The 157th Air Refueling Group, a small New Hampshire Air National Guard aerial refueling tanker unit, used the system for the Atlantic Tanker Task Force, which coordinated all aerial refuelings for flights from Europe to North America, including for Air Force One. Also, Pease Tradeport, when it used to be Pease Air Force Base, was a favorite vacation stop for President George Bush and his family, so a terminal was installed and kept at the airport. Cazaux's organization had bribed several of the Guardsmen at the airport to do a variety of things, such as alert them when any state or federal inspectors were inbound, monitor the status of the state police patrols, and procure fuel and other aircraft parts and supplies.

For the flight of their fake Air Force One, they would have one of the Air National Guard controllers input a military flight plan into the system, originating not from Portsmouth, New Hampshire, but from Manchester, New Hampshire, the site of an upcoming and widely publicized debate between the expected 1996 presidential candidates, organized by the League of Women Voters. The flight plan, using the call sign SAM-2800 (SAM stood for Special Air Mission, the standard call sign for military flights such as this; 2800 was the tail number of one of the two VC-25A Air Force Ones in the inventory), had to be filed not earlier than sixteen hours from the proposed takeoff time, although the exact takeoff time could not be recorded.

Immediately after the counterfeit Air Force One was airborne, the Air National Guard controller would issue an ALNOT, or Alert Notification message, to a special office in the FAA Air Traffic Control Command Center known as ATM-200, requesting special priority handling and revising SAM-2800's call sign to Executive One Foxtrot, signifying that a member of the President's family or White House staff (but not the President himself—that would be too easy to verify) was on board the aircraft. The ALNOT would be retransmitted by ATM-200 to the various Air Route Traffic Control Centers along the route of flight as well as the Air Force Air Defense Sector Operations Command Centers, letting everyone know that a member of the President's entourage was airborne. The plan after that was that the controller would be knocked unconscious so he could claim that he was overpowered and his equipment used without his knowledge—of course, Cazaux would see to it that he was executed to keep him quiet.

"I'll take care of all those details," Cazaux was saying. "Now get moving." Townsend and Ysidro turned to leave, but Cazaux stopped them by adding, "And I want no more slipups. Security will be tight and everyone will follow the plan to the letter, or I will spend the rest of my days on earth hunting down and executing each and every one of you. Now get going."

PART 5

Andrews Air Force Base, Camp Springs, Maryland
Early the Next Morning

Tomas Ysidro had made his own green active-duty U.S. military ID card long ago—his was Army, showing his home base as the Defense Language School, the Presidio of Monterey, California; he carried a set of orders showing him as a visiting instructor in Farsi and Mandarin to the 89th Air Wing to teach some of the aircrew members some basic foreign language skills for an upcoming presidential trip. But getting onto Andrews Air Force Base, the place where the President of the United States' planes were kept, was child's play, and he didn't need to show any of his carefully prepared credentials. The guards at the Virginia Avenue gate were still doing hundred-percent ID checks, but there were no dogs, no searches, no questions asked. The smiling Air Force bitch in her toy-soldier blue fatigues, silly black beret, white dickey, and pretty spit-shined boots waved the car right on through after a quick flash of the card, and four international terrorists were on a major military air base with ease.

"No vehicle checks or searches," one of the terrorists remarked after they were well past the guard gate. "Not even a thorough check of your card."

Ysidro had been careful to scuff up his ID card and not make it look too new or too perfect, but the apparent lack of diligence did puzzle him. Weren't they concerned about Cazaux any longer? "We can still be monitored electronically," Ysidro warned, "so everyone stay sharp." That did not need repeating—driving right into the jaws of the enemy, the ones that were out looking for them—was not a comforting or casual activity at all. But the apparent lax security made them breathe a bit easier and helped them concentrate on the tasks ahead.

They drove north on Virginia Avenue and followed the signs about a half-mile to the base golf course—and found, to their amazement, that it was open. It had been closed for days because the Army had placed an entire Patriot missile battery there, assigned to protect the Capitol, Andrews, Washington National, Dulles, and other high-value targets in the D.C. area from air attack. Ysidro turned right onto South Wheeling Road and there it was, right in front of them—an entire Patriot missile battery, less than a thousand feet away on Wyoming Road. The Army Patriot missile encampment, within sight of the end of runway 36 Left, was well in the process of being dismantled—the back nine holes of the course were still not usable, but the front nine were open, and golfers were out there just a good five-wood shot or two away from some of the Patriot launchers.

"Well, what the fuck . . ." Ysidro said, surprised and pleased by what he saw. "Maybe we should've hidden our gear in fuckin' golf bags." They could see all eight Patriot missile launchers lowered and configured for road march, and the large flat "drive-in-theater" antenna array still raised but with soldiers working on and in front of it—obviously it wasn't radiating, because that man in front of the array would be fried to a crisp by the amount of electromagnetic energy that thing put out when it was radiating. The electrical power plant vehicle was still running and the command vehicle was apparently still manned, but the Patriot site itself was apparently decommissioned. Ysidro's assignment had been to destroy it.

"What do we do now?" one of the commandos asked.

"We do what we've been assigned to do—it'll just be a hell of a lot easier," Ysidro said. "The electrical truck is still running, so this could just be a maintenance period—the Patriot site at Fort Belvoir or Dulles might be taking up the slack." Two other commando squads had been assigned to take out the Patriot sites at Davison Army Air Field at Fort Belvoir and at Washington-Dulles International Airport, but if those Patriot sites were closed down as well, they would have a much easier time of it. At last check, the Hawk missile sites at East Potomac Island Park Golf Course near George Washington University, Rock Creek Golf Course near Walter Reed Hospital, and the East Capitol Country Club golf course were still operational;

other teams were assigned to take out those sites as well. But this Patriot site at Andrews was the Integrated Command Center, or ICC, which controlled all of the Hawk and Avenger air defense units in the region.

The terrorist group took a right turn on Wisconsin Road, a left onto South Perimeter Road, and headed for the housing area and east runway side. Andrews Air Force Base had two, two-mile-long parallel runways, with the main part of the base on the west and the enlisted and junior officer housing area to the east. The fighter alert area was on the south side of the east runway, with two fighters on alert with ladders attached, ready to go; two more fighters were parked nearby, but neither appeared to have weapons loaded. Surprisingly, the guards at the entrance to the housing area had been removed. They doubled back onto South Perimeter Road, heading for the main base side. A small lake south of the west runway had numerous creeks and ditches flowing into it, all leading toward the airfield—that was the best way to approach the runways.

They drove north on Arnold Avenue along the rows of hangars on the main base side. Every Air Force VIP plane in the inventory was visible—small jets to big helicopters to a huge white E-4 Airborne Command Post, a modified 747 resembling Air Force One but specially designed for the President and military leaders to run World War III from the air. They did not see an Air Force One itself. But then again, they didn't need to—they were bringing their own.

They turned right on C Street and tried to go north on Eagle Road, the street right in front of the newer hangars, but roadblocks ahead steered them back onto Arnold Avenue—that told them that the hangars behind that section of Eagle Road had the really valuable hardware. Still, there were no patrols, only barricades. The two hangars that were accessible from the one block of Eagle Road they were allowed to drive on had a clear view of the alert fighter area across the airfield, and by using binoculars they could even see the upraised Patriot antenna array to the southwest, pointing westward toward the capital.

"Let's remote-control everything from here—no use in risking exposure if it ain't necessary," Ysidro said. "We'll use the short-range radio detonators for maximum efficiency, and we'll station ourselves within missile range of the runways in case we're needed."

"May not be able to remote the Patriot stuff," one of the other terrorists said. He pointed to a red-and-white block building at the end of the runway. "ILS transmitter. Could interfere with the radio signal, or it could activate the detonator as soon as the mine is armed."

"Fine—we'll do it face-to-face. I like it that way," Ysidro said. "Security is a joke anyway—this looks like a walk in the park. If this isn't some kind of setup, this will be the easiest job we've ever had to do."

Atlantic City International Airport
Later That Evening

At precisely sunset, the formation leader radioed, "Ready, ready . . . now. Three, clear to depart."

"Three," Lieutenant Colonel Al Vincenti acknowledged, gently pulled on the control stick and put in a notch of power. He was flying the third F-16 ADF Fighting Falcon in a V-formation of five, passing over the base headquarters building near the Air National Guard ramp at Atlantic City Airport. From the ground, the V-formation stayed intact but with a large gap between the leader and the number-five aircraft to the right of the leader—the "Missing Man" formation, signifying that one of their comrades had died in the line of duty. Vincenti, as the main fighter representative to the Executive Committee on Terrorism in charge of the Cazaux emergency, had requested and was given the honor of flying as the "missing man" in the 177th Fighter Group's memorial-service flyover for Tom Humphrey, who had died in the crash of his F-16.

Vincenti climbed to two thousand feet, turned on his transponder so air traffic control could pick him up on radar, then checked in with Atlantic City Approach Control: "Atlantic City Approach, Devil Zero-Three, overhead Atlantic City International, passing two for five thousand."

"Devil-03, radar contact, climb and maintain five thousand, expect twenty minutes holding at NAADA intersection for arriving and departing traffic."

The delay made sense—in fact, he was hoping for it. Air Traffic Control had shut down all traffic in and out of Atlantic City International for thirty minutes so the New Jersey Air National Guard could do this memorial, so it was only fair that all the civilian traffic be allowed to depart. "Roger, A-City," Vincenti radioed back. "Devil-03 cancel IFR, requesting radar flight following, destination Atlantic City International via the Beltway tour, overfly if able."

"Roger, -03, remain this squawk and frequency, maintain VFR routes and altitudes on the Beltway tour, I've got your request for an overfly clearance."

"-03, roger."

It was far more restrictive now than when Vincenti flew F-4Es out of Atlantic City Airport a million years ago, but it's still a pretty good ride, even at dusk, he thought—that is, if the lights are on. He knew that exterior illumination of most of the historic buildings and monuments of Washington, D.C., had been turned off during the Cazaux terrorist emergency; no announcement had been made, but rumor had it that the President was going to order the National Park Service to lift this restriction. It was pretty lucky for him to be flying at all, let alone as part of the Air National Guard unit's memorial flight. Few guys want to fly Missing Man formations—they believe it tempts Fate to fly close formation in a high-performance bird in tribute to a fellow pilot that . . . well, erred. Crashing and burning in combat is one thing—getting excited and accidentally blowing away an identified civilian plane, and *then* committing suicide, was not cool. Everyone was sorry for Humphrey and his family, but no one wanted to get too close to his bad jujus. That's the way fighter jocks are.

Of course, the Learjet shoot-down and Humphrey's subsequent crash was not being called a suicide or a screwup, at least not by the Air Force or the White House. Along with the usual "the investigation is under way, I can't comment on that," Hardcastle and Vincenti had explained to the press all about the TV crew's errors, about how they broke the law, stopping short of saying they deserved to get shot. A few veiled hints about mechanical or electrical failure on the F-16 because of the constant flying during the emergency, some more hints about incorrect "switchology," mixed with more comments like "if it had been Cazaux, Atlantic City International would have been a smoking hole otherwise." The press needed massaging. More than most military men, Hardcastle—once the leader of one of the most controversial paramilitary organizations in American history, the Hammerheads—understood that it was important not to tell the press the facts, but to meter information bit by bit, letting them form their own conclusions that, not too coincidentally, were the ones you wanted them to have. It didn't always work, but it was an efficient way to go.

Humphrey was a victim of circumstance. Yes, he screwed up. Military jets did not have cockpit voice recorders or flight data recorders, so everything was speculative until the final accident board's report. Hardcastle often used familiar "goofs" to explain failures in multimillion-dollar military hardware: like causing an accident while using a cellular phone in busy rush-hour traffic. Humphrey had wanted to film the Learjet with his gun camera during the intercept; he saw the floodlight hit his leader's cockpit canopy, saw him go out of control temporarily, assumed that it was an attack, and launched a missile. Under the emergency situation, such a response was understandable. Of course, Hardcastle explained, the deaths of the "Whispers" TV crew were unfortunate, but it was probably avoidable—it wouldn't have happened if the TV and Learjet crews had been following the law and not out for a scoop. For once it looked like blame was going to be placed on the right party.

By being up in Atlantic City instead of in Washington, Vincenti was really just postponing the inevitable: the intensive debriefing that Judge Lani Wilkes was giving Hardcastle and Harley right now in Washington. Vincenti's turn was next. These all-day, half-the-night sessions were nine-tenths retribution and punishment and one-tenth information. Wilkes was claiming that there were tons of evidence to make everyone, including the President of the United States, believe the body of the motorcycle rider shot by the V-22 crew was Henri Cazaux. The gun camera videotape from the third V-22 of one of the two riders that escaped was inconclusive. It was a thermal image, almost useless for trying to identify someone. But in Vincenti's opinion, any one of the two that got away could have been Henri Cazaux. Wilkes and the rest of the Justice Department disagreed. To Al Vincenti, it was all just educated guesses and assumptions—and politics, of course. The more this air defense emergency went on, the more uneasy it made the public. The President needed this emergency over with soonest.

Vincenti admired Harley for standing up to Wilkes and most of the rest of the FBI. She was definitely someone he wanted to get to know better. He still wasn't exactly clear what her relationship to former Vice President Kevin Martindale really was, but Vincenti never liked to take a backseat when it came to the pursuit of women. He could take on Martindale any day of the week. That aside, he wished Harley would at least take some pride in knowing that Cazaux's organization was busted up, his sources of funds cut off and confiscated, his butt being chased closer and closer every hour. Vincenti hoped

Cazaux would dive back under whatever rock he crawled out from—Harley didn't believe he would. But the U.S. Marshals and the FBI were hot on Cazaux's organization's heels, so if Cazaux's wasn't one of the bullet-riddled bodies she pulled from the mansion in New Jersey, he was as good as captured anyway.

Cambridge-Dorchester Airport, Maryland
That Same Time

The little airport on Choptank Bay in south-central Maryland was a busy and favorite destination for fishermen from all over the northeast United States, but at dusk it was as dark and as quiet as the countryside around it. The Patuxent River Naval Air Station was just thirty miles southwest, where the U.S. Navy trains all of its test pilots and conducts tests of new and unusual aircraft—it was the Navy equivalent of the Air Force's Edwards Air Force Base—and the area just south of the little airport was often filled with Navy jets dogfighting or practicing aerobatics or unusual flight maneuvers. But promptly at nine P.M., at the very latest, the Navy jets went home. No one dared disturb the peaceful little Chesapeake Bay resort town in summertime unless you had a lot of political or financial pull . . .

. . . or unless you were an international terrorist, and you didn't give a damn.

Inside a hangar rented for this mission, Gregory Townsend checked the attachment points of the devices under the wings of the single-engine Cessna 172. He had slung one BLU-93 fuel-air explosive canister under each wing, just outboard of the wing strut. It was a simple two-lug attachment, connected to a mechanical-pyrotechnic squib that used small explosive charges to pull the lugs out of the attachment points and let the bombs go. The charges were bigger than what was needed and would probably punch a hole in the Cessna's thin aluminum wing, but that didn't matter as long as the bombs were able to free-fall properly. As the bombs fell, a simple cable would pull an arming pin out of the canister. Three seconds later the canister would disperse the explosive vapor, and two seconds after that three baseball-sized bomblets in the tail cone of the canister would detonate in the center of the vapor cloud, creating an explosion equivalent to ten thousand pounds of TNT. The fuel-air explosive blast would incinerate anything within a thousand feet of it and destroy or damage almost any structure within a half-mile.

Once the canisters were properly attached and checked, Townsend and two of his helpers threw tarps over the wings to hide the canisters and towed the aircraft south down the parking ramp and onto the parallel taxiway to a runup pad at the end of runway 34, using a rented pickup truck and a nylon tow strap. Cambridge-Dorchester Airport had a lot of airplanes parked there, but there was no fixed-base operator to service planes, so it was not unusual to see private autos towing them. There were a few onlookers outside the Runway Restaurant at the entrance to the little airport, the usual assortment of people that hung around airports day or night, but when they saw the airplane with the tarps over it, they assumed it was being fixed, so few paid it any more attention—onlookers came to see takeoffs and landings, not engine runups or fuel tanks being drained or scrubbed out. By the time Townsend and his soldiers reached the runup pad, they were away from most of the lights and the spectators.

Townsend towed the Cessna onto runway 34, then stepped into the cockpit and started its engine. His soldiers meanwhile moved the truck behind the plane, attached the tow cable to the rear tie-down bracket and the other end to the truck's rear bumper, and pulled the nylon tow-strap tight so it held the plane in place.

Inside the cockpit, it took only fifteen seconds for the Global Positioning System satellite navigation unit to lock on to enough satellites for precision use. He checked the navigation data in the set. There were only three waypoints in the flight plan—an initial takeoff point about two miles off the departure end of the runway, a level-off point over Chesapeake Bay, and a destination: 38-53.917 North, 77-27.312 West, elevation twelve feet mean sea level, the geographical coordinates of the Oval Office in the White House, Washington, D.C. programmed to the nearest six feet. Townsend checked that the GPS set was exchanging information with the Cessna's autopilot, then activated the system. The GPS immediately inserted the first altitude into the system, which was one thousand feet, and its initial vertical velocity of three hundred feet per minute. The Cessna's horizontal stabilizers moved leading-edge down slightly, ready to execute the autopilot's commands. Townsend then stepped out of the cockpit and motioned to his soldiers to get ready for launch. He began to push in the throttle control for takeoff power and . . .

The Cessna's one VHF radio suddenly crackled to life—Townsend didn't even realize he had it on: "Cambridge UNICOM, Cambridge UNICOM, Seneca-43-double Pop, ten miles northeast of the field at two thousand five hundred, landing information please, go ahead."

Before Townsend could respond, someone else on the airport radioed back, "Seneca-43 Poppa, Cambridge UNICOM, landing runway three-four, winds three-one-zero at five, altimeter two-niner-niner-eight, no observed traffic. Airport is closed right now, parking available but no fuel or service available, over."

"Shit," Townsend swore, pulling the throttle on the Cessna back to idle until he decided what to do. "What in bloody hell is he doing here?" In the past few days, as his men monitored activity at the airport, there had not been one takeoff or landing after nine P.M., not *one.* Their whole mission was in jeopardy, and he hadn't even launched it yet!

As if to answer his question, Townsend heard, "Hey, Ed, this is Paul," the Seneca pilot replied. "Yeah, it's just me. I gassed up at Cape May this time—their gas is down thirteen cents from last week. I had dinner out at Wildwood, too—that's why I'm late. Hope the condo association doesn't give me too much grief. I'll try to keep the noise down."

Townsend grabbed the microphone and, trying to tone down his British accent as much as possible, radioed, "Cambridge traffic, this is Cessna-125-Bravo. I'm doing a little engine and brake maintenance at the end of runway 34. I'll be done in about five minutes."

"Hey, Cessna-125B, are you running engines out there?" the guy on the ground asked. "You know you ain't allowed to run engines out here after eight P.M. County ordinance."

"This is very important," Townsend said. "I'll be done in a minute."

"You the one that got towed out there with the tarps on your wings, -125B?" the guy asked. "The homeowners' association listens in on UNICOM. They'll probably call the sheriff and complain. I'd pack it in for the night if I was you. Don't dump any gas out of your sumps onto the dirt, either—county gets pissed off about that too."

"Kiss my bloody ass," Townsend said. He unplugged the microphone, then shoved in the throttle again, locked it tightly, closed the pilot's side door, and motioned for his helper to remove the tarp on the right wing . . .

. . . and, sure enough, by the time Townsend had removed the tarp on the left wing and gone back to the pickup truck, blinking red-and-blue lights could be seen back by the main part of the airport—a sheriff's patrol car. Also, by that time, the twin-engine

Seneca was on downwind, just a few minutes from landing. As the soldiers got their suppressed MP5 submachine guns ready, Townsend released the pelican clamp on the tail of the Cessna, and the plane shot down the runway.

The Cessna didn't look like it was going to make it. It pitched onto its left wheel as it accelerated, it skittered over to the left side of the runway precariously close to the VASI lights, and the left wingtip dipped so low that Townsend thought it was going to flip over and spin out. But just as he thought it was going to hit the dirt edge of the runway, it lifted off into the night sky, its wings leveling off as it gracefully climbed and proceeded on course. The GPS flight plan coordinates must've been off slightly, and the plane had immediately tried to correct itself. Luckily it had not run out of runway first.

The sheriff's patrol car looked as if it were going to drive down a taxiway and perhaps block the runway. It shined its floodlight at the plane, as if trying to read the registration number. "He's going to see those FAEs under the wings, Mr. Townsend," one of the soldiers reminded him.

"Well, let's give the constable something else to think about, shall we?" Townsend suggested. He pointed to the Seneca, which was just turning final for landing. As the patrol car backed up to get back onto the main taxiway, the second soldier took cover behind the pickup truck, out of sight. As the Seneca came in over the approach end of the runway, flaps extended and engines at near-idle power, the soldier opened fire. He emptied one thirty-two-round magazine on it, reloaded, and fired again.

Nine-millimeter bullets raked across the left side of the plane, one bullet grazing the pilot's head and knocking him unconscious. Most of the bullets chewed into the left propeller, breaking off huge pieces and throwing them in all directions. Unbalanced, the engine began to violently shake out of control. The Seneca skidded to the left, pirouetted around almost in a complete circle, and crashed. It skidded over across the parallel taxiway just a few feet from the patrol car, then flipped over and tumbled end-over-end into the south park of the parking ramp, destroying a half-dozen planes along the way before bursting into flame with a spectacular explosion.

The only clear way around the wreckage was down the runway, and that's where Townsend and his soldiers sped away. The patrol car tried to pursue, but had to turn back to help the survivors in any way he could. There was no pursuit—it took the sheriff's patrol and fire department fifteen minutes to respond, and the call to find the men in the pickup was drowned out by the call for ambulances and doctors. Townsend and his men went north across the Cambridge Bridge to the town of Easton, picked up their Cessna-210 escape plane at Newnam Airport, and were already flying outside the state to safety less than thirty minutes after the crash.

Over Chesapeake Bay near Annapolis, Maryland
That Same Time

Vincenti was flying west into the beautiful yellow, then orange, then red sunset, still killing time until his scheduled landing time. Northern and central Maryland and Chesapeake Bay were dark except for the occasional farms and rural subdivisions and the white dots of vessels' running lights on the Bay, but soon the lights of Baltimore and Washington could be seen, and they were spectacular. The city of Aberdeen was to the right, with the famous Aberdeen Army Weapons Proving Grounds nearby. The big splash of light to the right was Baltimore, and off the nose was Washington and the Virginia suburbs. He was headed right for the Annapolis–Chesapeake Bay Bridge.

Vincenti started a descent to fifteen hundred feet, only a thousand feet above the surrounding terrain and a thousand feet under the Class B airspace around Washington. It was a bit dangerous flying into such congested airspace at night, but flying was always a bit dangerous, and any chance he got to enjoy it, he took. He was still legal, taking advantage of all available assets to keep separated from other planes, and he was talking to air traffic control. The airspace structure around DC and Baltimore forced VFR (Visual Flight Rules) pilots either very high, above ten thousand feet, or very low. But he was still hoping for a friendly controller and a lot of luck to get a really good look at the capital area.

Of course, the reason he was allowed to be up here at all was because the Justice and Transportation Departments had recommended they do away with the air defense emergency, a move that puzzled and infuriated Vincenti. They had dismantled all the flight restrictions, fighter coverage, and Patriot missile protection in record time. The President wanted things back to normal so he could begin campaigning and tell everyone he had a handle on the situation, and the so-called Executive Committee on Terrorism okayed it.

Vincenti overflew the three-and-a-half-mile-long Annapolis–

Chesapeake Bay Bridge, skirted south around the U.S. Naval Academy and the city of Annapolis, then turned westbound toward Rockville. Vincenti could see the Goddard Space Flight Center, Walter Reed Hospital, the Mormon Temple, ablaze in lights, and Bethesda Naval Hospital. After passing about five miles north of Bethesda, he heard, "Devil-03, are you familiar with Special Routes 1 and 4, sir?"

"Affirmative, Devil-03."

"Devil-03, clear to Atlantic City International Airport via present position direct Cabin John intersection, Special Route 1, Hains Point, Special Route 4, Nottingham VOR, direct, at two thousand feet, do not overfly the observatory, the Capitol, or Arlington National Cemetery, keep your speed above two hundred knots, report passing the Wilson Bridge."

"-03, copy all, thank you." Vincenti pulled back power and used override to lower two notches of flaps, then thanked his lucky stars. Special Routes 1 and 4 are helicopter routes that generally follow the Potomac. It was going to be a quick but very spectacular tour.

And it was spectacular. Starting at the Taylor Naval Research Laboratory, he cruised over the Potomac south, with the entire expanse of Washington and the Virginia suburbs spread out before him in blazing glory. Vincenti saw the U.S. Naval Observatory, Georgetown University, Teddy Roosevelt Island, and then the Capitol came into view on the left. The memorials, monuments, and historic buildings were all brilliantly lit—he could not see the White House, but almost every building and monument along The Mall was clearly and beautifully visible, all the way to the Capitol itself. It felt as if he could reach out and touch the Washington Monument. He saw everything—the lights surrounding the Vietnam Veterans Memorial, the Reflecting Pools, the Jefferson Memorial . . . it was simply spectacular.

He cruised east of Arlington National Cemetery, and he could make out the Iwo Jima Memorial and could even see the lone dot of light that marked Kennedy's gravesite—just follow the Memorial Bridge west and the bright-yellow glow of the Eternal Flame could be seen through the trees. The Pentagon was plainly visible, a definite five-sided outline against the lights of Pentagon City. There was a helicopter landing on the Pentagon helipad, Vincenti noticed, and he wondered who was on board that helicopter and hoped everything was quiet down there at the Puzzle Palace.

Aboard an Air Force E-3C AWACS Radar Plane Over Eastern Pennsylvania

The mission crew commander aboard the Airborne Warning and Control System radar plane, Major Scott Milford, diligently continued to scan all five of the vital sectors assigned to him—Boston, New York, Philadelphia, Pittsburgh, and Washington, D.C.—but he always came back to check out Executive One Foxtrot.

The modified Boeing 747, Air Force designation VC-25A, commonly referred to as Air Force One (but actually only called that when the President of the United States was on board; its call sign tonight was Executive-One-Foxtrot, meaning that a member of the President's family or some other very high-ranking White House official was on board), had been assigned a standard FAA air traffic control transponder code, and everything appeared to be normal. It was flying Jet Route 77, an often-used high-altitude corridor used by flights from New England to transition routes into the Philadelphia and Baltimore areas. Usually the VC-25A was cleared direct airport-to-airport, even if it would bust through dense or restricted airspace, but since the President was not on board, the crew was apparently taking it easy and following published flight routes to avoid totally messing up the air traffic control situation all over the eastern seaboard. The White House had learned from the Los Angeles haircut incident, when the President tied up air traffic at Los Angeles International Airport for an hour by having Air Force One block a taxiway while he was getting a $200 haircut from a famous Hollywood stylist, how sensitive the public was to the Chief Executive stomping on common people while using the privileges of the office.

The senior director on Milford's crew, Captain Maureen Tate, turned and saw her MC scowling into his radarscope. "Still bugged about that VC-25 flight, sir?" she asked with a trace of amusement in her eyes.

"It's not the VC, it's the whole White House policy jerking us around," Milford complained. "We set up this whole complex air defense system, and we get blamed when it fails, but when the President wants to go on the campaign trail, he dismantles the whole thing overnight. Now the White House is taking one of its heavies right through our airspace, and we didn't hear word one from anybody until twenty minutes ago."

"That's FAA's fault, not the White House's fault," Tate said.

"We checked—they got the flight plan and the Alert Notification. The Northeast Air Defense Sector scrambled those two F-16s from Otis, too, and they got a visual—it's a VC-25 all right." It was standard procedure for Air Force One to get a military fighter escort anytime it was in or near hostile airspace, and these days, with Cazaux on the loose, the airspace over the United States was definitely considered hostile. But the fighters' standard operating procedure was not to come closer than three miles—close enough for a big plane like a 747—and there was to be no escort after sundown unless requested, so the fighters from the little base on Cape Cod had gone home shortly after the intercept. They probably got some dynamite pictures.

"I guess I'm bugged because usually we hear from Air Combat Command or the 89th before they launch a VC-25," Milford said. It was not standard or required procedure, but during most special operations and especially during an emergency situation such as this, the Support Missions Operations Center (SMOC) of the 89th Air Wing, the Air Force unit that flew the VIP jets from Andrews Air Force Base, usually notifies Air Combat Command and the Airborne Warning and Control Squadrons that they were going to fly a SAM (Special Air Mission) through their area. It was a simple "heads-up" that was encouraged to expedite VIP traffic. Milford saw Tate's little amused grin, and added, "And I'm bugged I didn't get my invitation to the President's barbecue, either."

"Situation normal, all fucked up," Tate offered. "Want to call and raise some hell with Andrews? I can contact the SMOC." Milford hesitated for a moment, not wanting to bug the VC-25's crew unnecessarily, but Tate took his hesitation to mean yes. "Comm, this is the SD, get the 89th SMOC on button four for me, okay?"

"Copy," the communications officer responded. A second later he responded, "SMOC on button four, SD. Call sign 'Midnight.' "

"Thanks."

"Hey, who's that?" Milford asked. He had flipped over to the Washington, D.C., sector radar display, where a large electronic arrow was pointing at a low-flying, fast-moving radar target flying right through the middle of D.C., just a few miles from the Capitol. "Jesus, *who is that?* Who gave him clearance to fly down there?"

"Washington Approach has him, sir," Tate reported after checking with the Comm section. "It's an F-16 from Atlantic City, Devil Zero-Three. Looks like he's on a Beltway tour."

"Who gave him *that?*"

"Washington Approach cleared him, sir," Tate responded. "National Tower is talking with him too. He's VFR."

"I don't believe it, I just don't believe it," Milford said angrily. "Two days ago we were ready to blow planes like that out of the sky twenty, thirty miles away—now we're letting them fly practically up to the front door of the White House. And he's not even under a proper flight plan! What are we doing up here if ATC keeps on clearing guys to cruise around anywhere they want? Are we supposed to be able to stop this guy if he turns out to be a terrorist?"

Milford switched his comm panel to Washington Approach's direct phone line. The reply came: "Washington Approach, Poole."

"Mr. Poole, this is Major Milford, aboard Leather Niner-Zero, the radar plane assigned to your sector," Milford responded. "You've got a Devil-03 flying VFR through the center of National's Class B airspace—I'd like him out of there as soon as possible."

"Any particular reason, Major?"

"Any particular *reason* . . . ? Sir, we're in the middle of an air defense *emergency!*" Milford shouted, trying to keep his composure on the landline. "The FAA may have taken down the special flight restrictions and approach funnels, but we're still responsible for stopping possible terrorist aircraft from entering Class B airspace. It really complicates our job having unauthorized VFR traffic flying through the middle of one of the most vital airspaces in the country. Is that good enough for you, Mr. Poole, or do I need to talk with the TRACON supervisor?"

"All right, all right, Major, I get the point," the controller responded, clearly exasperated at the threat but not wanting to make waves. "How about we give him present position direct Nottingham direct Atlantic City International, and no more Beltway tours unless we coordinate with you first?"

"That sounds fine, Mr. Poole, thank you," Milford said. "Leather-90 out." He punched off the phone line, stripped off his headset, and wearily rubbed his eyes and face. "Man, what is it with these controllers?" he murmured. "It seems like every one of them believes it's not going to happen to them, so they treat everything like situation-normal. I'm sick and tired of FAA controllers giving these pilots anything they ask for, and then us getting blamed when the pilot turns out to be a terrorist . . . look, there's another VFR flight, busting the Class B airspace." Milford pointed at a new target just marked as UNKNOWN by the Surveillance section. It was a slow-moving target flying northwest toward Washington Executive Field or Potomac Airport, traveling less than two miles per minute—a light plane doing some sightseeing. "We ought to blow that guy away just as a warning."

"Executive-One-Foxtrot's been cleared to descend," Tate reported. "He's twenty miles northeast of Pottstown VOR."

"He's going to have to get his tail down if he wants to make RONNY intersection by eight thousand," one of the weapons controllers behind Tate remarked as he watched the VC-25 make its descent. RONNY intersection, fifty miles north of Andrews Air Force Base, was the usual turnpoint for VIP planes landing at Andrews—it gave the pilots a nice long straight-in approach, with little traffic and few turns to disturb the passengers.

"Good thing the President's not on board," another WC said. "I heard the Steel Magnolia pitches a fit and tries to shit-can the whole flight crew if her ears do so much as pop while she's in Air Force One."

"She's got bigger things on her mind these days . . . like how to keep her and the President from being indicted."

Everyone chuckled.

"There he goes," the first weapons controller reported, monitoring Executive-One-Foxtrot's data block and mentally calculating the descent rate by watching the altitude readout. "He's doing at least fifteen hundred feet a minute in the descent. I think heads are going to roll tonight."

"Just everybody settle down and monitor the transponder changeover up here," Tate said. Before passing through ten thousand feet, Air Force VIP aircraft like Executive-One-Foxtrot switched their transponders to a discrete code, usually 2222, used only in the terminal area to alert controllers so they can give the plane expedited service. When the changeover occurred, the target usually disappeared off the radarscreen for about twelve seconds until the new code was picked up by the radar computers—if the controllers weren't ready for the changeover, they got very frantic and sometimes pushed the panic button.

Milford went back and scanned his other four vital sectors. Everything seemed to be running smoothly. Air traffic had not returned to normal by any means, but in the past few days travel at night had virtually disappeared, and now it was making a comeback. Fewer restrictions on flight routing, more controller discretion, and less reliance on published arrival and departure procedures really helped to clear things up. That newcomer, the slow-moving VFR flight that had originated somewhere in eastern Maryland, was now over Nottingham VOR, still headed northwest—its course would take it south of Andrews Air Force Base, but it was definitely on its way to busting the Class B airspace. That idiot deserved to get his license pulled, Milford thought.

"Any ID on that VFR flight out there, AS?" Milford asked the Airborne Surveillance section.

"Still checking, MC."

Jesus, Milford thought, *what an asshole.* The air defense emergency had not been officially canceled, although the FAA did announce that flights were not required to follow the special-arrival corridors into the nation's busiest airports anymore. It was also not hard to hide all of the long-range Patriot missile sites being taken down all over the country.

"MC, no IFF changeover on that Executive-One-Foxtrot flight."

Milford immediately flipped back to the Washington, D.C., Class B airspace radar display and zoomed his presentation in, putting the VC-25A on the top of the scope and Andrews Air Force Base, the plane's destination, on the bottom. His heart immediately started to beat a bit faster. Executive-One-Foxtrot was at RONNY intersection, inbound on the ILS approach to runway one-eight left, passing through eight thousand feet—and still no transponder code changeover.

The crews flying those VIP jets never made mistakes like that, *never.*

The next question was how to notify the crew of their omission. Although it was certainly not required that the VC-25 crews change their transponder codes or accept any expedited service, it was generally not a good idea for any of the President's jets to be delayed in the air, especially when the President was on the road. But blabbing it on an open-frequency was probably not a politic idea, either. Milford flipped his radio panel over to the 89th Air Wing's Special Mission Operations Center, the ones that were in constant contact with all of their VIP planes: "Midnight, this is Leather-90 on SMOC common, over."

"Leather-90, this is 89th Wing SMOC, stand by." There was a lengthy pause, probably so the senior controller at Andrews could look up in his call-sign book to see who "Leather" was. Then: "Go ahead, -90."

"I'm tracking your SAM-2800, Executive-One-Foxtrot, fifty-two miles north of ADW inbound. Can you ask him to change over his IFF? Over."

"Say again, -90?"

"I repeat, I am tracking Executive-One-Foxtrot inbound to ADW, and he has not changed over his IFF to terminal procedure codes. Can you notify him to change his transponder code? Over."

There was another slight pause, probably so the senior controller could ask the VC-25 crew if they were squawking the right code and to change it immediately if they had forgotten. Milford watched his radar display, expecting the code to change at any moment . . . but it did not. "Ah . . . Leather-90, sir, we can't verify the location of our SAM flights to you on this channel. You'll have to contact us on a secure landline or secure datalink. Over."

"What the hell is this guy talking about?" Milford muttered. "The whole friggin' world knows that this plane's up there." On the radio, he said, "Midnight, I've got a valid military flight plan for SAM-2800 and an FAA ALNOT on Executive-One-Foxtrot, IFR from Manchester, New Hampshire, to Andrews. He's less than fifty miles north of Andrews inbound for landing. He's been airborne for well over an hour. I think it's a little late to play hide-and-seek games with this one. All I want is to have him change over his IFF. Over."

After another interminable pause that was about to drive Milford nuts and had now gotten the attention of the entire AWACS crew, the SMOC controller came back: "Leather-90, I've been directed to tell you by the senior controller here that there is no SAM-2800 or Executive-One-Foxtrot inbound for landing at Andrews. All of our assets are accounted for, and none are inbound to Andrews at this time. You have a faker on your hands."

Milford felt the blood drain out of his face, and his stomach muscles tensed so tightly that he felt as if he were going to throw up. "Shit, shit, *shit,*" he cursed loudly. On the radio, he shouted, "Midnight, are you sure?"

"I can't tell you on this channel where the VC-25s are, Leather," the SMOC controller said, "but I can tell you they're not inbound to Andrews. All of our other assets are nowhere near ADW. Closest one departed a half-hour ago, destination Langley."

"Damn it, I can't believe this," Milford said. Tate and the other weapon controllers were waiting for their instructions—he had to act *now* . . . "Comm, this is the MC, contact Washington Approach and Washington Center, advise them we're declaring an air defense emergency for the Baltimore-Washington Class B airspace. I need the airspace cleared out and instructions issued to that 747 to stay out of Class B airspace. Surveillance, MC, mark radar target P045Y as 'unknown.' Maureen, do we have anybody suited up? Do we have a chance to get this guy?"

"Yes, sir," Tate responded immediately. "Two F-16s—tactical birds, not interceptors—on ready five alert at Andrews."

"Scramble them," Milford ordered.

"Yes, sir," Tate acknowledged. She had her finger on the SCRAMBLE button as soon as she heard there was something wrong with Executive-One-Foxtrot. On aircraft-wide intercom, Tate announced, "All stations, all stations, active air scramble Andrews, unknown target P045Y designate as 'Bandit-1' . . . MC, Alpha-Whiskey One-One and One-Two acknowledging the klaxon; Weapons One, interceptors coming up to you on button two."

"Who else we got, Maureen?" Milford asked.

"Next-closest units we have are F-16 ADF interceptors at Atlantic City and tactical F-15s at Langley," Tate responded. "ADFs at Atlantic City are on ready five alert, but their ETE is at least ten minutes at zone 5. The F-15s at Langley can get there in five minutes, but they're not on ready five alert."

"Call Langley and tell them to get anything they can airborne," Milford said. "Put A-City on engines-running cockpit alert at the end of the runway in case Bandit-1 tries to bug out or if the fighters at Andrews are bent. Get a tanker from Dover or McGuire airborne and put him over Nottingham VOR for refueling support—all the out-of-towners are going to need gas if they arrive over DC on full afterburner."

"What's the order for Alpha-Whiskey flight, sir?" Tate asked.

Milford checked his radarscope. The now-unknown 747 was only forty miles out; at his airspeed, traveling six to seven miles per minute, he would be over the Capitol in five minutes. "If Bandit-1 turns away and does not enter Class B airspace, the order is to intercept, ID, and shadow," Milford said. "If Bandit-1 enters Class B airspace, the order is to engage and destroy from maximum range. Comm, get the National Military Command Center senior controller on button four."

Milford then reached up to his primary radio channels and selected the common channel linking the fifteen Hawk missile sites and the twenty Stinger man-portable shoulder-fired missile platoons assigned to Washington-Dulles, Washington-National, Andrews Air

Force Base, Baltimore International, and the Capitol district, and said, "All Leather units, this is Leather-90, air defense emergency for Washington Dulles, National, and Baltimore Tri-Cities Class B airspace, radar ID P045Y is now classified 'unknown,' target designate 'Bandit-1,' stand by for engagement, repeat, stand by for engagement."

For the moment, the slow-moving VFR flight was forgotten . . .

Andrews Air Force Base
That Same Time

"Andrews Tower, Alpha-Whiskey-11 flight, active air scramble, taxi and takeoff northwest."

"Alpha-Whiskey-11 flight, Andrews Tower, taxi runway three-six right, wind one-seven-zero at five, altimeter three-zero-zero-one, expect immediate takeoff clearance crossing the hold line, intersection Bravo takeoff approved, seven thousand five hundred feet remaining."

It took considerably less than five minutes for the two F-16A crews from the 121st Fighter Squadron "Guardians," District of Columbia Air National Guard, to run to their jets, start engines, and begin to taxi. No matter what someone at the Department of Justice said, they knew they were the last line of defense for the nation's capital. Not only did the Guardians refuse to revert back to normal air defense operations, but they kept themselves in advanced states of readiness in order to cut down on response times. All idle-time crew activities had been moved from the alert facility to the aircraft shelters, so crews were no more than six ladder steps from their cockpits, and runway 36 Right had been designated the "alert runway," so it was always clear and unused except for absolute emergencies. By the time the echoes of the three long klaxon blasts were gone, immediately the roar of two Pratt & Whitney F100-P-200 turbofan engines replaced them.

Both planes—not ADF (Air Defense Fighter) F-16s, but standard battlefield combat models—carried four AIM-9L Sidewinder heat-seeking missiles, ammunition for the 20-millimeter cannon, and one centerline fuel tank. They reached the hold line in less than a minute, performing last-second flight-control checks and takeoff checklist items on the roll. "AW flight, clear for takeoff to the northwest unrestricted, contact approach," Andrews Tower radioed.

"AW flight, clear for takeoff, go button three."

"Two."

For safety's sake at night, the fighters performed a standard in-trail takeoff instead of a formation takeoff. The leader turned onto the runway, not bothering to set his brakes but plugging in the afterburner as soon as he was aligned with the runway centerline. The wingman started counting to himself when he saw his leader's fifth-stage afterburner light, and although he was supposed to wait ten seconds, he started his takeoff roll on eight. Smoothly he pushed his throttle to military power, checked his gauges, cracked the throttle to afterburner range, watched the nozzle swing, and checked the fuel flow and exhaust pressure ratio gauges, pushed the throttle smoothly to zone five, and . . .

There was a bright flash of light ahead, like a lightning strike on the horizon or a searchlight sweeping down the runway. The pilot heard no abort calls, either from his leader or the control tower, so he continued his takeoff, clicking off nosewheel steering and shifting his attention from the gauges to the runway when he passed decision speed. He then . . .

There was another bright flash of light, and then the pilot saw a ball of flames tumbling across the runway, spinning to the left across the infield, then back to the right across his path. He was already past his decision speed—he was committed for the takeoff because he no longer had enough pavement if he tried to stop now. He still considered pulling the throttle to IDLE, but his training said no, you'll never stop, take it in the air, continue, continue . . .

The second F-16 plowed directly into the fireball that was his lead F-16. He thought he had made it through safely, but his engine had ingested enough burning metal and debris to shell it out in seconds. The pilot tried for a split second to avoid the fireball by turning left toward the other runway, but when he saw the FIRE light, saw his altitude as less than a hundred feet above ground and sinking rapidly, he did not hesitate to pull the ejection handle.

"Shit the bed, we got *both* those motherfuckers!" one of Cazaux's soldiers shouted gleefully.

"Damn straight," his partner responded. They were in a hiding place between two maintenance hangars on the west side of the western parallel runway, in clear view of both runways and especially the alert fighter ramp. They wore standard military fatigues and combat boots, except both wore no fatigue shirts—that was common during after-duty hours in the summer. After nightfall, they had successfully planted a series of radio-activated claymore mines along both runways, which they activated when they heard the klaxon and were tripped when the hot engines of a plane were detected by infrared sensors. "Now let's get the hell out of here. We got thirty seconds to get to the rendezvous point or Ysidro will go without us." The terrorists activated switches on the radio detonators, which would set off small explosives in the devices several minutes later or if they were disturbed so investigators wouldn't be able to use them as evidence or as clues to their whereabouts.

They tried to leave their hiding place on the street side near a dark parking lot, but the explosion on the runway had attracted a lot of attention faster than they anticipated, and they had to wait for several security police cars to whiz past. But as they crouched in the shadows waiting for the cars to pass, there was a sharp *bang!* right behind them, followed by the sputtering and sizzling of burning wire and circuitry. One of the self-destruct devices in the mine detonators had gone off early—and it had attracted the attention of a security police patrol on the ramp side of the hangars. The blue-and-white patrol car skidded to a stop, and the security police officer saw the smoking and burning box and shined a car-mounted floodlight in between the hangars, immediately impaling the two men hiding on the other side in the powerful beam.

"You two between the hangars!" the SP shouted on the car's loudspeaker. "Security police! Kneel down with your hands on your head, *now!*" The two men ran off, together at first and then in diverging directions.

As they bolted from their hiding spot, another security police cruiser passing by saw them running and heard the other officer's alert on the radio, hit his brakes, and stepped out of the car. He shouted a perfunctory "Halt! Security police canine unit! Stop!" but he was already opening up the right rear passenger door of his cruiser. He shouted a few instructions to his German shepherd partner, pointing out one of the fleeing suspects until the dog barked that he had the suspect in sight, and then commanded the dog to pursue.

Spurred on by the wail of sirens all around him, the first terrorist ran north on Arnold Avenue as fast as he ever recalled running in his life. The fire trucks from the base fire station at Arnold Avenue and D Street were rolling, heading for the flight line, and for a moment the terrorist thought he could loose himself in the confusion of vehicles if he could just make it to D Street. Beyond the fire station was the base exchange, commissary, and theater, with plenty of places to hide, cars to steal, hostages to capture.

But the chase did not last long. Trained to be perfectly silent throughout the chase, the terrorist didn't hear the animal, not even a growl, until he felt the dog's teeth sink into his upper-left calf muscle. The terrorist screamed and went down, rolling across the ground with the dog's incisors still buried in his leg. As he tried to rise, the dog released the man's leg and went for the right wrist, the main appendage a K-9 patrol dog is trained to clamp down on, and began pulling in any direction possible, trying to keep the suspect off-balance until his human partner arrived. Teeth struck bone several times, and dog and man went down together. The dog was a dynamo, never staying still, but twisting in several directions, shaking his head as if trying to rip the suspect's arm free from his torso.

But the terrorist was left-handed. He drew a 9-millimeter Browning automatic, and, before the dog spotted the gun and went for the other wrist, put it up to the big furry body and pulled the trigger. The one-hundred-pound bundle of teeth and muscle blew apart in a cloud of blood and hair, still trying to keep hold of his suspect until life drained out of his body—even so, the terrorist had to use the muzzle of his Browning to pry the animal's teeth out of his mangled right arm so he could . . .

Headlights, squealing tires, a furious, high-pitched voice shouting, "Freeze! Don't move or you're dead!" It was too late. He was already dizzy from the exertion and the loss of blood—there was no resistance possible. Capture was not an option. If the cops didn't kill him, Cazaux would. Failure was inexcusable; capture automatically meant betrayal, punishable by death. He would rather have the cops do it quick than watch Henri Cazaux rip his beating heart out from his chest.

The terrorist sat up so as to present as large a target as possible, aimed his Browning at the headlights, and fired. The security police returned fire with an M-16 assault rifle.

He was not disappointed.

Army Colonel Wes Slotter, commander of 108th Air Defense Artillery Brigade, Fort Polk, Louisiana, was the overall commander of ground air defense forces for the nation's capital. From the Patriot

Integrated Command Center van at Andrews Air Force Base, he was in constant contact with all of the Patriot, Hawk, Avenger, and Stinger units in the Washington area, as well as the E-3C AWACS radar plane and the National Military Command Center at the Pentagon, where the Joint Air Defense Commander was headquartered. Although his headquarters was at Fort Belvoir, Virginia, like his mentor, General H. Norman Schwarzkopf, he hated being stuck in his office with his units deployed in the field—even if "in the field" only meant The Mall or a golf course on East Potomac Island Park—so he was on his way to the integrated central command for all of the ground air defense units when the air defense alert came down.

And as he trotted over to the control van, he also had a perfect view of the crash of the two F-16 fighter jets, less than a mile from where he was standing.

Slotter ran back to the control center van, wedging his six-foot-two frame past the maintenance technicians and over to the Patriot battalion commander, Lieutenant Colonel Jim Buckwall, who was seated at the communications officer's station behind the battalion fire control officer and battalion radar technician. "Jesus, we just had two fighters crash on the runway," Slotter said. "What do we got, Jim?"

"AWACS radioed an air defense emergency about two minutes ago, sir," Buckwall reported. "We're tracking a single heavy airliner inbound toward D.C. from the north. Apparently it made its way from New Hampshire calling itself Executive-One-Foxtrot."

"A VIP flight? No shit," Slotter exclaimed. How that bastard made it all the way like that was almost unbelievable. "First that, then they crash a couple F-16s—the Air Force is dicking up by the numbers." He wasn't one to dig on another branch of the service, especially during an emergency when anything could happen to anyone at any time, but the prima donnas in the Air Force really deserved it sometimes. "Let's try not to make any mistakes ourselves. Everybody reporting in okay?"

"Yes, sir," Buckwall said. "All Avenger ground units deploying as per the ops order. This ICC is in contact with all the Hawk batteries except for Baltimore, but the AWACS had full connectivity with them. We're checking our comm relays to find out what the problem is."

"That AWACS has full control of all ground units, eh?"

"Yes, sir," Buckwall said. "We launch our missiles, but Leather-90 tells us who and when and how we attack. If we lose connectivity with them we have full authority to launch, but as long as the hookup is solid, Leather-90 has the red button.'' Slotter didn't like that idea, either. An Air Force guy with authority over a dozen Hawk missile batteries and two dozen Avenger units, and with full launch control over the Patriots if they were still on-line—well, the idea was unnatural.

Slotter could tell that the maintenance techs wanted to get inside to start checking over the systems to regain contact with the Hawk units at Baltimore-Washington International. There was no room in the control van for an extra person, especially a high-ranking extra person. ''I'll be en route to the NMCC at the Pentagon, Colonel,'' he said. ''Notify me as soon as possible on the secure line on the engagement status.''

''Yes, sir,'' Buckwall responded.

Slotter squeezed past the maintenance techs and exited the hatch, nearly colliding with a soldier coming up the steps toward the ICC. The soldier, wearing an ALICE harness and web belt, had his Kevlar helmet strapped down tight and pulled over his eyes, so Slotter couldn't recognize him. It was unusual to see a soldier in full combat gear up in the ICC—the security guys usually stayed on the perimeter. ''Excuse me, sir,'' the soldier said. ''I've got a message for the commander.''

''Battalion CO's tied up right now,'' Slotter said. ''I'm Colonel Slotter, the brigade CO. Let's have it.''

''Yes, sir,'' the soldier said. His right hand came up—but there was no message, only a small submachine gun with a long silencer on it. Before Slotter could cry out a warning, he felt the sharp, sledgehammer-like blows on his chest, then nothing.

Tomas Ysidro shoved the body off the rear deck of the Patriot ICC, pushed open the entry hatch, threw a tear gas grenade and two hand grenades into the ICC, slammed the door tight, and jumped off the truck. Seconds later, the hatch opened and the tear gas grenade sailed out, but it was too late. The other two high-explosive grenades were never picked up, and the explosions inside the steel box of the Patriot ICC destroyed everything inside instantly.

"Move it, move it!" Ysidro shouted to his partners. He should have set the explosives on the antenna array, but the array was still deployed and the electrical power plant was still operational. He unbuckled the last two grenades he carried, pulled the safety pins, and ran toward the antenna array truck when he heard, ''Halt! Drop your weapon!''

Always playing cowboy, Ysidro thought. *You're in combat, you idiot Americans—why do you insist on trying to order the enemy to halt?* Ysidro threw the first grenade at the antenna array, then wheeled around and rolled the second grenade under the electrical power plant truck—just as three Army security guards opened fire, catching him in a murderous crossfire from their M-16s. His shattered body hit the ground just a few feet from where his partner lay, shot by another security guard as he tried to plant the remote-detonated mines around the antenna array and electrical power plant.

But the first grenade did the trick. Ysidro's toss was perfect, bouncing off the back of the "drive-in theater" array and landing right on the waveguide horn on top of the unit. The explosion ripped the entire array and waveguide assembly off the top of the van. The second grenade rolled all the way under the EPP, but the force of the explosion toppled the vehicle on its left side, spilling diesel fuel and starting a fire.

Along The Mall
That Same Moment

When the alert went out from Major Milford aboard the E-3C AWACS radar plane that Washington was under attack, the air defense ground units that had so very carefully been under wraps for the past several days immediately deployed to their fire positions.

From First Street, east of the Capitol, to the Lincoln Memorial, Avenger units rolled out of their parking garages and took up positions on The Mall, with one Avenger stationed every six thousand feet; at the same time, Avenger units deployed to positions around the approach ends of main runways at Dulles, National, Andrews, and Baltimore airports. Avenger was an HMMWV (High Mobility Multipurpose Wheeled Vehicle, the Army's new "Jeep") truck with a rotating turret installed on it that contained two four-round Stinger missile launchers, a .50-caliber heavy machine gun, a laser rangefinder, and a telescopic infrared sensor. The gunner sat in a cab between the two Stinger launchers and electronically spotted and attacked airborne targets as far as three miles away. A driver/loader and two security troops completed the Avenger crew.

"All Leather units, Bandit-1 bearing zero-one-eight degrees magnetic, range thirty miles and closing. All units stand by for status poll."

Sergeant First Class Paul Lathrop pushed open the bulletproof Lexan canopy of his Avenger FAAD (Forward Area Air Defense) unit to get a little fresh air into the cockpit, and stretched to try to smooth out the kinks in his muscles. He was the unit gunner, sitting in a tiny, narrow cockpit between two four-round Stinger missile pods. The cab was not made for anyone over six feet tall, nor anyone with any hint of fat—the turret steering column was right up against his chest, and his knees were bent all the way up practically to the dashboard. But even worse than sitting in the hot, confined cab was sitting in the cab when the vehicle was moving. He was wearing no tanker's pads to protect himself, so every bone in his body ached from being thrown around in the bucking-bronco HMMWV.

Lathrop's Avenger unit was stationed on the west side of the Washington Monument, with an almost unobstructed view of the sky in all directions—except, of course, for the sky blocked out by the monument. He could clearly see the front of the White House, the Lincoln Memorial, the Jefferson Memorial, and of course the Capitol itself. There was another Avenger unit east of the Washington Monument, near the Capitol, with a clear shot of most of the sky that Lathrop couldn't see to the east; there were other units over at West Potomac Park guarding south D.C., Ft. McNair, Arlington National Cemetery, and the Pentagon, and east of the Capitol as well.

You don't deploy units like Avenger in the middle of The Mall in Washington, D.C., and expect not to get noticed, and almost as soon as they rolled out of their hiding places near Union Station, West Potomac Park, the Navy Bureau of Medicine, and George Washington University, a crowd had gathered to watch. D.C. Police and Army security troops were trying to close off The Mall and chase all the bystanders away, but on a warm summer evening in D.C., with the lights of the monuments on for the first time in days, there were a lot of folks out wandering around. The lights had not yet been turned off, and Lathrop idly wondered who would have the switch to the lights of Washington, D.C. Certainly not the President—or the Steel Magnolia.

It was then he noticed that the poll of the air defense units had stopped. On interphone, he said, "Mike, how do you hear?"

"Loud and clear," Specialist Mike Reston replied.

"What happened to the poll?"

"Dunno," Reston replied. Lathrop heard a squeal in the radio as Reston deactivated the squelch control. "Radio still works. Hang on." On the radio, Lathrop heard, "Control, Leather-713, radio check . . . Control, -713, radio check."

"-713, this is Leather-601, stand by." That was from the lieutenant in charge of the four Hawk missile sites stationed around D.C., based out at East Potomac Island Park, south of the Capitol, along the Potomac.

"Control must've gone off the air," Reston said.

That got Lathrop worried. With a bandit only a few minutes away, he needed radio contact with someone with a long-range radar to spot targets for him until the bandit got close enough. The passive infrared sensor on the Avenger was good out to a range of about five to eight miles, so long-range spotting was crucial. The Patriot ICC (Integrated Command Center) stationed out at Andrews provided radar coverage for the Hawk and Avenger units—what a shitty time to have radio problems.

"All Leather-600 and -700 units, this is Leather-601," the commander of the Hawk battalion said on the command net. "ICC is down, repeat, ICC is down, -601 is taking operational control. Bandit-1 bearing zero-one-zero magnetic, twenty-eight miles, status is batteries released tight, repeat, status is batteries released tight, all units—"

And then that transmission stopped.

"What the fuck . . . ?"

"Hey, guys . . . er, Leather-700 units, this is -711, I see a fire over on East Potomac Island Park," one of the crew members on the Avenger at West Potomac Park radioed. "I see . . . holy shit, man, I see big explosions south across the Inlet, over on East Potomac Island. I think the Hawk site just got wiped."

"Say again, Winfield?" Lathrop radioed. "You say you saw explosions?"

When Lathrop released the mike button, the gunner on Leather-711 named Winfield was already reporting: ". . . and I see several guys headin' this way . . . shit, man, shit, they're *firing* at me, all units . . . you motherfucker!"

"Win, what the hell's going on?" But then Lathrop looked to his left and saw two men dressed in jogging shorts but carrying rather big knapsacks or duffel bags running down the long walkway to the west of the Washington Monument. He rose out of his seat and shouted to his security guard, "Hey, Kelly, watch those two guys to the west. Don't let anyone near the unit! Some shit's going down out there! We lost contact with Winfield in -711."

The Army guard named Kelly moved over to the left rear corner of the Avenger unit and spotted the two guys trying to casually jog over toward them. Kelly shouted, *"Hold it!* Stop where you are!" The joggers didn't stop. A D.C. Police cruiser on Seventeenth Street spotted the joggers and turned on its lights, trying to get them to stop. The first one hesitated, jogging in place a bit until the second guy caught up with him, then they continued. The Police cruiser jumped the curb and started down the walkway, issuing a warning to stop on their PA system. The joggers kept on coming. Kelly leveled his M-16 and shouted, "I said, *halt! Last warning! Stop!"*

The joggers angled over away from the Washington Monument, about fifty yards or so away from the Avenger, near a small information kiosk . . . then suddenly stopped, both of them, and put their duffel bags down.

"What's the problem, man?" one of the joggers shouted. "What's going on?"

Kelly shouted, "Leave those bags on the ground and raise your—" But he was interrupted by a terrific explosion that rolled across The Mall. A bright yellow fire was burning, somewhere near the Capitol.

"-712, you read me?" Lathrop radioed. "Wood, man, answer up . . . -712, you read me? What's that fire . . . ?" But Lathrop knew what it was—it was the burning hulk of the Avenger stationed west of the Capitol. Someone was picking off all the air defense units around the Capital, one by one . . .

. . . and now they were attacking here. The two joggers had leaped behind the information kiosk, out of sight of the Avenger crew—and suddenly a burst of automatic gunfire erupted, sweeping across Lathrop's Avenger. The D.C. Police car that was speeding toward them slammed on its brakes, and another burst of automatic gunfire sprayed it with bullets. Kelly ran behind the Avenger and returned fire with his M-16, chopping holes in the fiberglass kiosk. The D.C. Police cruiser was getting chopped up badly—they had some heavy firepower . . .

Lathrop closed his canopy and swung his turret westward toward the kiosk. Machine-gun fire peppered the polycarbonate canopy, and 9-millimeter bullet holes dented it, but thankfully did not penetrate. One of the joggers bolted toward the police cruiser, firing on the run. Lathrop tracked him with ease in his infrared scanner window, flicked his arm switch to GUNS, hit the ENABLE button on the left turret control, and squeezed the trigger on the right turret grip.

From only about two hundred feet away, the Avenger's .50-caliber heavy machine gun—designed to blow fifty-thousand-pound aircraft out of the sky a mile away—chopped the first jogger up into several large chunks in less than a second. Lathrop immediately swung the turret back around and reacquired the kiosk, ready to blow the shit out of it as well . . .

. . . but the second jogger had pulled out a LAWS (Lightweight Antitank Weapon System) rocket from his duffel bag, aimed and fired, and from less than two hundred feet away he could not miss. It seemed as if the rocket was headed straight for the space between Lathrop's eyes. He felt an incredible blast rock his eight-thousand-pound vehicle and saw a bright flash of light, and then he saw and felt nothing . . .

Hoover FBI Building
That Same Time

It was the closest thing to an interrogation any of them had ever been subjected to. Deborah Harley, Ian Hardcastle, and the Deputy U.S. Marshal of the United States, William Landers, along with several Marshals Service agents and U.S. Navy pilots had been questioned in the Director's conference room for the past nine hours on the CV-22 raid at Cazaux's estate in Bedminster, and the attempted intercept of Harold Lake and Ted Fell in Newburgh. They had been subjected to "tag-team" questioning by a small army of investigators—asked to draw detailed maps of their route of flight and movements in the mansion once the attack was under way, describe all of their communications routines, and provide exhaustive records of everything concerning the mission, from where they bought fuel for the PAVE HAMMER tilt-rotor aircraft to a full list of all the weapons used.

Finally, Judge Lani Wilkes, the Director of the FBI, came to visit the group. While staffers and other witnesses had been shuffling in and out all day retrieving records that the FBI requested, Harley and Hardcastle had been there the entire time, and they were stiff and tired as they got to their feet when Wilkes entered the conference room. "Good evening, Agent Harley, Admiral Hardcastle," she greeted them. "I appreciate your assisting the Bureau in preparing our report to the Justice Department and the White House. I'm told you've been here since early this afternoon."

"You know damn well we've been here all day," Hardcastle

snapped angrily. He had ditched his coat and tie long ago and had changed into a short-sleeve shirt and comfortable loafers; Harley was in a business suit but had removed her jacket—she still looked as calm and fresh as she did when she began the marathon "debriefing" session.

"Something wrong, Admiral?" Wilkes asked sweetly.

"We should have been allowed to submit our reports on the incident first before all this began," Hardcastle said. "I think it would've been more *efficient* to take our report and *then* fill in the details later. We're essentially duplicating our reports and being kept here like prisoners. We should—"

"Admiral, I've been FBI Director for three years, and I've been involved in thousands of criminal and interagency investigations in my thirty years of law enforcement," Wilkes interrupted crisply, "so I think I know a thing or two about how to conduct an investigation and how to take a report. Frankly, judging by your actions in the raid on the Bedminster estate, I question whether you have any idea on proper or legal law-enforcement actions. Do us both a favor, Admiral, and let the Bureau do its job—for a change." She surveyed the room, noticing empty drink cups and sandwich boxes in the trash cans. "I see you're being taken care of here. This shouldn't take too much longer. I'm sure you agree that it's better if we just get this whole thing over with."

"Judge Wilkes, do you still think the body recovered at the mansion was Henri Cazaux?" Harley asked, a hint of annoyance in her voice.

Wilkes narrowed her eyes in irritation at the question. "I'm sorry," Wilkes replied icily, "but I can't talk about an ongoing investigation with you, Agent Harley."

"She's as much a part of the investigation as you are, Judge Wilkes," Hardcastle announced. "Perhaps much more so."

"Just because you flagrantly disregarded Justice Department policy and procedures and shoot up a nest of terrorists doesn't give you a need-to-know," Wilkes hissed. "If we weren't talking about Henri Cazaux, I'd see to it that you had your stars yanked, you and Deputy U.S. Marshal Landers. You don't seem to care or realize that you interfered with the biggest Bureau investigation since the World Trade Center bombing. However, I will say that the cannon you used to kill him and the eleven other persons inside the place really did a good job in obscuring their features and making identification more difficult—"

"So this whole interrogation is your way of getting back at us, right, Judge Wilkes?" Landers asked, refusing to be cowed by the Director of the FBI or anyone else. "You don't have to lock us up—just 'debrief' us for the next six weeks until the press is done raking us over the coals for the 'brutal' attack on the estate and the 'incompetent' way we handled Harold Lake's capture."

"Deputy Landers, all these little problems you've encountered have nothing to do with me—you caused them all, you and Admiral Hardcastle's damn-the-torpedoes, full-speed-ahead and attack-dog solutions to every problem that crops up," Wilkes said. "You interfered with an FBI investigation, and I've got to clean up your mess. Congress is going to question us next week on what happened, and I'm going to be ready, and frankly, if you're inconvenienced by this, I don't really care. Now, I've asked for your cooperation. If you refuse to give it, I'll have no choice but to schedule a deposition and compel you to attend."

"And make sure that such a summons is made quite public," Hardcastle interjected.

"All such summonses are a matter of public record, Admiral," Wilkes said, not bothering to hide her contempt. "Now, if you'll excuse me . . ." Just then her pager went off, and she went over to a nearby office phone on the conference room table. "Director Wilkes . . . a *what?* When . . . ? I'll be right down . . . no, I don't want to deploy BLACK TI . . . I said, I'll be right down." She slammed the phone down and hurried to the door.

Both Hardcastle and Harley were on their feet—by the look on Wilkes' face, they both knew something terrible was wrong. "What is it, Judge?" Hardcastle asked.

"Nothing . . . I'll brief you later."

"Receiving a recommendation from your command center to deploy BLACK TIGER is not exactly 'nothing,' Judge," Deputy Chief U.S. Marshal Landers pointed out.

"What's BLACK TIGER?" Hardcastle asked.

"That's none of your concern" Wilkes warned.

"BLACK TIGER is the classified code name for the joint federal and military team designed to protect the capital," Harley said to Hardcastle. "In peacetime, it's mostly to protect against rioters and civil unrest. The Attorney General is the commander; senior representatives are from the FBI, the U.S. Marshals Service—Bill here is the Marshals' rep—the Secret Service, and the two-star commanding general of the Military District of Washington, plus other military reps. There was an attack somewhere in the capital—wasn't there, Judge Wilkes?''

"Deputy Landers, you're with me. You two, I'll talk to later,'' she said, and hurried off. Landers gave Harley a friendly squeeze on the arm and followed Wilkes to the underground FBI Emergency Operations Command Center.

Suddenly, outside the open conference room windows, they saw a flash of light, like a huge flashbulb going off, followed seconds later by a loud rumble that was like a short, sharp crash of thunder. They all went to the window. The flash had come from the south, in the direction of The Mall, but they could see nothing.

Hardcastle was reaching for the phone to call his assistant Marc Sheehan: "That wasn't thunder—it reminded me of a bomb attack in San Salvador I witnessed once,'' he told Harley. "Something's going on out there near The Mall.''

"Forget the phone call—let's get out of here,'' Harley said. "Talk on the way. We'll take my car.''

Aboard the E-3C AWACS Radar Plane Leather-90

"MC, Comm, we just lost contact with the Hawk unit at East Potomac Park.''

Milford was dumbfounded. The fake Executive-One-Foxtrot was less than thirty miles away from the Capitol, and at the exact point where the medium-range air defense units would have engaged, they went off the air. First the fighters launching from Andrews were destroyed, then the Integrated Command Center at Andrews that had overall control of the Hawk and Avenger units around the city, now the close-in Hawk radar system.

The Avenger units—if there were still any Avenger units down there—were virtually blind. The gunners on the Avengers had IFF (Identification Friend or Foe) interrogators, so they could pick out any aircraft that was not squawking air traffic control codes, but the tracking sensors on the Avengers had limited range. Even if they spotted the fake Executive-One at the absolute maximum range, they would have only a few seconds to attack before the plane got within range. The Stinger missile was designed to attack targets flying less than two hundred knots airspeed—the fake Executive-One was flying almost twice that speed.

"Status of the runway at Andrews?''

"Closed, sir," Tate reported. "There are only two other fighters assigned there; neither are ready to fly."

"Status of the Patriot batteries? Any of them operational?"

"The Patriot site at Dulles was destroyed by commandos," the Senior Director responded. "The site at Fort Belvoir is not damaged, but it was decommissioned this morning and was ready to road-march in the morning. It won't be able to respond."

Milford checked the radar display with an almost feverish feeling of helplessness and dread. He had nothing to respond with, *nothing.* A single F-15C fighter carrying one Sparrow radar-guided missile had launched only moments ago from Langley Air Force Base, near Hampton, Virginia, but even at fuel-sucking afterburner power it would take about ten minutes to fly within missile range of the fake Executive-One. Two fighters had launched from Atlantic City, but they would not be in range for almost fifteen minutes.

Not only that, but now they had a new concern. That VFR slow-moving plane from Maryland was right on the outskirts of Andrews Air Force Base's Class B airspace, about sixteen miles southeast of the capital. It had not announced itself on any emergency frequency, was not squawking any transponder codes, and it had not deviated from course one bit to try to avoid any restricted airspace. It was dead on course—for the capital. It had been marked now as "Bandit-2," but like the fake Executive-One, they had no way of stopping it.

"Comm, MC, get me the White House, Capitol, and Pentagon communications centers, Flash priority alert," Milford said. "If you need to get their damned attention, tell them the capital is under attack."

"MC, Comm, National Command Authority Joint Emergency Communications Network, call sign 'Palisade,' button four," the communications officer said just seconds later. "No problem at all convincing them something's going on."

"Go ahead, Leather-90, this is Palisade."

"Palisade, this is Milford, Mission Force Commander Leather northeast sector, we have an unidentified aircraft inbound, about four minutes north . . . make that three minutes north of the capital." Milford found himself hyperventilating, and he consciously slowed his breathing and got his voice back under control. "I have declared an air defense emergency for the Washington and Baltimore Class B airspace. Be advised, all of my air defense systems have come under simultaneous terrorist attack in the past few minutes, and I have no aircraft or ground-based systems left to respond. I recommend the Leadership be notified and they evacuate to underground shelters. I am also tracking a slow-moving target sixteen miles southeast of the capital at fifteen hundred feet, groundspeed one hundred knots, ETA to the capital about twelve minutes. We have not been able to contact either aircraft; they are hostile, repeat, hostile aircraft. How copy?''

''Leather, I copy all, stand by.''

The response was almost instantaneous: ''MC, SD, Marine Two and two other helicopters airborne from Anacostia,'' Tate reported. ''Three aircraft launching from Quantico.'' The Anacostia Naval Station, just a few miles south of the capital, is a satellite base for HMX-1, the Marine Corps unit that flies VIP-configured helicopters from Quantico Marine Corps Air Facility, including Marine One and Marine Two, which carry the President and Vice President, to reduce their response time to the capital. Obviously, the senior director at the National Command Authority Joint Emergency Network command post was trained not to take any warning or threat lightly. The helicopters would touch down on the south lawn of the White House to take the President or Vice President; other helicopters would land on the east side of the Capitol to take any members of Congress or any justices of the Supreme Court to safety, if it was necessary. Others would land near the FBI Building, Justice Department, State Department, and the Pentagon, all to ensure that the most senior members of government, if they were still in the capital, would be safe.

''Give those choppers full priority, SD,'' Milford said as he studied the sudden flurry of aircraft over the capital and the surrounding area. ''Get their tactical frequency from 'Palisade,' or use GUARD to vector them around Bandit-1 when they're ready to—''

Then he stopped, and his jaw dropped open in surprise.

Washington Approach and National Tower was clearing out the airspace around the city—inbound air traffic was stacking up as high as forty thousand feet in orbit areas all around the Class B airspace—and Milford was mentally dismissing the outbound flights . . . all but one . . . ''My God . . . Jesus, Maureen—Devil-03. He's an F-16, isn't he?''

''Devil . . .'' The senior director had completely dismissed the flight from her mental catalog of aircraft around D.C. after the mission commander kicked him out of the airspace, but now it was coming back . . . She punched up his call sign and expanded her scope until she saw the blinking datablock: ''God . . . Weapons One, you still got Devil-03? He's three miles west of Nottingham.''

"I got him," the weapons controller said.

"Take Devil-03 on—no, disregard, take him on GUARD channel, don't bother with a discrete channel. Maybe whoever is flying Bandit-1 will hear what's going on and get the hint."

"I got him, I got him," First Lieutenant Ed Flynn, flying the Weapons One control station, repeated excitedly. He switched his radio to 121.5, the GUARD international emergency channel, and radioed, "Devil-03, this is Leather Control on GUARD, how do you read?" To himself, Flynn and everyone else on that AWACS radar plane were praying that the pilot of Devil-03 would respond . . .

. . . and Vincenti was praying that someone would call him, because air traffic control or anyone at Andrews Air Force Base command post was not taking his radio calls. He had been trying frantically to contact someone, *anyone,* and offer his assistance ever since he heard the air defense emergency declared. "Leather Control, this is Devil-03 on GUARD, I read you loud and clear, how me?"

"Devil, I need you to turn left to a heading of two-niner-five and descend and maintain three thousand feet, right *now,* acknowledge."

Vincenti had racked his F-16 ADF into a tight, seven-G turn and was on the new heading in three seconds. He began feeding in throttle until he was at full military power. "I'm on your heading, Leather," Vincenti reported. "Is this a vector to the bandit?"

"That's affirmative," the controller replied, trying to keep his breathing and voice as normal as he possibly could. "Your bandit is one o'clock, forty miles low. I need your best speed to the intercept, Devil, what can you give me?"

Checking his fuel gauge, Vincenti made a quick mental calculation, then turned the throttle past the detent and clicked in zone 3 afterburner. The airspeed gauge slowly eased upward, the Mach meter hovering very close to 1.0, the speed of sound. "That's it, Leather," Vincenti said. "Are we going over to tactical frequency?"

"Negative, Devil," another, slightly older voice cut in. "No time for that now—besides, I want our bandit to hear all this. Devil, we believe your target is a Boeing 747. It may be painted to resemble a VC-25 or some other VIP aircraft, but it is not, I repeat, it is *not* a VC-25. This has been verified by numerous independent sources. It is not carrying any VIPs or any government officials—it is believed to be carrying hostiles. We are tracking a second aircraft south of the capital, slow-moving, tracking toward the capital. Whoever they are, they have not responded to our radio calls to turn away from Class B airspace. Both aircraft are definitely hostile. I want you to keep both aircraft away from the entire area, but especially Prohibited Areas P-56, Washington-National and Dulles airports. Your priority is Bandit-1 west to the north; we have other interceptors inbound that might be able to catch the guy to the south. Take Bandit-1 west or north if you can do a visual intercept on them; take Bandit-2 south. Are you familiar with the prohibited areas, Devil?''

''Affirmative,'' Vincenti responded. P-56A and -B was prohibited airspace over The Mall and the U.S. Naval Observatory.

Vincenti checked his weapons status, which was a joke. He carried no weapons or ammunition, just videotape for the gun camera. *At least I'll get some great pictures of the chase,* Vincenti thought wryly. *Of course, maybe the bandit is really radio-out, or maybe a passenger is flying the thing and can't answer, or maybe he'll turn away when he sees me or he'll give it all up and follow me out of the area.*

Just then, a large yellow MASTER CAUTION light illuminated on Vincenti's eyebrow panel, and he heard a female voice on interphone saying, ''BINGO . . . BINGO . . . BINGO.'' It was a reminder that he had enough fuel to get back to Atlantic City. *Plenty of airfields out here,* he thought. *No way I'm turning back.* But it was a bad sign. At afterburner power, he was burning fuel at fifty thousand pounds per hour—he was going to be running on fumes very soon.

''Devil, your bandit is one o'clock, thirty miles low.''

There were lots of radar targets out there—dozens of planes were stacked up over Washington-National and Dulles—but only one at that azimuth and range. Vincenti locked the radar blip up, using the F-16 ADF's IFF interrogator to see if the target was transmitting any air traffic control codes or signals—nothing. *This had better not be another fucking hot dog TV show crew,* Vincenti said to himself. ''Devil-03, judy,'' he reported to the AWACS controller.

The fire control computer put the bandit at two thousand feet, just a few hundred feet above ground. His groundspeed was 360 knots and his closure speed was 250 knots. He was going to intercept the bandit only about ten miles north of the capital, so he nudged the throttle to zone 5 afterburner. The airspeed indicator went over 1.0. There was no sudden sound as he broke the speed of sound, no jolt, no vibration, nothing except the ground was going by real damned fast. ''One o'clock, twenty-eight miles.''

''That's your bandit, Devil,'' the controller said.

"Control, Devil, say my engagement instructions again for this target," Vincenti radioed. He thought he'd try a little gamesmanship here—hopefully the crew of that plane would get spooked and turn around. "Your last instructions to me were to keep this bandit clear of P-56 and Washington-National Airport. No matter what I hear on the radio, even if they claim to be an authorized TV crew on assignment, am I clear to engage at will? Over."

"That voice sounds familiar," another voice came on the frequency. "Do we know each other, Devil? Have we met?"

The voice sent chills down Vincenti's spine. *It's him,* he thought. *Shit—it's Cazaux.* It was the same voice he heard over Sacramento before Linda was killed. *It's Cazaux. He's on board that fake Executive-One-Foxtrot.* Vincenti keyed the mike button: "Cazaux, this is Lieutenant Colonel—this is Al Vincenti, the partner of the pilot you killed over Sacramento. Remember me?"

"Who can ever doubt the existence of the Fates now, I ask you?" Cazaux asked with laughter in his voice. "There are indeed mysterious forces at work, Colonel Vincenti, that have put us back together once again. But aren't you the one that is supposed to be keeping the skies safe from men like myself, dear Colonel?"

Vincenti was going to reply, but the MASTER CAUTION light snapped on again, and he saw a FUEL indication in his heads-up display. This time the caution light said AFT FUEL LOW, meaning that the fuel quantity in the aft reservoir tank had dropped below four hundred pounds. It would run dry in just a few moments if he stayed in afterburner power. When the FWD FUEL LOW light came on, he had about two minutes of fuel remaining before they flamed out—perhaps only about twenty or thirty seconds in afterburner power. A normal landing would be impossible if he stayed in afterburner power. He ignored it and keyed the mike: "I'm not going to warn you again, Cazaux. You will turn westbound, lower your landing gear, and head west or north, right *now,* or I'll blow you out of the fucking sky. This time I won't hesitate. I've got plenty of reasons to flame your ass, Cazaux. Do it, or you die. That's my final warning."

The answer was immediate: "Very well," Cazaux said simply, and, to Vincenti's surprise, the 747 banked right and turned toward the west. "Now you have promised you won't fire on me." Cazaux snickered. "I have your word, don't I, Colonel? We are on an open frequency—there are probably thousands of people listening to us. You promised not to harm me if I turned away."

"I promised," Vincenti said. He immediately chopped the throttle back to 90-percent power to try to conserve every pound of fuel possible. "But if you try to evade me or don't follow my instructions, I won't hesitate to open fire."

"I assume your Leather Control has heard our conversation as well?" Cazaux asked.

"We're listening, Cazaux," the controller replied. "You're within range of a Hawk missile site right now. I suggest you keep going westbound."

"Very well," Cazaux radioed back, chuckling. "I will take my chances with your federal court system. I understand your federal courts have no death penalty, correct? Life in one of your fine American prisons will suit me just fine."

A few moments later, as Cazaux's plane was about to fly over the Potomac just south of Rockville, Maryland, Vincenti banked left and joined on the tail of the massive 747. Sure enough, the plane had been painted to look like Air Force One, except the paint was peeling off in several locations and the lettering was not perfect, although very believable. From a distance, it definitely looked like Air Force One.

"Devil, Control, I show the bandit headed westbound, targets have merged. Do you have him in sight?"

Before Vincenti realized he was talking on an open frequency, he replied, "Affirmative, Control, I'm joined on the bandit. His landing gear is down. The aircraft is a 747, resembling a VC-25. It—" Just then the 747 started a steep left turn, the landing gear retracted, and the airliner began to accelerate rapidly. "Cazaux, stop your turn. Head westbound *now.*"

"Too bad, Colonel Vincenti," Cazaux said firmly. "Too bad you were given a plane with no weapons. You could have been a hero today."

"I'm warning you, Cazaux, turn back or I'll fire."

"You have not been truthful with me, Colonel." Cazaux snickered again. "I am the man who killed your Linda McKenzie, the man who terrorized the world's supposedly greatest nation, the one who destroyed your fighters and rendered your entire air defense system useless and inadequate. I am your nemesis, Colonel Vincenti. If you had weapons, Colonel, you would have not hesitated to attack. You have obviously closed inside both missile and gun range, and we are over open territory, with little danger to innocents on the ground—

you would have fired on me if you had the ability. You do not. Nor do I expect any of the Hawk missiles sites you lied about to engage. My men have taken care of all of them very effectively.''

The 747 rolled out, now heading eastbound, and Cazaux added, ''And look, Colonel—with typical government efficiency, your National Park Service still has not turned out the lights in your capital. We are perhaps twelve miles away, and I can see your Capitol Building very clearly. It is so simple—line up on the Iwo Jima Memorial and the Washington Monument. How convenient of you to provide me with such beautiful landmarks. I was hoping to hit the White House, but I'm afraid I won't see it in time. But I can see the Capitol Building very clearly, up on that hill by itself lit up so brightly, so that shall be my target. Good night, Colonel. You did everything you could. Your government certainly cannot fault you.''

Vincenti swore loudly in his oxygen mask and pushed the throttle back up to military power, banking hard to cut off the turn and stay close on the 747. But as soon as he moved the throttles to the mil power detent, the MASTER CAUTION light came on for the third time, this time with the FWD FUEL LOW caution light on. At military power, burning ten thousand pounds of fuel per hour, Vincenti had less than sixty seconds of fuel left . . .

He knew what had to be done—it was the only option left to him now.

Near The Mall
That Same Time

The radio in Harley's car was already a jumble of confusion. She had automatically pulled out of the FBI parking garage onto E Street, heading west toward the Treasury Department, but after pulling onto Pennsylvania Avenue, passing the Hotel Washington, she heard another radio report of terrorists sighted near the Washington Monument, and she turned south onto Fifteenth Street and roared off in that direction, her little emergency light flashing away atop the dashboard.

''Why wouldn't they let us get our sidearms back?'' Hardcastle asked in between radio reports.

''Because the FBI is filled with paranoids,'' Harley said, ''or else they were told not to release them—that might be Judge Wilkes's idea of throwing her authority around. Doesn't matter—we don't need the popguns anyway. There's a reason I wanted to take my car." Hardcastle had never considered his trusty Colt .45 automatic a "popgun," and he hoped Deborah had something better in mind.

They raced down Fifteenth Street, across Constitution Avenue, and found a plain sedan stopped on the east walkway, about two hundred yards from the Washington Monument. A chunky, gray-haired black plainclothes or off-duty D.C. Police officer with an "ass-duty spread" was standing behind his sedan, pointing a .38 revolver toward the monument and trying to raise someone on his hopelessly jammed police radio. Harley skidded to a stop, popped open her trunk, and jumped out of the car, holding her gold Secret Service badge up for him to see. "Secret Service. What do you got, officer?"

"Automatic gunfire from two perps near the monument, hit a D.C. cruiser over there," he said, pointing to a stopped D.C. Police cruiser just barely visible on the other side of the Washington Monument. He was a good three hundred yards away—obviously the cop had no intention of getting any closer with just a .38. Smart thinking. "Just blew up an Army missile jeep with a damned bazooka."

Harley met Hardcastle at the trunk of the car—he was wisely reaching for the heavy, dark-blue bulletproof vests he found. "You always carry two vests in your trunk?" Hardcastle asked.

"Sometimes I *wear* two vests, Ian," Harley said. "I'm not proud, believe me." She flipped down a flap on the front and back of the vests, revealing the words TREASURY AGENT. She then lifted the floor carpeting, unlocked a padlock, lifted a large metal door covering her spare tire well, and lifted out two short, futuristic-looking bullpup rifles with green plastic stocks that seemed to comprise the entire body of the gun itself. "Steyr AUGs. Familiar with them?"

"Used them all the time in the Coast Guard and the Hammerheads," Hardcastle said. He shoved two 30-round magazines into his pants pockets, slammed one magazine home, charged the weapon, and set it on SAFE. They hopped back into the car and drove off toward the Washington Monument.

Over Arlington, Virginia
That Same Time

The 747 was over Arlington now, skimming over the trees and buildings. It looked as if it were going to hit the apartment buildings north of the Iwo Jima Memorial, but Vincenti knew they were not Cazaux's target. The 747 now filled the windscreen. They were almost at the memorial, yet he couldn't see anything but the reflection of the lights of Arlington and Washington off the mottled white paint of the 747.

"What are you doing, Colonel?" Cazaux radioed. "Are you enjoying the view? I am."

"The view I'm enjoying is the one with you crashing into the ground and dying once and for all."

"I don't think so, Colonel," Cazaux radioed back. "Unfortunately for you, I am not on board the 747. But thank you for thinking of me."

Vincenti's color drained. *Cazaux isn't on the 747?* He hissed, "Cazaux, you're a dead man, you don't know it yet, but you're *dead.*"

"While you waste your breath on threats, flyboy, I shall stroll down The Mall, watch my 747 crash into the Capitol Building, and then see what other havoc I can raise in the ensuing panic," Cazaux said. "Perhaps I'll take my remaining soldiers and visit the White House. *Ciao,* Colonel."

"Fuck you, Cazaux!" Vincenti raged on the radio. He shoved his throttle to full afterburner power to try to catch up with the 747—but as he did, the WARN symbol appeared in the heads-up display almost immediately afterward, and a large red ENGINE warning light illuminated on the eyebrow panel. He was out of fuel and the F-16's engine had flamed out.

Near the Washington Monument
That Same Time

Just then, a man appeared from behind the Washington Monument, about a hundred yards away—they could see his outline against the floodlight surrounding the monument. Harley immediately slid her car right, with the left side of the car facing the man, when suddenly a burst of machine-gun fire sent a swarm of bullets in their direction.

Hardcastle had swung open his door as soon as he saw the man, and he threw himself out of the car even before Harley completely stopped it. He felt a hand on his leg as he was leaping out, and he thought Deborah was right behind him. Hardcastle took cover behind the right front wheel, leveled the Steyr, flicked the safety to the upper five-dot full-auto position, and fired a full one-second burst in the terrorist's general direction. "Deborah!" he yelled behind him.

He could no longer see the terrorist—either he was on the run or was on the ground. "Deborah, you all right?"

"Shit, no!" Harley yelled. Hardcastle leaned his Steyr against the car beside him where he could get to it easily and crawled around to the passenger-side door. Deborah Harley was lying on the car seat, the left side of her face and left arm bloody. Her left arm looked like it was hit just below the bulletproof vest, but it appeared to be only flying glass that caused the facial injuries. "When you're getting out, Admiral," Harley said in a remarkably clear voice, still with a trace of humor despite her injuries, "don't waste time. I'll have to crawl over you next time."

"You do that," Hardcastle said. "You got a first aid kit anywhere in—"

"Forget about me. I'm all right," Harley said. "Where's that gunman who fired?"

Hardcastle heard sounds of running. He reached for his rifle—only to face a tall, fearsome-looking warrior dressed in black, wearing a balaclava facemask, a web harness filled with grenades and weapons, standing less than fifteen feet away. The man was carrying a small submachine gun with a long suppressor. The warrior raised his SMG, aimed . . .

. . . then stopped, lowered it, and said in a definite French accent, "Admiral Hardcastle, I presume?" Hardcastle made a move for his rifle, but the gunman fired a short burst into the ground beside him. Hardcastle heard only faint cracks when the gun fired, but he could feel the impact of the bullets along the ground. The gunman then ran over, grabbed the Steyr, tossed it aside, then stood over Hardcastle, just a few feet away. He was tall and powerful-looking, with an athletic body that could not be hidden even by all the combat hardware on his combat harness.

"This officer is hurt," Hardcastle tried. "Who the hell are you?"

The gunman pulled off his balaclava hood, revealing a narrow face and close-cropped hair. "I am your old friend Henri, Admiral . . . Henri Cazaux."

Hardcastle's face registered shock, then pure white-hot anger. He tried to jump to his feet and tackle Cazaux. The terrorist merely kicked Hardcastle aside with a sharp snapping kick to the head, accomplishing the move quite easily.

"This is perfect, Admiral, just perfect," Cazaux said. He peered into the car door, checking Harley and taking away her rifle. He quickly checked the glove compartment, removing a .380 automatic backup pistol. "She looks beautiful even with her wounds," Cazaux said. He turned back to Hardcastle and said, "First I encounter my old friend and your colleague Colonel Vincenti, and now you."

"Vincenti?"

"He is out there," Cazaux said, waving toward the Lincoln Memorial and the Iwo Jima Memorial to the west, "trying to stop my 747 from crashing into the Capitol. He—"

"What?"

"Oh, yes, Admiral," Cazaux crooned. "You and the young lady have wonderful seats for my final spectacle. You will witness the destruction of the Capitol as my 747 crashes into it, and then witness the destruction of the White House when my fuel-air explosives destroy it. Of course, I think we might be a bit too close to the explosion at the White House—they assure me everything within a half-mile will be damaged or destroyed by the explosion. If the Fates let you live, then you probably deserve it. Unfortunately, I won't have the opportunity to see any of this—it is a poor soldier who stops to admire the destruction he causes. *Au revoir,* Admiral. I hope to—"

"*Freeze!* FBI!" a voice behind them shouted. "Drop your weapon!" Cazaux let the submachine gun clatter to the ground. "Now raise your—"

Cazaux didn't hesitate—he ducked down behind the car, drew a sidearm, and dragged Hardcastle to his feet, holding the pistol to his head. It was Judge Lani Wilkes, drawing down on Cazaux from about twenty yards away. "Drop the gun, *now!*" she shouted.

"My luck is running true to form tonight," Cazaux cackled. "It is none other than the beautiful FBI Director, Lani Wilkes! I think you should drop *your* gun, Madame Director, or I'll blow the Admiral's brains out right now. Don't you move in that car either, Treasury agent!" he shouted as he noticed movement inside the car.

"Bad move, Henri," Hardcastle said, his voice weakened by the steel-like arm across his throat. "The lady would probably give you a citation if you pulled the trigger. Judge, meet Henri Cazaux. Henri, FBI Director Wilkes." He could see Wilkes' stunned expression even in the semidarkness of the lights surrounding the Washington Monument.

"My extreme pleasure, madame," Cazaux said gallantly. "Admiral, it was convenient of you to wear a bulletproof vest tonight. Madame Director, I'll make you a sporting proposition. If you don't lower your weapon, I'll kill the Admiral and I'll still escape. Toss your weapons away, give me a head start, and the chase starts anew, on equal terms. Agreed?''

''It's not going to happen, Cazaux,'' Wilkes said, her voice faltering from the strain, confusion, and outright surprise. ''No one is going to give up their weapons.''

''Ah, your voice says otherwise, Madame Director,'' Cazaux said. ''You have faith in your agents, I assume. Surely they can capture me in the nation's capital? Now drop your gun. This is my final warning.''

To Hardcastle's surprise, Wilkes let her service revolver roll on her trigger finger, barrel pointing upward. ''Wilkes, don't do it.'' Hardcastle groaned. ''He'll kill me anyway.''

''Freeze! D.C. Police!'' they heard.

The plainclothes D.C. Police officer had chugged his way over to the monument, drawing down on Cazaux. Cazaux instinctively raised his pistol toward him . . . and Hardcastle reached up and grabbed his right wrist, shoving it upward. The officer fired, but he was too far away and missed. Cazaux shrugged out of Hardcastle's grasp with ease and fired three shots at the officer, two rounds hitting him in the chest. Wilkes dropped to one knee, swinging her service revolver back up.

Cazaux aimed . . .

. . . and they fired simultaneously.

Three .45 caliber rounds hit Wilkes, one in the shoulder and two in the chest; two .38 caliber rounds hit Cazaux in the stomach and left shoulder. Wilkes collapsed onto her back and was still. Cazaux stood there, a hand over the stomach wound, but he was still standing. He swung his pistol down at Hardcastle, but suddenly his knees gave way and he went down on one knee. Realizing he was really hurt, Cazaux stood up shakily, ignoring Hardcastle, and started running south toward the Sylvan Theater and the Tidal Basin. He started to pick up amazing speed. Before Hardcastle could react and reach for one of the Steyr rifles, Cazaux had almost reached Independence Avenue and was lost in the darkness.

Hardcastle's first thought was to go after Cazaux, but not with three wounded officers around him. The D.C. Police officer was dead. Lani Wilkes was alive but hurt very badly. ''I was on the way to the White House . . . heard the radio call . . . where . . . where's Cazaux?'' she gasped.

''He got away,'' Hardcastle said. He tried to stuff a handkerchief into one of the wounds and tried to compress the other with his bare hand—the bleeding was serious.

"Don't . . . don't let him get away, Hardcastle, damn you . . ."

"Lie still, Judge. Help is on the way," Hardcastle lied.

"Violence . . . this violence is sickening," Wilkes gasped. "When will it end? When will it . . . ever . . . end . . . ?" And her voice trailed off into a whisper, then nothing.

"Shit!" Hardcastle swore aloud. "You bastard!" He turned to retrieve his Steyr bullpup rifle, and found Harley on her feet, headed toward him. "Deborah, stay down."

"Is she dead?"

"She's hurt badly. The cop is dead," Hardcastle said. "I'm going after Cazaux. Stay here and see if you can help Wilkes."

"No way. Where did he go? I'll call it in."

"Call it in, but you're—" He turned and looked toward the Lincoln Memorial as the loud scream of an airliner got closer and closer. "Oh, my God, there it is!" Hardcastle shouted, pointing toward the Iwo Jima Memorial. "It's headed this . . . Jesus, Deborah, *get down, get down!*" Harley ran over, grabbed Wilkes by the arms, and dragged her behind the Washington Monument to safety . . .

. . . just as all hell broke loose.

Near the Iwo Jima Memorial
That Same Moment

Just as the 747 was north of the Iwo Jima Memorial and over the interstate, Vincenti closed his eyes and flew his F-16 Fighting Falcon into the right rear portion of the fuselage, between the wing trailing edge and the forward edge of the horizontal stabilizer.

The impact sliced off most of the 747's rear empennage, and it nosed over, then tumbled, the crushed F-16 adding its own remaining jet fuel vapors to the tremendous explosion over the Theodore Roosevelt Bridge. The airliner impacted just east of the Rock Creek Parkway, on the interchange west of the Navy Bureau of Medicine and Surgery complex, tumbling end-over-end in a tremendous flaming fireball two hundred feet high. The bulk of the burning wreckage missed the Lincoln Memorial by less than four hundred yards, spraying burning metal, fire, and destruction across the Reflecting Pool, across the Kutz Bridge, and the Bureau of Engraving and Printing Building on the east side of the Tidal Basin, destroying everything in its path.

With a terrific mushroom-shaped cloud of fire, the Francis Case Bridge exploded when it was hit by the wreckage, but it stopped the careening hulk from tumbling any farther. Flying debris and burning fuel spread out in a half-mile-wide, two-mile-long fan, spraying buildings from the Smithsonian Institution and the Energy Department all the way to South Capitol Street with an incredible firestorm. In less than two seconds, almost two square miles of the District of Columbia was on fire.

Near the Washington Monument
That Same Moment

Hiding behind the square stone face of the Washington Monument, their breathing rapid and shallow, hands and legs shaking, eyes staring in terror, Hardcastle and Harley tried to close their eyes, then found they couldn't bear to *not* watch, and they waited for the fires to engulf them.

The crash was utterly devastating.

Hardcastle caught a glimpse of the huge white 747 just to the right of the Iwo Jima Memorial. It appeared to be landing except that it was moving at an incredible speed, the engines shrieking louder than at takeoff, the landing gear up. And, of course, there was no runway in front of it, only the three-mile-long Constitution Gardens and The Mall.

But then Hardcastle saw a blur, a streak of light to the 747's left, then a brief puff of fire, and suddenly the huge airliner simply dropped out of the sky right before him, like a huge pelican diving for a fish in the Potomac. The cloud of fire and debris obscured all view in that direction, and that's when Hardcastle dove for cover, holding Harley close to him as if to shield her from the awful concussion that he knew he had no power to stop. The terrible sound of wrenching steel and Capitol-sized flames hissing in the humid night air moved across and seemingly over them at tremendous speed. Hardcastle always remembered the slow-motion TV shots of plane crashes, but of course they always slowed the images down so you could somehow savor or try to analyze the crash, and the airliner had to be moving well over three or four hundred miles an hour when it hit the ground. The earth rumbled with the force of a hundred earthquakes; the lights around the Washington Monument exploded as if being shot out by machine-gun fire. The air felt hot and electrified, as if they were standing in front of a steel smelter, and a sudden windstorm sucked the air out of their lungs as a huge mushroom-shaped blob of air was consumed in the fire.

But they didn't die.

Hardcastle stayed put for what seemed like a long time, and finally looked up when he heard a large piece of debris fall close by. His and Harley's bodies were, surprisingly, still whole. He crawled around the north side of the monument and peeked westward.

It was raining burning debris and slippery moisture that Hardcastle knew was jet fuel, not rain. The stricken 747 had somehow careened around to the south, between the Lincoln and Washington monuments, across the middle of the Reflecting Pool, coming to rest in a massive flaming pile beyond the Tidal Basin. The sky was glowing far to the southeast with several fires, but Hardcastle did not see the massive Dresden-like firestorm he was expecting. By just a few hundred feet, the 747 had miraculously missed most of the important government buildings and monuments.

"It's over," Hardcastle said to Harley, who had gotten to her feet and followed him around the Washington Monument to inspect the destruction. "I think Vincenti rammed it. I thought I saw either a missile or an F-16 itself hit the 747 just before it cleared the Potomac."

"My head is still ringing," Harley said. "I've never heard or felt anything like that before in my life." She walked around the monument, her eyes tracing the destructive path of the stricken 747. "Didn't I see Cazaux running in that direction?"

"Yep," Hardcastle said proudly. "He was all the way down to Independence Avenue. He ran right into the path of that 747. Man, I hope he got fried. What a great way for him to go—cooked by his own weapon."

"That would be the perfect definition of justice," Harley said. She trotted over to her car, retrieved a first-aid kit from her well-equipped trunk, and began dressing Wilkes' wounds. The FBI Director was not conscious, but most of the bleeding had slowed to a manageable level. "I just wish he had gotten it sooner." She looked back to the west and spotted the Avenger air defense vehicle, sitting on what looked like the scorched edge of the fireball across the Constitutional Gardens. "What's that? Is that one of the Army air defense things?"

"It's an Avenger Forward Area Air Defense System," Hardcastle said. "Must've been one of Cazaux's targets. He had to take out the ground air defense units to make his air attacks work."

"We better go see if anyone's in there."

"I'll go—the fire might have destabilized the missiles on board," Hardcastle said. "They might have a radio on board."

"You better call the Bureau and tell them Wilkes is hurt badly."

"She got a piece of Cazaux before she got it," Hardcastle said. "She was going to play by the rules, even with the Devil himself standing right in front of her." He shook his head as he trotted toward the Avenger. "Lani Wilkes saved my life. How am I ever going to live that down?"

Aboard the E-3C AWACS Radar Plane Leather-90

Milford saw the fast-moving low-flying radar targets, the F-16 and the fake Executive-One-Foxtrot, get closer and closer, saw the targets merge . . . and then both disappeared, right over the Potomac, just west of the capital. "Oh, Jesus . . ."

"Lost contact with Bandit-1 and Devil-03," the Senior Director, Maureen Tate, reported. The entire AWACS crew was silent, everyone realizing what had just happened—a terrorist 747 had just hit Washington, D.C.

"Bandit . . . Bandit-2 now twelve miles southeast of the capital," Maureen Tate stammered, trying to force her brain back to the task at hand. "Groundspeed ninety-three knots, in a slow descent. ETA to the capital area, nine minutes."

"SD, Weapons-3, I need to bingo Lima-Golf-31," the weapons controller reported. Lima-Golf-31 was the F-15 out of Langley that had tried to chase down the 747. "He has less gas than he thought. He won't make it to the capital." The F-15 had been in full afterburner power ever since takeoff, and he probably didn't start with a full load of fuel anyway. "Andrews is closed, and National is a zoo right now, with planes stacked up all over the place—I recommend Navy–Patuxent River." Tate turned to Milford, who nodded his agreement. That was their last chance of stopping the new bandit. All they could do right now was wait for it to hit . . .

. . . no, *no,* there *had* to be something still out there. He once had several dozen air defense units operational in the D.C. area—it was inconceivable that Cazaux or any army of terrorists could have gotten them all in just a matter of minutes.

Just one shot was all they needed to stop this last threat . . .

"Comm, MC, sweep all the tactical channels and try to raise any of the Leather air defense units," Milford ordered. "Someone out there must still be operational. If possible, try to get some of the Avenger units from the Pentagon, Dulles, or National over to the capital area to try to stop Bandit-2."

"Any Leather unit, any Leather unit, this is Leather-90 Control," the communications technician radioed. "If you hear me, come up on any tactical frequency or on VHF 105.0. Repeat, if you hear me, come up on any tactical frequency. Over."

Near the Washington Monument
That Same Time

The entire front of the top turret of the Avenger was crushed inwards and blackened, obviously by a hit from a small but powerful antitank weapon. The front of the HMMWV itself was still smoking from the fire in the engine compartment, and the turret looked cockeyed, as if shoved off its moorings. Hardcastle used a fire extinguisher he found on the rear deck of the Avenger to put out the last bit of fire in the front so he could reach the driver and gunner. Both were dead. He found the third man in the Avenger crew nearby, shot to death by machine-gun fire. Cazaux was nothing if not a very efficient killer, Hardcastle thought. "Dear God," Hardcastle said half-aloud, "you may not want it, but I'd give all of my remaining years for an assurance from you that Cazaux is really—"

Hardcastle started on the grisly task of removing the bodies from the Avenger. As he removed the driver's helmet, he heard through the headphones, "Any Leather unit, any Leather unit, this is Leather-90 Control. If you hear me, come up on any tactical frequency or on VHF 105.0. Repeat, if you hear me, come up on any tactical frequency. Over." Somebody was still calling, trying to see if anyone was still alive. Hardcastle tried to remember who "Leather" was, but it really didn't matter. This Avenger unit was definitely dead. It wasn't going anywhere, and the turret and sensors were cooked.

"Unknown rider, unknown rider," another radio in the

Avenger blurted, "unidentified aircraft on the Washington National one-two-five degree radial, two miles, this is Leather Control on GUARD, turn south immediately or you may be fired upon without warning. You are in Washington National Class B airspace and are approaching prohibited airspace. Turn south immediately and squawk 7700. Attention all aircraft, stay outside Andrews or Washington National ten DME, air defense emergency in progress. I say again, unknown rider . . ."

Holy shit! Hardcastle gasped.

Cazaux's second terrorist aircraft!

He had almost forgotten—Cazaux said he had a *second* aircraft inbound to bomb the White House with a fuel-air explosive.

That "unknown rider" was it—and it was only a few miles away.

He donned the Avenger driver's thick bulletproof Kevlar helmet, moved the microphone toward his lips, and keyed the transmit button: "Leather Control, this is . . . ah, this is Admiral Ian Hardcastle, on board an Avenger unit on the Mall. How do you read this transmitter?"

"Calling Leather Control, say again."

"Leather Control, this is Admiral Hardcastle on board one of the Army Avenger units on The Mall. Can you read me?"

"Person calling Leather Control, this is an aviation emergency channel only, if you require medical or police response, change to VHF 121.5 or UHF 243.0, over."

"Listen to me. Henri Cazaux is flying some kind of aircraft toward Washington, D.C., and it's loaded with explosives. I'm on the ground near one of your Avengers. Your crew here is dead. I need to know how much time I have and if there's anything I can do to help avert disaster. Over."

"Listen, sir, if you are at The Mall, stay away from any military units you might encounter. The authorities will be arresting or shooting any looters. I advise you to get away from the area as quickly as possible. If you are injured or your home has been damaged, you should contact the proper authorities imme—"

The controller's voice suddenly cut off, then another voice came on the channel: "Is this Admiral Hardcastle, the White House air defense adviser?"

"Affirmative. I'm—" Suddenly Hardcastle remembered back from his unit and situation briefings who "Leather" was: "Is this the senior director of the AWACS orbiting over eastern Pennsylvania?"

"This is Major Milford, the force mission commander," Milford replied from Leather-90. "Admiral, we're tracking an unidentified aircraft about nine miles south of you, about three hundred feet aboveground, groundspeed about eighty-seven knots, heading right toward the capital. What's your situation there? Over."

"A 747 crashed just west of the Constitution Gardens section of the capital, and it destroyed or damaged everything from the Lincoln Memorial to the Capital Yacht Club," Hardcastle said. "We found an Avenger unit that was hit by an antitank weapon just west of the Washington Monument. The crew is dead, and the front of the vehicle and the turret and gunner's cockpit are badly damaged. That plane you're tracking belongs to Henri Cazaux. He says he's got a fuel-air explosive weapon on it and that he's going to bomb the White House. Is there any way to reactivate this unit, maybe by remote control? Over."

"Affirmative," Milford said, stunned by what he had just heard. "There should be a remote-control computer unit up with the driver. You should find a spool of fiber-optic cable about fifty yards long. You should be able to operate the unit with that."

The computer was in a strong plastic case on the right side of the HMMWV, plugged into a mounting unit under the dashboard, with a round reel beside it. The case unclipped easily from its mounting; the fiber-optic cable was thin but strong. "I found it," Hardcastle said. "Stand by."

The remote control unit was a laptop computer with a flip-up two-color LCD screen, a sealed plastic-covered keyboard, and a finger-sized joystick built into the base below the keyboard. To Hardcastle's surprise, it was working. A simple menu selection displayed on the screen, and by touching a few buttons he got a radar depiction of the skies around the city. After a few moments, Hardcastle could understand the symbols on the scope—the unknown aircraft, labeled "^" on the screen, was only ten miles to the south. "The remote control is working, and I've got a depiction of the area here."

"Good," Milford said. "That means the telemetry between the AWACS and the unit there is functioning. Do you see the up-caret symbol at the bottom of the screen? Zoom the picture in or out to see it."

"I see it."

"Just move the cursor with the joystick onto the caret symbol at the bottom of the screen and press the button below the trackball." Hardcastle did, and a diamond symbol surrounded the symbol. "What happened?"

"I got a diamond around the caret."

"Good. You should see a menu on the bottom of the screen, with a button or function key that says something like ENGAGE or ATTACK. Do you see it?"

"Yes. It's a covered switch that says ENGAGE."

"Good. Get out of the unit, clear yourself and everyone else away by at least fifty feet, and press the button. The turret should turn and the missile launchers should start tracking the target. You can plug your headset into the side of the remote-control device. The missiles will launch when it gets within range. Go ahead."

Hardcastle plugged the driver's Kevlar helmet communications cord into the computer, got out of the vehicle, unreeled the fiber-optic data cable at least fifty feet, and knelt. Harley was well behind him, tending to Wilkes. He made sure the diamond designate symbol was still on the hostile "^" symbol, then hit the ENGAGE button. It turned yellow, then began to blink. The turret, which was pointed west, did not move. "The turret didn't move, and the ENGAGE button is blinking yellow," Hardcastle radioed back.

"I'm not sure what that means," Milford said. "Deselect the ENGAGE button, then go to the unit and see if the turret is jammed and that it can turn freely." Hardcastle did it, then ran to the Avenger unit. Sure enough, the entire circular track that the turret rode on was twisted and almost completely sheared off the base. There was no way it was going to move.

"I don't think it's going to move," Hardcastle radioed. "The antitank missile twisted the turret track all to hell. There's hydraulic fluid all over the place."

"Can it slew in the other direction?"

"Negative. The whole turret is off the track. It would take a crane to lift it back on."

"Then you better get out of the area as fast as you can, Admiral," Milford responded. "You've done all you can. The plane will be overhead in about five to six minutes."

Hardcastle wasn't ready to give up, but he didn't want anyone else nearby. Their car didn't look like it was going anywhere, either. "Deborah, start heading toward the Capitol Building—we've got about five minutes to make it."

"What about the Director?"

"Just get going—I'll bring Wilkes. Cazaux's going to bomb the White House, and the explosive he's using could fry us all. The Capitol will be the safest place for us. Can you drag Wilkes over there?"

"I don't think so," Harley said. "I'm staying here with you, Ian. There's no other choice."

"I'll take Wilkes in a minute. You head for the Capitol. Get going." Harley reluctantly got to her feet and began trotting east toward the Capitol Building. Hardcastle found a four-cell flashlight and examined the interior of the Avenger—and immediately struck paydirt. He dragged two green steel-and-plastic cases out from storage racks behind the passenger seat and opened them to find a large shoulder/pistol grip assembly and two cylindrical cans.

"What are they?" Harley asked behind him.

"I said *get moving* toward the Capitol."

"I can't make it—I can hardly see where I'm going," Harley said. "I'll help you. Do you know what they are?"

Hardcastle cursed and pulled a yellow-and-black tab on one side of the pistol grip. A metal grilled device resembling an open animal cage popped out of the right side of the unit. "It's a Stinger missile shoulder grip assembly," Hardcastle said. "I think we can fire the missiles from this unit from the shoulder. All we have to do is figure out how to get the missiles out of the launchers."

"Looks like the Army already thought of that," Harley said. She shined the flashlight into the lid of the carrying case, where they saw color-cartoon-like pictures detailing how to do it. Two latches on the bottom side of the right Stinger launcher opened an access panel, where they could see inside the launcher itself; two more latches on the side of one of the green aluminum tubes allowed it to slide free out the rear end of the launcher. She helped slide the aluminum tube onto the pistol grip assembly and lock it into place. Hardcastle took one of the cylindrical cans, inserted it into a hole just forward of the trigger, and twisted it to lock it in place. A green light on the side of the grip told him the unit was on.

"Get that computer over there," Hardcastle said. "It has a map telling where Cazaux's plane is." Harley retrieved the computer, opened it, and studied the screen. Meanwhile, Hardcastle keyed the mike switch on his helmet headset: "Leather, this is Hardcastle. I've found the Stinger shoulder launchers. I'm going to try to shoot it with a Stinger."

"You ever shoot a Stinger before, Admiral?"

"How hard can it be?" Hardcastle asked. "The instructions are printed in cartoons."

"Three miles," Harley said, "heading right for us."

"Can you describe those instructions to me?" Hardcastle asked.

Harley studied the drawings for a moment. "Looks like a button on the left side of the grip is for the . . . the IFF?"

" 'Identification Friend or Foe,' " Hardcastle said. "It'll tell us if the plane is transmitting proper codes. Doesn't matter—if it flies near here, I'm shooting it. Next."

"Large lever behind the grip. Pull down with your thumb when the target is within range. Powers the missile gyro, cools the seeker head, and charges the eject gas cylinder."

"What's the range?"

Harley checked the computer screen: "Two miles."

The time seemed to drag on forever. Hardcastle couldn't see a thing in the sky—the few lights and the remains of the fires to the south were destroying his night vision, and now the sirens wailing around the city prevented him from hearing anything. "Range!" he shouted.

"One-point-five miles . . ."

"I see it . . . Jesus, it's low!" Hardcastle shouted. It was a small single-engine Cessna with a fixed landing gear, and it looked like it was less than a hundred feet in the air. It was just south of the Tidal Basin, skimming the treetops. An occasional gust of wind or thermal current from the fires pushed the plane sideways or caused it to lose altitude, but it always regained its heading—it was homing directly for the White House. Hardcastle moved the large lever behind the pistol grip down until it snapped to the stop, and he heard a sudden shot of high-compression air and a loud whirring sound. "I think it's on. What next?"

"Large button on the very front of the grip—squeeze it with your thumb and hold to open the seeker-head shutter. Look through the sight and center the target in the sight."

Hardcastle looked over the sight, first to line up the Cessna, then looked through the sight. There was a sawtooth frame under a tiny round circle in the center of the sight. When Hardcastle placed the Cessna inside the center of the circle, he heard a loud *beep beep beep beep beep* . . . "It's beeping. What next?"

"Pull the trigger and kill that motherfucker," Harley said.

Hardcastle squeezed the trigger.

There was a very loud *fwoosh!* with very little kickback. The missile popped out of the aluminum tube and sailed skyward . . . and immediately fell to earth about fifty yards ahead of them. A second later the missile's motor fired, and it skittered across the ground for hundreds of yards until it was lost from sight. "Shit! It didn't track! It didn't go!" Hardcastle shouted.

"It should've *gone,*" Harley shouted. "We did everything right." But Hardcastle was already scrambling to remove another missile from the Avenger launcher. He removed the launch tube from the shoulder grip, twisted off the hot battery cylinder, loaded another missile on the shoulder grip, and twisted on another battery unit.

By the time Hardcastle hefted the Stinger onto his right shoulder again, the Cessna was over the Jefferson Memorial, swooping lower and lower. Its wings swung wildly as it caught in the hot lower air currents as it passed over the flaming ground path of the terrorist 747. Hardcastle lined up on the Cessna once again, flipped the BCU activation lever down, and . . .

. . . as soon as he did so, white acidic gas began streaming out both ends of the missile. Hardcastle threw the missile and launcher on the ground. The gas was coming out at high pressure now, and the battery unit underneath the grip was smoking. "The missile must've been bad," Hardcastle said. Harley was already moving toward the Avenger launcher to pull off another missile, so Hardcastle opened the second case to get another launcher—and he had a chance to study the instructions himself . . .

That's it! he exclaimed to himself.

The missile was pushed out of the launch tube by compressed nitrogen gas, and there was a 1.5-second delay before the rocket motor fired. The launch tube needed to be "super-elevated," or raised high enough so the missile would not hit the ground before the rocket motor would fire. The last drawing before squeezing the trigger described the final lineup of the target in the sight and how to superelevate: after the target was acquired and locked on with the beeping tone, the Stinger had to be raised until the target nestled into one of the sawtooth notches on the bottom of the sight, depending on the direction the target was flying, to lead the target. The missile's seeker head would still be tracking the target all the way, and when the rocket motor fired it would home in and kill.

By the time they loaded the third missile and screwed in a new battery unit, the Cessna was almost directly overhead, flying less than the length of a football field west of the Washington Monument. Hardcastle could clearly see two objects under the wings of the Cessna—those had to be the fuel-air explosives. He let the Cessna fly north of his position, then, as it flew over Constitution Avenue, activated the battery unit, squeezed the seeker head uncage switch, heard the beeping sound, lined up on the Cessna for the last . . .

"Freeze!" someone shouted behind him. "FBI! Drop that missile launcher *now!*"

"No!" Harley shouted. "I'm Harley, Secret Service!" She held up her U.S. Treasury Department ID wallet, hoping that the FBI agent would notice the standard federal agent "safe signal"—looping one finger over on the badge side and two fingers on the ID card side. "We're trying to stop that plane!"

"I said *drop it!*" Obviously he was too keyed-up to notice Harley's safe signal. To the FBI agent who had driven up to the group at the Washington Monument, it looked as if Hardcastle were trying to launch a bazooka round at the White House or the Commerce Department Building.

"No!" Harley shouted. "I'm Secret Service! He's authorized! Don't!"

Hardcastle felt the bullets crash into the middle of his back like two sharp rapid punches—but the bulletproof vest saved his life. He superelevated the Stinger launcher, placing the target in the middle notch on the bottom of the sight so the muzzle of the launcher was raised well over the Cessna, and squeezed the trigger . . . just as two bullets hit the back of his Kevlar helmet. The FBI agent couldn't get the shooter in the back, so he tried for a head shot, and this time he got him.

The missile popped out of the launch tube and sailed high overhead, nearly out of sight—but nowhere near the Cessna. Hardcastle thought it was flying out of control again. *It was our last chance, damn it,* he thought as he fell forward on his face, dazed and immobilized by the shock.

Our last chance . . . God, no . . .

He looked up toward the White House when someone shouted, "Look!" Two quick puffs of fire could be seen on the wings of the Cessna as the fuel-air explosives canisters released, just as the Cessna passed over the Zero Milestone at the north end of the Ellipse and continued on toward the White House.

"Everyone get down! Get down!" Hardcastle murmured. "The bombs . . . the bombs are going . . . going off . . ." But he couldn't seem to make his mouth move anymore.

Just as the Stinger missile started to nose over and head back to earth, the rocket motor ignited with a bright orange tongue of fire, and a split second later the missile arched gracefully and smoothly right into the front left side of the Cessna's engine compartment, near an exhaust stack. The one-and-a-half-pound warhead exploded on contact, and the Cessna nosed over, spiraled down, and crashed on the south lawn of the White House.

But as the canisters began to disperse the deadly high-explosive mixture, the Stinger missile exploded. The cloud of explosive vapors had no chance to properly disperse and mix with the air that would have given it its tremendous explosive power. The fireball that erupted just over the south lawn was still a thousand feet in diameter, large enough to blacken the entire south lawn and blow out windows at the Old Executive Office Building and the Treasury Department. The polycarbonate antisniper windows of the White House rippled and shook from the explosion, but remained intact. Harley could feel the intense heat of the fireball a half-mile away. There were several loud explosions as the bomblets from the fuel-air explosives harmlessly hit the ground, tossed several hundred feet away by the force of the blast.

Harley and the FBI agent ran over to Hardcastle together. The agent had his gun out and aimed at Hardcastle's head, but Harley shoved her badge and ID in the guy's face. "Call an ambulance, you idiot," she ordered. "He just saved the White House. The Director is hurt too—she's over there."

"The Director . . . of the FBI?"

"No, the damned director of 'I Love Lucy.' "

"Well, Jesus, Agent, how the hell am I supposed to—"

"Just get an ambulance, damn it!" Harley yelled. She carefully unbuckled the helmet—it fell apart in pieces in her hands. "Ian! Are you all right? Can you hear me?" There was no response. The back of his head was covered with blood, the glistening red blood contrasting well with his thin gray hair. "Ian? Stay with me, stay with me!"

"All right, all right, Deborah," a subdued, strained voice murmured into the ground. "Just answer the damned phone, will you please? The ringing is driving me crazy."

Epilogue

The Next Morning

The closest undamaged airport to Washington that could be totally secured was Naval Air Station Patuxent River–Trapnell, about forty miles southeast. The airspace for fifty miles in all directions was closed from the surface to infinity, secured with rapidly reactivated Patriot and Hawk surface-to-air missile sites and constant fighter patrols. At precisely nine A.M., Air Force One—the *real* Air Force One—touched down on Trapnell's two-and-a-half-mile-long runway. A formation of three VH-53 VIP helicopters was waiting, and the President of the United States, the First Lady, and a group of Cabinet members boarded the middle one, ignoring the small knot of reporters and photographers that had been allowed to cover the President's arrival. It was obvious to all that the President didn't feel like talking to the press.

After lift-off, the three Marine Corps helicopters did an aerial shell game, changing position in the formation so that no one on the ground—no gunner, no terrorist, no assassin—could tell which one carried the President. They flew high and fast, heading first toward Arlington to trace the final flight path of the 747 as it crashed into the city. The only planes allowed to be anywhere near the President were three F-16 fighters—one was on high patrol at twenty thousand feet, the other two orbiting at low altitude, separated from Marine One by three miles. They had orders to shoot any aircraft that strayed within twenty miles of the President, no questions asked, no warnings issued.

The group of three helicopters flew over the impact area near the Lincoln Memorial, then traced the two-mile-long path of destruction across the Reflecting Pool, the Kutz Bridge, the Tidal Basin, and south Washington to survey the damage. The burned, twisted hulk of the 747 was still piled up against the Case Memorial Bridge, but cranes had already been put in to start removing the wreckage—the blue-and-white Air Force One paint scheme could clearly be seen. Fireboats were still spraying water on smoldering boats and buildings at the Capital Yacht Club, the Washington Marina, and other buildings along Water Street, and a thick rainbow of spilled jet fuel could be seen streaming down the Washington Channel toward the Potomac. The Auditors' Building, the Sylvan Theater, and the Holocaust Museum were heavily damaged. The southwest corner of the Bureau of Engraving and Printing, the Outlet Bridge, the Kutz Bridge, most of the cherry trees on the east side of the Tidal Basin, the Japanese Lantern, the John Paul Jones Memorial, and the Tidal Basin Paddle were completely destroyed. Army and National Guard troops had been dispatched to seal off the Bureau of Engraving and Printing to protect against anyone looting the valuable currency and note plates inside. A few large-scale fires had broken out near Southeastern University and Sixth Street, and the area was alive with emergency lights and streams of water being pumped onto apartments and high-rises.

The three helicopters then flew over to the White House, all three coming in together in formation a thousand feet in the air on a fast, high approach west of the Washington Monument, north over the Ellipse toward the south lawn, duplicating the flight path of the Cessna on its computer-controlled bomb run. The westernmost helicopter touched down first, discharging ten heavily armed Secret Service agents and lifting off again, before the middle helicopter came in, bringing the President and the First Lady, followed by the third helicopter with other presidential advisers, a few reporters, and more Secret Service agents. Army gunners with Stinger missiles and machine guns were deployed on the roof of the White House and in several nearby buildings, scanning the skies in all directions for any sign of trouble.

The White House didn't look so white that morning.

Its front had been slightly damaged, with some missing stone and long streaks of black and gray across the south side. The Old Executive Office Building, the Treasury Department Building, and the south lawn were battered and heavily blackened, with trees and gardens still smoldering in all directions. A steel helicopter combat landing zone mat had been anchored to the south lawn for Marine One, and a raised walkway had been set up so the President would not have to walk across the scorched earth. A wooden platform had been set up for the members of the press, about sixty yards from where the President would be walking toward the White House.

The Q & A podium had been set up near the press pit, but the walkway did not extend over to it and no one expected the President to make a statement on this very grim occasion. But as he emerged from Marine One, several heavily armed Secret Service agents took positions in front of the press pit, facing toward the crowd with weapons highly visible at port arms, and the President walked across the scarred earth to the podium, with the First Lady on his right side. The bulk of the bulletproof vests they wore under their business suits were obvious to everyone.

"I'm not going to take any questions," the President said solemnly, "just the following statement: I wish to convey my sincere condolences to the families of all those who lost a loved one in this . . . this devastating tragedy. I share their pain, and the pain of all Americans as they try to comprehend this disaster.

"I wish to thank the federal agents, District of Columbia Police, and the members of the military who responded when the disaster struck, especially FBI Director Lani Wilkes, who was wounded in an exchange of gunfire with Henri Cazaux himself. The disaster would have been much worse if it had not been for their efforts.

"Finally, I want to ask for the cooperation of all Americans as we work toward rebuilding the capital and as we intensify our efforts to bring those responsible for this disaster to justice. I pledge—"

Suddenly he stopped as something caught his eye and a stirring in the crowd grabbed his attention. The President was staring at . . .

. . . a paper airplane that had sailed over the reporters' heads, bobbing and flitting directly for him. Four Secret Service agents grabbed the President and pulled him and the First Lady toward the White House, and suddenly unmarked Secret Service trucks and D.C. Police cars were racing for the group of reporters from parking areas near the Treasury Department Building. The reporters and cameramen were instantly surrounded by armed agents. "Wait a minute! Wait!" the President shouted, twisting in the Secret Service agents' arms. "I want that note! I want to see it!" But the Secret Service hustled him and the First Lady away to safety.

The entire twelve-square-block area around the White House

was sealed off by the Secret Service and D.C. Police, and all streets were cordoned off. As the D.C. Police got more units into the area, the dozens of Secret Service agents deployed were able to withdraw into the White House compound itself, leaving the D.C. Police and National Park Service officers to deal with the sudden crunch of traffic and the flood of curious onlookers. In the confusion, no one noticed one of the Secret Service agents standing in the shadows near the statue of Alexander Hamilton as he removed his earpiece, then his jacket and tie, and casually walked off down the street toward the Hotel Washington and a waiting limousine.

"That was a really silly thing to do, Henri," Gregory Townsend said as the limo headed off down Pennsylvania Avenue. He lowered the Browning Hi-Power semiautomatic pistol he held. "We should be a hundred miles from this bloody city."

"I like Washington, Gregory," Henri Cazaux said with a glint of humor in his eyes, adjusting the bandages that were tightly wound around his chest and ribs to try to make himself a bit more comfortable. "I think we will set up our new base of operations here. What do you think?"

Townsend motioned to a metal suitcase on the seat across from them. "I think you should take your cash, use all of the survival skills you possess, and get out of this country as fast as you can," Townsend said. "You know where Lake's ranch is in Brazil, you can access his Swiss bank accounts, and you must have a plane or boat stashed somewhere—go to Brazil and relax for a while. The Americans will go back to business as usual soon, and that's when you can consider coming back."

"The Devil never takes a holiday," Cazaux said. "My work is not finished, Gregory. You noticed how easy it was to slip into a closed presidential press conference as one of their own Secret Service agents? They are calling in even more agents, unrecognizable to each other. My goal is to get inside the White House itself, perhaps into the First Lady's bedroom, fuck her, and finally destroy that place. Nothing will stop me."

"Henri, the business accounts and contacts Lake set up for you are worth billions to us," Townsend insisted. "If we go back into business, we'll be the toast of the international arms market. We'll command top dollar, and no one will screw with us. You are the top dog, Henri. Why waste all that on a scheme like buggering the Steel Magnolia?"

"Because I have a score to settle, Gregory," Cazaux said, wincing as a muscle in his chest pulled one of the gunshot wounds wider. "Because I have been blessed with immortality. The money doesn't matter, don't you see that? Madame Vega was right—why waste my gift on selling a few weapons or smuggling drugs, when I can use my powers to destroy the greatest nation on earth? No, I have big plans for us, Gregory. I will have hundreds of soldiers that will rally to my side. I will destroy this entire city, and by doing so bring an entire nation to its knees. I will . . ."

"Oh, bloody hell," Townsend muttered, rolling his eyes. "Henri, I've had enough." He turned the Browning on Henri Cazaux, pulled the trigger, and squeezed off a half-dozen rounds. Fortunately, the Black Talon super-expanding low-velocity bullets did not bust out of the armored side doors of the security stretch limo. Cazaux looked at the glistening red bullet holes in his chest and stomach, and Townsend saw his eyes flare in red-hot, intense anger as he drew a knife from his behind-the-neck sheath—but Townsend was able to easily deflect Cazaux's weak stab, disarm him, put one more bullet into Cazaux's forehead, and topple the body to the floor. Townsend then calmly raised the privacy screen between the cabin and driver and aimed the smoking Browning at the driver.

"Who do you work for?"

"I work for Captain Townsend," the driver replied immediately.

"Correct," Townsend said. "Now find me a nice, quiet place to get rid of this mess."